It Happens in the Hamptons

Also by Holly Peterson

FICTION
The Manny
The Idea of Him

NONFICTION
Smoke and Fire: Recipes and Menus for Entertaining Outdoors

It
Happens
in the
Hamptons

A Novel

HOLLY PETERSON

WM
WILLIAM MORROW
An Imprint of HarperCollinsPublishers

IT HAPPENS IN THE HAMPTONS. Copyright © 2017 by Holly Peterson. All rights reserved. Printed in the United States of America. No part of this book may be used or reproduced in any manner whatsoever without written permission except in the case of brief quotations embodied in critical articles and reviews. For information, address HarperCollins Publishers, 195 Broadway, New York, NY 10007.

HarperCollins books may be purchased for educational, business, or sales promotional use. For information, please email the Special Markets Department at SPsales@harpercollins.com.

FIRST EDITION

Designed by Diahann Sturge

Surfboard illustration © Sergio Hayashi/Shutterstock, Inc.

Library of Congress Cataloging-in-Publication Data has been applied for.

ISBN 978-0-06-239150-6

17 18 19 20 21   LSC   10 9 8 7 6 5 4

*To Stick-em-Up, Bedford, Toddler, Java, Ass-man, J-Po, Hawaii
Joe, Shane, Wingnut, Joey Wakesurf, Fardaddy, Chef Henri,
Fetus, and Sunshine for teaching me to love the salt water*

"Moderation is a fatal thing. Nothing succeeds like excess."
—OSCAR WILDE

It Happens in the Hamptons

Chapter One

One Small Step onto Planet Hamptons

Sorry, lady," the taxi driver said to the woman in the backseat. "I don't see number thirty-seven marked on a porch or mailbox. Sometimes they nail the numbers on trees, but I can't find the house."

The woody station wagon taxi rounded a corner and slowed alongside one stretch of Willow Lane, then turned around and back again. The midmorning sunlight burst through the tree canopy and heated the wet street, burning the fog so it swirled off the pavement.

"I know that's the right number," Katie Doyle said. "I'm positive. My friend said it was a little hidden."

"You've been there before?"

"We're from Oregon. I've never even been to the East Coast."

"Um-hum," answered the driver, knowing this out-of-towner was in for a few shock waves this summer.

"Let me get out of the car and investigate," said Katie. "Maybe the number is blocked."

Katie longed to breathe in the curative salty breeze instead of the stale, fruity air freshener in the car. Her eight-year-old son, Huck, was asleep next to her, his white-blond hair mashed against the clumpy pillow he'd fashioned out of his knapsack and jacket. She would let Huck nap in the house before exploring the new town, though he'd slept well on the six-hour red-eye flight from Portland, two and a half hours jolting on the Long Island Railroad to Southampton, and then fifteen more minutes encased in the stench of this taxi.

She yelled back to the driver, "This is it for sure!"

Katie never found a number, but she did spot a metal pail on the crumbling porch that looked like it was last painted around the era her taxi came off the production line. She walked up to the old steps and found the pail bore a welcome offering: summery bing cherries inside—the same type she and George Porter had picked with her son at a Hood River farm back home.

Looking down at the cherries, she thought back to that early May afternoon. Huck had sat in the grass under the shade of a tree making a pyramid of cherry pits, his lips turning a darker crimson as his pile grew. On a blanket warmed by the sun, Katie laid her head back on George's outstretched arm. He traced his finger down her profile and neck to the top button of her blouse. She took a deep breath to disperse the arousal from his touch, and wondered if they'd fall into bed again before his flight back home that night.

He blurted out from the calm silence between them, "Come east to Long Island for the summer."

"Yeah, sure." Katie smiled softly, keeping her eyes closed.

"Be sure."

She pushed her chin out resolutely toward the sun. "No problem. Huck and I will just pick up and move to the opposite coast, just like that." She elbowed George to quit it with the silly talk, and placed her finger on her mouth to get him to be quieter so Huck didn't hear.

He kissed her forehead gently and then whispered in her ear. "I want you. I want us together all summer."

"Huck and I are staying put. You can come visit anytime." She jutted her jaw to the side to suppress a smile.

"No strings. Just come. The family cottage is yours. I never stay there. I've got my own a few miles away."

Katie turned to him and propped on her elbow, looking back to make sure Huck was consumed with his cherry pit project. "Are you serious?"

"Very. And you'd love it."

"It's already May," she answered, squinting her eyes at him to gauge his resolve.

"It is, thank God," George said, upping the challenge. "And your teaching seminars are completed and you've got the summer off. Perfect timing. In the Hamptons, you'd find plenty of students to tutor and time to write your studies. Hood River may be the windsurfing capital of the country, but you haven't tried the pre-vailing winds off the Atlantic. Ever."

Katie wrapped strings of grass around her fingers, tighter now that she felt he meant this. "Using wind and water to entice me is pretty clever. But, are you serious?"

"Very."

"Aren't the Hamptons just a rich playground where a bunch of people spend too much money?" Katie asked. "We've discussed this, that's not my thing, all the snobby . . ."

"I'm not going to lie and say some of the summer people aren't a little over the top, but you make the Hamptons what you want. There are perfectly normal families that have lived out there full-time for generations. You can hold the August tomatoes and bite into them like an apple, the shellfish is amazing, and the Atlantic is so much warmer than the Pacific."

"You mean it."

"I do. I really do." He kissed her neck softly, sexually in that way he did in the dark.

A moment passed. "Well, then I'll let it settle a little. I promise. A change is not a crazy idea at this point," she let out in the most noncommittal tone she could. She faced the sun again, wondering if this man was falling for her more than she had understood. Since Huck's father had skipped town before the kid could even sit up, Katie's trajectory was her own design. She could say yes and own a new life plan right this minute if she wanted.

"We've only known each other for a month," she reminded George.

And he replied, "Four perfect weekends, why not try a dozen more?"

Chapter Two

Try to Hang on for the Ride Known as Summertime

Anyone could have predicted that the summer's turmoil would start the moment Kona's rusty Jeep blasted through the wooden white entry gates that Saturday night. The car skidded around a rare Japanese tree and screeched to a stop. He marveled at the deep tire marks he'd made in the cinnamon pebbles raked like frosting.

Luke stepped out from the passenger side first. He swiped his hands down his black pants and stiffened the collar on his white shirt, his handiwork with the iron now ruined by the ride in Kona's damp Jeep. His soft, dark eyes itched from a day in the salt water, and a trace of white zinc remained in a small patch of stubble on his handsome jaw. He patted down his shaggy mahogany hair, particularly on that stubborn part on the top. No matter how hard he'd worked, nothing felt right.

The guys were trying their best, but that didn't extinguish the "fish out of water" neon signs blinking on their foreheads as they entered the fray of the .001 percenters at the Chase estate. The mansion, which they'd only seen from the beach shoreline, bulged with impossible weight over the fragile oceanfront dune. The party above was filled with warlocks who controlled every lever of Manhattan's industries—from Wall Street and media to advertising, fashion, and the arts.

"You think we're dressed right?" Luke asked. "*Hamptons Festive* might mean those pink ties and blazers."

"Nah. Black and white. Always the safe bet. All good," answered Kona. Years battling waves and climbing up Hawaiian palm trees to pick coconuts had sculpted his burly frame, now sheathed in a wrinkled white button-down he'd found in the depths of his dresser. Kona had inherited his Nordic father's bushy blond eyebrows and blue eyes and his Hawaiian mother's high cheekbones and caramel skin. "When you're tan and good-looking and not a fat banker, it doesn't matter what clothes you got on. Fuck these people: we look good. And forget Simone for a night. C'mon. Let's find you a higher grade woman."

Luke fist-bumped the young valet parking attendant he recognized from town. "Thanks, man," he said, as Kona threw the kid his keys in a large arc over the exposed roll bar of his Jeep. "We teach the Chase kids to water-ski and surf; I'm sure little Richie made them invite us."

Luke didn't like gaining entry to the Chases' exclusive party when the twenty-three-year-old parking valet couldn't get in, and he promised himself he'd sneak him a beer on the way out. He remembered this same kid had dented the shiny right bumper of the owner's new four-seater Porsche Panamera "family car" when the automatic driveway gates had opened on their own last summer. Jake Chase, the forty-seven-year-old, corpulent owner of the otherwise pristine vehicle, didn't much mind. He knew he'd simply have someone tell someone to tell someone to repair it.

At the scene of the fender bender, Jake, amazed by his uncanny ability to keep everything so well in perspective, had assured the young man: "It happens, kid. Don't sweat it. Hell, why should a fifty-thousand-dollar gate function properly when you push a button?"

The legendary Jake Chase was like that, always trying to prove he was on even par with the local guys because he started out driving a laundry truck to get by in college. By the time he was thirty-five, that stint behind the wheel led Jake to create the country's largest Laundromat chain. Developing entire malls followed, and the cash rolled in with the same certainty as those pounding waves in front of his summer home.

Jake would punch the guys too hard in the upper arm to make sure they were alert when he recounted tales of his career. He'd then throw his balding head back in laughter, hoping deep down in his short, stubby build that they got his inane jokes. Cool is a gift bestowed. Luke and Kona knew one couldn't buy, rent, borrow, or steal it.

But at this moment, Luke was feeling anything but an arbiter of cool, even among posers. It was an accepted fact of life on this rarefied outer tip of Long Island that many of the local families' incomes were reliant on wealthy Manhattanites with their clan-like customs and infantile impatience. Every summer, these invaders crashed into town on Memorial Day weekend and vanished at the stroke of 6:00 p.m. on Labor Day.

"C'mon, man," yelled Kona, shaking his stringy blond hair that graced the lower part of his shoulders—a perfect length to attract the lady folk, while still thrusting a middle finger at any semblance of a desk job. "Julia Chase is waiting for me upstairs; I just feel it." Julia Chase, the buxom hostess of tonight's Memorial Day weekend cocktail affair, had pushed the guys hard to show, insisting her glamorous friends wanted to meet real surfers.

Luke, thirty-one, and Kona, thirty-four, had both grown up in the same Southampton school district. Their local friends and relatives were electricians, land surveyors, restaurateurs, AV technicians, shop owners—normal American folks who actually lived in one residence all year round. Though Kona had spent many school years in Hawaii on an Air Force base with his parents, both men had grown closer than brothers. They knew middle-class childhoods, nothing more—and a lot less when times were tough.

The gray slate steps were illuminated with a subtle line of lights flooding the stairs as if they were leading to the entrance of a royal Egyptian tomb. Kona didn't appreciate that the entry was conveniently lit for his bare toes in black rubber flip-flops, nor did he know that a few steps cost more than he and Luke made all summer.

As he strode up to the event, Kona couldn't decide if Julia Chase's supersized wealth and married status were an inconvenient reality, or one of those thrilling challenges that tended to smack him in the face.

"The beach was empty, my towel was like a goddamn postage stamp in the sand," Kona declared, with boorish confidence. "And Julia chooses to do a down-dog yoga move like five feet in front of me? She's dying for it."

"She may have not even noticed you were there," counseled Luke. "She'd just dropped her kid off at camp and maybe wanted to stretch a little. Don't get us in hot water with Jake Chase. The season is just starting and that kook is sharper than he looks."

Entering *her* territory and this grandiose house, Kona began to question everything he'd felt on *his* territory: the water sports camp on his beach. Whether he could properly evaluate Julia's stretching needs or not, he resorted to his fail-safe stance and walked up those illuminated steps like he owned the entire forty-million-dollar beachfront property.

The guests inside reveled on this Memorial Day Saturday, drunk with the sweet aphrodisiac of summer's arrival. Kona reminded himself that life was all about making moves—on bored, horny housewives, on job connections with the city people, on any opportunity that befell him. He rubbed the stubborn sand out of his eyebrows and shook his head a bit to cast off these rare schoolboy inhibitions.

Chapter Three

Shoreline Sideshow

Near the twelve-foot-high privet to the side of the estate, a young woman escaped the party and raced behind the pool shed, her heart beating violently. She tried to create moisture in her dry mouth by sucking on the insides of her cheeks. Pulling her glorious, curly mane off her bare back, she knotted it up into a bun so as to better perform the business she had in mind.

Waiting for her, he lay like a starfish in the dark, tangled brush. His blazer flapped open against the sandy earth beneath him, exposing the Lilly Pulitzer pink-and-yellow gardenia lining he found so festive and reassuring all at once. He passed the time deciphering the sparkling constellations above, his eyes eventually settling on the hunter, Orion.

The shoulder straps of her orange silk romper got caught in the branches as she dashed along. An undulating field of high sea grass shielded the spot they'd agreed on. She knew sneaking here was not the best idea, but it was funny that he'd suggested that they should do it now. An Instagram of the spot would be awesome. No one would ever recognize the patch of grassy sand where he waited, but she would make clear what transpired there. And she would never tell anyone with whom.

He checked his vintage Rolex Daytona. Indeed, she was eighteen minutes late. Off in the distance, the waves of the Atlantic pounded the shoreline, making the ground beneath him reverberate with a gentle rumbling. He had all night to mingle, and he knew all the arrivistes sipping their colorful cocktails on the other side of the hedge wouldn't discover them. His reasoning, honed on the debate team at Exeter, usually did not fail him. But tonight, with his mind consumed in the sparkling sky and his loins captivated by her sheer roundness, his thinking was not sound. After all, ensuring a young woman's discretion was far more difficult than pinpointing the archer's bow above.

As she opened the wooden gate, it creaked loudly, and she carefully closed it back while covering it with dangling branches.

"Over here," he said quietly, calmly. She liked his voice. It was so gentlemanly, so evolved, so not like men her age.

"I'm coming!" she whispered loudly, hopping on one platform espadrille as she pulled off the other. She walked with both shoes hanging from her two fingers as she moved along the pathway toward him. Before reaching the clearing where he was lying, she noticed the stars flickering above as the evening sky transformed the landscape into a hazy, Hamptons purple hue. She snapped a photo to be posted later. *For sure.*

"You smell delicious," he muttered as he pulled her down toward him. He kissed her furiously for good measure, then, not too subtly, pushed her head down his torso to get on with it already.

Chapter Four

Preposterous Posing

"I t's not like we're saving some hedge fund client in rough currents; they hardly need us here," Luke whispered loudly to Kona. He was taller than his childhood friend, but much slighter in composition. He looked back at the lawn, which was as long as the five-par golf holes he used to caddy. "Let's hold back a little, look at the line of cars arriving now." He pointed at the never-ending driveway behind them. A dozen cars snaked along, while uniformed valets raced around to open doors as if they were saving children from a burning building. First rolled in a vintage 1970's Mercedes convertible 280SL, then a Porsche Turbo S, and then an Aston Martin V12 Vantage.

"C'mon man, I'm hungry," Kona yelled back to Luke. "*A'ole pilikia*. Stop sweating this. Let's go crush the buffet." For the first time, the men were able to check out the grounds of the famous Chase house, normally hidden behind twenty-foot-tall hedges. Only in the late autumn and winter, when the leaves fell and the green walls turned to barren branches, could anyone get even a glimpse of the landscaped Southampton estates filled with outdoor art installations, tennis courts, and infinity pools stretching out toward the sea. Like many of his neighbors, Jake Chase had labeled his home with a wooden plaque out front as if it were Windsor Castle on the English countryside. He fretted over the possibilities for months until he settled on *Pine Manor*. That many of these homes were contemporary in design or had titles that had nothing to do with the local landscape (no pine trees nearby) didn't much matter. It was the aura of gentility and massive wealth that the monikers announced.

Kona and Luke passed an enormous sculpture that looked like a poodle made up of long balloons that clowns twist into shapes. Luke knew he'd seen that same image in pictures from a museum exhibit, but he couldn't remember the name of the artist. He wondered if it cost over a million dollars, or over ten million, or possibly even more.

Just then, both men heard laughter on the other side of the hedge.

"Let's start some trouble if you wanna wait," said Kona, trying to peer through the bushes at a couple in the sea grass. "We're going to find something we shouldn't."

He grabbed Luke's shoulder and pushed him behind the pool shed so they could both get a better look. They cleared the brush from above a small wooden gate. Though the clusters of high sea grass obstructed their view, they could see a man was lying on his back. He looked older; they could make out grayish hair, with his elbow draped on his face while a young woman had her mouth bobbing up and down between his thighs.

"Check it out," whispered Luke, who never wanted to follow Kona's often disastrous lead. "He's really getting worked on. And look at her, on her knees getting so busy. Check out his blazer, what is that, yellow flowers inside it? I told you they'd all be wearing stuff like that. You recognize the guy?"

"No idea."

"Let's go," cautioned Luke.

"Nope," replied Kona. "Stay here, we gotta nail this old asshole. She looks too young." He waited a few more moments, and then yelled "Yo!" at the couple to get their attention and freak the older man out.

Suddenly from behind the pool shed on their side of the hedge, a muscled man dressed in a white polo shirt with *Pine Manor* stitched on the left chest tapped Luke's arm with enough force to inflict a bruise. "Can we help you boys? Whom are you yelling at?" He elbowed his partner.

"No, uh, we were . . ." answered Luke, rubbing his arm.

"You were what?" The two security goons looked at each other, trying to divine if Luke and Kona were nosy guests or criminals. "Should we escort you up to the cocktail area, or is there a problem here we should alert Mr. Chase about?"

Through the high sea grass that lined the deck ahead, the young woman completed the artistry with her expensive mouth. She then ran back to the party, her short silk romper outlining her curvy legs and water balloon breasts, as the man disappeared to the darkened beach below.

Luke said, "All good, all fine." The men walked up the stairs, while the guards muttered to themselves.

"I think we should figure out who the guy was," said Kona. "I got a nose for bad stuff and I'm telling you . . . sicko preppy pervert."

On the expansive deck overlooking the Atlantic Ocean, a sea of kelly green and Tweety-bird yellow now greeted Luke and Kona, as if they had suddenly walked onto a life-size board of Candy Land. Orange and pink weather balls were strung across the pool. Waiters meandered through the throngs with cantaloupe mojitos curated to match the guests.

The guys didn't know where to move first, as wealthy summer people converged in tight, impermeable circles. On the couches, a media CEO who had just merged his company with a te communications giant pontificated gleefully about spineless anti-trust legislation. And inside, a black artist, dressed in a Gucci bomber jacket, track pants, and snakeskin Balenciaga high-tops, mesmerized a crowd about his blockbuster show in Chelsea. While waxing on about cultural signifiers, his devotees jockeyed to secure one of his tar-covered sculptures they knew would triple in value by next summer.

Luke and Kona walked strategically around the herd of party-goers toward the bar, the drink less important to them than their dire need to look occupied and purposeful. This kind of money would make anyone nervous. Luke tapped his toe impatiently. "Like I predicted, we don't know anyone." The wind turned slightly, and they got a whiff of the wood burnt pizzas the celebrity chef created in the Chases' new outdoor pizza oven.

"Relax, man," answered Kona, grabbing a slice with heirloom baby artichokes and truffle shavings. "We look fine, professional." Of course "professional" to these two meant they had "a job," such as running a water sports venture in summer. In winter, Kona worked as a Hawaiian landscaper and Luke, a part-time marine biology teacher. To everyone else at the party, "a job" meant "own, run, or be the majority stockholder in a multinational conglomerate."

"C'mon," whispered Kona, glaring into the crowd before him. "Let's nail the lecherous guy in the grass."

Luke and Kona waded around huge floor pillows covered in Mexican tapestries, an attempt by Julia Chase to make the "intimate" affair for one hundred and fifty guests seem thrown together and casual. The party planner had charged the Chases a twenty-eight-thousand-dollar design bill just to get the "bohemian" décor on paper, fifty-five thousand dollars for a tent complete with Latin American planters flown in from Belize, and a sixty-four-thousand-dollar food and beverage bill that included a shellfish taco bar with

ervers hacking open stone crabs flown in from
beef sliders and the hip-hop Pandora station
ackground helped boost the Chases' bourgeois
hey were playing it down.

"C'mon, Luke, let's cop some drinks," Kona demanded, suddenly fed up with feeling inferior. He grabbed two pink, girly shot
glasses from a passing waiter who looked annoyed they considered
themselves guests.

"Doesn't it look like an airport hangar, all the glass and steel?"
Luke asked, noticing how the ten-thousand-square-foot house lit
up the sky. "If I had fifty million dollars, I think I'd build something that looked like a home where people actually watch TV,
fuck, and sleep."

Kona elbowed Luke, saying, "Hot babe at nine o'clock." On
their left, a married mother of four brushed her butt into a bestselling author's side, as she gobbled her meal for the night, three
radishes from the crudité tray.

Minutes later, Julia Chase spotted Luke and Kona lying back
on loungers by the pool, several black cod ceviche crisps they'd
hoarded balancing on their thighs. As they chomped, she appeared
before them like a Missoni mermaid, with a long knit skirt in
shades of peach that strategically matched the setting sun. A slinky
white silk tank top left no one guessing as to her nipple size and
shape: half-dollar sized, coffee-with-cream in color, and showing
the beginnings of chilly air.

"Kona, Luke, there's so many people who want to meet real
surfers!" Julia's blond curls framed her beautiful, angular face,
and her lips were permanently poised as if to whistle. "Let me
introduce you." She blew out her breath slowly.

"Sure." Kona slowly lumbered up as if he didn't really need to
meet anyone, because, well, he was fitting in just fine.

But before they could take the seven steps over to her, Julia had turned away to infiltrate another group of men and women who would rather swallow an orange beach ball than talk to someone who wouldn't advance them socially or professionally.

At this point, Luke and Kona only wanted another free shot of expensive Patron tequila, or three . . . and hopefully to embarrass the pervert in the brush, when a young woman appeared and said, "Hey, guys! It's so cool you showed."

Neither Luke nor Kona could respond at first—they were both so alarmed by the transformation that a year could inflict on a teenage girl. They remembered Alexa Chase, their camper for four summers, as the girl with braces, teeny little budding breasts, and twig legs.

"What happened to you? You look so, well, so different, Alexa," sputtered Luke, still struggling to accept this woman with rambling curves was the skinny girl who acted as DJ on his water-ski boat instead of getting in the water like the rest of the campers.

"What is it?" she asked with faux naiveté.

"You look like you grew up five years. I swear if any tenth-grade boys get . . ." Luke stammered, his paternal instincts kicking into turbo gear.

"What? I'm sixteen. You guys are acting silly. There are no boys. I just gained like twenty pounds this year." Alexa swiveled her butt around and grabbed a chunk of flesh.

Both guys looked up at the sky, their cheeks flushing red.

"So this summer I swear I'm going to get in the water more to work it off."

Kona ruffled her hair like she was his kid sister and put his arm around her. "We're glad to see you," he said. "But Luke's right. Look at you! What are you wearing, honey? How short is that? Did your parents okay your outfit?"

Alexa twirled around for them, her curly ponytail whipping around her head. She took off her long sweater and fidgeted with the straps of her silky orange romper. Just then, in the exact same millisecond of the exact same infinitesimal tilt of the Earth's axis, Kona's and Luke's faces turned as white as the plush loungers behind them.

"What is it?" she asked, smiling.

"Uh, nothing . . . it's just . . ." Luke said, trying hard to delete the image of the man getting pleasured in the sea grass.

"You guys are being weird. Go get a drink or something, I'm not checking my outfits with my mom!"

Alexa strutted toward the Beluga caviar tapas bar as if she were on a catwalk.

"I can't handle this; she's so young still," said Kona.

"She's sixteen years old. The guy was like forty. In her parents' home, or near it?" said Luke. His eyes glazed, colorful humans, drinks, and pillows now blurring together.

Like twins in their monochrome black pants and white collared shirts, Kona and Luke stood there dumbstruck one moment too long.

Just then, a man dressed in Pepto-Bismol-colored pants shoved his empty highball glass in Kona's one hand, mushed a pesto marinade–covered napkin and shell-encrusted toothpick in the other and said, "Waiter. Be so kind. Fetch me two gin and tonics."

Chapter Five

An Innocent Stroll

K atie and Huck waited in line at a deli positioned between a Chinese take-out spot and a carpet chain in a small shopping strip before the town of Southampton. She studied the six or eight men around her wearing Timberland boots, worn work pants, and utility vests. They grabbed BBQ-flavored chips and Arizona iced tea in big cans on a ninety-nine cents special while they waited for their chicken Parmesan and meatball heroes. Katie's two turkey and American cheese sandwiches, Snapples, and potato chips cost nineteen dollars, which she didn't find expensive. A young teen helped his father wrap up a bagel at the counter. The man kissed the top of his son's head while he counted out change for the customer ahead. *Nice people around here*, she thought.

That morning, after organizing their clothes in the small Porter family cottage, Katie wanted to take Huck to explore the town. They'd spent their first day napping and getting used to the creaks in the house where they would spend the twelve weeks of summer.

George wouldn't be out for seven more days, and Katie was relieved to discover the Hamptons first on her own terms, not as a beholden tourist, with him playing the role of insider guide. He had left her an old pale green Volvo station wagon in the driveway, cautioning against driving it on a highway or at any speed over fifty miles per hour. That sounded good to Katie. Slowing down was just what she needed.

"Can we go to the beach tomorrow?" Huck pleaded as he climbed into the back of the beat-up Volvo in the deli lot. "I don't want to get sandy for a picnic, Mom. I'm cold anyway."

"I'll find a little spot near town in the grass with no breeze, honey. We can eat the sandwiches there." Katie looked into the rearview mirror and sent her son a little kiss. She longed to put her feet in the sand and feel the slosh of soothing salt water on her body. But she knew not to push her son more than she already had.

For their lunch, she pulled into a protected bay with a small dock and yellow flowers blooming along the embankment. As they threw bread scraps to the ducks in the water, Katie told herself she needn't have been worried about snooty people in the Hamptons. Catapulting their life out here still felt like a prudent decision, even if it were a little rash. The farm stands were country in feel—cute red wagon–style trailers filled with baskets of jewel-colored flowers and produce. Maybe George's assurances were on point: the tutor hours would pile up, Huck would love a new coastal environment, and the Hamptons *were* populated by kind people drawn to water sports and nature, who also fed fuzzy ducks paddling for crumbs with their children.

Katie watched her son throw the crusts of his sandwich into the flurry of ducks gathered by the bank. She thought about her mother, and how strange it was that she would never know she'd taken Huck here. Having died in early March, her mother had advised her to leave home when she felt ready for a new life chapter. Today, it felt both natural and bizarre to have landed here at the dawn of Katie's first summer without her.

As she faced the warm Hamptons sun, her mind flashed back to day one of the Portland education conference series, near the remnants of the Danish breakfast spread, when George had walked right up to her.

"Your morning talk was damn good," he'd said. "I want to hear more about your dyslexia papers. My company is investing in some of the learning software you mentioned." He'd pulled his long bangs off his forehead and locked his blue eyes on hers like a dare. "But I'm more interested in your brain than all the studies we are hearing about, frankly."

"Thank you. I've published other . . ."

"Let's leave."

"Leave now?" Katie asked, shocked by his bold suggestion. "It's only eleven-thirty, we've got four more panels . . ."

"Let's slide out. Now, before the next session starts."

And so it was that Katie and George replaced the sessions on fostering academic grit with an early lunch at a bistro on Portland's Willamette River. A frenzied session tangled in the Hilton's starchy sheets followed. The couple barely participated in the education conference over the next three weekends, favoring wine and heated calisthenics in their hotel rooms.

Katie looked at the still bay, reflecting like a mirror off the bright sky. She said to Huck, "It's so peaceful, how can anyone be anything but happy here?"

Huck smiled up at his mother, his contagious, youthful innocence fortifying her own convictions. "You'll see, we'll meet people and we'll both make great friends. They can't be that different from the folks back in Hood River. Let's go walk down the Main Street in Southampton town, and we'll see some new faces." She remembered locking the door of her Oregon loft for the final time just forty-eight hours before.

"This was the right move, honey, I'm sure."

Chapter Six

Close Encounters with Another Kind

On Main Street of Southampton town, Katie and Huck entered a gourmet-style market called the Silver Apple where she paid six dollars for a small bottle of water. *Strange,* she thought, *what exactly is in this water at these prices?*

She placed a twenty-dollar bill at the counter, where people were packed in like a tight elevator. Below her, Huck could barely get oxygen in the dense crowd. As the waitress took her money, Katie squeezed Huck's hand tighter to signal that this plan to move all the way across the country wasn't ill-founded. The town was just a little more crowded than she imagined.

Katie tried to get the attention of the waitress behind the counter. "My change for the water? I, just, didn't get . . ."

"I forgot. Sorry!" the girl said. "I'm dealing with another order, give me a little!" The espresso machine gurgled as it steamed up milk.

A woman in line behind Katie reached for a Fair Trade raw hemp bar on the counter, elbowing her in the ear, and screamed at anyone who'd listen. "An almond milk chai latte with Stevia and a wasabi tuna Swiss chard wrap! Do you mind dusting it with some turmeric?"

Katie's mom had always reminded her to find the funny in annoying situations. She wanted to bark out an order for a donut with pink frosting and sprinkles just to make a point, but she'd be just as likely to find a can of Spam here. Finally, the waitress placed her fourteen dollars on the counter.

Before leaving the upscale Silver Apple with her son's overpriced water, Katie looked back at the aggressively thin housewife pointing her finger at the local waitress. She was yammering on about the obvious difference between Stevia and Splenda and that they should really know to put turmeric in their food for its anti-inflammation benefits. She resolved to forgive the young woman who'd taken forever with her fourteen dollars.

"TWO BIKES. NOTHING fancy, just for us to tool around in, please," Katie asked the distracted man behind the counter of the Gyrations bike shop, about six doors down.

The store owner, Harry, looked over his reading glasses to estimate the cost of Katie's shoes and bag. He didn't need to look at her son's Teva water sandals to discern this probably wasn't his biggest sale of the day.

"Not fancy? What do you mean by that?" the man asked, without bothering to glance up from the ledger.

"I mean, just what I said," said Katie matter-of-factly, not wanting to jump to conclusions about this guy. Maybe he was busy during a holiday weekend. "Like, three speeds at the most for me. And just anything for my son that rolls down a street safely."

"Uh-hmmm. So just two . . ."

"Yeah. We're two people, who need two bikes." Katie bit her lower lip and squinted her eyes at the salesman. She wanted very badly to believe that all the Hamptons' snobby-ness she'd been wary of wasn't going to materialize on day two.

The fifty-something Harry lumbered off his stool. "Well," he muttered. "We are having a Memorial Day special." He led her to the front of the store where a dozen, brightly colored three-speed bikes were lined up. "William, pull out a few, please," he asked his employee, a kid who looked hardly old enough to be in high school.

"Oh great, I don't know if you have any sales if we buy two but . . ."

Harry interrupted her. "Everyone who isn't training to do triathlons, and wants a little three-speed clunker to drive around town in, takes this model." He shook his head. "And I mean *everyone*. It's called the Townie. Twelve colors, all pretty run-of-the-mill Easter-egg palette. We got dozens in the warehouse next door."

Katie figured that these people must know something if they are all buying the same model; it must rarely break down, or be easy to ride. "Well, okay. It looks like what I'm after."

Bang! The front glass door swung as if it had been blasted with a significant explosives cache. The wooden door molding almost clipped Katie's nose, and the force knocked over a small biking glove display case. An almost visible cloud of gardenia-scented perfume nearly asphyxiated Katie and Huck.

Helping to tidy up the gloves now strewn on the floor did not enter the mind of the forty-three-year-old Margaux Carroll. She moved swiftly, witch-on-a-broom style, her silky Calypso St. Barth's–brand caftan flowing behind her. A floppy white straw hat hung out several inches farther than her shoulders and looked absurd on her skinny frame. It was as if someone had placed an entire beach umbrella on her head.

She screamed to no one in particular, "Can I get some help, please? *Hello?*" (That "hello" pronounced as "*what the hell is wrong with you people?*") Her enormous black round sunglasses made her look like an oversized insect in a horror film. The Botox and Juvéderm injections stretching every corner of her face in lopsided directions didn't help.

The owner, Harry, looked over Katie's shoulder and yelled to the back of the store for the floor manager, "Roger! Customer coming in hot."

Katie continued on her task. "So this bike looks fine, my son needs a little one, too. What . . ."

"I'm so sorry to do this to you," Margaux said to Roger, who now sped to the front of the store. She played with the curls of a recent blow-dry. "I've got a *thousand* houseguests, and we all got this sudden, *really* fun idea to go on a bike ride. All together. We want to cruise down Beachwood Lane to the ocean before sunset."

Roger responded in a tone reminiscent of a meditation tape. "We have everything you need in stock, Mrs. Carroll, I'm sure."

"Can you send over a ton of the bikes?" Margaux spat back at him like bullets from an automatic weapon. "You know, the ones everyone . . . like the Old Schwinns we used to ride, the cute . . ."

"You mean those in the window? The Townies?" Roger asked.

"Is that what they're called?" She snorted. "Oh, that's so funny. Like, yeah, we're townies. Helloooo?! If you could see two of my houseguests who are gay designers, definitely not townies, definitely very chic city people, but okay! That's funny, I like it."

Margaux marched back over toward the window near Katie and the owner, banging Huck's head with her Celine bucket "it" bag on the way. "Oh, so sorry, sweetie!" she said as if she didn't mean it at all, and kept moving. "I really like it when houseguests match. My friends do that. They get bright printed sweatshirts with something like TEAM CARROLL JULY 4TH, 2017 waiting on their beds, and I always think to myself, *I have to do that!* Can I get like ten Townies or so? Maybe call it an even dozen?" She widened her eyes like a four-year-old wanting her way in a toy store.

Katie pondered getting on the next flight back to her Hood River hamlet before her landlord rented out her old apartment. She watched Margaux fish into the bottom of her purse, her toned upper arms exhibiting the hours she'd spent all winter in power Ashtanga yoga. She whipped out her black American Express card, a metallic, thick, heavy purchasing machine with a credit line of over five hundred thousand dollars. Roger reached for it.

"Just, can you just please write down the card number," she demanded. "Could you actually, just, file it? Then I never have to wait for the little machine that takes forever?"

Roger nodded. He knew summer lady invaders wanted total capitulation from shop people, cementing their serf-to-empress relationship.

"Good. You sound like you can handle this," Margaux said, as if Roger had an I.Q. of fifty-five. "My home is 325 Pridwin Lane. It's got a really long driveway, I mean *really* long, you'll get to the house eventually. I have to tell everyone that. The house is called Sailor's Way."

Roger nodded. "Sailor's Way?" He shot Harry a glance.

"Yes. My daughter took a few sailing lessons the summer before we built it. Of course she stopped. But the name stuck," explained Margaux. "And, oh . . . can I have these bike racks?"

Roger had to pause. "Well they are part of the store display. We need them for . . ."

"I need them all next to each other outside. Without the racks, they'll tip over in the wind and . . ."

"Harry?" Roger gave up all sense of reasoning to the boss.

Harry walked from his less wealthy client, Katie. He had bought the racks in a retail supply catalogue for forty-nine dollars. "Mrs.

Carroll, they do belong to the store. But I'll give you a deal, you can have three for three-hundred dollars each."

"You're the best!" Margaux pumped her arms hard as she stormed back into the middle of the store. "I need baskets. Those cute white ones . . . that hold, say, a towel and bottle of rosé? And you have orange plastic wineglasses? The kind everyone has around the pool?"

"Mrs. Carroll, we are a bike store. Most don't carry glassware. And I'd bet you would not like the plastic bottles the athletes use . . ."

"Hideous. Never."

"Halsey Hardware has the plastic wineglasses in all colors. My buddy runs the store. I know they have them, aisle right off the counter."

"Do you think you could go get, say, twenty of them and throw them in the baskets when you deliver everything? I would really appreciate it."

Harry shook his head *NO* back at Roger, as he returned to Katie and found a small bike for Huck. He whispered to Katie, "You have to treat these women like toddlers and at some point draw a line."

Katie resolved to do the same should she ever encounter one at close range.

Roger explained to Margaux, "I can't go to another store and purchase glasses for you, that's just—" He shook his head at her sternly as if she should know at some point not to ask certain things of her subjects. "That's too much."

The cash register pinged. "Just so you know, the charge will be $13,843.53."

"Look, I'm not an idiot," Margaux said. "I went to Dartmouth. How much of a markup are you making on the bike stands alone? Or should we calculate your commission on a fourteen-thousand-dollar sale, done in eight minutes of your time . . . and you can't get me sixteen plastic glasses? Really?" Then she added, making quotation marks with her fingers, "From your 'buddy'?"

Roger wanted to smack this woman. But, on some deeply demented level, he knew she had a point.

Margaux relented. "It's fine. I'll send my guy." Then, her mood brightened with a brilliant inspiration. "Maybe I'll tell him to get a dozen orange beach towels at that little Aerin Lauder store, one for each guest. It'll be so cute when we get to the beach. Like a little orange sunset army announcing summer! We'll just, you know, take off!"

And that she did, into the purring Lexus LS sedan her chauffer had waiting for her outside.

KATIE TOOK A breath and tried to remember the good folks back at the highway deli. "I'm sorry, can I ask again? How much is this sturdy Townie bike that everyone has?"

"Eight hundred ninety-five dollars," Harry answered.

"Oh, that's a lot. I just need a little . . ."

"I'm sorry, you seem like a nice woman, but I can't give you a deal." He leaned in. "There's a Kmart with a very good bike department. I know they have plenty of those Huffy brand bikes. They last years and cost only sixty-nine bucks." He smiled.

"Thanks," Katie answered quietly, beginning to understand there were two distinct worlds with two distinct economies out here: one with meatball heroes and one with wasabi tuna Swiss chard wraps. "We only need a bike for this summer. I'll survive if it isn't a Townie . . ."

"Mom," Huck looked up at her and announced loudly, "I don't like the bikes in this store."

Katie knelt down on her knees and smiled so hard she could feel her ears pulling backwards. She kissed Huck's perfect forehead and thought, just maybe, she could alone raise a son with judgment, a gut for instincts, and good taste.

Chapter Seven

The Binary Beachfront

I got four watermelons, a huge tub of Crisco, and nine dozen eggs," Luke announced as he walked up to the instructors waiting for him at the patch of land between the sand and the public parking lot. "I figured it's a beach games day."

"Good move," Kona answered. "Look at the ocean. Flatter than my third grade girlfriend."

Memorial Day Monday marked the end of the first weekend of Kona and Luke's Tide Runners Camp, where dozens of kids would show up and pay one hundred and fifty dollars for three hours of water sports lessons, rain or shine. Their friend Kenny, who worked at the camp part-time, busied himself inflating inner tubes for activities in the bay. "Luke, Kenny, you guys count the kids," Kona told the instructors he'd assembled that day: men with no official training besides a lifetime in the water. "No waves, no surfing for sure. Slather up the watermelons with the Crisco and we'll throw them in the water and they can try to hang onto them."

Tide Runners Camp offered surfing and ocean safety lessons

on the Atlantic side, and their two dilapidated motorboats took small groups water-skiing and tubing on the bay side of the parking lot. Three rusted Jet Skis were available for lucky adults over eighteen.

The instructors' shoddy equipment and mellow surfer demeanor did not translate into reckless behavior. In reality, no one had greater respect for the power of the ocean than these men who battled it every day. And that was a good thing: their clients ranged from age four to seventy, many wanting to try out surfing for the first time.

It was a simple fact as clear as Kona's ability to "harvest pussy": the locals respected the power of the ocean and the city people often did not. Their ignorance, hubris, and stupidity would lead them to walk into crushing waves they couldn't handle, with riptides they couldn't see. The guys figured their colossal estates weren't enough to hold them over: these people felt entitled to own Mother Nature as well.

By 9:00 a.m., the parking lot that led up to camp resembled an arms dealer convention in Kuwait City with expensive sedans, SUVs, and two-seater sports cars jamming in and out of tight spots. Kids piled out of the cars dragging wetsuits, plush Frette beach towels, and monogrammed tote bags loaded with coconut water and tubes of seventy-five-dollar Orlane Pure Soin Sun Cream SPF 30.

"Do you know if Alexa will be at camp today? It's nuts how girls from the city grow up too fast," Kona told Luke, tying his hair back into a ponytail. "Julia Chase didn't stop by the shop all weekend that I saw. I was hoping to cop a little feel of something."

"Julia is your whack concept of who you should be fucking, not mine," Luke answered. "I haven't seen her, but I also haven't been on the lookout for a married mother in a see-through shirt."

"She usually brings Richie around to buy a T-shirt or some skim milk chick latte next door, but I haven't seen her since we bolted that lame affair."

Of course they hadn't planned on leaving the "Hamptons Festive" cocktail party so early that Saturday night. Unfortunately, the humiliation of a shell-encrusted toothpick rammed into Kona's hand had forced them to leave without saying goodbye or ever nailing the older guy getting his way with a sixteen-year-old in the sea grass. On the silent ride home, neither man knew what to say to each other, except, "Fuck those people."

This morning, about ten women in the parking lot unloaded bags with young and teen children. Some of them headed to the Seabrook Club next door, while some nonmembers headed to the water sports camp meeting grounds at the top of the lot. All of them looked the same: toned figures draped in crisp Tory Burch tunics fresh out of the orange tissue paper for their virgin summer 2017 appearance. On their feet, they sported pricey-looking, beaded sandals they'd bought on their boozy girls' trip to Mykonos the previous summer while their husbands slayed the market dragons on Wall Street.

The housewives had emailed Kona and Luke early in the week, imploring them to occupy their children at surf camp for three hours to free them up to get their houses "weekend ready," as if for an impending missile strike. Once the kids were happily at water sports camp, the moms could get after their staffs to iron the Porthault cocktail napkins, buy the farm-raised chickens at the overpriced butcher, and stuff the vases with extravagant bunches of peonies that played off the new curtain fabric.

These women felt a huge sense of accomplishment knowing their houses would be functioning in order while the children were out a hundred yards in the rough currents of the Atlantic Ocean, monitored by a group of hungover guys, whose names they didn't quite catch.

Colette Spencer, her child terrified of waves, ran up to Kona. "I've got to do errands and then I have an exercise class. Can you keep Charlie out of the water?"

Though a strange request for a water sports camp director, this was not unusual. Kona knew these city women prioritized their Power Pilates classes over common sense parenting. "Mrs. Spencer." He locked his dashing blue eyes on her. "He will be fine without surfing or water-skiing; we'll keep your kid happy. Go take your class. We'll teach them how to fix a boat motor or something." Kona then glided his fingers up her arm. "Just, go on." And he winked, signaling silently, *I got this little butterfly fluttering technique with my tongue, so very light between your legs, it'll drive you insane.* "Trust me, I got this, or as we say on the Big Island, *Malama pono.* Take care."

"Well," Colette answered, flustered by Kona's ruthless stare, and aroused for the first time in at least three years. "Just, uh, no water anything for Charlie, please." She kissed her miserable son on the forehead who would rather have been anywhere on the planet besides this camp.

Just then, Jake Chase's restored white 1977 International Harvester Scout that he'd bought from Billy Joel's personal collection roared into the public beach parking lot. This vintage Scout gas-guzzler cost him about ninety thousand dollars, a vehicle pretty much every American surfer bum would give their left testicle to own.

Jake possessed the same ability to handle his new Scout toy as a three-year-old boy would a bucking rodeo steer. This was, after all, a man who had no interest in putting his pinkie toe in the ocean. He knew there was a possibility he didn't look legit peeking over the top of the wheel as he drove this ultimate surf vehicle, but he wanted to show it to the surfers anyway. Maybe their cool would rub off on him. Or, of course, vice versa.

Jake figured he'd impress his local buddies first time out with the Scout by gunning it full speed onto the soft Hamptons sand.

"Dad!" wailed his son Richie, who was already in camp starting an egg toss. "You can't drive on this beach. It's only down near the jetty you can drive!"

The Scout made it about fifteen yards before it began to whip up sand that had the consistency of confectioners' sugar. Soon the undercarriage chassis was sitting directly on the earth with the tires dug in so deep they couldn't grab anything. The smell of burning rubber wafted down the beach, while the newly restored transmission (costing thirty thousand dollars) whirred at a screeching pitch as it headed to ruin. Jake stepped out and marched around to survey the damage. His gut protruded on his short frame, making his walk more a waddle than a stride.

Luke and Kona rushed up to Jake Chase, motivated not by wanting to help so much as fear this would make their camp look even more unruly than it already was. Kona said to both Kenny and Luke, "Watch, it'll just give the town board more ammunition to shut the camp down. Let's dig him out fast."

Members of the Seabrook Club were far from enamored with the idea of filthy camp surfboards and coolers adjacent to "their" beach. Some overreaching ladies had formed a committee the previous summer to lobby that Tide Runners be shut down on the legal grounds that money wasn't allowed to change hands on town beaches. Kona and Luke always made it a point to accept checks and cash in the public parking lot, which was, according to the rules, legal.

Jake Chase lumbered a few feet across the sand, defeated, confused but grateful these men had more 4x4 know-how than he did. His dark, curly hair now blew in his face, long on the sides to counteract the middle-aged, thinning spots on the top. "Thanks guys, I feel like a fool. I just wanted to say hi, hang out a little."

Kona said, "You know, Jake, when you drive on the beach, you've absolutely got to air down first."

"Air out what?" Jake chuckled and punched Kona's arm too hard. "It's a fuckin' safari vehicle with the whole sky open to the passengers." He wondered what the hell Kona was referring to, and hated not knowing.

"Jake. Take a breather, man. I'm talking taking air out of the tires. It is actually called 'airing down,'" answered Kona, returning the verbal volley. "If you want to drive on sand, you have to air down the tires."

"The guy who sold it to me never said I had to do that," Jake responded, cranky over his disastrous Scout unveiling. He'd had a completely different entry in mind: he'd roll on the sand, the guys would hop on the side runners, they'd all plow down the beach to a good Kanye West song Jake had already queued up in his playlist. "If you knew what I paid the guy to . . ."

"It actually doesn't matter how much the truck cost. Regardless, you gotta 'air down the tires' when you're driving any vehicle down the beach," answered Kona calmly, like he was putting a mental patient into a straitjacket. "The softer tires with less air in them allow it to stay on top of the sand, making them wider, instead of getting stuck. When you plan on driving on the pavement, you gotta air back up to normal, hard tires."

During this explanation, Jake had his hands on his hips, shaking his head back and forth furiously like a five-year-old who didn't want to eat his peas. He cut Kona off, saying, "No fuckin' way am I doing that."

Just then, Julia Chase rolled up to the lot in her own clementine-orange 1974 Porsche Targa, which she thankfully had the good wits not to drive into the sand. Kona spotted her and took off his shirt as he gallantly shoveled her husband out of the mess he was in.

"Hey, Julia!" Kona couldn't help but yell. "We got this!"

"I wouldn't have bought this fucking car if I'd known I needed to go to mechanic trade school to . . ." Jake whined.

"It's pretty basic. It's not like the guy who sold it needed to explain," lectured Kona.

"Dude," Jake clarified, his need for acceptance driving his blood several degrees warmer. "Let's get real here. I'm just a working guy like you. I ain't actually like these rich city assholes who think they're better than you locals who grew up here. I'm sure you know them."

"Yes, I do actually, my fair share," Kona answered, curious where this line of reasoning was going.

"I'm just like you guys. No different and no better," Jake, a titan controlling half a billion dollars of Laundromats and mall properties, contended. "My dad never once made more than fifty K in a year, my mom was a substitute teacher."

"Well, now I wouldn't . . ."

"Put myself through school. Drove a laundry truck to get by. Swear, if luck didn't fuckin' follow me around. If it hadn't, I would'a been happy teaching water-skiing for a living like you guys!" Jake thought hard about how much that would suck. "Point is, I work like a sweaty son of a bitch to run my properties. *Never* will I air a tire up, down, or even fuckin' sideways."

"So why don't you hire someone to lie down in the trunk anytime you want to go on a little off-road adventure?" Kona laughed and shook his head. "He could just pop out when you need him."

"I'm not, I just meant, I fuckin' work all week already. It's not fair on my weekend when I'm trying to relax to have to . . ."

"C'mon guys! Let's shovel him out before the Seabrook people come down," Luke yelled. Kona fell to his knees to shovel the sand away from the buried tires. He hoped it would make him look like a stud in front of Jake's wife, Julia.

After only two minutes, Jake's patience on the dig-out wore thin.

He yelled at the guys, "How long is it going to take you to work me out of here anyway?"

The fact that it wasn't Kona's job to work him out of there didn't enter Jake's mind. Neither did the fact that it might present a problem that his wife, Julia, was digging out the exact same tire Kona was working on. In fact, she was now kneeling in front of Kona at the perfect angle, so that her bulbous butt bumped into his inner thighs as she helped shovel her own husband out of humiliation.

Chapter Eight
Goliath v. Goliath

Raging over how this week's market hammered the meager trust his aunt Bunny and uncle Tripp had left him, Bucky Porter clambered down from the Seabrook Club. A summons he'd get signed today over the truck in the sand incident would be a step toward restraining the Tide Runners instructors' ill-found sense of privilege. This summer, he'd decided to run for a trustee slot on the town board that would give him formal municipal levers to shut down the wretched camp for good.

The Seabrook Clubhouse, well in sight from the camp drop-off, stood high up on a bluff overlooking the sea. It was an imposing fortress, with a slate roof, red shingles, and white-paned windows. The six cement cracked tennis courts, unrepaired since 1962, stood between the club and Beachwood Lane.

The High Episcopalian members of Bucky's club, already plying themselves with barrels of alcohol before lunch, nodded to him as he passed. The older ladies with hair so gray that it had a blue tint sat in circles playing bridge in the enclosed patio area. The younger women gathered at other tables, or chased after children, their

A-frame Lilly Pulitzer uniforms signaling a strictly missionary, no orgasm zone.

The bar counter, adjacent to a veranda-style restaurant, stood next to a pee-filled Olympic pool. Today, the male members washed down their drinks with Ritz crackers and cheddar cheese spread from a black earthenware tub. They chomped on Chex Mix, and guffawed about one of them missing putts all morning at the nearby Emerald Links Club, then miraculously draining a thirty-foot snake on the eighteenth hole to win the match.

Bucky, forty-three, worked in New York, but, truth be told, didn't really have a job. He had a broker spot at an investment firm that paid on commissions, but he wasn't much good at it. He knew that, the firm knew that, but he was allowed to sit there because his great uncle Tripp had started the firm during its heyday in the 1950s. None of this mattered to Bucky; he had means other than his professional accomplishments to express his authority and aptitude.

He marched down several splintered gray steps to the sand, shoddy from beach erosion. He waved a friendly hello to the Seabrook beach boys who busied themselves laying out dozens of rickety wooden chairs under matching yellow-and-white striped umbrellas. Ropes leading to large metal buoys on the shore delineated the sandy area that the club could control for their members only. Of course, in higher tides down by the shoreline, club members tended to put their chairs and umbrellas too close to the water, clearly encroaching on the public property . . . strikingly similar to those Israeli settlements they blamed for all the world trouble "we" were in.

Bucky, having passed the figurative and literal line in the sand that separated Seabrook people from "other people," now marched to Tide Runners' camp headquarters.

Luke nudged Kona as the two of them, having gotten Jake off the beach successfully, stared out at the flat ocean before them. "Asshole coming at us at three o'clock on your right. Don't make eye contact or he'll think we give a shit. I told you Jake's truck was going to cause huge trouble for the camp."

"Damn it!" Bucky yelled at himself. His worn loafers with the big gold horse-bit buckle loaded up with more and more of that flour-like New England sand as he marched toward the Tide Runners instructors. First he dumped sand out of his shoes and then, for some reason that made no sense to any of the guys, put them back on just to slide into each step and fill up again ten yards later.

Kona whispered to Luke, "He looks like a walking billboard for an erectile dysfunction commercial."

Standing before them now, Bucky pondered the camp head-quarters. It resembled a low-rent yard sale. Before him: a few Lands' End navy-and-red striped towels with children's initials left behind from last summer's kids, two coolers filled with juice boxes, a huge bag of Cheetos from the Riverhead Costco, several life vests, four paddleboards, four uneven paddles that didn't match the paddleboards, three *Star Wars* boogie boards from last century, and thirteen long surfboards with soft tops for beginners, also scraped to hell and dinged, showing pockmarks of the Styrofoam layer underneath as if they had been riddled with machine-gun fire.

Kona, standing five foot ten, puffed out his bare and tanned chest to prepare for battle. He walked straight up to Bucky who was dressed in a teal-blue polo shirt. It didn't go unnoticed by onlookers that Bucky's upper torso and biceps were larger and more sculpted than Kona's, who'd spent hours at the gym to work on getting his body right for the ladies.

Bucky was a man who did not work hard at anything. His muscles, like his handsome face, were God-given.

"Bucky, so good to see you," said Kona. "If you don't mind, I'll take two egg salad sandwiches and a glass of that cheap Chardonnay you serve."

"Before you start," Luke interrupted immediately, rolling his eyes at his friend, "the Scout truck was not ours, and we got the man out of the sand quickly. We're simply helping a citizen of this town."

Bucky surveyed the disarray before him. "You sure that dangerous safari vehicle didn't belong to a camp parent?"

"I have never seen that man in my life," Kona lied.

"Hey, Kona," Bucky said. "C'mon, work with me a little. You know this is a town beach, no vehicles, no businesses that attract such vehicles, no . . ."

"Exactly. Town: as in catering to the citizens. Meaning we, as lifelong residents of said town, can do what we want here," Kona answered, sounding like more of a stuck-up ass than Bucky. "Including teaching kids and adults to respect the power of the ocean. And keeping them safe."

Bucky guffawed, "Safe? With boats that don't work, Jet Skis that are a dozen years old? Just look at this equipment!"

"Yeah, safe. Speaking of which, we noticed you foundering around in the flat shore break today. If you want a quick ocean swimming lesson, there's a spot in the six-to-eight-year-old swim class, we could squeeze you in. But you're going to have to wait about twenty minutes for that egg salad to digest. I don't want you to cramp up in those scary, ankle-high waves."

"Your camp is a joke, barely legal," Bucky scoffed.

"We've been over this every summer. We do what we want on the ocean as long as we take payment in the public lot," Luke claimed, noticing that Bucky once again turned his back to him, only talking to Kona.

"Why do you have to gather here, at the top of the beach entrance, with this vista," Bucky answered, ignoring Luke, then waving his hands over the Atlantic like Jesus at the Sea of Galilee.

"Just curious," asked Kona. "How exactly do twenty pieces of equipment laying in the sand destroy a 'vista,' and your two hundred yellow chairs and umbrellas and ropes do not obstruct our view?"

"The Seabrook serves *the community*. We provide a wholesome family environment that generations of . . ." As Bucky listed his people's superior attributes, he witnessed a rather attractive young mother running down to camp headquarters. She was clearly rushed.

Kenny, a huge beast of a bearded man and a few years older than the rest of the crew, raced to go talk to the mother, away from this group. Mrs. Saltzman reached into her purse and grabbed her wallet while Kenny tried to yank her up the lot. Too late, she pressed several bills in his hand, screaming, "It's all there plus tips!"

Bucky smiled. *Bingo. Exchanging cash for a business on a town beach: very, very illegal.* Even better, this Kona from some loser Hawaiian island was so busy defending his filthy enterprise, he didn't notice. These guys were nailed, done, and it wasn't even June.

"You may feel comforted to know we are, in fact, doing the same thing as your club. Catering to our clients. Now if you'd . . ." Kona made a quick head-butt motion at Bucky.

Bucky jerked his head back and then leaned right into Kona's face. "You do know I'm running for town trustee? And you do know trucks driving on sand in public areas could run over and kill people?"

"Wasn't us and . . ."

"Are you sure your ledgers are clear and copacetic?"

"Copa-what?" asked Kona slowly, trying to sound like a doofus surfer dude. He made another head-butt motion right at Bucky.

"You know what? I'm not making any progress here; you don't get it," Bucky answered, pulling his head back in defense, with no particular riposte in mind except, *"Jesus H. Christ!!!"*

It was important to know one's limits when dealing with people who had less of a brain in their heads, like that Lenny character in *Of Mice and Men.* Bucky matched up physically with this gorilla before him, but he realized Kona could still do something to harm him. After all, he was hardly accustomed to fistfights, as this local shithead surely was.

And so, Bucky retreated, spinning around to mingle with the more genteel types behind the ropes, and silently vowing, once elected, to get these local, uneducated, unrefined pieces of crap back where it counted.

Chapter Nine

That Memorial Day Monday Thing

Huck studied the wrinkled Lego manual with defeat. "Mom, can you help me find the piece with six holes? It's flat and red and I think it didn't make it with the rest."

Katie closed her eyes to summon patience and knelt on the floor with her child, an old peach-flowered pillow barely providing cushion under her knees. After eight minutes of separating Lego pieces into piles, she walked back into the kitchen to get cereal bowls. "Honey, we'll put them in bowls by colors. That way you can keep better track."

"Okay, Mom." Huck smiled. There was nothing Katie hated more than Legos, but her son would never know. She spent half an hour helping him construct a wing of a Lego heli-jet they'd brought from Hood River in a huge Ziploc bag. Once Huck hit a stride, she left him to finish the next stage on his own. She had more organizing of her own to do before George arrived in less than a week.

Next, she lined up her cosmetics in neat, obsessive lines on the bathroom windowsill. She then folded her son's shirts as if they were new and for sale, all physical steps to giving an upended life a sense of order.

Katie felt fidgety this early Monday evening. She had so much to do, but, she remembered, none of it needed doing just then. While Huck constructed his flying masterpiece, she plunked herself down on her bed, the springs creaking loudly beneath her. She'd wiped the bedroom dresser several times since they'd moved into the Porter family's second cottage, and it was even dustier now.

She stood up suddenly to open the windows. The cooler breeze and the sounds of cicadas buzzing like tractors flowed into her teeny bedroom. She knew she felt out of sorts; a half-happy and half-sad cocktail that, when mixed together, turned melancholy.

Today was only ten weeks since her mother died. The carved ebony box she'd brought from home beckoned her from the crooked shelf of the bedroom closet. She'd carried it on the plane in her purse, the velvet pouch inside holding half her mother's ashes. Katie had purposely placed the box behind sweaters when they arrived. She didn't want to see it every day. Some days, she hoped, she'd forget it was there.

Now she grabbed the box and held it in her hands as she again sat on the edge of the bed. The thin mattress listed, and she had to push her feet against the floor so as not to slide off. She traced the pattern of inlaid enamel flowers of the box. Once the cancer vanquished her mother, she implored her daughter to face life with a strong, authentic smile. Though Katie felt her eyes get hot, she used the box to summon resolve over sorrow.

The early evening sun now streamed sideways through the lace curtains of the musty cottage. Speckles of dust floated in the air and reflected like bits of mica. Katie reminded herself this was simply the beginning of her eastern adventure. Everything that could be in place was in place, just like those products on her bathroom windowsill.

Her landlord in Hood River had thankfully allowed her to end the lease four months early, and she knew it would be easier to move out here with nothing holding her back. Six hours a week were already guaranteed by the tutoring company, and that newly posted Bridgehampton Middle School job for a special ed substitute had her name on it. She'd have her couches, boxes, and car sent in September if all went as planned.

Katie stood to touch the scrimshaw etchings of ships on the bedroom wall, wondering which members of the Porter family had a history of whaling. Nautical charts hung everywhere. Heavy doorstops made of shipping rope held doors ajar, and an antique brass telescope dominated much of the living room. She figured the family must be attached to the quaint flea-market aura of it all.

In old family photos, she studied George on a college tennis team with championship cups thrust in the air. In another, George with his father, now deceased, at the stern of a sailboat, both looking up at the sail's tack in the wind. They were ruggedly handsome men. Some of the photos and maps were nailed to the hallway walls an inch apart, others several inches. The mismatched angles all over the hallway jarred Katie's methodical brain.

Katie was hardly in a position to tell the Porter family she preferred the clean white lines of the lofty one bedroom in an old Hood River, Oregon mining factory she and Huck had just moved out of. The white Formica shelves had given her possessions a sense of geometric order, all fitting together like Legos.

After a quick shower, Katie was upbeat about the progress she'd made unpacking. She changed into clean yellow shorts and a T-shirt, and then said to her son, "Honey, let's bike, look around a little. I want to get out of the cottage before it gets dark and see the town again."

"I don't want to leave, Mom. Now I can't find the yellow light for the wing, can you . . ."

"C'mon," Katie said. "I'm getting excited about living here. They seem to surf more than windsurf from what I can see, but I'll figure that out. And for you, good news: there's a really good candy store on Main Street. Let's go."

Her son bolted up and ran out the door to jump on his sixty-nine-dollar Huffy bike. Mother and son steered their new bikes out the driveway and onto a street they didn't recognize at all.

Interlude: August Sneak Peek

The bay constable cast his light across the wake once again to be sure. The waves lapped the nearby shore in a gentle rocking motion that belied the chaotic search for the man.

Irregular sand bars, a few feet in depth, lightened patches of the bay during the day, but now hid themselves in the monotone inky water. Several officers walked the length of the jetty with searchlights swinging back and forth, illuminating the sharp and shiny rocks for an instant on either side. A Zodiac police raft sped by in the distance.

Members of the country club last saw the man on the docks late that afternoon. They told police he had had an "animated" discussion with the water sports instructors. Something about renting a Jet Ski with a child, even though the rules about sixteen and under riding on a Jet Ski had been made clear. He wanted a lesson to navigate the channels, the jutting boulders, and the quick changes in depth of the sandy bottom. His caution and foresight made sense, according to the members who had grown up with him. They described a thoughtful man, someone apparently drawn to the order of rules.

Moments later, the constable radioed back at the two other boats in the water. "An object forty degrees north from the clubhouse," he said, his walkie-talkie crackling. "Not a buoy for sure. But something's in the water. I'm going to get a look."

He pushed the boat gear into forward and idled closer, a cloud of gasoline fumes stagnant in the humid August night surrounding him.

Indeed, the underbelly of a Jet Ski now appeared amidst the small waves. And nearby, swaying back and forth, another upturned object: the sole of a soaking wet Gucci loafer.

Chapter Ten

Downtime in Town

On that same Memorial Day, Kona, Luke, and their fellow instructor Kenny demolished their one weekly indulgence, overpriced scoops of blood orange and mint chip gelatos from the fancy Italian café. Today, it served to help calm their collective nerves.

"Such bullshit, the town board isn't even open. I don't get how Bucky could even file the complaint on a holiday," said Kenny, tightening his eyes with brain freeze from the cold. "I'm sorry guys, I didn't know he was watching. Mrs. Saltzman just literally threw the cash at me on the beach. I can't believe he saw . . . I thought he was yelling at you."

"He even cited her in the complaint, the nicest camp parent we got. She was just rushing and doesn't know the rules," lamented Luke.

All three men silently scraped the bottom of the gelato cups with their wooden spoons, many more times than the remnants of gelato required, calculating how they could pay rent, mobile phone, and car payments this summer if Bucky succeeded in closing down their camp.

"I'm going to sweet-talk the clerk," Luke told them. He played with his cleft chin, pushing the skin together with his index finger and thumb, a nervous habit of his. "Plus, when's the last time any of us got C.P.R. training? We checked that box on the town forms, but we gotta sign up for a real class, get some certificate . . . wait, whoa, look at that . . ."

Three faces and three pairs of eyes slowly moved in unison from left to right, following the woman and her son on the sidewalk across the street, as if they were watching a slow lob in a tennis match.

"Who is that?" Luke asked, flying his hands in the air. It was the first time he'd allowed himself any tumescent stirring since Simone's demolition of every fiber in his soul. Something about this woman's gait, her delicate femininity, the way she'd just knelt and brushed her son's face made his stomach ache with a need to know her. *"Very, very pretty."*

The town was mostly empty at this hour. The last of the urban throngs had left in a long line of vehicles snaking west up the main Route 27 out of the Hamptons. For those unfortunate city folks not owning a personal aircraft, all conversations centered on the quality of the beach day and the best time to beat the traffic on the Long Island Expressway back to Manhattan.

Of course, one notch better than not having to panic about when to pile into one's plush sedan was not having to leave the beach at all. At treasured times like this, the lucky ones who lived full-time in the Hamptons all collectively took one big, deep sigh like Cheshire cats.

The guys were sitting outside the Sun Spot Surf Shop in town, smack in the center of Main Street, where their usual bench tended to be command central of a large crew of locals who shared a kinship born in the ocean. Behind them, young men and women, teens to late thirties, talked in small groups outside the shop, many of them employed by Kona and Luke at some point during the summer. The older guys grabbed private-lesson clients after work, many holding regular jobs as carpenters or landscapers, but were often able to convince their bosses to give them leeway in summer to seek other income. People around here had the same mutual understanding that the rushing waterfall of summer cash was something to grab at while they could, and when they could.

"Down, boy," said Kona, patting Luke's head. "I see you finally got some blood flow back to the tip of that little penis of yours. You over your post traumatic stress of Simone leaving you?" He hit Luke's head this time, and Luke stopped short of shooting him a nasty look. He didn't like being teased about something too real. "Anything, jump on a whale, if it gets Simone out of your brain . . ." Kona couldn't help himself. He added, "Of course, you're never going to grip an ass like that again."

"Enough with Simone," Kenny ordered. Kenny had grown up on the rough side of the tracks in nearby Flanders, and was known as one of the most able fishermen and strongest surfers on Long Island. He had inherited his family's landscaping company, which was a glorified way of saying that he owned four John Deere lawn mowers with chronic mechanical issues, and worked part-time for the camp when he could. He added, "Simone's a whore. A mean one. Move the fuck on, Luke. Go for that woman in yellow shorts with the kid you haven't stopped watching. I like her flow. She seems, I don't know, not advertising that she's hot, but still game."

Kenny's protective love for this crew on the bench was the real reason he strayed from his John Deere lawn mowers on the sprawling lawns; he was hell-bent on making sure no shithead rich kid died on his friends' watch. And, besides, what the hell, he could skip out on work for private surf lessons or camp when he wanted: his clients only spoke to him or his illegal day laborers to say, "Keep the noise down out there, guys!"

"She looks game, but not as game as Julia Chase," said Kona. "This is the summer I'm gonna do it. Take notes, boys."

"Never gonna happen. Julia is playing you to make her husband jealous," said Kenny. "Stay away."

"She was here earlier; she sat here. Said she wanted a wakeboard lesson, something about firming up her thighs, which she then massaged. *On the inside.* I'm telling you, she wants the dick."

The men turned their attention from Kona's delusions to the woman strolling down the street just in front of them, a brunette in her late twenties or early thirties, with a round beautiful face, pale skin, bright red lips, and clear green eyes.

"I'm going to talk to her," answered Luke. "Or, at least try . . ."

"I'd move on that," Kenny advised. "She looks like Snow White in the flesh. Jesus, closer up, she is really pretty."

The woman wore tight, straight-legged, yellow shorts that were tattered at the ends and hit her mid-thigh. On her feet were flat white Top-Sider sneakers, now gray with age, and a Portland Trailblazer's T-shirt on her slender frame. Her thick brown hair fell in a bob just above her shoulders. The child with her, a young boy of about eight or so, had a blond bowl cut, chubby cheeks and thighs, and was stomping his new sneakers to make tiny red lights on the soles go on and off. She was hunched over, guiding his bike by the little handlebars.

Luke felt a gentle pat on his shoulder. He looked up and saw his stepfather, Frank. "You making so much from camp you can afford that fancy Italian gelatin?" Frank asked, never a fan of extravagance. He was the owner of the small-sized, but consistently successful, Forrester Plumbing.

"It's *gelato*, Dad." It had been a long weekend handling a bunch of bratty kids on a boat that tanked out every fifteen minutes.

"Excuse me? You need a ten-dollar cup of gelatin?"

"Never mind, it's just, I don't know, a little treat after a big day." It was hard for Luke to yell at Frank, a man who'd married Luke's young mother when he was two, replacing a father who'd left the moment she got pregnant. Fifteen years after her death in the ocean during Luke's teen years, Frank was still hell-bent on guiding the boy he'd raised.

"You don't need that. Why don't you come home? I got plenty of vanilla in the fridge—we can watch the game?"

"All good, Dad, another time," Luke answered, as he continued to follow the woman.

Luke hated thinking about Frank alone at nights, but what could he do? His mother had been gone for more than a decade now, and Frank still hadn't found anyone to fall in love with.

Luke had been with Kona at a skateboard park in Riverhead in Luke's tenth grade year when Frank had yanked them off the ramps and physically thrown them into his pickup. Driving eighty miles an hour back to the boat docks, Frank delivered the news that Luke's mom had gone missing in the currents. She and the girls took a boat out that seemingly clear Saturday in September before the storm came in. Frank and Kona spent seven days and nights searching the waters for her. Luke stayed with an aunt at home, too terrified to leave his room. They kept looking, not even giving up when the local Coast Guard turned the search from "search and rescue" to the dreaded "search and recovery" mission for bodies. When Kona, crestfallen, relented to Frank's wishes and gave up the search after ten days, he also vowed to spend his life watching Luke's back.

"C'mon Luke. Kenny's right," Kona cajoled. "That woman is hot in a way Simone isn't. Look at her. She's way cooler, more confident."

Luke didn't love the guys all ganging up on him about his obsession with Simone over the past year, but they had a point: he needed to step out of the fog.

"She's not from here. I would'a seen her," answered Frank. "She's got some beautiful legs, I tell ya. Luke, she looks like a nice girl, a few years younger than you. You oughtta go introduce yourself. Go, c'mon."

"I think she's from the city," remarked Kona. "She's got style that isn't from here. Got money. Playing it down, though."

The guys let that settle, and considered Kona's observations because he did play women better than any of them. But this night, like most nights, Kona was dead wrong about the facts.

"I'm going to go watch the Mets game at home," Frank said, wiping the gray strands down on his balding head, then placing his hands on his portly hips. "If she's from the city, you guys stay far away. Those women are only trouble. I've told you . . . Kona, you especially, stay away from those married moms. You're gonna get your ass whipped by a husband one of these days if you keep at it."

Frank, sixty-eight years old and set in his ways, did not believe in fraternizing with city people under any circumstances other than payment for work fairly done. Luke's mom had gotten tangled up with a city person long ago in a messy situation, and Frank was not one to forgive or forget.

"Dad. Please. We've all heard it, like seven hundred times you've warned us."

"I happen to be right. Your mother, God rest her soul, would want me to keep you away from them. But I'll shut up only because I got a game to watch. You dopes waste your hard-earned cash on overpriced Jell-O and go solve the world's problems," Frank said, massaging Luke's shoulders warmly. "Dinner this week, son?"

"Yeah, sure."

As Frank walked to his pickup truck, Luke felt bad for dismissing the man who'd always been kinder to him than anyone. But only for so long, as the woman came into their crosshairs again. "I know we've never seen her."

Luke watched the woman as she meandered through town,

coming in and out of the shops. A few times he stood up from the bench to feign a stretch and make sure he kept a hold on her exact coordinates.

As THE MOONLIGHT bore down on the abandoned town, the conversation between the Tide Runners instructors bounced between topics big and small: the height of the waves heading in (measured by buoys far out at sea that could predict), how they would get the city families, possibly even Jake Chase, to help fight the town board to secure the camp's very existence this summer, and, most animatedly, who would be paying the thirty-dollar June fee for the Porn Hub password they all shared.

Several minutes later, the woman in yellow walked right in front of them. "One shark necklace," she said to her son. "Just don't ask me to find another Lego piece. I beg you."

Watching her as she passed into the store, Luke stood up. The Sun Spot Surf Shop behind their bench was the guy's version of a general store, a homegrown establishment that offered beach shovels for a reasonable eight bucks, and Coppertone spray for four. All the kids from Manhattan coveted the graphic T-shirts, skateboards, and surfer gear sold inside. The store was one of the few places in town frequented by locals and city people alike. Locals appreciated the fair pricing, and city people would stumble in, relenting to their children, to see how regular folks across America shopped. If she even cared to enter, this woman had more than an ounce of cool, Luke was willing to hope.

"She looks kind of settled, maybe married," cautioned Kenny, as Luke walked away from the group toward her. "Jesus, I hope you don't land another psychotic woman. But I didn't see a ring."

Neither did I, Luke thought to himself and he walked in behind her casually as if, at 7:00 p.m., he had a sudden need to buy a tube of zinc oxide.

Chapter Eleven

Surf Shop Shenanigans

Katie Doyle knew the guys were checking her out, and she noticed that the best-looking of the bunch followed her inside. She smiled to herself, biting the outside of her lip to hide any trace of the inconvenient flutter he caused. His cool manner attracted her, as did his unruly, dark chocolate hair. She knew she had a weakness for messy, and found it daring compared to her fastidious nature.

She decided to focus on a small gift for Huck rather than flirt back. George would be arriving the following weekend, and there was no need to complicate her carefully crafted summer plan. She liked the sudden quiet ambiance with the New York people apparently gone for a workweek in Manhattan.

Inside the Sun Spot Surf Shop, summer goods swelled out of the cramped shelves. Huck touched everything he could, the graphic T-shirts with the coveted NEW YORK SUNSHINE brand blazoned across them, the boxes of inflatable pool rafts piled to the ceiling (swans to sit on, half pizza slices with holes for drinks to lie on, donuts to curl into), surfboards—some short, some sky high—lined up vertically, boogie boards wrapped in plastic, Go-Pro cameras, and other mechanical gadgets designed to make any child salivate.

Katie could sense the guy near her, tracing her steps around the store. He looked her age, maybe a tad older, early thirties. His upright posture signified a self-assured person, but the way he followed her from afar also read careful, with an air of kindness. Just what the doctor ordered after the hell she'd been through this past spring with her mother dying.

Huck tugged hard at her shirt from behind. "Mom, we really need a drone."

"Honey, I promised candy. Possibly a shark tooth necklace. We came into town to explore, and buy one small thing. Remember, *explore* was the plan."

With all the water sports paraphernalia in the shop, Katie imagined herself windsurfing on the bays in the Hamptons, boom in hand, sea spray in her face. It all made her desperate to get summer going already. Katie had discovered the soothing salt water of the Atlantic for the first time this morning. Dunking her body in had felt positively baptismal, as salt water always washed the demons away. She'd found salvation all year back home in Cascade Locks—a windsurf mecca, with the winds blowing into the gorge from the Pacific, her heavy wetsuit keeping her warm in forty-five-degree water.

The Sun Spot store was even messier than the cottage, but she was excited to shake up their senses with the new sights, sounds, tastes, and even aromas in the Hamptons. This morning she'd inhaled humid, salty fog rather than the dry Pacific Northwest air. For lunch, Huck had scarfed down his first plate of fried clams from a truck by the sea. Katie chose a lobster roll. She couldn't remember if she'd ever eaten lobster on a hot dog bun. As they biked around the back lanes of Southampton, Katie had yelled back at

Huck, "Even the light is different out here! Look how the thick trees make these streets all shaded even in the middle of the day." Katie and Huck were used to the blinding sun on the open lavender field outside her Hood River door, reflecting off the snow-capped peaks of the largest mountain range in America.

Katie watched Huck in front of a row of bathing suits, perusing the bold colors with patterns, stripes, and images of the sea. "Look, it says SURF on the side. I really need one."

She flashed on an image of Huck standing like this, his back to her as it was now, before her mother's resting place after the funeral in March. They had strewn half of her ashes in Flathead Lake by their home. For a moment, while Katie said goodbye to mourners, the child paid homage to his grandmother alone, walking down to the shore again. He stood there, his chubby physique thinned out in the dark suit with baggy pants she'd borrowed from a neighbor. The delicate waves of the lake lapped at his big-boy shoes in the muddy sand.

This is my first glimpse of the man Huck will become, she'd thought. During the entire ceremony, he'd grabbed her arm, squeezing it hard, knowing he was sending love up her limbs, telling her they'd carry on in life as a duo now without her mom next door. Watching Huck standing so tall reminded her of her mother's dying credo even as illness spread: she'd told Katie it was easier to live out her days grateful, rather than glum. Katie breathed in deep, channeling her mother, fortifying her resolve to embrace all the newness out here and stand firm in her decision.

The guy walked closer to her now. It was getting more difficult to ignore him. He wore jeans that curved on his strong build, and a T-shirt that hung a few inches farther down on one arm than the other. His thin frame was muscular and tight.

As she feigned interest in a small boogie board for Huck, she smiled back at him, even though she wanted to keep the segments of her new life simple, easy to put together, just like the jigsaw puzzle from the musty closet she and Huck had started on.

Katie thought about the relationship space George kept mentioning in phone calls. He was so intent on giving her distance and time so she didn't feel pressure. Was it possible, she might even date a little when George wasn't here? How weird. This great-looking guy now trying on a sweatshirt made her anxious with possibility.

George couldn't have been clearer, or more convincing. He'd laid out the summer plan in detail after that day picking cherries when he took her out to a dimly lit restaurant for dinner. "I swear on my life and yours. I like the other house. I haven't slept in the little cottage for fifteen years. We just give it to someone who is writing a novel or needs a break from a marriage. We don't rent it, ever. You don't have to pay. Just stay. No strings." At that point he'd asked the waiter for a thick felt-tip pen and written on a cocktail napkin in the light of a candle: COME EAST, NO STRINGS, KATIE OWES GEORGE ZERO.

But Katie had never maintained she owed him zero. She never said she needed monumental amounts of this so-called space. And that nagged her back in Hood River, on the long plane ride, and even now in the store. Her close friend Ashley had advised her when she'd visited Hood River to help her pack, "What man pushes a woman to cross the country if he isn't into her? He's just acting cool by saying you get your space . . . maybe you're giving him standoffish signals? Maybe you seem tentative about the summer in the Hamptons?"

"I'm sure I am, but I feel like I'm falling hard," Katie told Ashley as she'd taped up boxes. "I want to go out for work and a new life for Huck and not count on this relationship. Yet sometimes, when I'm feeling challenged by mothering Huck alone, or missing Mom, I find myself getting hooked on George in a way that makes me nervous, especially when he's all like, 'Yeah, you got the cottage, I'm not out much.'" She'd stopped taping and just sat on a box for a moment, wondering out loud, "What the hell is he doing when he's not out in the Hamptons much besides working?"

"Well, he's probably working honestly. But try to fall hard when you spend a summer together, not before," Ashley cautioned. "Go and keep your mind open about men in general. You can't take care of yourself and Huck in this huge change if you let a man sway you too much. Don't swing from intrepid to insecure. Go windsurf a lot out there to remind you of your strength. And the pieces will fall in your favor. I promise. You're an independent woman, always have been. It'll serve you out East."

Independence can have broad meaning. Katie was living in George's family cottage, beholden to him for that. She assumed they'd at least fall back into the initial pattern of dinner, a vodka or two, and sweaty, if a little too kinky, sex.

Good plan. Stick with that plan.

So why court trouble with this man studying the Maui Jim sunglass display case six feet down the aisle? She'd never been very good at paying heed to life's silly rules. Katie knew herself, and the strange pull she felt toward this man was potent.

She hesitated at the shark tooth display. Perhaps she could come up with a reason to ask the guy a "man" question about shark fishing or boats.

Katie then backtracked a little—what was she going to ask, *what is the best kind of shark tooth to own?* There were hundreds of little necklaces in the basket to choose from. The plastic packages weren't even labeled, and all the teeth looked the same.

Katie longed to call Ashley: *You sure it's not bad that George isn't even here for my first week? Or is it good to settle in with my ornery ways?*

And a far more pressing question: *Is this other guy bizarrely cute, or am I crazy?*

"All kids like those necklaces, good choice," the man said, watching Katie and Huck take several more out of the basket. His voice was kind.

She looked at him, her green eyes against her fair skin translucent in the fluorescent lighting in the store. "I, uh, it's just a little gift. He's tired." He looked a few years older than her twenty-nine years.

Luke smiled back at her, as he pulled his longish, dark hair over his ear. He played with his cleft chin, considering her beauty, and whether it would silence him. Maybe he could come up with a witty joke on the fly.

"All kids get tired at this hour." He thought to himself, *Stupid move, if the kid was tired, then he couldn't show them the ice cream store next door.*

"Yeah, it's just a little gift," she answered. *Couldn't she think of something about the town, then maybe he'd have to explain, then show her in person?*

"Mom. We decided. Can we go now? Can I wear it?"

Katie kneeled down to kiss Huck. Talking to this man wasn't wise on many fronts, she told herself again, unconvincingly. She turned to him, wishing she'd thought of a shark tooth question after all. "So anyway, I guess we'll buy it."

"Yeah, it's a good choice," he answered, wondering why he couldn't be more like a suave Casanova in situations like this. Kona would be whispering sweet Hawaiian nothings into her ear, and pouring her a glass of red wine by now.

They stood there for a long pause, neither having any idea how to keep talking.

"So, anyway, thanks," said Katie, looking at his gorgeous cheekbones and full lips.

"Yeah, anytime." Finally, Luke got up some nerve. "You from here?"

"Not at all," she smiled. "From out West."

"Got it. And you're visiting or . . ."

"Here. For the summer."

"Mom, c'mon, let's go. You said candy, too. Please?" Huck yanked her to the cash register.

Despite this man's allure and the NO STRINGS rumpled paper napkin document, Katie defaulted on the flirtation match. She paid quickly, deciding it was better to put the hormones on ice.

Katie stepped onto the sidewalk, lined with folded beach chairs and plastic baskets of primary-colored shovel sets. She couldn't help herself: she smiled back at the man who couldn't take his eyes off her, no matter how hard he tried.

Interlude: Memorial Day

The man with the pink-and-yellow gardenia lining inside his blazer needed a little more action before he faced a week of work. That young store employee with the gargantuan tits entered his mind. She was a local girl, surely not thinking of college, trying her best to advance herself in a life of retail at the Club Monaco shop off Main Street.

She wouldn't make it at the more exclusive Ralph Lauren down the block with her pale blue eye shadow and generic bracelets from a shopping mall that, frankly, advertised *middle class*. She was a woman who knew her limits. But he could change her life. Up to a point, of course. But, then, he was that way. He was generous. Not only with career guidance, but in the sack, too.

He parked behind the store and used the back door. Inside, he marveled at the all-white clever branding: spiffy floors, white orchids in little white pails, white sofas, white cotton throws. Good value clothes for Manhattan housewives here, always something they could buy to throw on for a lobster bake where one got messy anyway. And local women could find a suitable blouse for an interview or event, posing as if they'd been raised in a hydrangea-filled summer estate.

Diana Doherty was standing at the counter, stuffing crisp Oxford shirts into a bag. "Sixty-nine dollars retail, but only forty-eight dollars today on the holiday sale, that's a savings of 30 percent."

She was competent, self-reliant, he noted, could do math in her head. She'd never want anything from him. Feminism was a great thing!

"Take a break now," he whispered at her, while he considered a big table of coffee table books near the back of the registers. Her looked over at her tending to customers and tried to decide if her calves were a tad full. Good ankles, though, that saved her. Townie girls let themselves go a little more, ate too many cheeseburgers, fried what-have-you, with beer.

Maybe the calves were easier to hang onto when he'd fold her in two. It was fine, he'd only see those thick legs flailing around in the dark. It's not as if he'd take her anywhere in broad daylight. Flipping through a fancy book on outdoor entertaining in the Hamptons, he instructed her, "I'll meet you in the back storage closet."

"I can't." She smiled, relieved he'd come in. "Not again. C'mon." She motioned her hand at a short line before the counter. She'd checked her phone about seven thousand times since last week when they'd had the bedroom to themselves. He hadn't called or texted once. She knew she should give him a hard time, but he might take it like she was clingy, and then he might never . . .

"You can. Take a break, tell the manager something, uh, came up . . ."

She loved his persistence, even his stupid jokes. Maybe they'd get together for dinner that night. There was a lovely spot on the bay with fish tacos she'd wanted to try. He would consider her in the know, even elegant, for suggesting it.

Nine minutes later, they were tussling on a huge pile of sweaters in plastic bags used as cushions in the dark storeroom. She'd locked it of course, but didn't tell him other salesgirls and the manager had keys. She unbuckled his belt and rather aggressively yanked his pants and boxers halfway down his thighs, knowing it pleased him when she seemed all excited before they'd even started.

However, happy to see him, hoping they'd actually go on a date that night was different from wet-in-her-panties turned on. She pretended to moan a little.

And, though he was older, he was hot in his own way. If only he had a nice convertible. It would be so awesome to drive around with the roof down, with some cool new sunglasses on. Maybe Neil, who'd just dumped her, would see them.

As she wriggled and writhed beneath him, she heard footsteps in the hallway. He was too occupied between her breasts now to hear. *God*, she thought, this would really be bad if her manager came in. If she lost her job, he'd have to realize it was his fault, and that he'd made her leave the register.

But it'd be worth it, especially if he set her up in an apartment, maybe got her a cute little MINI Cooper convertible. If they got really serious by next Easter, he'd surprise her with a pale pink one or something thoughtful like that.

Okay, maybe he was pretty good at going down on girls, like better than anyone actually. As he twirled his tongue around her like a master, she figured his prowess was due to his lifetime of experience. No one her age moved his mouth slowly and softly like that. Guys she grew up with never understood girls don't jerk off like a jackhammer the way men do.

As she was almost there, he started to lick lower. "Not there, up higher it's better," she whispered down at him, so close to coming. He was nice; it was always all about her. She thought she heard something outside, but at this point, she didn't care.

"Just lemme try something here . . ." He flipped her over.

"C'mon," she pleaded. "That's too much, I don't think . . ."

And you know what? He was right. He slid himself into her, and it was strangely amazing. And then, wow, she came in successive waves like she never had in her young life, the explosions in her body feeling eternal and nuclear all at once.

Chapter Twelve

And Pop Goes George

The following Friday, Katie rushed to get Huck ready for his day at soccer camp. The magnificent summer sun streamed through her windows, and she hoped it would brighten Huck's mood. He'd been decidedly lukewarm about the competitive camp atmosphere. Though the counselors had promised to watch out for him, she'd picked up a rather reticent child in the previous few days. She hoped the perfect weather would help his comfort there.

As she neatened her hair into a ponytail in front of the bathroom mirror, and put blush on her soft, cream-colored cheeks, she heard a noise out the window beside her. Tires of a car crunched as they slowly rolled over the cracked little asphalt potholes on the driveway. No deliveries had been ordered, and George had said he wasn't coming until Sunday. She was supposed to have ten days to settle—that's what they agreed on. Or more precisely, that's what he told her the best plan would be. She pulled back the grandmotherly lace curtain from the small-paned window in the bathroom, but couldn't see the car because of the overgrown hedge branches.

Katie walked briskly through the small living room of the cottage, smoothing the top of her ponytail. She'd had a fitful night; the worry fairies kept sprinkling their persuasive spell on her. She missed her mother's wise counsel and wondered whether it might have been nicer to have George here her first week. She also felt unnerved about her flirtation with the adorable man in the surf shop earlier that week.

And then her finances agitated her: she'd done the same calculations all night to reassure herself. But every hour or so, she'd counted the numbers up: tutor hours per week, her take-home after the agency took their cut, the five-hundred-dollar monthly rent she insisted on paying, and costs she hadn't anticipated, like bicycles. How many more would there be? She was determined not to touch the fifteen-thousand-dollar inheritance her mother had left her.

The morning sunlight exposed the yellowing patches on the white-painted floor that had been covered by rugs or chairs over the years. On the red Americana dresser in the front, the eyes of George and his mother and now-deceased father stared at her in photographs from years ago. She swore their eyes were following her gait.

Her premonitions proven right, Katie looked out the front door panes to watch George step out of his 2002 BMW 320i with a bag from Dunkin' Donuts. She raced back to the bathroom to put on mascara.

"Huck!' she yelled into the adjacent room, where he was constructing a new Lego she'd bought (another expense she hadn't counted on). Indeed, the child had been right, and they had left parts of the heli-jet set back home. "We need to leave soon for camp, sweetie, five-minute warning with the Legos. And George is here a couple of days early!" She was a little upset he hadn't called to say he was coming early. Or called enough this week, period.

Katie looked into the decades-old bathroom mirror, the sides flecked with black spots from years of corrosive, salty air. Her cheeks flushed. She knew she hadn't felt this drawn to a man in several years. The vulnerability prickled more than she liked. Her mind hurtled from guilt to embarrassment, as if she were doing something wrong, standing in this bathroom that wasn't hers, enveloped in this strange, decaying home.

She studied her round face in the mirror, and squinted her bright green eyes back at her reflection, hands on hips now. This anxiety wasn't like her. But then again, she was due to feel a bit rattled; perhaps she'd been bottling it up to stay strong for her child and resilient her first week.

Katie strode back to the living room. She grabbed Huck's entire body and whooshed him out of the house.

"Mom! I wasn't done!" he yelled. Katie bounded out to the front porch, remembering eager didn't work on many fronts with men, but neither did ice-cold and unappreciative. She knelt against a pillar on the steps, smiled at the sight of cute George getting out of his car. He looked damn good with the sunlight highlighting his blond hair and strong build. She then placed her hands in her pockets just to stop them from shaking.

Pointing to the donut bag in his hands, she said, "George. You're spoiling him again." She sounded like she'd just sprinted to the corner stop sign and back. "Did you just get here this morning?" She longed to call her friend Ashley and laugh about their favorite topic: how grown women tap into those potent middle school nerves.

"No, I got here yesterday. Just getting settled in my own house and I figured I'd said Sunday, and this is two days early, but I couldn't wait to see Huck again." He winked at her.

Katie wondered, *He got out yesterday and didn't call?*

George walked across the small, unkempt lawn next to the cracked driveway and held Huck in his arms up high above his head, which made the child giggle. He then smiled warmly at Katie, slid Huck piggyback around his back and asked him, "Can I show you something kind of cool?"

As she watched George hold her son tightly, then grab a little bag from his car and walk away, she noticed his hair had grown a tad over his ears since she'd last seen him four weeks ago. His forty-something years weren't showing anything but a little gentlemanly elegance. George's arms shone in the morning light as he held Huck up to a bird feeder in a tree: they were strong and masculine in his navy, tattered polo shirt. She wasn't one for khakis on a man, but George's were so old and wrinkled, they looked good. His moccasins pretty much ruined his look, but she'd work on that.

She'd only been with him in Portland on his business trips, and he'd worn suits or jeans and light jackets in the colder Pacific Northwest air, both with freshly dry-cleaned, folded button-down shirts. This look was foreign to her, relaxed and decidedly preppy. They were equals out West: strangers connecting in a Hilton Hotel conference where she'd had solid command of her topics on stage. If anything, she gained a little control by taking him to restaurants *she* knew on the Willamette River in town. He looked different out on his turf; the ease, the comfort granted him a degree of power and took away some of hers. Perhaps, she figured, that explained the persistent anxiety in her stomach.

And now the man she had flirted with in the surf shop popped into her mind. His arms weren't this good, not as solid and muscular by a long shot—and she wasn't one for a lover with a slight build. Still, the man from the shop's clothes were better, more like people from Hood River, and his jeans fell off his hips in an inviting way. He had a cool style, and she instinctively liked that better than the Brooks Brothers uniform George now had on.

George probably had at least ten years on the handsome guy in the store, forty-three to his thirty-three or so. Or maybe he was thirty-five, she wondered to herself, shielding her eyes to try to see what George and Huck were doing in that tree.

George yelled back at her, holding Huck up to see something hidden. "You know this is a bird feeder from my childhood. Did my mother, Poppy, stop by? My father and I painted it when I was Huck's age."

"Didn't hear anything from her yet, but I'm looking forward to meeting her."

George walked back to the porch, holding Huck's hand, and released him to go into the house. "She wants to take you to the Seabrook Club for lunch, which is going to be a little bit of a culture shock for you. She's going to call you. She likes a late lunch and wanted to see you there, alone."

"Sounds fine. What does she know about us? Any topics I should avoid?"

"I didn't tell her anything. She just assumes there's a woman in the house, and she wants to see her herself. She talks better without me, you'll see." He kissed her softly on the lips. "I cannot wait to show you both around. Clamming, tennis, the perfect ear of buttery corn."

"Of course. I'd love to see her. I'm good with women only." Katie put her hands on her hips again to stand firm. She was feeling better now. This George was really handsome, and so kind with her child. He seemed genuinely happy to have them living here.

"Nothing's off-limits with my mother. You'll like her. She's kind of irresistible in her own Ayatollah way."

At the very least, she'd see the inside of that dilapidated country club George had referenced once, which probably looked like this cottage on the inside. She remembered a pink blouse that could be steamed. Did she even bring that here?

Then, she convinced herself clothes didn't matter, so it was silly to focus on them, either her own or George's. She was fine. All was in order. The glorious sun warming her back slayed the nighttime worry fairies.

She liked how George walked, not like he owned the world, but in a sexy alpha way, like he'd be able to take charge of situations. The guy in the T-shirt could barely talk to her in the store. George was more substantial. He had walked right up to her in the Hilton by the breakfast spread like he was a sexy caveman ready to drag her by her ponytail into his lair. *Let's leave. Now.* Huck came out of the house, and George placed him again in his arms to get more birdseed out of a box in his trunk.

Katie had never been one to consider "breeding" as a plus, but this George did have some intangible hint of class that she now understood as she watched him in his element. His frayed pants and polo shirt held historic substance of some kind, worn for decades on golf courses and stubbornly unchanged, like the fabric on the couches or the steps peeling with paint beneath her. It all reeked of an elite, laissez-faire, don't-show-too-much-effort-in-life style.

Middle-class people in Portland didn't like old clothes and furniture; they liked their houses neat, clean, presentable. Ikea had worked for her because she was drawn to the uncomplicated nature of white and spare, an environment where, unlike this cottage, Windex could do its job.

George was so old-world he couldn't help it, she decided. Katie didn't think he had a ton of money, for he flew coach on airplanes and his company only put him up in mediocre hotels. But he did have some kind of lineage, some roots to bankers and investments that settled him squarely in the upper class. Two family homes in the Hamptons signified a certain level of wealth, even if the cottages were old and small and falling apart. Although she hadn't seen his mother's home, he'd told her it was a cottage just a tad bigger than this one, and that both were nestled into cul-de-sacs and not near the estate section of town nor the ocean.

After a good five more minutes with her son and the bird feeder, George returned, and put Huck down. "Let me at least properly say hi to your mom before you go to camp." While Huck ran into the house, he grabbed Katie's hips and yanked them into his, whispering into her ear, "I know I said I'd give you space, but I don't know if I can wait."

She felt an instant longing for this man she'd fallen for fast. Their familiar feel together helped her body stop shaking. As he'd embraced her, she knew that his "take it slow" plan wouldn't work; she'd felt the hardness in his pants from the brief, but erotic embrace. Her mind flew to the first moment she lay beneath him in Portland when, shimmying her jeans down her knees, he'd whispered, "*tell me what you want, I need to know, I want to know exactly . . .*" She'd been too shy to answer in words, barely knowing him; it wasn't easy to explain anyway. Turned out he knew just fine without a bit of instruction or guidance.

"Can I take you to dinner?" George asked, "I have a sitter we know, the girl a house down. There's a place on the bay in East Hampton. It's a drive but at sunset it's perfect." His azure-colored eyes stared into hers with a safe hint of romance.

Dinner would be nice. He'd tell her everything she needed to hear: the tutor hours would pile up higher than the summer cornstalks, that job in the Bridgehampton school would be hers for the asking, and her research would get noticed at child-study centers in Manhattan once she'd had time for more follow-up calls. He'd look into her eyes the way he had in Portland, determined to make her his.

Tonight, she'd have one of those Kirs he'd ordered for her in that little bistro in Hood River, a rose-colored drink she'd never tried before, crème de cassis liqueur and white wine, something he always had in Paris. Then she thought about the possibility of Paris—she'd never been—of sex in Paris, of a little inn in Paris with couches covered in tattered fabric, of white wine Kir in Paris . . . yes . . . okay this wasn't a faulty plan. Katie allowed herself to smile. Her finances were fine, the jobs would come, and this relationship might even work for real. Those anxieties would be fleeting.

Huck shook his head vigorously at the dinner date suggestion, slamming Katie back into reality. She didn't even hesitate, knowing her son wasn't a champ with new sitters. "Sorry, let's have drinks here. I can cook. I've never even cooked for you and it's the least . . ."

"You're not cooking. That's too much work. I want to spoil you with the amazing food of the Hamptons. There's my spot on the bay, it's . . ."

"It's fine. We've got time. I'll shop now after I drop Huck at camp. He'll be asleep by eight anyway; he's exhausted." Katie looked at George's eyes in that womanly wiles way, trying to make very clear that she'd do the same thing to his body she'd done the last time they'd fallen in bed at his Hilton Hotel on weekend sex marathon four. They didn't need to wait a week. She wanted it, too.

"Okay, that sounds like a plan. I love home cooking. I never get it. *Anything* you prefer." And George added with special emphasis, "I mean that across the board, Katie. You do what you want here. Take your time; enjoy yourself. You deserve it, what with the sad changes, you know," he whispered, "and of course the dead-beat . . ." He twirled his hand in the air, rolling his eyes a bit, referring to Huck's dad who sent Hallmark cards with fifty-dollar bills every six months or so.

George grabbed the orange-and-brown donut bag and handed Huck his favorite: French Cruller. "I got three more in the bag if you want."

"George! Sugar high. Please?" Katie pleaded, knowing she'd get little reaction from either man or boy by her side.

"Too late," answered Huck, sugary glaze plastered all over his mouth and chin.

As George laughed and ate the opposite end of Huck's cruller, this variety being his all-time favorite as well, she knew just then, sugary glaze now stuck to his manly stubble, it was good she'd come here: he was kind, generous, handsome, not forcing her too fast into anything. All good, right?

Chapter Thirteen

Helipad Heaven

Julia and Jake Chase landed promptly at 10:00 a.m. at the small Beachwood Lane helipad out near the Southampton jetty. The blasts of sand shot out from under their Sikorsky helicopter, announcing to all that yet another Manhattan chieftain was feverishly arriving to relax. (And that there would be hell to raise with anyone within one hundred yards if he couldn't.) The Chase driver waited inside his shiny black Cadillac Escalade SUV on the other side of the street, license plate reading, BEACH1, (out of the Chases' seven vehicles) to avoid the Saudi sandstorm before him.

The two pilots came out of the cockpit first. They ran with their heads hunched to avoid the thud-thud-thud of the propellers overhead, and started unloading the mounds of matching Goyard luggage for the five Chase family members. Like the driver, the family was also practiced in the art of helicopter arrival on the sandy lane helipad. They remained in their seats another four minutes to allow the windswept dirt to settle, and for the men to place their bags in the SUV.

Tote bags, larger weekend bags, a few giant-sized duffels, all marked with the distinctive brown Goyard background and the owner's initials and varying red-and-yellow, and orange-and-pink stripes were ferried to the SUV. On the family's last stroll down the Rue St. Honoré in Paris over spring break, they agreed it would be "so cute" if they all matched when they traveled together. Jake enjoyed not flinching at the $4,470.00 price of the smallest "Croisiere" duffel and ordered nine larger pieces in perfectly ascending sizes.

Julia Chase came out first, taking the hand of the copilot. She felt beautiful in the sunlight. It didn't hurt that her husband had spent half his time reminding her he was the luckiest fucker on earth to have bagged her. Her honey-colored hair blew in her face. She wore tight jeans on her short, but shapely legs, Stan Smith–style sneakers from Barneys that cost six hundred dollars instead of the original ones costing eighty dollars, a white Gucci button-down blouse showing her signature, slightly too much, gorgeous, silicone-enhanced breasts, and a gray Alexander McQueen zippered sweatshirt with a jeweled skull on the back hanging over her shoulders. A snow-white bulldog named Betsy, with an S & M gold-and-black dog collar, toddled down after her, pulled by his matching Goyard leash.

Next, the eldest son, Evan Chase, peered out from the helicopter cabin, proudly assuming his twenty-year-old, urban, super douche stance. He squinted his eyes, and pulled his new Tom Ford sunglasses down from the top of his head. His black hair was overly coiffed to mimic the latest David Beckham short-on-the-sides-and-straight-up-fade-on-top style. He wore a Salvatore Ferragamo gold medallion-ed belt that matched his jeans, a stiff baby-blue button-down shirt, and bright orange J.P. Tod's suede driving shoes.

Next came Julia's mini-me—that young brunette, illegal-to-touch, sixteen-year-old Alexa Chase, in a crocheted miniskirt and a tight V-neck body suit that cut low on the back. She expertly maneuvered her Jimmy Choo rope platforms down the helicopter steps with ease, as the multiple Hermès enamel bracelets, and two Cartier Love bracelets clanked on her wrist (her mother had the white gold and diamond ones costing $15,600 each; hers were *only* yellow gold at $6,300 each).

Aware that the family's handsome pilot tried to avert his eyes as her skirt blew up in the wind, Alexa made sure to flaunt her inherited sexuality with every step just to drive the poor guy nuts. She thought about how *crazy* it would be if she blew him. Some of the staff in her young life (pilots, chefs, that one doorman) were, like, really hot, but, it wouldn't be right to do them. Her parents' guests at parties were much fairer game.

She had fuller legs than her mother, a smaller waist, larger breasts, and a rounder, J-Lo ass, an attribute she made sure to highlight with each day's well-planned outfit changes. Her long tresses were held up most days in a high ponytail that still reached the middle of her back.

Young Richie descended next with his curly brown hair, and slightly pudgy eight-year-old build, wearing nondescript jeans, running shoes like any American boy, but a "Free in St Barth's" $140 T-shirt that gave him that superior Manhattan rich-kid badge. Finally, the patriarch, Jake, surveyed the adjacent parking lot across the road just to check out any less-monied onlookers who stopped to gawk at the arrival of a helicopter. He reminded himself it was a great thing that, just by showing up, he could remind anyone in the near vicinity of his monumental success in the Laundromat sphere.

In the car, the oldest sibling, Evan, sat up front in his usual seat and instantly plugged his iPhone into the car stereo AUX jack. He played the latest ASAP Rocky song at a volume that he knew would annoy his mother.

"Turn that down!" she yelled on cue as she pulled herself into the second-row seat. "That hip-hop gives me headaches. You know that, Evan. If you're going to live with us this summer in the city and every weekend, there are certain rules of mine that have to be respected."

"Mom. Stop," cooed Alexa. "You have to let him live his life now. He's got a real job and he needs to unwind." Things had been on the upswing after that episode a few years back in his junior year spring in high school where Evan had been caught dealing Xanax. He'd collected it from the adult medicine cabinets at his friends' houses. (His father had to give the school enough money to construct a rooftop art center to get them to give him a diploma.)

Life for her brother had been very stressful, and he was finally getting everything back on track before his delayed first year at University of Miami this fall. He had repeated tenth grade, and also took a gap year to "calm down" and "work in the real world" after those rough years in high school. A few months ago, Evan had finally found an internship he'd liked (he'd quit half a dozen after one-week trials), and seemed to be flourishing in the music video–producing firm his father had largely financed with a golfing buddy from Boca.

Evan turned from the front seat. "Since when do you defend me?"

"I'm not. Mom's just being ridiculous. Like when she tried to tell me I couldn't go to Tide Runners today. It ends at noon and it's only 10:00 a.m." Alexa then raised her voice, so the driver could hear her. "I'd like to be dropped off at water camp please, Mario." She was in the far backseat of the three-row SUV and was already draping a towel over her body to change into the outfit she'd instructed the housekeeper, Edviane, to leave in the car for her. Mario wasn't, like, hot at all, so she didn't need to flash him anything in his rearview mirror while she changed.

"Give me a break," Evan yelled back at his sister. "You're not going to honestly spend another summer with those idiots. Why don't you get an internship at the Southampton magazine, or with some P.R. party company here, rather than hanging out on a water ski boat all day?"

"Your job at the video company that Dad forced those guys into hiring you for is not really a job if you're taking every Friday off to 'wind down' with your Xbox and FIFA game. And besides, I get in shape in the water."

"All right, all right." Jake stepped in. "It's not up to you all to judge each other's choices. Your mother and I decide what is an appropriate way to spend the summer. Alexa, you honestly want us to drop you from the city right into the camp?"

"Yep," she groaned from the third row, shimmying out of her miniskirt and into an even mini-er bikini under the shield of her towel. "I promised Kona I'd be there. I just *have* to be there."

That got Julia's attention. "You what? What does Kona have to do with any of your choices?" she asked, aware her daughter was growing into a woman way too fast. "Kona is not aware of every single kid who's there; he can't be that concerned who shows up."

"Since when the fuck do *you* know what Kona wants and doesn't want?" answered Jake, protective of his ability to cull local "buddies." "I know that guy better than you do. I was the one who talked to him about his business plan last summer, not that he knew what the fuck I was talking about. I could tell my advice was fuckin' Mandarin to that guy. But this summer I'm going to help him get his ass in gear to . . ."

"No fair!" yelled Richie, yanking off his headphones and taking his eyes off his Candy Crush game on his iPad for a precious three seconds. "If Alexa goes, I want to go. If Luke is teaching, I want to see him."

"You don't have your bathing suit or wetsuit, honey," said Julia. "I wasn't planning on having you all go to camp today. It's so early in the summer, I just want family time at home, I'm not . . ." Julia, who sensed she wouldn't get her way, suddenly decided to save her arguing capital for another fight. It was easier to let the kids and husband believe they were in charge so she could squash their demands like insects when it really counted.

"They have so many wetsuits for kids always. Old ones for kids who forget, come on, Mom, pleeease? If Alexa gets to go, I get to."

Jake patted Mario on the shoulder. "Stop the car at that water sports camp. We'll drop off the two kids. Who cares, Julia? We've got all weekend."

Once in a while, Jake had to trump his wife. He loved her to death, but still, she had to let him act like a man when it counted with the kids. He was happy she had a bigger brain than him, and wasn't one of those women who obsessed over exercise classes to keep her ass from drooping. On the other hand, nothing worse than a droopy ass, Jake thought to himself, as various moms' rear anatomies shuffled through his head like a deck of cards.

MARIO GUIDED THE Cadillac Escalade up through the public parking lot toward camp, and Alexa bounded from the back row and out the side door, stepping into her gold flip-flops on the hot pavement. Into a rubber Birkin-style fuchsia beach bag, she stuffed her plush Hermès bedsheet of a towel and her patchwork designer Cynthia Rowley wetsuit (which was so tight it gave her breathing issues).

Richie ran out past his big sister. He headed directly for the plastic bins filled with wetsuits that dozens of children had peed in. They smelled like a combination of teenage boys' feet and rotten fish.

Evan, meanwhile, waited in the car, disgusted by anything having to deal with the local leeches on the beach, lost in their inane, underclass notion that instructing children in the water was an actual vocation.

"Hey, man, happy summer once again," Jake said as he fist-bumped Kona, who was rushing up from the bay area to the ocean side with a boogie board for one of the kids. "I got two very late kids here who want to jump in. You cool with that?"

"Yeah, we already started camp, but if you want to sign up for a full morning now, you can do that. We don't do half fee on late arrivals, but, hell, you wanna pay full fare, that's fine. And you know, we've been meaning to talk to you. That day on the beach with your Scout truck, you know there are these people at the club who weren't so happy with that. They are trying to shut down the camp which would pretty much ruin my life, so it caused some . . ."

"Hey, lemme settle in for my weekend. You wanna call me next week?" Jake said, checking the weather app on his phone. He was hoping that sand incident was long forgotten.

"Yeah, fine, but I do need to talk," Kona answered, desperation clear in his voice.

"I said, call me. I meant it, buddy," Jake answered, loving that he was needed by one and all.

Alexa pulled her new patchwork wetsuit up her thighs and leaned over for several beats too long, just to make sure there wasn't a man within a five-hundred-yard vicinity who hadn't noticed that *purrrrfect* wedgie, rammed up inside her full butt cheeks.

Jake went on, his back thankfully facing his daughter's sideshow. "You know, come to think of calls, Kona, something's bugging me and I'm a very direct guy who's gotta say it."

Kona cracked his neck purposefully, feigning interest in Jake as his eyes tried hard not to look at Alexa's bending and stretching. The way she walked around the lot sickened him as if she were his own child. Last summer, this girl was a kid. The image of her Memorial Day weekend in that orange romper, on her knees in the sea grass still haunted him. Maybe he'd force her to wear a sensible, black wetsuit with long legs and arms like most of the other kids did. That'd be a start in the right direction for her.

"About that music gig I promised you last summer," Jake said. "So sorry we never got that done. I know I sent you on a few interviews, but I should'a, could'a gotten a few more until we got you a real fuckin' job you were happy with. That wasn't right. I just, you know, man, I tried . . ."

"It's fine," Kona lied, trying not to reveal any disappointment. "I know you're a busy guy with a lot going on. This camp thing, though, is serious. We're trying to get city families supporting our cause or we're going to have to shut down for real."

Meanwhile, Julia had gotten out of the air-conditioned SUV in time to witness Alexa jam her breasts inside the wetsuit and then struggle to zipper it up her neck. "Honey, that suit is just too small. Can we please go into town later and get another?"

"Stop, Mom."

Julia watched her daughter strut around, fear and maternal anxiety now pumping through her body. "I'm not stopping, honey. We'll talk later." The girl didn't have any smarts about the mesmerizing power her balloon breasts would have over men. Julia got back in the car and sat with her head in her hands, concerned about the trouble her daughter could get herself into this summer.

Alexa took a photo of a little drink shack on the side of the beach where she'd hooked up with a guy a grade older from the Riverdale school the previous weekend. She immediately posted it on her anonymous @DIDITHERETOO Instagram account that pretty much showed the locale of every expert blow job she'd ever delivered.

That was her favorite way to taunt her twenty-three thousand social media followers: just give them a hint, not really a full idea, that maybe she had blown someone there in the photos she posted. The great shot she'd posted the night of the Memorial Day bash, with the purple sunset and the grassy dune, had been her most popular this spring. She got thousands of likes. Sunsets always got likes, but sex and sunsets, even better. The suggestion that she "did it here too" was a *really* clever way to use her Instagram when all the other girls were posting selfies in bikinis. Like, no one knew it was her account. And, like, no one would ever find out.

Thank God she knew how to handle boys and men so well at age sixteen; it helped that she was born with no gag reflex, which was a *really* great thing in life. Something to be really thankful for.

She hoped she'd see the older man from the party this weekend, so she could play with his head a bit. He said he might show up here today to see her at camp. He was really handsome, and so mature. And she liked how hot and desperate he got around her.

When her parents questioned why she still wanted to go to surf and water-ski camp after four years, when she hadn't noticeably improved since season one, she explained it all made her feel happy and fit. She mostly sat on the boat with Luke acting as camp DJ, blasting music while the kids water-skied behind the boat. Plus she got to buy a lot of new swimsuits every spring, and bags for her beach belongings and awesome flip-flops in colors that coordinated it all. And it made for good posting photos for her other Instagram account with her real name on it. All the surfing photos she posted made her look really athletic and down to earth, which she so was.

"It's *not* right," Jake said to Kona, using his best patrician tone, as he headed back to his SUV. "I promised I'd deliver some kind of job for you and I'm a man of my word. I just get pulled in so many directions and, Jesus fucking Christ, I can't help everyone." He slapped Kona's shoulder.

"I got it. Maybe another time," Kona answered. "But I'm going to push on the camp closing. They're sending summons for infractions, building a case. It's very serious, Jake, and we need . . ."

"You know what?" asked Jake, nodding thanks at Mario who'd run around the open car door like it was an Olympic track meet trial. "Let's do this. Let's celebrate the start of summer. You guys, you know, Luke, that teacher guy, whomever, the older one who doesn't talk, you all come over after camp soon. I'll have my chef lay out a spread. And we'll talk about your camp problem."

"We'll come, we're there, for sure, man," Kona answered. "It's really important. We can't shut down after ten summers. We need the income, your kids need safety in the water."

"2206 Beachwood Lane? Best food you ever had, guaranteed?" Jake slugged Kona's back a little too hard, and climbed into the climate-controlled comfort of his car, marveling at his own magnanimity as if he'd cured every case of malaria in the Third World.

The corner of Julia's mouth turned from frown to naughty smile at the news that Kona was coming for lunch, while Evan smacked his forehead in disgust, just like his daddy always did when he was astounded by other people's idiocy.

Chapter Fourteen

Conscious Coupling

At the end of Katie's third week in the Hamptons, George arrived at the cottage at 3:00 p.m. bearing bags of succulent blackberries and cherries he'd picked up at his favorite Halsey farm stand. From her room, she heard the sound of the kitchen faucet running. She walked out to find George flipping berries in a colander. He took a bunch of bright wildflowers out of newspaper and placed them in a mason jar.

"George, this is really kind. I don't need flowers."

"You do, actually."

"Thanks." Katie smiled at him. "Okay, maybe I do. I love them."

"And I promise this is the last time I come here unannounced. I wanted to take you to the new tutor client, and then for a Kir cocktail on my favorite bayside spot, Sag Harbor Point. We'll have oysters and watch the sunset after your session."

"How could any woman say no to that?"

"And I want the sitter next door to understand the rules in this house when you all are here." He then pulled her toward him and kissed her forehead, keeping his mouth pressed against her for a long while, expressing that he wouldn't be letting go any time soon.

"Did you go for a swim?" she asked. He smelled clean from his afternoon shower.

"Of course. In the ocean. After a brutal tennis match I've been losing since boarding school. My friend Oldie was captain of the team, and I never caught up. Still trying." He laughed. "You know . . . boys."

"I know. I got one, but mine isn't such a competitor. He hates it actually."

"Let me work on that this summer. There's plenty of sports at the club for the kids. It'll be good for him. He likes Cynthia, right? She could organize some games," George asked, referring to the sitter next door. "That family has lived in that house for thirty years. She's the grandchild of the owners, and worked for the club a bit as a waitress and she's a good young woman."

"We like her so far. I feel more comfortable that you know her."

"Did she stay while you found the windsurfing bay the other day or did you bring Huck?"

"No, I got her, it was a godsend. The southwest wind is the prevailing wind in summer at Napeague Harbor. It comes up in the afternoon at about fifteen miles per hour. It funnels in there nicely, just like it does back home in the Columbia Gorge. But, it still feels very different here when I'm on the board."

"How come?"

"I can't quite define it. I'll let you know, though."

"Did you get an instructor? They have a shack out there of some kind where they teach."

"Nah, I do it alone, that's the whole point. Just me and the boom and the sail. There's people out there, about thirty the day I was there, so we watch out for each other. But I love it, it's like an elixir, I told you that."

"That's why I wanted you to try it in the Hamptons first thing. And good you feel secure with Cynthia here. I went by this morning to their house. I asked they check on you often to make sure all is okay over here when I'm in the city."

"George, you're being an angel." Katie grabbed the back of his belt and brought him toward her. She rubbed her pelvis hard against his. "I love flowers and berries, you know that, but I can drive alone to the tutor appointment if you want to get stuff done before dinner. What do you think I do out West? I find places on my own, there's Google Maps when I'm lost, I drive all the time to . . ."

"I think you manage brilliantly." He swayed back and forth, pushing his body back into hers, allowing into his mind the possibility there was time to ravage her now without the child knowing. "You raise that gorgeous boy on your own, you turned your degree into a career, and now, you take a chance at a new life. Maybe even a chance at real happiness after a terrible spring. I never knew your mother, but I know she'd want that and more. Maybe I even hear her saying that now." He cupped his ear toward the sky as if he were listening to her mother from above. Katie smiled hard at first, but then blinked the stinging out of her eyes. He kissed a tear away that ran down her cheek. She tried to pull back, but he'd have none of it. "You're not going anywhere." He pushed her against the old fridge with the rounded front door. "I'm here for you. Any way you want. You can discard me as a lover, and I'm still here for you. It's a wonderful community to start a life. When you do your new tutor client session today, pretend it's for real and you're getting that full-time gig in Bridgehampton."

"Why are you kissing my mom again?" Huck asked, trying to open the fridge door for a juice box, shoving George in the kidney to get him to move.

Katie wiped her salty wet face with a dish towel. She then turned on the faucet and patted cool water on her cheeks to reduce the ruddiness that always erupted when tears came. She went to gather her notebooks.

With Huck ensconced with his Angry Birds games on an iPad and Cynthia on the back porch, George drove Katie to her new session in East Hampton. All four windows of his BMW were open and the afternoon foggy mist left a soft dew on Katie's cheeks. She laid her head back and closed her eyes, content to be driven after all.

She turned her head lazily to look at George. He looked fit after his tennis match, and handsome in a starched white shirt that showed off his good tan. His blondish, graying hair was askew, flying around now with the wind from the open windows. She loved the way he always yanked his too-long bangs back with his fingers. His haircut was more French writer than American preppy, and it was one of the things she always remembered in her mind's eye. His hair made him look cool, but responsible. A man you could count on with a bad-boy look. His wide shoulders gave him the air of a man who took care of himself, and who didn't put up with anything he shouldn't.

Katie knew her mother would like him (mostly his kindness and care).

Her friend Ashley back in San Francisco would be the only voice advising her not to get too wrapped up in George. She had called that morning to make sure. "Just because you're in his family cottage and he's a masterful lay doesn't mean anything."

"Well." Katie laughed at the predictability of Ashley's constant protective watch. "There you go again, just like we say . . ."

"I know," Ashley answered. "Everyone's advice is autobiographical."

"Exactly. Just because you don't trust men, doesn't mean I have to be so cautious. Good sex and a nice cottage with a beat-up Volvo can also mean he's generous and thoughtful. A masterful lay is a man who cares about a woman's pleasure. And that he does—it's all he focuses on. He says he can't get turned on if I'm not, so . . . it's not all bad."

"Where's your heart? That's what I want to know. Does your heart stop when he walks in?" Katie could imagine Ashley's image burning through the phones, all hunched over, one eyebrow cocked, waiting breathlessly for the answer to this key question.

Katie paused. "Well, yeah . . ." Yes, her heart fluttered, but sometimes it felt like nerves around the newness.

"Doesn't sound like true love," Ashley responded like a prosecutor.

"Well, I mean, c'mon. You told me to wait until summer was over, not to get too attached, take my time. Now you're saying either I have to fall hard or leave town?"

"I'm asking a simple question. Are you really into him?"

"I'm into him," Katie answered, trying to provide her friend the right answer, without annoying legal ammunition to be used later on. "But it makes me nervous sometimes."

"Why, because you think he's going to ditch you, too?"

"No, c'mon, I'm not that fucked up and scared of life. It's something else. I don't know. Maybe the newness of the East. Just, I'm totally responsible for Huck and my finances, and I can't assume everything will be working here yet."

"Okay, like I said, take your time to figure out where you are . . . in every which way."

"Trying!" Katie yelled into the phone.

"Love you. Bye."

As GEORGE DROVE and explained back road Hamptons savvy, she thought about what she'd divulged on the phone. She didn't relay to Ashley that they'd only slept together a few times since she'd arrived in the Hamptons, not dozens a weekend like they had at the Portland Hilton.

The sex here was just as powerful, but much less frequent. Katie felt it wasn't due to Huck asleep in the next room; they could have found stolen hours while he was at camp. It was some limbo George had manufactured "for her." She and George had even had one surprisingly chaste dinner date with stolen kisses only. She'd been sure they would fall into bed afterwards. But one night he'd gone home early, reminding her he'd made a pact.

"I'm going to leave now," George had said, at about eleven on a balmy, humid June night, after furiously kissing her on her porch. "Before it's too difficult to leave, I have to go."

"Huck's asleep. You don't have to," Katie had said.

"I don't want to crowd you." Then he'd left her wanting him sexually, but convincing herself she could have him if she insisted.

As she'd watched his BMW roll into the night, she'd remembered the weekends back at the Hilton after the seminars, the scent of sex so pungent on their bodies they'd had to shower several times a day.

Now George caressed her bare knee in the car. The silence in the car allowed her to remember they felt at ease with one another. Why, when he was absent, did she get a little anxious? It was offputting how he let days go by with total radio silence—no calls, no emails, no texting—not normal in this era of iPhone ubiquity. She blamed his age, fifteen years older than she, for not checking in more often. And it was strange to leave the house that night and not stay for sex. As she he watched him drive with those sexy long bangs whipping around his head, she reminded herself he was at least stable, strong, and consistent. But still . . .

"How come you don't call or check in more?" she blurted out.

"What do you mean? You wanted to take time to settle in. I'm not going to make you claustrophobic. We got years ahead if we want." He looked at her as if she were crazy. "You serious?"

"Yeah, I am. I think it's a little weird. You're in town, but you don't tell me. You don't call for a few days."

"Well, first of all, you call me anytime," he stated.

"I do, when I need, but . . ."

"And secondly, I'm kind of a wise man. I mean that. Give me a little credit here. I'm smarter than I look. It's only mid-June. Let's spend more nights a week together in August. Let's let it build on a slow time frame."

"I know you're trying to do the right thing."

"Well, you're really smart. I'm sure more so than me, women always are. But trust me on this," he said. "You're an accomplished woman, published papers under your belt, well launched on your career, and you've been living alone. You think I'm going to be some guy who watches ESPN eating Doritos in your living room every free moment? And you'd find that attractive?"

"I wouldn't like that." She had to laugh.

"Okay, so relax. We got this. You just got here. Give yourself some space, forget about me. I've got a busy life, too. I'm working on some big investments, for years now, that might actually pan out. Go hold that windsurfing boom out in the bay. If that's pure nirvana for you, glide away your days. We got plenty of time."

"All right. I guess you have a point." She smirked a little. He was damn cute. And sexy. And he didn't crowd her. Not dumb.

"We'll be at your appointment ten minutes early. I'll go into town for the papers, then come back and get you for an all-out oysters feast after."

"I could have taken myself, but I'm happy you took me. It means I can just relax a little and feel totally prepped for the session. This kid is a mess." Katie put her hand on his now. "There's one thing I know, I can change his life if his parents allow me. I'm going to give her my study on resilience. It's in my bag here and every parent seems to respond to it. His mother was a freaky worrier on the phone." She got out of the car.

He yelled out the window, "Oh, and you're Miss Cool Cucumber all the time?"

"Shut up." She laughed, and slammed the car door.

TWO HOURS LATER, the setting June sun showed the last vestiges of its own resilience. Katie and George sat dockside at a low-key restaurant on Northside Harbor. She put a frosty white wine and cassis liqueur Kir to her lips. The blush-colored drink went down smoothly, bitter and sweet all at once.

"This is a crisp nice white from a local vineyard, Wölffer," George told her, grabbing the cold bottle out of the ice bucket and topping off her glass. He handed her a just-shucked oyster on a big round tray with crushed ice and seaweed. On top, it was crowded with fresh shrimp, half lobsters, clams, and oysters. "Now, while the Kir is still on your palate, suck this baby down. Nothing better." The sun reflected off his hair like a halo.

"Wow," Katie said. "I've never eaten something so fresh."

"This place sells seafood at a shack in the lot. We can do takeout one day and eat it on a bench at the marina. They catch everything same day and serve it at night." He pointed to a fifty-three-foot Viking sport boat docked out front. "That boat belongs to the owners. Everything here they catch on their own, or that's the story anyway."

Katie took another sip of the wine and swallowed an oyster while the tartness remained on her tongue. She smiled and shook her head. Everything felt good.

George brushed her cheek with the back of his hand. "I told you. Pure Bliss. It happens in the Hamptons."

Chapter Fifteen

Happy Campers

H oly shit," said Luke the next Monday morning at camp. "That woman. Is here. "

"Which woman?" asked Kona.

Luke didn't want to point out that that woman with the yellow shorts whom he'd been stalking predator-style inside the surf store three weeks before was walking up to him. She may have been a married housewife for all he knew. But the way her smooth and toned thighs glistened in the morning sunlight in shorter shorts than she had on that night made him extremely hot for her.

"I said, 'which woman'," asked Kona again. He whistled with two fingers to no avail. "Hello? Wake up, shithead. What the fuck are you talking about?"

"I don't . . . know," replied Luke. "I just thought I saw someone from last summer. And I don't think it's her after all."

The woman took her son's hand and marched up the lot with a striped overflowing tote bag. She stuck out from the other women only in her effortlessness. She had on white cutoffs and a simple navy tank that hugged her slim frame. She wore beige rubber flip-flops on her feet and black hair up in a ponytail. She walked up to the four guys, and hesitated a little, looked down, and then, as if she'd just decided, what the hell, life is short, walked to Luke and Luke alone.

"Hi," she said, pulling her hair out of her ponytail and back into another one, her clear green eyes astonished that this was the same guy from the shop. "I heard about Tide Runners from a poster in town."

"Well, had I known you were looking, I would have suggested by the shark teeth in the store." *What an idiot he could be.* Of course he should have suggested water sports camp for her son that night in the shop. Kona would have had her kid in camp and this clear-eyed beauty horizontal in the sea grass by 9:00 a.m. the morning after they'd met.

"My son isn't liking his soccer camp. No one answered your main number all day yesterday. I didn't know if it was okay for him to attend?" Katie couldn't look him straight on; she'd thought she had fully worked the electric bolt from that Memorial Day night in the shop out of her system.

"Of course it's okay. We just take people who show up, and I'm sorry, my partner Kona is supposed to check messages more than once a week . . . oh, never mind, does your son have a wetsuit?" He stared at her hard. "We rent them." He smiled. She smiled back. "It's cold in the water for an hour or more and he'll need one."

"I got Huck one," she said, thinking that just as she was feeling settled, something like this had to come along to uproot her. Ashley was going to have a field day with this one. "We bought one yesterday because the ocean was so cold." She turned to Huck. "Let's get your cool new wetsuit out." Katie grabbed it out of the bag and struggled to bite off the plastic tag with her teeth. She remained crouched down, not wanting to face Luke's sexy stare, which she could feel over her head.

She closed her eyes and thought about how George's hair was damn good in the sun: blond, a little flowy, thick. And his muscled body was crazy attractive naked. Okay, he didn't text or call all the time. Even so, he was also polite, fun, game, and not clingy. He was exactly what she needed now. *Don't fuck that up; don't let the thrill of this high drag you in.*

"Hey, Huck," Luke said. He checked and didn't see a ring on her finger. "You're not too young to water-ski, are you?" Huck hid behind his mother, yanking the tank top so much that it exposed the right side of her pink gingham bikini top.

Huck nodded "yes," clearly not liking the idea. His shoulders slumped now. His face remained in his hands. He was pretty sure he didn't like anything about this new camp already.

"Well," said Luke, "then you must like tubing. We have a big blow-up tube with kind of a couch built into it. It has handles and I'll sit with you so we can ride together. I'll hold you tight. You're not too young for tubing, are you?"

Huck pulled his hands down and looked at Luke's face on the other side of his mother's hip. "I'm not too young."

That worked with the little shy boys every time. Luke had never met one who didn't love to be dragged behind a boat on the tube, flying between the wakes and bouncing to and fro like a rag doll.

"I didn't catch your name. I know this little man Huck now," Luke offered, straightening up, grabbing the clipboard, trying to be businesslike to assuage the tension he felt in his throat. "I need it for the signing of releases. We ask all parents to sign one. Sorry, just a formality. Not to make you worry."

"Katie Doyle. And yours?"

"Luke Forrester."

"What will he be doing today exactly? I only know from the

poster that you are water-oriented, but I don't really want my son in the big waves."

"We don't let any kid in who can't handle themselves. We teach them how anyway fast, even ones much smaller than this guy."

"You're one of the instructors?"

"Yeah, I run the camp. In the summer. In the off-seasons, I'm still kind of submerged in the ocean. I'm a marine biology teacher. Mostly young kids like yours."

"You teach?"

"I do," he answered, not looking up at her. "It's an elective in the school, but the kids love it. We do all our classes in the sand, even when it's cold, we learn right on this beach. Anyway . . . Huck's birthday is . . ." Luke asked, looking at his clipboard.

Being with this man, whoever he was, made something inside Katie ache with a mixture of angst and exhilaration. She smiled and stared at him for a moment, letting her eyes glaze over a little. She had to rein it in and remember she'd come here for someone else; someone to whom she owed a fair, focused trial.

Just then, Kona walked over to Julia Chase, who had just arrived. He threw her son Richie up in the air three times to make him laugh. And for more strategic reasons, he knew this talent with her son would cause Julia to melt with burning desire.

Next, something strange happened: Kona and Julia walked right into Kona's Jeep. This did not go unnoticed by the other instructors and a few of the envious mothers dropping their children off. Kona and Julia disappeared down Beachwood Lane right at the start of camp.

Luke tried to concentrate on this beautiful woman with green eyes, but he made a *what the fuck?* expression over at Kenny, who had also witnessed Kona and Julia's sudden departure at the busiest moment in camp.

"Here, honey, step into the legs," Katie instructed her son, just to occupy herself and not look up at this man. She realized they'd forgotten the sun cream in the car, so she walked back with Huck. "We'll be back in ten minutes."

Back in the lot, she took her sweet time getting Huck's suit on, making sure his swim trunks weren't all bunched up, the shoulders weren't tight, and that he had room under his arms. As a local teacher, this guy must know something about the school system, so she could just keep it formal, professional, and keep in touch with him. With her child now more ready, she walked up the lot and right back to the cute camp director.

From the little creases in the sides of her kind eyes, Luke figured she must be about two to four years younger than he, somewhere in her late twenties or perhaps just thirty. Mature, though, not desperate for marriage since probably she'd already been through all that. Nice age, not that rough period when all they wanted was a ring, and not so young she had time to play mind games like his ex, Simone, whose body he still couldn't get out of his mind.

Kenny poked him way too hard from behind and whispered in his ear, "She'll be begging for it if you charm the son like Kona does."

Luke shoved Kenny back with his elbow a little too hard so he got the point: *shut the fuck up, Kenny; don't fuck this up for me. I'm not like Kona that way; she's gonna think we are all idiots.*

Luke knelt down, partially to get out of Kenny's air space and partially to focus on little Huck, who looked somewhat lost in a sea of entitled kids. Most of them knew each other from New York City private schools. Her child was adorable, and she was a parent who didn't roll in like the world owed her something. She'd even asked him what he did year-round. That had to be the first show of interest in his life from a camp parent.

Katie zippered up the thick neoprene wetsuit onto her fidgety boy. Now that she could actually talk to this man, her mind wound all the way back to spring of tenth grade, at the end of a day in April: Tommy, the baseball player (in sloppy uniform), stood on the other side of her locker in a bustling hallway. When she slammed the door, he simply smiled and said "hello," and she was lost in his spell for years. This damn guy from the shop smiled just like Tommy, and his look was all messy the same way.

"Where do I go, Mom? How do I know I don't have to go into the ocean if I don't want to?" asked Huck.

Luke jumped in. "We don't let any of the kids in the ocean who aren't ready for it and aren't wanting it. Today, it's pretty calm out there, not many big waves, so today would actually be a great day for Huck to do the ocean-side activities. If he wants to be with me though on the bay side, not saying he has to, just . . . kind of . . . like it seems he wants to."

Huck had now inched closer to Luke, so he continued. "I'll be on the bay side in the boat doing waterskiing, wakeboarding, and tubing, or whatever the kids are in the mood for. We don't really impose anything on them, so . . ." Huck was now holding Luke's hand, his expression still frightened. Luke cocked his head at Katie, knowing his instincts were right. "Why doesn't he just stick with me?"

Luke looked for Kona's Jeep in the far-off spot, and realized it was gone. Kona couldn't be doing Julia Chase right at the beginning of camp. In his car? *Really?*

"That sounds really fun," Katie answered, looking Luke right in the eye in that adult-understanding-of-kids'-needs way. "Thank you, I'm sure Huck would prefer to stay with you." She nodded as she watched him pick up Huck. "And for the lessons, you'll be with him . . . ?" She was trying hard to sound official, efficient, and safety-first oriented. Her eyes noticed the dark hair on the top of his chest coming out of the T-shirt.

Luke answered, trying to focus on this woman with perfect green eyes and not on the possibility his oldest friend would be murdered by a certain Jake Chase if he were, in fact, getting blown by a married Mrs. Chase in his Jeep at this moment. "We say we do skill-oriented lessons and all that, but we pretty much just do whatever the kids want in the bay and that's 90 percent tubing, honestly. No lessons a ton of the time. For tubing, we'll pull him slowly behind the boat. We're not really regimented, to put it mildly."

"What about the propeller? What if he gets caught up in . . ."

"No propeller," Luke answered, shielding his eyes from the sun's glare and surveying the lot for a returning Jeep. "We thought of that, and got old used jet boats with jets way underneath, in the middle. No way they can harm you. No propellers. All good. And it's Huck Doyle, right?"

She smiled. "Yes." She knew her face was beet-purple. Her light cheeks always flushed when she cried or got nervous. So she grabbed her baseball hat out of her bag and pulled it down hard on her head. "He's my son. This is my son." She knew she sounded strange and awkward.

"I got that part early on, with his grabbing your leg for dear life." His voice cracked ever so slightly and Kenny came back again with one of his hugely obnoxious, but encouraging punches, which Luke tried to ignore with a cough.

"Yeah," she said. "He's shy. He doesn't really know kids yet. This is new to him, and to me. All this. . . ." Katie held her palms up and motioned toward the private club down the beach and the Gatsby-style estates lining the bay behind her.

"You said you were from out West, back in the shop?" Luke asked.

"Like, really, *not at all* from here. I live in a small town near a lake outside Portland, Oregon. It's called Hood River. I was a teacher there. I might be a teacher here if things work out."

"I can certainly tell you all about the system here. It's pretty solid with the huge tax revenues."

"I know."

"You do?" He smiled, wishing she needed him to explain it all.

"I'm a learning specialist. I also write studies. I'm hoping to publish some with institutes in Manhattan. And there might be a special ed position in one of the local middle schools."

Interesting, Luke thought. She wasn't from here, but she taught. Special ed always meant nice and understanding and patient. "And, you're here for . . ."

"The whole summer." She smiled. Shit. She shouldn't do this.

Just then Kona's Jeep pulled up way too fast. He got out, no Julia inside now. Interesting. He had a stupid, satisfied grin on his face. This wasn't good for anyone at the camp. He walked up to the group, and studied his buddy handling this beautiful new girl in town.

"She wants to suck your little dick," said Kona way too loudly after Katie finished signing forms.

Huck was squirming and yelling as Katie slathered more white zinc oxide on his face. It didn't seem she heard Kona's gracious observation. Luke closed his eyes and prayed to the Good Lord Jesus, the Savior Moses, and the Prophet Mohammed that she hadn't.

Chapter Sixteen

Yes, Her Real Name Is Poppy

K atie. It's Poppy Porter." She sounded stern on the phone.

"Oh, hello. I'm looking so forward to meeting you," Katie said. "I hope you got the flowers."

"They were beautiful, dear."

"George said he would get us together and I was leaving it to him, but perhaps I should have called myself."

"We women can't leave *anything* to men. Haven't you learned that, child?"

Katie laughed. "I do unfortunately know something about that!"

"Come to the Seabrook Club. Today. I like a late lunch. Two p.m. The first trials for the children's swim meet are done this afternoon, always the first Wednesday the kids are out of school for good. Please tell me your Huck can swim?"

"Yes, of course he can, but he's not the most competitive kid."

"It's good for him. Leave him with the lifeguard at the club. We need to talk and I need you to do something for me, for the club and community."

At 2:04, Katie ran out to the restaurant veranda. She sensed from Poppy's schoolmarmish photos in the cottage that she did not tolerate tardiness. Getting Huck settled with a new person by the club pool had taken longer than the thirty minutes she'd allotted. She left him crestfallen, legs dangling into the water, sitting right under the lifeguard's chair. If he sat there and didn't cause trouble, Katie bargained they'd finish the entire lighthouse jigsaw puzzle later.

On her way to find Poppy, Katie passed Seabrook members sipping their prized Southside cocktails made with gin, simple syrup, crushed mint, lemon, and a splash of soda. The elderly African-American bartender, Henry Walker, had amended the famous drink that originated during Prohibition in the South Side of Chicago, adding a sprig of flowering thyme.

Katie found Henry holding court behind the bar, shaking a fresh batch. "I'm looking for Poppy Porter?"

Henry smiled. "There's only one Poppy. And she's on the far right in the bright hat."

Katie looked out at the sea of club women. "I'm sorry. Everyone has a bright hat."

He laughed, his beautiful, white teeth shining from his dark complexion. "You're right, young lady. Let me take you. And may I introduce myself? My name is Mr. Henry Walker. And you are?"

"Katie Doyle. I'm visiting for the summer. This is my first time here."

"Well, there's a first for everything," he answered. Henry moved his large belly around the bar and offered Katie his elbow as if he were escorting her down the stairs to her cotillion. He was wearing a white polo shirt and crisp navy blazer with a Seabrook emblem on his pocket.

They passed a table of boisterous women, possibly over-served, all sporting peach-colored sweatshirts that said, THE DAVENPORT FAMILY SUMMER SOLSTICE DINNER 2017 on the front and *"Longest Night of the Year . . ."* on the back. Katie figured they were another case of those matching Hamptons houseguests.

"And this is the one and only Mrs. Poppy Porter." Henry motioned with the palm of his hand. He then leaned in, "She knows she's my favorite girl here."

"If only 1 percent of the men in this world were the gentleman you are," Poppy said as she smiled at Henry, tucking her longish blond-gray hair under her huge hat. "So, sit, Katie, please." She pointed to the seat, settling her own full figure back into the chair. "It's fine you are a little late."

"I didn't know if Huck would ever let me leave. Even though he's eight, he's still a kid who takes a little while to get with the program."

Poppy put her index finger into the air. "Waiter, two Arnold Palmers, please."

Katie thought it wise not to point out that she preferred plain seltzer or unsweetened iced tea instead of the sugary lemonade drink Poppy ordered for her. She smoothed out her shorts, and settled into her seat at the small white table. Poppy explained first, "I don't drink until three. *Ever.* That's when Henry makes me a Pink Lady."

"It's fine, honestly," answered Katie. "If you'd like some wine, I'm not going to join you but . . ."

"Never." Poppy pushed her lips tightly together. "Pink Lady at three."

"Okay then. A Pink Lady?"

"Gin, grenadine, one egg white. Garnished with a cherry." She smiled.

"Raw egg whites?" asked Katie. "In this day and age when everyone's so worried about salmonella?"

Poppy chuckled. "Silly modern worries don't interest me. You should try one. They're delicious. Henry adds four cherries to mine." Poppy wore bright pink lipstick that matched her hat, but no other makeup on her fair and freckled skin. She had a small turned-up nose and warm blue eyes, punctuated by deep lines when she smiled. At seventy-four years old, she had assumed her age gracefully, clearly not a fan of Botox or hiding the gray. "Are you enjoying your time in the Hamptons? Is my son doing all he can to make you feel welcome?"

"Well, he's been extremely kind. He had someone bring me my favorite bing cherries in a big pail when I first got here."

Poppy nodded knowingly.

"That was you?" Katie smiled.

"Of course that was me. But he told me to do it, so let's us girls give him credit. He can be very thoughtful, my George," Poppy said without any conviction. "Now, I did teach him the Porter family values that come from years of adversity in the sea. Did you know both sides of his family started whaling off the coast of Nantucket in the later 1600s?"

"I did not, but I figured with the compass in the living room, maybe . . ."

"They hunted the world's oceans for whales, whose blubber was burned into valuable whale oil, in ships named the *Aurora*, the *Catawba*, and the *Essex*, the latter having been sunk by a whale who crested . . ." Katie pondered all the nautical equipment in the cottage, the harpoons, and the scrimshaw while Poppy recounted Porter adventures through the centuries until she concluded with, "Well, now, let's go to the buffet before I tell you what I need you to do."

Famished after the dissection of colonial whaling techniques, Katie followed Poppy into the screened-in buffet area. Young children ran around in dripping wet bathing suits. J.Crew–clad mothers chased after them. Out-of-touch fathers focused on getting food and drink after a punishing game of tennis with their college fraternity brothers. On the way, Katie saw that Huck was now giggling on the diving board with another young boy his age. The friendly lifeguard was egging them on to jump, which allowed Katie to relax.

Gray plastic tray in hand, Katie then perused the Episcopalian culinary choices before her: prison-grade turkey burgers on slightly frozen buns with slices of sweet pickles; deviled eggs (over-boiled and now covered with yellow, dried crust); and chef's salads of processed lunch meats filled with air bubbles. For a more substantial warm meal, the gourmet offering included cod soaked in a nondescript, pasty white sauce, white rice with carrots, and tomato aspic. The "chef" had thrown a few courageous flakes of parsley on top as a show of WASP whimsy.

Back at the table, Katie explained her rapport with George as best she could to the probing matriarch. "Your son is very thoughtful and deliberate, and certainly raised well. I can see he gets his handsome face from his father in the sailing photos. At the education conference, the moment he spoke to me, I was taken by his intelligence and honesty."

"Interesting," answered Poppy. She crossed her arms over her plentiful bosom and twitched her teeny nose.

"He's also wonderful to my son, Huck, so what more can any woman ask?" Katie's face told two stories: her mouth curled up in a smile at the thought of George's kindness toward Huck, but her eyes penetrated Poppy's with a nagging hesitation she couldn't shake.

Poppy may have been wearing a large sun hat with big cotton peony blossoms plastered all over it, a hideous pink caftan with bold orange stripes that screamed, "Palm Beach!" and sunny yellow pants that didn't match anything except the Seabrook beach chairs. But, like her great-great-grandfather who hacked whales for blubber, she was a hardy woman who didn't shy from the obvious.

"Relax, child." Poppy patted Katie's wrist with her freckled hands, her bright-pink nail polish playing off her sun hat. "Your independence is something to cherish. You can have the cottage no matter what. I am aware of your mother's passing and how close you were. I know you upended your life to come here. I hear the tutoring company hired you from afar. You must have a good reputation in your community."

"My training as a learning specialist might lead to a special ed job at the Bridgehampton Middle School." Katie cleared her throat. "I just want to say that if I do stay in the fall, I have no intention of staying in the cottage that you so generously have offered me. And I hope you got the first month's rent?"

"George told me you wouldn't come if I didn't cash that so-called 'rent' check. You don't need to pay anything. No one does. If you insist, I will, but it seems wrong to." Poppy shook her head. "My son and I have the other cottage several streets away."

"Well, I can't say I can match you with a similar family history, but my son, Huck, and I are grateful. And yes, please cash it. I'll be looking at the account until you do."

"Would your son Huck like to come see my museum?"

"I'm so sorry, come see what?" Katie was finding Poppy more entertaining by the minute.

"There's a small whaling exhibit in our attic in the main cottage culled from Nantucket—you know we are descendants of the great Coffin family?"

"I've never heard of them."

"They were stalwart seafaring folk who left a legacy of leather log books of each voyage, lances, duck decoys carved by sailors on long days at sea, what have you," explained Poppy proudly.

"Huck would love it."

"In the summer, we bring the kids from the women's shelter—it's a place where ailing single mothers, many with cancer, some local people, some immigrants, live with their children." She leaned across the table. "I thought Huck might like to learn how the scrimshaw was made from whale teeth, etched with a needle and ink and polished. Apparently, Miles Coffin was quite the artist."

"Well, perhaps I can put your family history into the summer curriculum work for my students." The people Katie knew back in Hood River didn't discuss relatives further back than grandparents.

"Now about that cottage," Poppy instructed. "I ask everyone to pull their weight. We do need a fair amount of weeding, and if there's a repair, I need to know if you or George can fix it. I prefer that because a squanderer I am not. No one in my family was, going way back to my great, well, I don't need to bore you with my family history," Poppy stated, apparently unaware of the sole lunch topic since Katie sat down. "And there's a bird feeder. George and his father first put it up about forty years ago; he's no longer here to see it. Please, keep that feeder full. He would want that."

"George and Huck are on it. Your husband passed away ten years ago, right?"

Poppy pursed her lips tightly. "George's father was a fine man. He had some faults. We had our issues, but then, yes, he was gone before we could resolve them formally."

"I'm sorry . . . that must have been difficult. I lost my father when I was a young child. I don't remember him. My mother did it all alone. Like me." Katie smiled. "But you are still so young."

"Well, I'm getting on." Poppy took a huge gulp of her Arnold Palmer and pushed her sunglasses tighter onto her face. "And as for your chores . . ."

Katie choked a bit on her bread stick, soft and stale from the sea air. "I did repair a bunch of very small things in the house. I put some geraniums in the window planters, I caulked the tub . . ."

"I did not mean chores in your cottage."

"Then your cottage, you want me to tend to what?"

Poppy laughed out loud. "Who do you think I am? No, not *my* cottage either. You're the potential girlfriend, not the hired help! I meant here!" And she pointed her finger at the hallowed club grounds. "We have an annual garden party at the library; we call it the Patio Party. It takes place on a Saturday afternoon at the end of summer."

"Happy to help, Poppy," Katie wisely answered.

Poppy leaned across the table again and squinted her eyes. "Don't forget, the hallmark of clubs like the Seabrook is civic duty. For over a hundred years, we've served Southampton by preserving historic homes, keeping the library and hospital coffers full, and maintaining town codes. All of our activities are crucial to the functioning of the town. We run can drives and soup kitchens in churches. I know we might look a little elitist from the outside, but that charitable element is the foundation of our values. I won't let anyone at this club forget that. And I'll be leaving here feet first!"

"Well, I'd be happy to pitch in. I'd be helping the other co-chairs?"

"Yes. I must warn you they are not the most decisive women. I tend to stick with my age group, women who, frankly, seem more modern than some of today's scattered housewives"—and she whispered, cupping her mouth—"*Social climbers, a little too excited about seeing themselves in society pages!*

"But hopefully you can help them decorate the tables with flair. You're an educator, you must be good with arts and crafts." Poppy wagged her finger at Katie, and stared at her from under the brim of her ridiculous hat. "There are tables to dress, cocktails to choose, décor to arrange, and it's all to benefit the young children," she whispered, "many, you know, *illegal immigrants*. I don't mind helping them one bit. Their families are just trying their best to earn a living—God knows what kind of education they get in the public schools!"

Katie decided not to remind Poppy she was honored to be considered for a job in that very public education system.

"I'd be glad to," Katie answered. "If George would want me helping in any way, I'll do anything."

"My son isn't the easiest person in the world, but he's very, very dear," Poppy said. "I'd love him to get married one day. I'm not suggesting anything here, darling, just a family would settle him down. And I'm not averse to arrangements people have these days. Not to pry into where your son Huck's father is, nor do I need to know, it's just . . . well, actually, I'd love to know . . .

"Waiter! Two more Arnold Palmers please! And tell Henry to start shaking me a Pink Lady soon—it's quarter to three!"

Chapter Seventeen

Bond Girls or Girls Bonding?

Katie rang the doorbell of a shingled home that was larger than most seaside inns. The uniformed housekeeper led her to the breakfast pantry, where the mother, Samantha Davidson, opened mail on the counter. She turned around only to ask, "The school sent you his evaluation, his neuro-psych test, right?"

"They didn't," answered Katie. "But it's fine, we can sit and talk a little about what you want for Jeffrey, and of course Jeffrey's own goals for . . ."

"I swear I asked my husband's assistant," Samantha said, motioning Katie to sit with her twelve-year-old son, who nervously pulled at his short brown hair. She had her biking shoes on already, and her feet clacked on the marble floors as she approached the breakfast table. "Anyway, it's fine. Honey, can you say hi to the lady?"

"It's Katie Doyle. I'm a learning specialist."

"Learning specialist, huh? Is that better than tutor?" Samantha tapped her Fitbit tracking device several times.

"All that matters is I'll be coaching Jeffrey on new techniques. We just need to understand how he retains information best. I've written several papers for parents on coping strategies, if you'd like I can . . ."

"Tell her, Jeffrey, tell the lady what your problems with reading are."

Jeffrey hesitated, not exactly sure how to explain all his academic issues that had plagued him since nursery school.

Thirty seconds passed while Samantha stretched her hamstrings against the back of the chair.

"Oh, never mind, I will," Samantha added as if she were doing both of them a favor. "Jeffrey's got word recognition issues. He's good through a few sentences, and then they bleed together, right? He's in a school that is too hard, and they say it's touch and go, but we're keeping him in."

"What school?" Katie asked. "Just curious why . . ."

"It's Trinity. His father went there. His siblings did fine." Samantha bounced her fingers down to her toes, then rearranged the tight biking shorts around the top of her racehorse thighs.

"Um, okay . . . well if Trinity's remedial support isn't . . ."

"We're sticking with the Trinity plan. Don't even ask what we had to do for the annual fund." Samantha patted Katie's wrist like she was sweet, but didn't know any better. "Anything Jeffrey needs, we always say. He's worth it." Samantha clipped her Fitbit inside her sports bra.

"Well of course any child, Jeffrey included, is worth the investment to . . ."

"Social studies and English trip him up. Oh, and biology, too. He can't do textbooks basically. Otherwise you're good, right, honey?!" Samantha clacked down the kitchen hall, and then turned. "Oh, and pretty severe A.D.D., you know what that is, right?"

"Attention deficit disorder can be a blessing." Katie turned to the despondent child now, her hand on his shoulder. "I know when you're not interested, you can't focus or even listen. But, when it's something you're into, like sports or machines, there's no stopping you, right?"

Jeffrey nodded, and let out a teeny hint of a smile. "Yeah, airplanes and basketball. I know a lot, I mean, a real lot, about them."

"I thought so. Honey, welcome to the land of the gifted. We're going to use your A.D.D. as a driver of . . ."

"I don't medicate him in the summer, hate the zombie effect the Adderall gives him!" Samantha screamed back from way down the kitchen mudroom, yanking the cushion for her bike seat off a high shelf. "So he might not be able to focus one bit on what you're telling him today, right, Jeffrey?!!" This time, the back screen door slammed shut, leaving Katie and the humiliated Jeffrey at the table, while three matching housekeepers arranged hydrangeas cut from the extensive gardens in vases at the counter.

Two hours later, Katie parked the old pale green Porter family Volvo in the public beach lot. She watched throngs of women arriving at camp pickup, frazzled on a lovely weekend day. They were yelling at kids to rush to their next lesson, throwing them into cars, legs flailing, only half changed out of wetsuits before the cars tore away.

If Katie could manage to handle that difficult tutor session this morning, why were the mothers around her so strained by simply getting their children at camp? This was, after all, a low-key water sports camp pickup moment, not a Best Buy television department on Black Friday of Thanksgiving week.

A brunette in the spot to her right, wearing a shimmering bathing suit cover-up more appropriate for Kim Kardashian on her St. Tropez mega-yacht than a mom in a parking lot, darted out of her cherry-red Porsche 911 to fetch her child, a dash of madness in her eyes.

Katie heard the distant sound of the fire station's nasal honk reverberating through the salty breeze. It went off every day at noon to test the system of the mostly volunteer force. She wondered if today the noon signal meant something serious, given the frenetic activity.

"Is everything okay?" Katie asked another mother dressed in black Stella McCartney workout gear. "I'm sorry to bother you, but I mean there's so much honking in the lot, the parents are kind of sprinting around, I heard the sound of the fire siren, and I was wondering . . ."

The woman flapped her hand back at Katie, implying that a plain mother in cutoffs and a baseball hat (an outfit telegraphing *not from here*) couldn't be expected to comprehend the stress this woman was under handling three vacation homes (Southampton, Casa de Campo, and Aspen). Not to mention all the effort she expended to make sure the staff performed crucial functions like folding origami fish on the end of the toilet paper rolls for easy pulling.

Even those staff people on this otherwise lovely Saturday morning were racing around, sweating in their ubiquitous uniforms of tan pants, white polo shirts (some with the name of the house like a yacht crew), and sensible white soft professional shoes. Katie watched a nanny make a child simultaneously rush to the car and hold his arms in the air so she could put his white tennis shirt on while hopping out of his thick, wet, sticky wetsuit. "Sorry, Jacob can't do playdate," the nanny yelled at Katie. "He has a lesson now . . ."

Katie hadn't even asked for a playdate.

Through the sea of lunacy around her, Katie found her son,

Huck, sitting on Luke's shoulders. Another child hung onto Luke's right arm and both boys laughed as Luke tickled them.

"Hey, honey, how was it?" she asked Huck, pulling him off Luke's tall shoulders. Katie tried to act official and polite as she turned to Luke and said, "Is everyone okay? The people here seem kind of in a hurry."

"All good," he replied. "This is what they do. They act like the town is being invaded by the enemy."

"But it's Saturday . . ." Katie's voice creaked, a grown woman of twenty-nine once again succumbing to middle-school nerves. She stood up straight and resolved to speak more firmly as she listened to his answer.

"I can only give this possible explanation," Luke responded. "They're like hamsters in a spinning wheel back in Manhattan, and they don't hop off when they get here."

"Okay . . . I guess that makes sense." Her voice sounded more normal now.

"You'll see, they're not all like this. Some of the moms are fine. *Some* . . . not so much." He smiled, staring into her eyes until the silence was palpable. "But . . . these kids had a great day, right, guys?" He blew out a breath loudly.

"I don't know how you can count them all and keep them safe," Katie answered. "I'm sure you do and you have systems, but I'm just grateful seeing Huck's smile when he's near the water. It's so . . . empowering for him." *Empowering?* She had never once used that word. Katie hated that word.

Now her eyes lingered on his too long. She forced herself to study the cracks in the pavement by her toes. She felt like a seventh grader with her first girl crush on a friend's older brother. Or, far worse, like the neglected housewives around her. Speaking of, out of her sight, a wife in a Beyoncé caftan walked through head-high sea grass with Kona to his lair. The two of them resembled lions disappearing into the dense savannas of the Southern Sahara.

Huck tugged at her leg. "Mom, can I go home with Richie? He said he's always allowed to have a playdate and he doesn't have to check."

Julia Chase strolled up to Luke, a bit more casually than the other moms and certainly with more of a friendly expression on her pretty, tanned face. She held out her hand to Katie. "Hi, I'm Julia, known around here as Richie's mom. I see our kids have found the nicest guy in camp." She pulled her Richie off Luke's limbs. Her blond curls gracefully framed her face in the noontime sunlight.

"Can Huck come over?" Richie asked his mother as she looked everywhere for Kona. "His mom said okay I think." Both boys, wide-eyed, placed their hands in prayer under their chins. "Is it okay, please?"

"Yeah, please, Mom, okay?" asked Huck.

"You want to go to his house now?" Katie had had her own hands in prayer mode for weeks before they arrived, hoping Huck would make friends in the far-off Hamptons. And here, on his second try at a camp, he'd already found one. "Well, I guess, sure, if his mom, Mrs. . . ."

"Oh, please, call me Julia," she said. "Your son can certainly come over. Do you summer out here regularly?" Katie shook her head, noting the use of "summer" as a verb. Julia pushed her luscious blond curls off her face. "I know we just met, but I'm heading to a great exhale Core Fusion class, just five minutes away. While the boys play, we can go if you like?"

"What is . . ." Katie prepared herself to feel deeply out of it, one of those things that's not like the others.

"Core Fusion? You don't know it? Fred and Elisabeth? All the celebrities go. It's an amazing workout."

"I was kind of hoping to join a gym today," Katie said. "I do have my exercise gear in my car. But I have to be back close to here, for a job thing I have, by two-thirty."

"Just come." Julia smiled warmly. "It's only an hour and close by. You look like you're in great shape. They won't bring you out on a stretcher, I promise. We could let the nanny take the kids home with the driver and you and I can go. It's challenging, but fun. They just announced a twelve-thirty barre class with Fred so I thought I'd rush to it now after checking in that Richie was okay. Next to your son, he appears to be better than fine."

Katie liked something about this woman, despite her cosmetically engineered figure, her hair bleached several shades too light, and her Technicolor exercise outfit—basically, the kind of woman she'd never thought she'd relate to. And though she felt silly jumping into a stranger's plan, she did need a workout. The boys would be occupied, supervised, and Luke Forrester knew Julia as a regular, so . . .

"Why not go?" Luke added. "Core Fusion classes are part of the mom routine. Give it a try?" He smiled.

"We sign up online on the first Sunday night in April at midnight for the entire season," Julia explained. "And by the following Monday afternoon, the good summer classes are full. They just announced a midday class, and I got two spots just for the hell of it. You know, I could probably sell them for three-hundred dollars each."

"Julia will take good care of you," Luke reassured her, amused that Katie was jumping into the Hamptons housewives loony bin. "You couldn't have a better guide."

"Can you give me clear directions? I don't want to be late or lose you in all the weekend traffic."

Julia put her hand on Katie's. "Stop. Please. Let me take you in my car and we'll have our own playdate."

Chapter Eighteen
Wacky Workout

Next thing Katie knew, she was flying down Route 27—the road that served as the central vein of the Hamptons—in Julia Chase's second sports car, a navy blue Maserati GranTurismo Convertible MC that purred like a snoring grizzly bear. As they careened down the highway, Katie tightened her seat belt and gripped the sides of her plush leather seat. The pavement, so close to the bottom of the car, seemed like mere inches beneath her feet. To her right lay the ocean and enormous estates, and to her left, the smaller, less desirable parcels of real estate dotting the potato field horizon.

As they turned onto the back wooded lanes, the expensive grip of the tires felt like the centrifugal force of a roller coaster. Katie thought about how the very rich must experience everything differently, even a simple curve in a road.

"So I don't see a ring. Are you dating anyone?" Julia yelled, the convertible top down and her lemon-yellow hair flying all around her head like a 1950s movie star on the mountainous roads of Cannes.

"Well, yeah . . ."

"That sounds noncommittal."

"Well, it's more than that, but just starting, I guess."

"You don't have to explain; I know so many men who are always looking, so I thought I'd ask."

"I came here counting on seeing a man named George. I don't need a setup for sure." And after a brief pause, Katie added, "We're just kind of trying it out, so I should give it a chance."

"And you came from out West, Luke mentioned. It's Portland? Seattle? It's all the same to us New Yorkers. Sounds horrible, but that's the goddamn truth. We voyage all over the world, but we can be the most provincial people, just sticking to our little insular zip codes—10021 in the city, 11968 here. Terrible, really, but it's paradise. So what am I going to do?" She turned and smiled at Katie.

"Yeah, well, it is beautiful. But I have to say, not quite as gorgeous as Hood River, where I'm from. It's at the base of Mount Hood and in the Columbia Gorge, and surrounded by orchards and vineyards. You can view Mount St. Helens in the distance and even Rainier on clear days. There are wildflower fields as far as you can see, and great hiking."

"I might mountain bike, but you're not getting me in hiking boots."

"Call me crazy," answered Katie, now wiping her fingers along the smooth mahogany dashboard of the Maserati. "But I figured that out."

"And you left family, or you were single or . . ."

"Definitely was single, or well, not married." Katie held her hand on her head, so her baseball cap didn't fly off.

"And his dad, is he active with the child and okay with you all being out here?"

"He isn't in the picture at all."

"Never mind. I'm sorry." Julia turned to Katie at a stop sign and patted her hand. "Really I am. Don't mean to push you. New

Yorkers can fire questions at people. It's not that we are super nosy. I guess we are, but it's more we are just direct. We love to know people well. I certainly like a good relationship with my girlfriends. So I ask, but it's fine if you don't want to answer."

"No, it's fine." Katie missed having Ashley close by and wasn't all that different in her desire to get to know people quickly. She and her friends out West certainly gabbed all day and night when they could. "It's just, his father never was in the picture. He sends money almost never, he sends cards at Christmas. Huck sees him twice a year.

"We fell for each other after meeting in a gallery show of his artwork and I got pregnant in a short four-month period. His name is Liam, he's Swedish. That's where my kid gets his hair; it's almost white by August. Huck's dad is an artist and a dreamer, and once he had to settle down and face reality, he freaked out and pretty much disappeared on us. He thinks it's better for Huck if he isn't around, if he isn't planning on being *really* around."

"Do you agree? Are you angry at that?"

Katie shook her head. "I don't really disagree with Liam. He's a sweet guy with his head in the clouds and I'm not sure showing up and then not showing is good for any kid. So, now that Huck is eight, and my mother, who kind of half raised him, is gone, it's all really on me to turn him into a good man."

"I'm sorry about that."

"Yeah." Katie looked out the window at the cornstalks now half-way grown up with teeny ears just budding out a third of the way through summer. She wiped her eyes a little with the tips of her pinkies, feeling stinging in them, but grateful the wind from the racing convertible dried them out quickly.

After a few minutes of silence, Katie filled the void. "After a full four weeks here, my kid seems happy. We're recently trying out this new Tide Runners Camp. I like it, he likes it, but are you sure they are safe? I met Luke Forrester and kind of grilled him New Yorker style on all the chaos and waves and boats. But I liked him." Katie wanted more Luke data if she could discreetly pull it out of this nice woman.

"Luke is a plain old great guy. Straight arrow. In fact, most of the guys in that camp are the absolute best. They always have an eagle eye on the kids to make sure they're happy and safe and never hesitate to tell the campers how to behave and what's expected of them. And the kids respect them, especially Luke. They roll down the beach in circles around him like he's the Pied Piper." She smiled and studied Katie at a red light. Katie instinctively neatened her T-shirt.

"You'll see," Julia carried on. "Luke will be your son's first true love, or at least purest form of worship he'll ever experience. I don't know much about him personally except that he used to have a girlfriend. I think she kind of tortured him, or at least that's what the guys always said. She looks like a real-life centerfold."

Great, thought Katie, even though she was giving George the fair and focused trial.

"Of course, then there's Kona, who's just trouble."

"Trouble? Like drugs?"

"God, no, they are pretty clean, those guys, just he goes after women like a shark."

"Married women?" Katie couldn't resist.

"Married. Single. Anyone. I like to screw with him. Give him a glimmer of hope, then crush him. It's good for him," Julia answered. "He deserves a little of his own medicine as they say."

"It's good for him?" Katie wondered if it wasn't good for Julia.

"Oh, yeah. He's from Hawaii, or I guess he moved there where his mother's family is. That's why he has that face, that caramel skin." She sighed a little. "Oh, I don't know, just all island-y, kind of a worldly adventurer. He shimmies up trees and picks coconuts, or works on sailboats and climbs up the masts to unfurl sails flapping in winds. Gives him confidence to go after pretty much every woman. Kind of a wild dude, must have gotten it from his native roots, but we'll leave it at that."

Katie wanted nothing more than to *not* leave it at that, relishing some much-needed girl talk and, perchance, even a little gossip, but they had entered a small, sandy driveway off a back road and slowly edged up to the top of the hill where a large barn structure housed the exhale Core Fusion studio. When they rolled up to a dusty lot, toned women were jumping in and out of luxury sedans and sports cars, not one weighing in at more than 125 pounds. Suddenly, Katie realized the frenetic, honking scene in the beach lot was like a calm Buddhist colony compared to this one.

"This sucks, word got out," Julia lamented, watching the exiting and entering cars in virtual gridlock, inching in and out of cramped spots and up and down the tight sandy lane.

"The other class is ending now and the new class always arrives right as they are leaving, which is what causes this mess," explained Julia. "I thought that for this extra class midday, during lunch, things would be calmer. But this is going to get ugly."

"Why?"

"Because there are twenty-five spots in the class. This extra class is like a bag of bread rolls thrown on top of a starving refugee camp. People are desperate to get it, grabbing, pushing, fighting, you'll see."

"Well, it does seem like some of these mothers have really bad manners," Katie offered. "Before at pickup, and at some stores in town, I saw them acting insanely."

"Bad manners? Try ruthless psychopaths." Julia pulled her $161,070 convertible an inch closer to the center of the lot, where other cars were trying to exit, driven by mothers rushing to a golf, tennis, or a lunch emergency.

"That's my spot!" a woman in a robin's egg-blue convertible MINI Cooper yelled at Julia. "I call it! That one!"

"You call parking spots like that?" asked Katie.

"You don't get it yet," Julia said, laughing. "The possibility of missing a chance to work four grams of fat off their inner thighs is like missing a chance to secure their kids a spot at Harvard. Watch, she's going to accelerate and kill someone trying to get the spot before me."

The women maneuvered their masterpiece vehicles like fourteen-year-old girls in their first parking lesson with Daddy. It didn't take an engineering major to divine that the woman in the MINI Cooper would have to physically bend the metal on her car in half to move it into the spot she'd "called." But then, Julia wasn't much better off either: she was trying to enter a too-tight spot, at a ninety-degree angle with a two-inch cushion of space. So far she'd spent about six minutes going an inch forward and then back, clearly not understanding her Maserati would never make it into the spot if she were going to tack it in by inches. Katie thought it rude to ask Julia if these people paid people to take their driving tests.

"Don't take this the wrong way," Katie said. "But let me park the car or you're going to smash it up. You gotta start again, roll back like ten feet, and do a wider turn to get in there. You go in, and sign us up. I'll be there in three minutes and change and meet you."

"You can do it? I'm so sorry; you must think I'm an idiot. I've never been a good parker." She smirked a little. "Truth be told, I get driven more than I drive and I'm out of practice."

"Yeah, I can park the car. All good," Katie said, smiling and happy to be useful. She found this Julia amusing in her honesty.

Five minutes later, as Katie entered the studio where Julia had saved her a mat, she wondered what in hell they would do in this class. Several different sizes of weights, cloth bands, and P.E.-style red balls lay in piles in a large room surrounded by mirrors and ballet barres. She felt intimidated, but also willing to give her sporty physique a test. She placed her chic but simple white leather purse she'd found for forty-seven dollars at Filene's Basement in the corner next to a pile of twenty-five different bags costing around four thousand dollars each from Celine, Gucci, Alaïa, Chloé, Stella McCartney, Prada, and Givenchy. The three in precious ostrich hides had price tags north of eight thousand.

Better that Katie didn't know the total cost of the strewn bags was well over a hundred thousand dollars. And that wasn't counting the twenty-five wallets inside costing another two thousand dollars a pop, nor wads of hundred dollar bills in the wallets the women had their husbands' offices send out. Call it an even two hundred and fifty thousand dollars littered in a big messy clump in an exercise class that absolutely no one was sweating over.

Chapter Nineteen

Time for Romance

That night Katie watched as George Porter walked up the slanted steps of his great grandmother's cottage and knocked on the rickety side panel of the screen porch. The door was so old and in need of repair that knuckles rapping on it made it bounce open and shut. Katie thought he'd said seven o'clock and this was ten full minutes early. She rushed to her room, threw the apron on her bed, flung her hair upside down and spritzed perfume while she let it hang below her head. Reaching inside her blouse, she hurriedly took off her bra because he preferred her without one, jammed her feet into sandals and walked to the door, straightening out her shorts on the way.

"Hey, you don't need to bring stuff for me every time you come here. It's your house," she told George. He stood straight up six feet two inches tall on the other side of the screen door with a huge bouquet of colorful zinnias that smelled like he'd just clipped them.

He smiled and swung open the door his family owned. "It's your house this summer, not mine. We were pretty clear on that.

"And besides, these are flowers I love. They're from Halsey Farm, their corn in August is unbeatable, their field is just better than the others."

"You can taste different corn at different stands? Come into the kitchen."

"I don't know what it is, but maybe it's like vineyards next to each other out in Napa with different-tasting wines. Maybe their soil is different? Their August tomatoes, with just a little sea salt, you bite into like a peach."

"Thank you, it's like these flowers are announcing summer," she said. As he kissed her forehead, her shoulders bunched up. Katie took the bouquet, wondering what her August days here with those ripe tomatoes and crunchy corn would look like. "Huck's just in his bedroom working on some Legos; he'll be out soon."

"Well, leave him be. Happy you like the flowers." George smiled. "They're from a charming local family. They grow all organic. They rely entirely on their land. I like to support them. They've been there since I was a kid, and I'm sure way before that. Amazing cider in the fall, they make the most delicious cinnamon donuts to go with it." George hugged her hard, and then kissed her neck with a hint of tongue. She let her shoulders relax back to normal position.

George walked into the kitchen area through a little hallway like he owned the joint (which he, in fact, did). He yanked his too-long bangs back with his fingers and stared at her like he would fall hard forever. "Katie. I'm not sure I've smelled good food here in two decades," he said, brushing her cheek with the back of his hand, and then tugging on her ear gently. "You didn't have to make me dinner again, but I do love it. And I suppose it's easier just to let Huck play or sleep while we are together rather than use the sitter."

"I like to cook. It's always simple, but it tastes better at home."

"Something I never knew. My mother can't cook; she just makes canned tuna with way too much Hellmann's on Triscuits, uses bottle dressing on iceberg, and calls it dinner. I cook a mean grilled cheese, but that's it. So, what are you making tonight?"

"Tuna steaks with capers and lemons, new potatoes with farm butter and dill, mozzarella and tomato salad. Can't get enough basil in me. Do you like pesto? I might add some to the fish."

"I like anything you make and everything you do to me," George whispered into her ear. "And if Huck is staying in there, can we . . . just I need to feel you against me again. Last time was too good. Excuse my hands all over you." He cleared his throat. "What do you want me to do? You're stunning now, in this light. Let me take a photo."

"Stop!" Katie posed with her hands on her hips for him. She didn't want to spoil the mood, but she thought his lack of contact wasn't nice, or even normal. She'd explain later in bed, once they felt closer and more connected. George grabbed her back hip and tried to pull her into him.

Katie twisted around and snatched the flowers, acting all shy and coy for no particular reason except that she felt he should work a little if he was going to be so distant when they parted.

"Can I get you wine? I bought a few bottles," Katie answered. He stopped her constant movement and held her tight, while he let his fingers glide down the inside back of her pants. It felt good to be held, she thought about his expert soft and silky touch. She considered calling the sitter and just going to a local hotel and forgetting the damn tuna steaks. Both of them had their minds now on what would happen afterwards.

Huck yelled from the other room, "Mom, I lost a piece again!"

She pushed George away, and started to prepare the meal. They had to wait, but she felt a strong tingling between her legs that made her want to yank him into the bedroom and just get on with it. The sun hadn't even set, Huck was wide awake, and she was hungry. Katie took a bite of small toasts from a box. "The crackers get so soggy here. The salt air is something I'm not used to. I bought some cheeses that I think are homemade by the farm stand on the corner. They are so creamy and delicious; you were right about the food out here."

"I don't need much," George grabbed her hip bone and let his fingers trail up her shirt a few inches. "I'm only thinking about that Huck going to sleep. Is it just horrible to ask if we can give him some wine to pass out now?"

She laughed. "Yes, that is horrible. Let me go deal with his Lego crisis. I'll be back in two."

Her body remained on edge and wanting even though George's hand had moved away minutes before.

When she returned, he asked, "You cook well. You like it, really?"

"I love cooking, I do. I love sharing food." Katie knew the small talk sounded formal. She threw the kitchen towel on the counter and turned to him.

"What?' asked George. He looked alluring and refined tonight, a bright yellow cashmere cable-knit on his shoulders. No one would say they didn't make a good match, even though they were fifteen years apart. Maybe it was all okay.

"Nothing, I'm just trying to read you," she answered.

"Well, I hope you're seeing that I'm so happy you're here. Where's the wine?" George chuckled. "I'm pouring you a glass, and serving it to you outside. Just, go out on the porch, now. I'll put the flowers in a vase and see you there in a minute. I said it was your house, but I grew up here, for Christ's sake. Let me welcome you properly, and get some things in order for you. I've been so busy in the city these past weeks. It's a gorgeous night, go sit in the porch swing, let's watch the sun set and just have a glass of wine, c'mon . . ." He shooed her away as he scoured the cabinets for a usable vase. "Jesus,

I don't think this place has seen a new dish since 1972. Seriously, go out there on the porch. Sit. Let me . . ." George slammed the 1950s-style linoleum cabinets opened and shut as Katie walked outside. She plunked herself on the swing, trying not to take his taking over as a declaration of his ownership.

"Huck, I'm out here," Katie yelled into the little bedroom window on the side of the house, where he sat obsessively working on a space shuttle launcher.

"Come say hi to George when you can, honey. When you're done with the booster rocket part. No rush, though; we're here." Katie had placed a small platter on the outdoor table filled with soft goat cheeses and a ball of mozzarella so fresh and runny, she'd had to put it in a small ramekin. In a circle, she'd neatly laid out various crackers from the Carr's assortment box she'd bought. All were softened by the humid sea air, but she slathered the goat cheese on a cracked pepper water cracker anyway. It tasted perfect. It would go down well with the crisp, cold wine the guy at the little vineyard off the highway had suggested.

Sex would reassure her. Tonight, they'd have to be quiet in bed like they had last week with Huck in the next room, a flimsy wall separating them. George would have to cool on the experimental, bold stuff. He meant it as festive and energetic; she was game to be manhandled with his immense strength, game to be wanted in the most elemental way. But, when not in a Hilton hotel room, she now had to cajole him to move slower, softer.

His puttering in the kitchen now unsettled her. She was cooking, and he took over. But did it matter who poured the wine? She felt like someone at the precipice of a mountain cliff, helmet and harness on, not sure why they signed up to bungee jump off.

Across the short lawn, on the other side of the overgrown hedges, the setting sun danced through the rustling branches in the slight wind. She wished her mother was alive to see this little cottage, this new land. Like most good daughters who loved their mothers fiercely, she rarely had taken her advice, or at least rarely admitted to doing so. Tonight, Katie wanted to ask her mother one simple question: Was this George Porter from the far end of the East Coast a good person to be with?

"HELLO? WHAT ARE you thinking about?" George asked, swinging the screen door open, a plastic Tupperware lemonade pitcher filled with blooming flowers in one hand, and the wine bottle, a wine opener, and two mismatched wineglasses in the other.

"Nothing really. Just enjoying the outside air."

George grabbed her hand. "It's so nice to have you in Southampton." He smiled warmly and put the wine bottle on the table. George placed the flowers in the Tupperware pitcher on a side table, saying, "Sorry, told you it wasn't fancy here. No one needed a vase in the house this century, I guess."

Katie took the wine bottle and opener and started opening the foil as George sat back in the white wicker chair in front of her swing. He leaned back, elbows in the air, right foot placed on his left knee, all confident and masculine, as if he controlled the ways of the planet. He stared at her beauty, how her green eyes became clear in the waning sunlight. Then he uncrossed his legs, poured the wine and then handed her a cold glass.

"Take a sip. It's like heaven, that first sip. I see you found that local purveyor, Duck Walk Vineyard, off the highway. Who needs Napa Valley, we have our own?"

She took a slow sip. He was right. The Chardonnay was sweet and buttery. George grabbed Katie's cheeks. "You look gorgeous and tanned in the sunlight."

"Thanks, I'm just, I don't know, a little melancholy tonight."

"You look like you are trying to figure me out and if I fit into some plan to . . ."

"I wasn't, I'm not expecting much of anything except adventure."

"You were staring at me like you were calculating something. Your shoulders were so tense when I walked in."

Katie smiled and took a gulp. "Maybe I was. I just like things settled, orderly. I've had to as a single mom, and it's hard to feel unsure about what I'm doing, especially with Huck. I'm used to being all set, I guess." She smiled, relieved he understood and she couldn't hide from him.

"You have a cottage as long as you need. You're doing gangbusters already with the tutor hours. You son is happy. So don't forget the key pieces are in place. I'm just here because I *like* you. You're a lovely woman. And I like what you do to me in bed. Whether I get lucky and that happens all fall, time will tell." George raised his eyebrows at Katie. "Okay? I'm going to kiss you now. Only because I think you're beautiful."

Katie felt better. She kissed him back, his lips tasting like sweet honey. George sucked on her bottom lip very softly. "Let me make you feel better later."

"Are you her boyfriend now?" Huck surprised them through the living room screen, his elbows on the windowsill. His clear blue eyes went back and forth at each of them.

They laughed. "I just kissed your mother because I think she's a pretty and kind woman. She'll answer that question about 'boyfriend' in a while, maybe at the end of the summer." He mock-whispered to Huck, so Katie could hear. "I'm working on that, though. It's a guy thing that you'll understand when you get older. We all hope they like us as much as we like them. In the meantime, I got something for you in the car." George stood, saying, "Come here, it's a Lego set I bet you never saw."

"Oh, my God, another Lego set, George you are fully responsible for the pieces in this one." Katie laughed, shaking her head. She grabbed another cracker, scooped up some chèvre that had the consistency of ice cream, and smeared it on top. Food could heal almost anything.

While the boys laid out the new Legos in the living room, Katie put dinner on the table. George asked if Huck could sit with them and, though he'd been fed some noodles and chicken much earlier, the child liked being asked. She studied how her son watched George. She couldn't tell if Huck was wary or in awe of his gentlemanly way, his perfect manners.

George stood to pull out her chair every time she got up. He grabbed the wine bottle from her and poured it every time she wanted a little more. She appreciated how he asked Huck for his every opinion, even on things he had no business talking about.

"What does this little man think, that's what I want to know," George asked Huck when they were talking about Katie tutoring kids, and if she should seek out only kids with learning disabilities. "To get as many little clients as possible, should your mom say she's really good with kids who don't read as well and as fast as you do? Or should she say she's just a tutor of English and reading in general?"

Huck looked up at George, with a look that said *this guy's weird.* "I don't know. How am I supposed to know what parents want?"

George laughed. "Okay, well, you're a smart kid. Do you think it helps that your mom is good at helping kids who can't read that well?"

Huck scrunched up his mouth into a little ball to one side of his face. "I think, yes, that makes her a nice person."

George and Katie laughed again. "Well, that she is."

After dinner, while George and Katie polished off the bottle of wine and half of another, Huck passed out on his floor, the Legos he was lying on stamping little circled prints onto his face. Like a paternal knight, George gently lifted him and carried him to his bed.

Being the owner of the house, he then decided to take Katie into the bedroom.

She sat on the edge and unbuttoned her blouse first, and then he walked in front of her and pushed her back farther on the king-size bed so she lay comfortably. She lit a candle to set the mood, a little slower perhaps, a little less calisthenics with her child in the next room.

Apparently George got the message and was more adaptive than she may have given him credit for. "Tonight, no mauling, I'm going to take it so slow, you're going to be in agony you want it so bad."

He kissed her neck, then her breasts, so slowly she could count the seconds ticking. She actually wanted him to move on. She tried to get on top of him, but he held her arms down hard above her head. Now, she could hardly stand waiting. She arched her back and circled her shoulders a few times to ease her body into this newer slow motion tactic. His shoulders and chest were more substantial than she remembered, his body heavier, clearly hard and ready. He played with her nipples with his tongue until finally he slipped both hands down her pants—one in front, one in back—his fingers meeting in between. He then kissed her stomach, slowly opening the buttons of her jeans.

As Katie guided George's entire head with both hands, biting lightly, licking like the master he was, she thought, *this is all going to be just fine.*

Chapter Twenty

Ridiculously Extravagant and Incredibly Cheap

On the way up to the Chase oceanfront estate for lunch, automatic sprinklers watered the expansive landscaping. Kona and Luke used them to rinse the sand off their feet before ringing the doorbell. After four years of taking care of their younger kids, this was the first summer they had ever been invited in the home as guests. *Twice.*

Only this day was not social in their minds: they were on a mission that could be career ending or career saving: to get Jake on their side to help them fight the town trustees. They'd received three more summonses, one over a boat registration issue, overcapacity at camp, and an overdue docking fee—all things they'd never before been busted on. Mrs. Saltzman having made payment on a town beach illegally and Jake illegally driving into camp headquarters wasn't helping. Over the weekend they received a menacing call from the town treasurer for a meeting to clarify "legal issues and matters."

Sixty consistent families, dozens and dozens of other random kids who'd come for a day or two, countless adults who'd learned to love the ocean, all screwed because of a group of overreaching people wanted a small area on a beach clear of messy boards.

"We're going to stick with the strategy, right? You lay out the big picture, and I explain the details." Luke knew he'd have to cancel his cable TV and eat ramen noodles all year if they couldn't get Jake on board to help their case. Camp pretty much doubled his teaching income, and the potential loss had kept him up all night. That was before the bay constable had even slapped them with to-day's summons over the docking fee.

"Our camp is literally the only area where locals and city people hang together, having fun in the same waves. I'm gonna hit Jake with that too, get him all amped on chilling with us."

The door opened.

"Yes?" The housekeeper Edviane glared. She didn't work hard to clean this house for guests who presented themselves like this.

"Kona and Luke?" Kona said. "Uh, Jake invited us . . . he asked us . . . to come?"

She reluctantly led them into the entry hall, a glassed-in cavern. The dark mahogany floor lay largely barren except for a small field of Takashi Murakami mushroom stools, about a dozen of them, two feet high, painted in psychedelic, swirly colors.

Kona muttered to Luke under his breath, "Is that an area where little kids are supposed to play, or we wait here and sit on these mushrooms? Or, are they art they bought to make the house look cool?"

"No idea."

"You can say what you want about Jake Chase and call him an out-for-himself poser, but his house is kind of dope," Kona said to Luke as he knelt to sit on the nearest mushroom. He decided against it once Edviane shook her head at him as if he'd put his elbows on the dining table with the queen. She asked them to take two steps into the living room, then left them standing alone.

After they'd waited many more minutes than was comfortable, Luke asked, "You sure these clothes are okay? I don't want to have another problem." They had managed to throw on some T-shirts they found mildewing in the back cab area of Luke's Ford F-250 van for a decade or so.

"Fuck these people," said Kona. "We surf, we drive boats. It's 1:00 p.m. on a workday, we got afternoon privates. They can get us as we are. We gotta talk to Jake, we gotta look authentic. And Julia is so horny, she'll take me in anything I wear."

On the entry walls, they stared at two eight-by-ten foot Marilyn Minter photographs: huge shiny, red sparkly lips dripping with liquid that, though golden in color, clearly signified recently ejaculated semen.

"Those lips are hot, but strange what too much money can buy and even stranger what parents are willing to put in a house with kids," whispered Luke back at Kona.

Beside them, Lucite floating stairs led to the second floor where presumably the family slept. The blinding noonday sun poured through skylights, making it impossible for the curious men to decipher the upstairs layout. The entryway opened upon a two-level living room that looked like a spectacular greenhouse. Out the ceiling-length windows that encased the room, they could see a black infinity pool lined with five modern sun beds on each side. Beyond that, stretches of Long Island sea grass, and ultimately, the great expanse of the Atlantic Ocean.

The white living room couches were centered with a tennis court amount of space between the furniture and walls, an architectural study in scarcity and geometric precision. In the middle, a liquid glacial table by Zaha Hadid slanted and curved every which way, not the most useful coffee table to place a drink on.

"Check out this shark. Super freaky," said Luke, motioning to a life-size shark floating in formaldehyde in a large rectangular vitrine. "You think someone caught this? Or is this a fake?"

"No idea."

"Let's Google it," said Kona, who grabbed his cracked phone out of his surf trunks. After one minute trying to decipher words through the humidity that had seeped through when he'd dropped it last summer, he declared, "Sold once for eight million dollars more than ten years ago. Damien Hirst made it. I've heard of him. *I think.* Another site says it was twelve mill."

"We could make one," said Luke. "We get Kenny to get his shark fishing buddies out at 4:00 a.m., we get my dad's friends to make the case. We buy tubs of formaldehyde from the same place my school gets it for the biology department." He studied its dorsal fin. "It's actually a tiger shark, genus Galeocerdo."

"Quit it with the boring teacher bullshit. Who cares what kind of shark we get? Let's just do this."

Luke peered in. "It's known as the Sea Tiger, a relatively large macro-predator . . . found in subtropical waters."

"I say, we catch a Mako off Montauk. This weekend, 4:00 a.m. like you said. We'd just have to be gentle with the tackle so we didn't destroy the mouth; that would decrease the price," Kona surmised, looking through the glass on the opposite side. "These people are nuts. And their kids surf. Doesn't this give them nightmares about *Jaws*?" Luke softly touched the glass with the tips of his fingers.

"What on earth?" A forty-something butler with very short, neat, gelled-back hair walked in. Like every member of the daytime staff, he had the Chase estate emblem "Pine Manor" stitched on his chest, and Italian Superga white sneakers on his feet with navy laces. "Sir, it's not a toy, it's extremely valuable."

"I was just looking . . ."

"It's a very expensive work of art. No touching." The employee wagged his finger and walked out of the room.

On the right wall, words painted onto a canvas with stenciled huge block letters read,

IFYOUCANTTAKEAJOKEGETTHEFUCKOUTOFMYHOUSE

And then another that read,

FOOL

"Are we the fools for looking at it, or is the artist the fool for painting it? I don't even care how much that costs," said Kona, pointing to the words, defeated by all the money around him. He was aiming to earn thirty grand after tax in a whole summer of twelve-hour days in rough surf. "I do know, though, I could paint that in an hour."

"I could order stencils from the school system and say it was for . . ." Luke offered, considering the possibilities for an easier way to earn an income.

Kona cut him off. "How about, **YOUARERICHBUTYOURDICK-ISLITTLE?**"

The Chase décor had the intimacy of an airline hangar, and differed in every way from the shag carpet and corduroy-covered, mismatched couches filling the small houses they grew up in. "On one hand, I kind of like it," said Luke. "On the other hand, the fact that a real family lives in here is so weird."

"'Real' family is not entirely accurate," Kona answered.

"Well, real enough," said Luke. "When exactly are you going to bring up the summons, the notice to appear, the bay constable after us, Bucky and the pole so far up his ass it's coming out of his mouth? Don't do it too early, or he's going to think that's the only reason we came. We planned you start, say like a quarter of the way through, and you mention Jake's high property taxes, right? Get him a little fired up on how he's got power he doesn't even realize. He'll like hearing that, he'll be into saving camp."

Edviane walked by and said without stopping, "I told Mr. and Mrs. Chase you were here, but they didn't come down. Maybe later."

With that ringing endorsement of their social heft, Edviane left them stranded there and returned to the kitchen. The door swung open behind her, revealing a colossal kitchen lined with stainless steel appliances and an army of identically dressed Brazilians.

On the pool deck out front, twenty-year-old Evan Chase, shirtless and wearing Orlebar Brown $275 swim trunks he'd bought in a cliffside boutique in Capri last summer, made the enormous effort to lumber to his elbows to see who had arrived. When he saw the leeches from the local water sports camp stranded in the living room, he plugged his headphones back in, Enrique Iglesias blaring, and turned his sweaty face back at the blazing sun. Betsy, the Chase bulldog, jumped into the lounger and snuggled next to him.

Evan considered cooling himself down in the pool. All of the natural elements—sand, salt water, even wind—didn't work for his refined composition. The few times he did step into his family's pool over the summer, he swam breaststroke with his head above water like an elderly lady protecting her fragile coiffure.

"This is *fucking whack*," Luke yelled in a tense whisper, his neck muscles constricting. "It's been ten minutes. We can call Jake later after lessons. That Evan out there knows we're here, he saw us. He doesn't come see what up. He's got those Beats by Dre headphones I want, he's probably listening to Pit Bull."

"You're forgetting," said Kona. "He's got a vagina and it's gotta be Adele."

"Maybe Jake doesn't remember he invited us," Luke said. "Or maybe he's just banging Julia now in one of her ten closets."

"This is the way rich people run shit: the butler announces you and you sit your ass and wait on a fucking mushroom field," Kona explained as if he were an old hand at seaside luncheons. "We're not going anywhere, this is too important." Kona was always hungrier—with women, with access to a scene he wasn't part of—and thus, more willing than Luke to power through moments of humiliation like this.

"Yooooooo!" Jake yelled from the top of the staircase, as he eagerly ran down to them. "Dudes! I was on a call, shit's hitting the fan with this deal I'm sunk into like quicksand. It's like 2007 all over again today. What the fuck, you guys want a brew or what?"

"Just a Coke, no problem . . ." Kona answered as if they'd just then strolled in.

Jake blew past the guys and out to the pool deck where he threw his hands in the air and yelled to no one in particular, "What the hell?" Next, he roared back into his house and pushed open the swinging kitchen door, yelling at the servants, "Hello? Lunch? Edviane? Claudio? Why isn't the table set outside? Where's the goddamn food? I'm hungry, we got guests out there . . ."

"No, no, sir," a man's voice answered. "Mrs. Chase told us you were having lunch at the golf club today."

"But I don't *want* to go out anymore!"

There was more muffled screaming from the kitchen that the guys couldn't quite make out. It wasn't quite Amnesty International level labor abuse, but it sounded close. Jake swung open the door with the chef Claudio trailing behind him.

"Well, then, Mr. Chase, we have food here . . . certainly we can whip up . . ."

"Sorry, Claudio. My temper got to me," Jake apologized. Claudio nodded with exquisite calm, used to these tirades. Jake was the third self-made C.E.O. he'd worked for in his thirty-year career as a chef. "The guys will have, what . . . hey, dudes, what do you want? Anything. Lobster salad rolls? Crab cakes? Prosciutto paninis? Oysters?"

"Uh," Luke answered. "Anything, cheeseburger, B.L.T., whatever . . ."

Jake cut him off. "Well, I'm having a quail egg sandwich on brioche bread. It's really tasty when they toast it with truffle butter."

"Never honestly ate a quail egg and I've got wakeboard lessons this afternoon, so just anything to fill us up. We kind of wanted to talk to you today about a legal problem."

"Claudio, grill him one of those wagyu beef burgers you got from Japan, but also make a quail egg sandwich on the side . . . Kona, what'll it be?" the tone-deaf titan asked, profoundly in love with his own generosity, conjecturing how great it must be for these local guys on the receiving side. It would make them like him better to see all his success in the flesh, to experience a piece of it today. "Lobster roll? I mean, trust me, they're great. I'm talking a fuckin' stuffed with way too much lobster meat roll. I know you never had one like this. Let me . . ."

Little did the guys know the Loaves and Fishes lobster salad cost one hundred dollars a pound, and untold articles in the Hampton and Manhattan society media had already commented on this outrageous Hampton offering. (The moment Jake read the clamor about the cost, he'd instructed Claudio to keep the fridge stocked with it and to offer it to every guest.) The guys were also not aware that it had taken the kitchen staff two hours to boil and peel the grape-sized quail eggs for the egg salad sandwiches that Luke would soon gag over and stuff in his napkin.

"Well, uh . . . sure, the lobster salad sounds great. And like you said before. You and I, Jake, we have so much in common, growing up the same way," said Kona. "I hope that means we are on same trajectory, so when I'm forty-seven I'm complaining about clumps of lobster in my sandwich that are too big."

"Anything's possible," Jake answered, hitting the back of Luke's head too hard.

Luke nudged Kona. "And, like Luke said, we need to talk about a problem we're having. It's a legal problem, right, Luke?"

"Well, business," agreed Luke, anxiously, wondering why Kona said "legal" when Jake Chase owned Laundromats. His fingers had been playing with his cleft chin for minutes now. They had to get Jake on their side. It was dead in winter here, and there was no way as a teacher, just doing the marine biology elective for now, to earn enough to sustain himself. "You've been very successful in starting businesses, the laundry services every hotel in the country uses, the malls you created, so we thought you are the exact person who can . . . well, we got a big problem and we need your help."

"Hey, come to the table, guys. I'll hear anything you got. I'm two-fifty an hour, plus 20 percent take!" This time he smacked Kona's ass and said, "Mokey, pokey wokey, man!" mocking Kona's Hawaiian roots and lingo. Kona had to breathe in deep not to throttle him.

They sat down as Claudio and waiters brought out appetizers.

Kona started right in before Jake got distracted with showing off something else about his fabulous lifestyle. "So, there's town trustees. They have always said no businesses can exist where money changes hands on town beaches . . . but we've always gotten around that."

Luke witnessed Jake's eyes glaze over on the third sentence, so he elbowed Kona. "The short version is you got immense power because of the high taxes you pay."

"You think I got power? I just got a fuckin' house. I never heard of trustees, except I know they gave me hell about the staircase to the beach, some old ladies."

"Yeah, them. Exactly," answered Kona. "Those old ladies pre-serve environmental stuff and old houses. All good most of the time because they prevent taking down historic cottages and they keep the bays clean. But, in our case, they've overstepped."

"They always fuckin' overstep." Jake nodded. "Party poopers, my architect calls them."

"Exactly, so they don't overstep and shut down camp, we need some big support from landowners who pay high taxes and have some sway, and since . . . well, you love camp, I mean your kids do. You want us to thrive, and then we thought you care about . . ."

"You guys get a lot of pussy online, right? That Tinder, Bumble, stuff like that?" Jake interrupted, motor-mouthing at the guys. "Actually, Kona, you're probably more in the Grinder camp. Heh!"

Luke pretended to laugh at his lame joke. "We, uh, were talking about camp closing? Not apps?"

"But I really need your input for this investment that I fucked up on."

Luke and Kona looked at each other and hit each other's knees under the table, signaling, *we need a different approach here.*

"I lost a shit ton of cash in a dating app, some idiot made me invest. It's not my space. I know bricks and mortar. And washing machines. Not pussy. *Well, not online pussy.*" He slurped down his iced freshly made watermelon juice. "Listen to this. Instead of Tinder where you swipe left to right to like or dislike a date, it was a new clever app that . . ." The guys nodded their heads, waiting for the part when Jake would ask them what they thought. Or go back to the topic of their livelihood in peril. But once Jake got going like a steam engine, the guys had to suck it up and crunch on the Parmesan crisps just toasted in the oven.

As another servant poured ginger iced tea, and Jake yelled at his son Evan, still stewing in the sun thirty yards down the deck, "Evan. Come join us for lunch. We're talking business here, you could learn something, They got a problem I'm going to help with."

Kona hit Luke's shoulder with his and whispered, "Progress. Psyched."

"No, thanks. I ate," Evan called back, hoping his playlist would shuffle to some really good Ariana Grande to help drown out his disgust. Wasn't it enough to tip these local moochers? Did his father have to invite them into the house? The only thing Evan despised more than these guys gorging on expensive lobster salad was witnessing his father pathetically try to act cool with them. *As if they were cool in the first place.*

"Well, why don't you get off your ass and take a wakeboard lesson with the guys, or even a Jet Ski rental? I'll go with you . . . c'mon, get over your fear of the sand, kid, and come with us after lunch."

Evan ignored his father, pointing to the Bruno Mars now blaring in his headphones. He didn't want to admit his father was right. He honestly didn't like the way sand felt on his over-lotioned feet. It stuck between the toes and then rubbed against his new Tom Ford leather sandals in a way that gave him the chills like screeches on a chalkboard. And then you had to wipe it off again with a wet towel. It was all just too much. If you want to check out the ocean, why not just do it from your parents' deck?

Everyone at that table was making Evan sick. His insatiable father always chasing something new, pretending he was more relaxed and less neurotic than he really was. And these idiot surfers: gobbling free fried oysters, working just as hard at portraying themselves as hard bodies who get laid, whacked the lip of the wave, and cared a lot less about things than they actually did.

Chapter Twenty-One

Meanwhile Back at the WASP Fortress . . .

A mile and a quarter down that same Beachwood Lane, George Porter put his BMW into park, turned off the key and then ran around to open Katie Doyle's car door.

"Really. I'm fine." She smiled. "I can get out of an automobile on my own, you know. I'm not wearing a petticoat and this isn't a horse carriage."

"They called it the Age of Enlightenment for a reason. I see no need to change manners that worked in the past." He bowed. Huck smirked from the backseat at how stupid grown-ups were. George then opened the back door. "And for you, young man, you don't get that kind of fancy treatment, you're just a little sack of potatoes to be . . ." George crawled onto the backseat, yanked a giggling Huck out, and threw him over his shoulder, holding tight as the child wriggled to get away. Huck thought this guy could be annoying, but sometimes a little fun, too. He was good with Legos if you didn't have to answer his dumb questions.

"You two silly guys just go up. I'll get the beach bag," announced Katie as she opened the back trunk.

"C'mon, two gentlemen here to do anything for you, at your service." George gently placed Huck down on the hot midday parking lot outside the Seabrook and then handed the boy a tote bag of sunscreen and towels. "You get this, young man, for your mother. Katie, you've had two tutor sessions today, you've worked hard, time to relax."

"It's fine," protested Katie, holding another bag even tighter against her rib cage. "I got it, I handle him on my own all the time, I'm . . ."

"You're not on your own."

She smiled at him, and handed him the bag as they walked across the small lane and into the one-hundred-year-old WASP fortress.

George nodded at the front guard who shot his shoulders up right at the sight of him. Katie whispered to him, "I'm noticing people are terrified of both you and your mother. What do you do, abuse them when I'm not here?"

"It's just a summer job for the kid. I have no idea," he said out of the side of his mouth as he moved toward the pool. "I sit on the bench all the time outside the club because we can't use phones inside. I talk to them, they like me, but I guess I make them nervous. You know, it's not easy, the guard is a local kid. He hasn't grown up like the rest of the kids who are members. Maybe he feels inferior, or maybe he really needs the cash. Who the hell knows, but it's not me. I'm an angel, remember?!"

George grabbed Huck's hand and brought him to the pool. There were more practices for the swim meet and Huck looked back at his mother like he'd been duped. His eyes round as the moon, he shook his head back and forth at her.

"Okay, kiddo. This is what I did every summer. It's a rite of passage. The club swim meet is next Thursday, more trials today so they know what team to put you on. Make damn sure you stay in your age group and they don't put you with the younger . . ."

"Huck isn't so comfortable with the pool stuff," Katie said. "I told him the first day I was here with your mother that he didn't have to."

Huck very much wanted this man to stop hanging around his mother. He wanted pasta with butter at home for lunch suddenly, not a grilled cheese at this strange club. He did not like people judging his swimming prowess, which even he knew was a notch below pathetic for his age.

George walked a few steps away so Huck couldn't hear. "C'mon, Katie, it's good for him to compete with the other boys. Builds some backbone on the kid. He's fine," he told her, as if she were out of her mind protective. "I mean, the kid doesn't have a male figure who pushes him like this. It's three laps; it's not like I'm throwing him in the ocean with those fools down the beach you sent him to. I wished you'd asked me before . . ."

"George, you don't call or text for days, I wasn't going to bug you with every confusion I had. Besides, he loves that camp. He's gotten over his fear of waves already this summer."

"Well, if you can try to get him into the Seabrook swim camp, this is the real stuff. It makes a kid grow up and test himself. You don't want him bouncing around white water on a boogie board all day. He's gotta push himself against his peers, right?"

"I guess." Katie looked at Huck, hypnotized by anticipation and staring at his toes. "He's just . . . he's scared, I can tell he's not into it and . . ."

"Just let me handle it, would'ya?"

"Katie! Come with me!" Poppy Porter yelled as she powered her skinny legs toward them, pumping her arms on her thick middle. "The girls are out by the veranda and we are discussing the Patio Party. George promised he'd have you here by noon and it's already twelve-fifteen. We are discussing your tables. I told you they get a little too excited about the details, but they are thinking you go nautical. Think whaling, like everything in the cottage, for inspiration: compasses, halyards, sailcloth even . . ."

Katie looked at the sea of people around her; she didn't know one person except that dear Henry, now mixing his Southsides in a shaker behind the bar. He smiled at her and winked kindly, as if he knew exactly how she felt being an outsider among insiders.

"Let my son handle Huck, it's fine, you have responsibility with all the cochairs. I already ordered you an Arnold Palmer and the Seabrook Club crab salad . . ."

"Crab salad, that's . . ."

"Oh, it's not expensive."

"I didn't mean, I meant I don't usually eat . . ."

"We at the club don't like anything that's too extravagant for a family atmosphere. Don't worry, it's not made with real crabs, it's the long strips of imitation, you know, kind of pink, but it's delicious and I don't think you've had it."

"I, uh, I'm not a fan of . . ."

"It's just perfect on Triscuits; we got a whole bowl waiting for you! They put pounds of mayonnaise in the salad, so you really need the crunch!"

Chapter Twenty-Two

Clash of the Ages

At the other end of Beachwood Lane, Kona and Luke inhaled fried rock shrimp in a spicy sauce copied from Jake's favorite dish at the Nobu restaurant in Manhattan. They had brought up the impending camp closure several times, and Jake had listened for a moment, given them hope he'd help, then switched to explain how his business minted gold because laundry would need to be done for eternity.

While Jake excused himself for a call, Julia Chase strutted down the floating staircase in a white crocheted bikini "covered" by a see-through green caftan with layers of material flowing under her arms, the butterfly getup only slightly less extravagant than those on the runway for the Victoria's Secret Angels' TV special.

"So," Julia said as she sat down next to Kona. "How are you all? Is Jake boring you with his silly tech investment mishaps this morning? I hope not. I would have saved you all earlier if I didn't have a conference call for my own business."

Kona nudged his chair closer while Jake finished his call down on a pool lounger. "I didn't know you have a mind for business as well. What kind of business? How *interesting*." He stared at Julia with his bedroom eyes and, in a lower, scratchy voice, added, "Back on the Big Island, we call that kind of acumen *akamai*."

Luke couldn't help but throw his hands in the air at these same thirty Hawaiian words Kona pulled out every single time he turbocharged after a woman. This was *not* the time to go after Jake's wife.

"Oh, God, no, it isn't acumen, it's just simple know-how." Julia pursed her lips as if to suck on a Popsicle, the image driving Kona mad. "I source twelve-ply cashmere from India, and I have beautiful shawls made in every shade of indigo. I send 50 percent of the proceeds to women's micro-credit groups in impoverished nations."

"Tell us more, Julia," Kona asked, slipping an oyster down his throat, savoring it on his tongue for a moment, and winking at her like this would mirror what he'd do between her legs. Kona thought to himself, *Life is so great when you are the pussy whisperer.* "That's so *weird* you mention indigo." Kona leaned in, his elbow brushing hers and staying put, shamelessly adding, "I've been working on the *exact same* palette with my artwork."

Luke was disgusted at the heights Kona would go to to get pussy. *What fucking artwork? The last time you made art, you were standing in your nursery school smock, finger-painting on an easel!*

Kona pressed on. "I'd love to see every shade after lunch. I always feel such connection with the blue-est of shades because of my intense relationship with the sea."

"I sell my collection at a room at The Mark Hotel for a few days and give everyone food and wine and they get tipsy and shop. The girls love it. And . . ." she added, "we're helping women all over the world to create their own lifelines by donating . . ."

Jake came back to the table and whispered to Luke, "Yeah, and the champagne and hotel room costs me more than she sells in a few years. Strange accounting practices some women have." And then to the table, "My wife is the most beautiful, intelligent woman in New York. She's gets to do whatever she wants in my book."

Now their eight-year-old son Richie, his chubby stomach bouncing out of his swim trunks, waddled to the table like his father. Next to him, Betsy the bulldog's stride wasn't much different. Jumping into Luke's lap, Richie knocked hibiscus tea everywhere. When Richie hugged the guys as if he'd never let go, for a fleeting few seconds, Kona and Luke felt welcome at the table and, possibly, that they could get the Chases to agree to the help they needed.

Midway through the meal, Luke went to the men's room because he *definitely* had always hated egg salad, even when made with miniature quail eggs peeled by a matching-uniformed staff.

Once inside the designer powder room, Luke ran smack into a deeply unfortunate situation.

"Dad!" exclaimed Luke, seeing his stepfather, Frank, on his knees, butt crack in the air, a wrench sticking out of the back pocket of his stiff jeans.

Unbeknownst to the guys, Frank had arrived half an hour earlier to repair a persistent leaky drain on the Jacuzzi outside that threatened to flood into the first-floor plumbing.

"What are you doing here, son?" Frank got up to his feet and rubbed the sweat off his forehead with the inside crook of his arm. His fingers were covered with dark grease. "Oh, hell, give me a hand. I don't want to mess up all these ironed hand towels in here. I saw some soap up there . . . can you grab me some so I don't have to use soap in the shape of a dolphin they got in this ugly soap dish."

"Here, Dad, I don't know, maybe they have, like, staff areas to wash in or something. I don't see a paper towel in here to . . ." He pumped lemongrass-scented liquid soap into his stepfather's hands.

Frank grabbed a blob of toilet paper and tried to dry off his hands. "You didn't answer my question. What the hell are you doing here? Do you have lessons now on their beach out front? I thought there wasn't a good surf break out in this area?"

"No. I mean, yes. I do." Luke knew there was no way in hell he wouldn't hear about this one moment all summer.

"You aren't making sense, son."

"Well, it's like this. They got this kid Richie who worships us . . . and then the bay constable this morning had a field day with a summons . . ."

"Who's 'us'?" Frank didn't like the sound of this.

"Well, it's just Kona and me, we're just here for a little between lessons."

"You know your mother wouldn't want you with these people. They have a painting with women's lips that I don't like around children. Some sexual stuff dripping from them. Don't forget, these people aren't your friends. They didn't get this rich by being friendly."

"I think you told me that maybe eleven thousand times," Luke responded. "First, they invited us here because the son looks up to me, for years now, like a big mentor or something. And then we thought Jake Chase could rally the trustees to help save the camp. So it was a win-win invite."

Frank slammed the door under the sink shut. "I know they pay some slick architect with fancy magazine covers under his belt who doesn't know how to construct on a dune. I'm here to save them from a flood, but I don't think 'helpful to you' is something they are even capable of."

"I understand your view," Luke answered. "Listen, I gotta go. I'm not feeling great."

Anything to get his father out, so Luke could figure out if he needed to puke. Hopefully the door would close, Frank would leave, and he wouldn't ever see that his son was breaking bread with these people, wiping the expensive plates with it, and soaking up their values in the process.

When Luke quietly opened the door, still queasy from the meal, he looked left and right to make sure his dad was indeed gone. He sat down to a dessert spread of small local berries, caramelized agave tartlets, and homemade raw almond butter "cookies" that tasted like cement mix.

Luke mouthed to Kona, *Any progress?*

Kona shook his head.

A staff member stood like a khaki-clad sentry at the end of the table and asked, "Tea with mint leaves and mulberry infusion? Macchiato . . .". They could barely hear the choices because of loud clanging noises from the far end of the pool deck. Betsy the bulldog started barking loudly at the clamor.

"What the hell," yelled Jake down toward his Jacuzzi. "We're trying to have a meal here, buddy, could you just do that another time? Call my architect would ya? He knows the rules about workmen here in the summer when I'm finally trying to . . ."

Julia shot Jake a wifely admonition to *please cool it* in front of the instructors. He could be so brash and thoughtless. She hated that, but she knew he didn't mean it; he just wanted a quiet lunch. Since he spent every waking second trying to make her happy, it was hard for her to stay mad.

Frank Forrester's face popped up from a plumbing access panel under the deck, twenty feet from the table.

"Yes, sir, sorry," he said. "It's just kind of a leaking emergency in here." When he saw his son Luke sitting at the Chases' fancy table, biting into an 89 percent cocoa-dusted, pink sea-salted caramel, the weatherworn wrinkles in his face instantly melted downward. "I'll, uh, yes, I'll be leaving right now."

Luke cringed his shoulders in silent anguish as he heard his father's loud work boots stomping down the endless slate staircase toward the driveway.

Kona started to stand. He was ready to defend Frank against this one-percenter Jake Chase asshole. The calmer, more mature Luke grabbed his arm, not wanting to cause a scene.

Kona couldn't help himself, "You know, it's hot out. I bet that guy is super overheated in his work clothes; he's probably trying to save your house from some plumbing accident that could cost you . . . you shouldn't just . . ."

"I agree!" Julia added. "That plumber, Frank, is such a nice man, Jake, don't . . ."

"What the fuck? You all taking sides against me? The plumber needs to fix the machinery at 1:15? He can't wait an hour? I don't barge into my colleague's offices while they are eating a sandwich at their desk and demand we do a killer deal. Hell, this guy doesn't respect *my* need to eat with my family . . ."

Standing behind Kona now, pinching his shoulders hard, Luke said firmly into Kona's ear ,"I got this." And then to the group. "I'm going to talk to that plumber, if you don't mind. It's just something I have to do. But, before we leave, Julia, Jake, we really need to talk to you about the trustees shutting down camp on town beaches. Basically our whole way of life might be over. Your kids' too. You don't want to send them to a faraway sleep-away camp. You've always wanted them safe in the water, and nearby all summer. Let's keep that plan going. We need your help. Kona is going to explain. I'll be back."

"I get it. It wasn't right of Jake. I'll take his head off later," Julia answered. "Tell us, Kona, what can we do?"

Luke tried to run after Frank, but it hadn't worked. Nothing was working today. Frank had been so steaming mad, he'd gotten into his truck and tore off. Luke knew there was no reasoning when Frank's temper had gone off the morality deep end.

Back at the table, Luke got back in time to see Julia pat her husband's arm, then say, "We'll find a way to get him focused. No one is shutting down your way of life." She raised her eyebrows. "And *no one* is screwing with my kid's fun and safety in the ocean."

"Hey, you didn't tell me they were coming! How come?" yelled the famous Chase daughter, Alexa, as she slid open a glass door to the deck.

Exuding more high-end Manhattan stripper vibe than prime-time television runway angel, Alexa then appeared in her black mini-bikini, a crocheted yarn cropped shawl that ended at her belly button and high black gladiator sandals to her knees. She placed her thick and well-muscled thighs in a straight line, one foot before the other, in her well-practiced catwalk. She so wished she had a photo of her walking like this to send to her tens of thousands of social media followers.

Alexa toured the table, leaning to kiss her father while arching her back, and shoving her barely covered but plentiful ass in the air so that both Kona and Luke would be forced into having a creepy peek. Their faces turned purple. Luke whispered to Kona, "Could we ask the parents to buy her one of those bathing suit burkas?"

"She's way too young to dress like that. It's not right." Kona whispered back out of the side of his mouth. "She's going to get in huge trouble that she's way too young to handle."

As they plotted and planned to dismember the man who lay in the nearby grass during the Memorial Day party, they realized that nailing him with an underage girl, who happened to be the innocent heiress of this very estate, would make her father, Jake, indebted to them forever. So indebted, so determined to keep their camp and livelihood alive, he'd either buy the Seabrook Club to shut down Bucky or run for mayor himself. Or both.

Chapter Twenty-Three

Views in a Vise Grip

When Luke pulled into the parking lot for his 3:00 p.m. lesson after the fancy Chase meal, his father's maroon two-tone Dodge Ram pickup was idling loudly, one of his favorite Janice Joplin songs pumping out the windows. Frank never saved up enough for a new transmission and figured he could fix most of the truck problems himself rather than get ripped off by some knucklehead mechanic toying with his baby. Luke drove around to the far side of the same lot to avoid his father's fury.

Luke shifted his van into Park, and looked out the side mirror to see a determined Frank marching up the pavement like a cowboy about to grab two Colt 45s from his holster. Frank opened the car door before Luke could even get his own hand on the handle.

"Yes, Dad." Luke wondered if it was normal for a thirty-one-year-old man to be so fearful of disappointing his father.

"They say, 'don't get too close to the sun or you'll get burned,'" Frank stated. "What the hell is going on? The Chases are suddenly your friends? Or that horny partner Kona you got, what, he's doing that wife now? That Jake Chase is on his third contractor now who had to beg me to handle the flooding shit-show they are in over there, that whole house is about to sink in the sand dune if the plumbing isn't overhauled, well, more importantly, I don't want to see you . . ."

"Dad, calm down. Jake Chase can be an ass. I deal with him all the time, I get it, I ran after you and you saw me, right? And still you just threw your hand in the air out your window and drove off."

"I know you know how I feel, son." Frank softened, never able to stay tough with the son he inherited. "It's just bullshit to be asked to practice my craft, and then not be treated like a human being." Frank pointed his finger at Luke, his nostrils slightly flared on his round, ruddy face. He then took off his hat and patted down the wispy salt-and-pepper hair that was sprouting out the top of his head.

"Dad, it's the first time, honestly, that we ever ate there. I've worked almost every day all summer so far. I haven't had time to sit with you and explain exactly how much these trustees are gaining ground on us. Kenny exchanged money on town property one time Bucky was watching, plus we've had a bunch of other little fuck-ups they've let fly any other summer, and they're trying to shut Tide Runners down . . . and I thought the Chases being so wealthy and connected might help, which they kind of agreed to, so it was more a lifesaving professional lunch."

"All right, all right, I'm telling you one thing, though: those people will use you and spit you out so fast, you won't even recognize yourself. Don't expect them to pony up help for you guys.

"Your mother, God rest her soul, knew that all too well. She did not take well to people from Manhattan who come out and don't respect the community we built."

"Dad," continued Luke, "I, uh, actually do understand more than you give me credit for. I hear you. I'm also thirty-one years old now. I've got to be polite to people who trust me with their children. You need to just realize . . . not everything is as black and white as when Mom was around. I'm very protective of Jake's kids, the two younger ones anyway who've come to camp. The ocean brings us together like you don't understand. It's an equalizer. All of us, it's like a family out there in the boats and on the waves. It's not the kids' fault their dad is a dickhead at times. Jesus, the Internet wasn't even around when Mom was alive. Technology brings people together, Dad. You don't even have an email, so you can't really see."

Luke might as well have been speaking in Swahili, or using Kona's lame Hawaiian catch phrases. Frank's ruddy face got ruddier. He yanked at his utility vest and cracked his neck a few times.

Luke plowed on. "I'm not saying we're all equal or anything. I'm just saying many of the guys with these huge houses on the ocean have come from nothing and made fortunes. They aren't the snobby Southampton people from the past who automatically thought they were better than everyone, even though sometimes, yes, they get testy and treat you like shit."

Frank stood silently and pushed the few hairs back on his head to ease his headache.

"Look, I know this is frustrating you because you do that motion with your hand on your head when you've had enough," Luke said softly. He hugged his stepdad.

Luke for once was relieved to recognize his most annoying client by her sun hat as wide as a large flying saucer. Margaux Carroll was waving to him like a madwoman from the top of the parking lot. She had four kids with her, which was typical, given that she'd only reserved one 3:00 p.m. lesson for her fat, sorry-ass son who despised the water.

Luke didn't have backup instructors for the bay side. He knew she wouldn't understand that four kids and one instructor was not a safe way to go. Tyler had serious anxiety in the water, and she couldn't accept was never going to be the water sports ace his Yale water polo team captain dad was.

"Dad. Let's have a beer later. I'm sorry, I have to go make a living, while I still have a camp." He patted Frank's back. "You can't make people do things or feel things just because Mom would have wanted it that way. She wasn't here to mold me for half my life. Who knows what she would have wanted now? *Jesus.* You've got to drop it once in a while, *please.*"

Luke walked up the hill to the camp meeting area, not at all satisfied he'd gotten through. His stomach was still sick from far too much shellfish and quail egg sandwiches.

So much for that dreaded American word "closure." He hated being reminded about his mother's wrath. She was long lost in the boating accident. When Frank focused on it, it drew him down the whole day. Luke knew they were both still making reparations fifteen years later: Frank by force-feeding her wishes down her son's throat and Luke by saving the lives he could in the rough waves.

And as Luke walked toward his client, Bucky Porter hid behind a large SUV in the lot, and the bay constable's boat idled in the long reeds by the docks, both hunting their prey.

Chapter Twenty-Four

Everything Good Happens in Summer

"Luke, I'm sorry," Margaux wailed like a branded heifer. "You're going to have to do this for me. *Pleeeeeease*."

Luke shook his head at her, counting boys with his index finger in a motley grouping behind her. "Four? With me alone? You know the rules, Mrs. Carroll. We've been over this."

"I know you don't like it when I have add-ons, and there's some official little camp policy, blah, blah," Mrs. Carroll declared, as if Luke and Kona were idiots for having safety concerns in the churning Atlantic with forty children at a time.

"Hello, Margaux, anything I can help with?" Bucky Porter strolled into the scene. "I just got out here for the day, have some papers to sign in town, then I'm back to the city, thought I'd check on . . ."

"I wanted to leave these boys there but there is only one lifeguard on the public beach and they can't just run around on their own."

"So you're bringing them to *Tide Runners*?" Bucky asked. "And you feel they are safer than . . ." He turned his back to Luke, as he had on the previous beach tirade.

Margaux whispered to Bucky, within earshot of Luke, "Honestly, I've got so much work with guests coming tomorrow on the 4:07 cannonball train, and my help is just horrible. I'd leave the boys with just about anyone. I'd take hooligans at this point, and . . ."

"Hooligans. Interesting," answered Bucky, crossing his arms on his large chest. "My fear, exactly." Just then, the bay constable's boat rolled into the front dock slip. The hefty captain roped it on the deck cleats, and marched to the group like the town sheriff. He stood about five foot six, his potbelly cinched in with a leather belt and glossy buckle. Luke watched Bucky salute him like a fellow Marine.

What the fuck?

"Excuse us, Margaux, we will just need to check some credentials with Mr. Forrester."

The constable yanked Luke's elbow like he was nine years old and in big trouble. "Watch yourself, Mr. Forrester. I have access to any and all businesses operating on my waters. We have information on how you're running things. You're overdue on town records. You could be done in a matter of days."

"You know what?" Luke answered. "I'm a public employee during the school year just like you. I've filed permits. If there's one that's a little expired, I'll go into town later and update the form. By the way, no one in Town Hall has ever told us it's out of date."

"I got my eyes on you," confirmed the constable. "You're not getting away with anything this year."

"Well, sir, that's a great thing. Thank you, sir." Luke saluted. "Good to know we are being watched, so the families are safe. And right now, I'm going to deal with my client." And then he turned to Bucky. "Lovely disposition by your lady friend Mrs. Carroll, by the way. She has such a gracious way about her." And Luke walked away, half confident these men were on a harmless power trip, and half petrified they'd shut him and Kona down for good.

"I'm sorry to saddle you with these kids," Margaux plowed on, "but I promised I would watch the kids all day, and then I have this corn and lamb chop disaster at home. I just called the mothers and said you'd take them on the boat instead. If you can at least, just please, God, do me that one little . . ."

"I'm not doing any favors here. It's my job," Luke explained. "If you'd like to sign up ahead of time for . . ."

"My Brazilian help don't speak English and . . ." And then Margaux whispered into Luke's ear as if they were on the same nobleman level and could openly discuss the serfs' ineptitudes. "It's sooo inconvenient, I could just rip my hair out." She huffed loudly.

The gloomy, preteen boy posse at her side were mortified to be anywhere near this woman, let alone in her care. They all wore surf trunks, flip-flops, and towels wrapped around their necks. Margaux Carroll's son, Tyler, age nine, was a few years older than the other kids, and looked like he was weighing the pros and cons of matricide. All of their eyes pleaded with Luke to placate her.

Margaux went on, oblivious, "Who buys packaged corn on the cob from the frozen department at Waldbaum's when there's a farm stand on every corner with fresh, local corn? *Frozen vegetables in the summer?* Honestly! *Helloooo?*"

"I uh, Mrs. Carroll, yeah, we all love that local corn, but it's not in season yet," Luke said, squinting his eyes a little at her on the remote possibility she could discern she was the fool in this situation. "It's only June, so no farms stands have it yet. Maybe your staff had to improvise the best they could and thought it a good idea to get frozen rather than nothing."

"Are you taking them out or not?"

Luke knew the bay constable in mirrored sunglasses was still scrutinizing his every move. "Mrs. Carroll, no adult can watch four kids on a boat in a bay or in the Atlantic, and . . ." Luke whispered this into her ear, "C'mon. You know Tyler, he crawls on my head every time the smallest ripple of a wave comes. He can't be sharing me with three other kids, especially little ones."

"Well, can you please just play on the dock or something, Jesus, I mean *I'm paying you*."

"You're paying me for all four kids?"

"No. I'm paying you for Tyler."

Luke felt a tug on his shorts from a little guy behind him. And then a woman's voice, "Can I help? We were just driving by and Huck wanted to see if any boys were tubing behind a boat or if we could join in."

It was Katie Doyle, that sunny flash of summer that made Luke believe that this season would be better than any other.

"I mean, I could stay with you and help. I've actually been listening a bit to this conversation," she said. Luke beamed his smile right at her as she continued, "I used to be a counselor on Flathead Lake near my home." Katie had recognized Margaux Carroll from the bike shop on her very first day in Southampton, ordering Luke around the way she had the shop owners.

"Okay," barked Margaux. "Then it's all set. I pay for Tyler, you'll just include the boys for free, I guess, just because, well their moms aren't here. This kind woman can also help you because her son's obviously young and needs his mother still. So we're all set?"

"C'mon, you and I can handle five boys," Katie whispered. "We'll take them for ice cream if we have to in your van. Let's just put everyone out of their misery and say okay."

"I'll say okay." Luke let out a huge breath of air. "I'm saying okay now. If you really want to be an adult spotter on the back of the boat, we can even take them out." Luke would have taken two hundred kids on the boat to have some time with this Katie.

Margaux swiveled with great purpose to deal with the corn on the cob crisis that had befallen her family. Her Mercedes AMG S63 sedan pulled away, Andover and Yale water polo team decals plastered all over the back window, just to pound daily pressure on her lackluster son.

With Katie and young Huck smiling by his side, Luke chose to focus on something so true his mother had always told him: *Everything good happens in summer.*

Chapter Twenty-Five

Rocking the Boat

All the boxes were checked in Katie's tidy summer plan when, bang, she'd driven by the dock and seen Luke with a group of boys. Huck had yelled from the backseat, "Mom! Wait! I want to say hi to Luke!" She had stopped, wanting to blame the visit on her son's adoration, but knowing she couldn't help but slow the car. The pull toward Luke was natural and undeniable, like the moon yanking the Atlantic tides ashore.

With George on one of his binges of alone time, where he didn't check in over several days, she'd used the open mental space to put much in good order: her work was becoming more stable, (she had gotten several more clients with ten sessions in week four alone), and she had met with administrators at the Bridgehampton Middle School. Huck was happily ensconced in his water sports camp, and having play dates regularly with new friends.

There was nothing crazy about a detour to the dock, she had figured. Just a little temperature check. As she parked her car, facing Luke's boat, Katie mouthed these little justifications to herself so resolutely that her head bobbed. There was something about the way she had had to convince herself that George was lovely and kind and *what she needed right now* that still didn't sit right a month into summer.

Damn this confusion.

She remembered George's handsome, rugged face in the car, smiling at her, when he'd driven her to a new client in a small out-of-the-way spot three days before. The creases by the sides of his blue eyes were pronounced in the bright sunlight. He'd told her, "I wanted to drive you because I wanted some extra time with a beauty."

Her flip-flops strewn on the car floor, her bare toes on the dashboard, he'd made her feel both secure and sexy that day. George gave her advice on best career moves, lent her a cottage, excited her sexually, and got her to go places in bed she hadn't with former lovers. She'd remembered the masterful way he'd handled her body a few days before—how he'd pulled her jeans down before they'd even kissed and gone down on her until she'd come so hard and furiously, she couldn't believe his sheer authority.

She and Luke could be friends. In the fall, maybe they'd work in the same school system, they'd meet in the teachers' lounge, share notes, split turkey sandwiches and chips from paper bags. That's all.

Huck had asked from the backseat, "Mom, are you talking to yourself?"

"No, honey, just going over a little list in my head."

"What list? For the grocery store?"

"Just, I don't know, honey. Like a to-do thing, or like *why*-to-do thing, actually."

"I do that too sometimes, Mom."

On the docks now, with the ropes getting untied for an afternoon on the bay, and the boat's motor spewing oil fumes in the air, Katie recognized that she had casually walked into a whole afternoon with Luke Forrester. She helped Huck and the other young boys to buckle their life jackets. She could not deny the seventh-grade flutter in her heart.

Chapter Twenty-Six

Blushing in the Bay

For his part, Luke knew foul moods could vanish in mere moments, like ocean gusts that blew storm clouds into the horizon. Life was all about perspective, and Katie Doyle had changed his in an instant. He'd been chilly that morning, and been put into a bad mood with overdue town permits that might shut down his camp. The tense scuffle with his father over the Chase lunch didn't help.

Now, the June sun streamed down, warming his back as he helped the children leap from dock to boat.

Luke watched as Katie knelt to help a child she'd never met with his suntan lotion. Never mind those good legs, her kindness alone turned him on. Hell, East Coast or West Coast, good people were good people. He was. She was. Pretty simple equation in life to count on. Frank wasn't wrong about that.

Margaux Carroll long gone, the bay constable nowhere in sight, Luke now had the boys in a good place to leave the docks. There were five safe children's life jackets, a couple of usable but unmatched water skis, a tube patched in a dozen spots but not actually leaking, and a boat that tended to crap out in the middle of the bay but, hell, the bay was shallow and the shoreline visible.

He liked the way Katie dressed, too: neat but showing as much body as she could in her white cutoffs and plain rubber flip-flops. Hot and confident and sexy? Check. Tramping around like he was one of dozens of men who'd had his way with her like Simone? Nope.

Luke rolled up his T-shirt sleeves in case Katie cared to view the biceps he'd been working on all spring since Simone dumped him. They weren't much, but still there were discrete lines of definition if the light and shadows hit him just right. About a week before kicking him to the proverbial curb, Simone told him that his upper arms looked more like baby fat than lean muscle.

Katie would notice the new muscle lines. She seemed like someone who sought the happy in most any situation, having blown in like those Atlantic gusts, dispersing all the rancor in the lot.

As they powered out to the center of the bay, Luke took care Katie didn't get splashed with wake water, though he liked that she didn't seem to mind. He threw her his zip-up sweatshirt and she donned it instantly as if she were already his girlfriend. Even Tyler Carroll, once liberated from his mother's clench, and secured in Katie's knowing arms now out in the bow of the boat, seemed to feel at ease on the water, a first for him. Perhaps the kid feared his mother's shrill voice more than the ocean's force.

"What are all those buoys out in the bay for?" Katie yelled from out front, still trying to justify to herself that it was a grand, harmless idea to make a nice, really handsome male friend. "Why so many in one long line? Are there lobster traps here?"

"No, the town puts them in. It's not fishermen. On the other side, there's a jetty that sticks out much farther than expected, some of it underwater. It's used for tidal flows, but speeding boats don't always expect it and it can be very dangerous at night for people who don't know the water. Along the sides, there are natural sandbars that make the depth go from about eight feet to about two feet with no notice."

"Glad I'm not driving," she yelled back. "I can see the lighter and darker patches showing the changes in depth."

"It's really dangerous, actually. When we rent out the two Jet Skis, we have to explain to everyone what the issues are. That is, if we have a camp."

Katie turned and faced Luke, then took the kids off the bow and sat on the bench right next to him and the steering wheel. She figured this might allow less forced conversation, less of this distant flirt-or-not-to-flirt dance. Time to start acting normal, relaxed, no big deal to sit next to Luke and relate to him like an adult.

"What did you mean by that, if we have a camp?"

"See that bay constable out there, the boat that looks like a police car? He was gone on the other side of the bay, but now he's back, just puttering out there a hundred yards, only to make me nervous. And, unfortunately, it's working. He's in sync with the town trustees to shut us down over a little technicality about where we exchange money. Some late fees. Maybe some forms, too."

"Why?"

"Just miserable, uptight people from the Seabrook Club who never learned how to share. We're trying to get some families to help, but the town has got a tough clamp that's tightening." He looked at her beside him and lingered his eyes on hers. "Listen, I want to stay happy today, so let's not focus on depressing stuff. The whole camp thing is freaking us all out."

As he drove around a lighter patch of water, Luke yelled to the kids, "Hey, kids, look on the left side, you'll see tons of mussels next to this sandbar, they are from families called bivalve mollusks that live in both saltwater and freshwater habitats. They all have a shell whose outline is elongated compared with other edible clams."

"Do all the adults ever listen to you about safety in the bays of the Hamptons? That water is so shallow now," Katie asked.

"The kids are awesome, the adults never listen. But let's get your vocab organized. 'The Hamptons' is not what those who actually live here call it."

"You don't . . . hold a sec." She rubbed her son's back as he leaned over the edge of the idling boat. "Honey, I had those exact same mussels two nights ago; you liked them with the tomato sauce . . . sorry, Luke, go on."

All Katie could think was *this guy is damn adorable just like that Tommy on the other side of her tenth grade locker.*

"So, yeah, no 'The Hamptons' please, because those of us who live here refer to it as Southampton or East Hampton or Bridgehampton. These are legitimate towns, places where people grow up, earn a living, form roots. It's not a Disney resort village," Luke instructed. "So, do me a favor, refer to our town by its name. Otherwise, it's gonna peg you as *one of them.*"

"Well, don't look at me like *one of them.*" Katie laughed a little. "I'm from a town smack in the middle of the Cascade Range that goes from British Columbia to Northern California. I think that qualifies me as pretty normal. The only *one of them* I like is Julia Chase. We talk a bunch at drop-off and get together once in a while, but the others . . . not so sure."

Luke touched her arm with his elbow. Her light skin was softer than he thought. "Nightmare time is when the hedge fund dads, who got to where they are by never listening to anyone, come to rent Jet Skis. You can't be whipping at forty miles per hour on a Jet Ski and think you're invincible with two-foot sandbars everywhere. We often say they're booked or broken."

"You have to lie to control them?" Katie asked. She was now hugging her good strong legs up on the bench, and smiling as he drove in big curves to make the boys laugh. Wisps of her hair were sticking to her face, which she kept pulling away as she concentrated on Luke's every word. "You must love teaching near the water."

"Yeah, the ocean is the classroom. We study marine organisms with plankton nets in this bay and use hydrophones and sonar to find schools of fish. I've taught them all about the satellite tags of the great white sharks and we follow them online. Of course, there's the conservation element that kids love; we do beach clean ups with a barbeque after on Fridays." He turned to her. "You should come. Or, on Wednesdays I just go with friends to cook and surf. Either works."

"Yeah. That sounds really good." Katie let her knees fall to the floor, and looked at him, her green eyes sparkling like the translucent bay.

ALL AFTERNOON, KATIE was skillful and thoughtful on the boat. Luke's mother had known the waters as well; she'd taught him a bowline knot and cleat hitch when he was only in kindergarten. He wondered if she'd have liked Katie as much as he did. All the tragedy in the water might have been easier to handle if at least he knew more. Luke and Frank never found out how his mother and her strong girlfriend perished that day. Neither body was ever discovered, the boat simply overturned in seas rougher than projected.

"I'm telling you, I got it," Katie reassured him while she handed the boys water skis in the water, or helped tighten their vests. "I grew up near a lake a thousand times bigger than Peconic Bay. You just drive, I'll watch the rope doesn't get caught." The younger boys were too frightened to try skiing, so they jumped into the huge tube to be pulled on the back of the boat and over the wake.

At one point, Katie pulled off her T-shirt to jump into the water and help young Huck, who was getting a little overwhelmed by the spraying water and speed on the back tube. Luke watched her shorts fall to the wet floor. His eyes trailed every line of her body and she climbed up on the edge and jumped in. She lay on the tube alongside her son, while Luke chugged along at a slower pace, paying far more attention to her bouncing bikini top in the rearview mirror than any safety issues. Luke couldn't remember one mom who'd ever gotten out of the boat and onto the tube before. Simone would have said that it would mess up her blow-dry.

The light was high, but a late afternoon breeze hinted that the sun's heat would soon fade. When Luke announced the hour was more than over, the boys pleaded for one more turn in a chorus of whines, whimpers, and protestations. Luke, usually firm on the need to return and fueled by his constant exasperation with too many kids and too many demands, for once had no motivation to head back.

Back on land, he thought maybe an iced tea or ice cream in town could unfold naturally once they tied up the boat. He could explain the school system to Katie. Maybe they could even take a ride down onto the beach in his truck at sunset.

As they approached the dock after another full hour, Luke thanked God for listening to his silent pleas, because Huck asked, "Mom, can we stay later if I help Luke clean the boat?"

"I'm sure Luke has everything in order and is busy with his equipment and other kids on the way."

"No more kids." Luke couldn't help himself.

She handed him his sweatshirt and, as he took it, his hand brushed her rib cage by accident. She twisted her hip away. "Well, then I'm sure he's busy with the way he needs to close up camp."

"Nope. I could use the help."

Katie stood just a foot away and stared right at Luke. She tried to decipher if he was just flirting, or if he meant it that he wanted to hang with an eight-year-old.

"You actually need Huck's help?" Katie said, trying to figure out if all this togetherness was the good kind of dangerous.

Just then, Julia Chase approached the dock and waved. "Luke, can you give us one sunset surf lesson? Richie's at home and just called and the driver can bring him."

"So sorry, I got a little man here I need to handle, he's got me full-time." Luke carried Huck piggyback.

Julia walked up to the group and warmly put her arm around Katie. "Oh, I see, another Luke love fest going on. Lucky kid you got here, Katie. Let's get together outside camp again soon. You want to take a class in the morning?"

"You're sweet, but I have too much work tomorrow, but maybe later in the week."

"Well, how about we have lunch. We've said at drop-off several times we were going to. This is getting ridiculous."

"I'd like that," Katie replied, thinking maybe she could even open up to Julia like she had before. She was in desperate need of female company. Ashley back home had never stepped foot on this eastern planet and it was impossible to explain all the idiosyncrasies of life in Southampton on the phone. "Really I would, let's do that soon."

"Well, then, I'll call. I mean that. If Luke is favoring your kid over mine, there's gonna be hell to pay, though, for both of you," she joked and started to walk back to her car.

Luke held Huck tight around back. In the summers, he worked every single day, and often he was so waterlogged and sunburnt in the late afternoons, he said no to all new lessons. But now, a beautiful woman with black hair and crystal-green eyes kept him alert and wanting the day to last forever. "We got man's work to do: got to scrub the salt water off, rinse and tie up the life jackets, untangle the ropes these monsters messed up. It's going to be a while. Good news is we pay the best helpers who do the job well." At this, Huck's eyes widened and he slammed his palms together in excitement. Luke ruffled Huck's hair, already white-blond from a month in the sea.

Julia lingered at the edge of the dock to look back at Luke touching Katie's shoulder lightly.

"Well, the problem is," explained Katie, "I have to go because I have a meeting that's going to last an hour, but if Huck can agree to be a good boy and to work hard and wait."

"Uh, and I don't think I remember saying we needed you here?" responded Luke. Huck giggled. "We don't really need you sitting around like we're having a tea party. He can come back to the shack with me to unload equipment like a man. All good. We'll see you here after you're done and we're done."

Katie found most men do the requisite kneel down for a moment with her son. They make a few "hey, little buddy" advances and then ignore the child, like a pet that becomes too plaintive. It was a simple test for Katie; if they blew off her son, she walked. If they understood Huck in a meaningful way, she was drawn to them.

"Hey, Huck, you hose off the life jackets like this so they don't go flying off the dock." Luke then sprayed Huck's toes, making him jump up and down.

As for Luke, he didn't feel he was courting danger by being with Katie because there wasn't anyone else in the picture to complicate his choices. It was all working out so nicely, like those gray clouds pushed miles off the coast, all peaceful, sunny, feeling so right.

Until, unfortunately, it wasn't.

Chapter Twenty-Seven

Inconvenient Intrusions

"Hey, Luke."

Luke hadn't heard his former girlfriend Simone walk down the dock because he'd been adjusting the power of the hose with Huck. She almost checked Katie sideways into the water with the sway of her plentiful hip on her way down the plank.

Simone wore tight white shorts and a little tank that covered up the turquoise blue Brazilian thong bikini he'd bought her at some trampy beach store in the middle of Long Island. When they were together, she'd wear anything Luke fantasized about: fishnet, crotch-less body suits, X-rated silk lingerie, and microscopic bathing suits. The bottom bikini barely covered her butt crack and the top had a crisscross design in the front and back, suggesting bondage was her thing. Luke prayed she wouldn't display the suit underneath, or mention he'd bought it for her.

Please, for once, keep your clothes on, Simone.

"Hey," Luke answered flatly. "Just working. Kinda busy."

Simone stood before him and in front of Katie, hands on her hips in Wonder Woman stance. It guaranteed Katie would witness her flawless legs all oiled up to shine in the sunlight.

"See you all soon. I will make that lunch date, Katie!" Julia turned to walk down the dock to leave, but it was hard not to rubberneck.

Katie also gawked as Simone knelt down and asked Huck for the hose, then rinsed off her feet and started rubbing sand and salt off her legs, massaging the higher part of her inner thighs longer than necessary to do the job.

When an inch of her shorts got wet, Simone said, "Oh Jesus, I'll just go ahead and take my damn clothes off." She then proceeded to wiggle her large bottom out of the shorts, and stood there with about three quarters of her butt cheeks hanging out. She adjusted her teeny bikini top a bit to cover her breasts. They were enormous, and, unfortunately for Katie, not even a little fake-looking.

"Luke," Simone sighed, dramatically, "I told you not to buy me bathing suits like this!"

Katie left without saying goodbye to Luke and her son, only murmuring, "I'll be here in an hour to get him."

Were a fight referee here, he'd now be ringing a loud bell and thrusting Simone's arm in the air as Katie lay K.O.'d, facedown on the splinter-filled dock.

She walked to the old Volvo, now reeking of spoiled shrimp she'd bought for dinner. She had forgotten about the perishable groceries once they'd veered toward the docks. Katie felt dejected, but also a little relieved.

Luke must have been flirting for fun's sake only. Her instincts must have been all wrong. In either case, he was occupied with that woman. This made things easier. She willed herself to feel better about her original plan.

Interlude

The man with the pink-and-yellow gardenia lining in his jacket kept his car idling, a block from Natalie's house. The Japanese maple's deep burgundy leaves hovered a few feet above his car. The husband inside, Charlie, was an affable guy with a damn good putting game. He'd be playing the front nine in Westhampton that morning. Charlie had a 10:00 a.m. tee time; he knew because he'd been invited to join the foursome.

But the man in the car canceled last minute, instead preferring to show Charlie's wife what she'd been missing all these years.

He watched incognito as Charlie finally walked out the front door of his small, white-shingled house, and down the front steps. He leaned down to yank a few weeds out of the cracks in the slate stepping-stones in the lawn. Charlie Duke was a tall man with a thick build in the middle, and thick sausage thighs. Big cheeks framed his persistent, good-humored smile. At forty-eight, the flesh on his flabby arms was dimpled in the sunlight. A kind fellow, just, evidently, a little clueless on pleasing the wife.

Natalie met her husband on the deck to kiss him goodbye, a

peck really, probably had always been that way. Her shoulder-length brown hair was neatly pulled up in a clip, and she wore a loose top with an extremely short tennis skirt.

Charlie tightened his golf visor to wage the eighteen-hole war ahead. Then he walked into his garage, grabbed his fifteen-year-old Wilson clubs, laid them in the back of his Tesla Model 3, and sped off for the half hour drive to Westhampton.

The man waited about ten minutes under the Japanese maple tree shade, just in case Charlie had forgotten something. Then he got out of the car and walked around parked cars and hedges to hide in her back lawn. He stopped behind an old barbeque covered in black vinyl, dusty with cobwebs. *C'mon, Charlie, you got to at least grill for your wife. Even cavemen figured that out. Otherwise they're going to feel lonely, uncared for, metaphorically unfed.*

Natalie opened the screen door, looking left and right nervously, and beckoned him in, while raising an eyebrow. A little moisture formed under her arms. She wasn't used to any of this, but she felt more excited than bad.

"Love the tennis skirt again, first time I saw you in that, all slippery with sweat." He grabbed Natalie's arm. "Do you have a guest room—can't do your bedroom. I would never do that to a close friend."

"I, well, do you want some iced tea first, we could . . ."

"Just, come here, honey. I've been meaning to see if I could cup that little ass in one palm for . . ." He pushed her up against the cupboards in her kitchen, kissed her softly, biting her lip a little, firmly, then gently, firmly, then gently . . . she sighed.

This was too easy.

"Wow, I haven't . . ." Natalie whispered, breathing heavily. "We really shouldn't, not here, the windows, the curtains are see-through, not . . ."

Housewives were such a slam dunk, especially in the kitchen. It probably reminded them of some stupid TV show they watched. She was right about the windows, though; he glanced left out the back lawn to assess the risk factor.

He considered that she was hardly worth the lay. He'd have to be nice to her socially now, but, still . . . those oiled-up legs by the pool. He'd told her he wanted to drag his fingers slowly up them until he drove her insane. She'd answered by saying to call, and, well, here they were. Charlie would be hitting his three-wood down the second fairway soon.

He looked out at the small lawn. God forbid some contractor or landscaper worked on Fridays. He picked her up while she wrapped her legs around his hard waist, and placed her on the dryer in the window-less washroom. As he walked with her, he figured he'd multitask, and so he reached four fingers from each hand up her short skirt, dancing them delicately inside the lace on her panties. She must have weighed one hundred and ten pounds. A shame he hadn't placed her on a bed. She'd spin like a little top.

"I'm going to do things to your body that . . ." Always a good thing to give women the impression he was only there for them, especially the harried wives. It got them hot quicker. That, in turn, got him hot, which meant he could start getting his way sooner.

She sat on the dryer, and he yanked her legs apart, placed some freshly folded towels to cushion her head, *liked he cared so much about her comfort*, and laid her back. He pulled her panties aside to fondle her expertly with one hand while playing with her perky tits with the other.

He sucked on her nipples a little to gauge her horniness temperature. The Southampton heat index was alarmingly high. She was too damn wet now. He preferred more friction, so he grabbed some socks off the top of a neatly folded pile of Charlie's tennis whites. He used them to wipe her down a little. *Jesus these neglected wives*: same thing every time, zero to sixty with no effort at all.

Just before he thought she might climax, he yanked her to the edge of the dryer. He then rammed himself into her, all rough like he liked it. He hoped she could handle it without whimpering.

While he kept at it, he placed one hand behind her ass and one in front, tickling her lightly again to keep her motor revved high. He slowed down his ramming a bit to give her a break.

Natalie now placed her impeccably toned calves over his shoulders to make him go deeper and grabbed onto his back like she was dangling off a two hundred foot cliff. He continued to dance his fingers on her with a feather touch. Seven seconds later, she moaned so loudly, he had to place Charlie's tennis shorts over her mouth to muffle the noise.

Slam dunk, indeed.

Chapter Twenty-Eight

Misunderstandings and Miscommunications

Katie called Luke about fifteen minutes after she left the docks, her voice sounding sanitized. "Sorry, Luke. Can you possibly drop Huck off at the house?"

Luke barely knew this woman, but he very much wanted to ask her, *"What the hell? Why the chilly tone?"* Or, *"Don't sweat Simone. She just likes to screw with my head and keep other women at bay by shoving her body in their faces."*

But, since he was, in fact, not remotely dating Katie, he agreed to her plan. "Yes, uh, fine. Sure. I'll do that."

"I appreciate it a lot. I have the daughter of my neighbor who will be there waiting for him. Her car is at the shop, so she can't get him. My tutor meeting is taking longer. The house is close."

"Yeah. Fine."

"You don't mind?"

"I don't mind, no." But of course Luke minded; he'd wanted to take Katie to the beach, with sandwiches, chips, and guacamole. He wanted to do something fun to celebrate his favorite season, bring them to a beach cleanup, teach her kid to understand marine life. He couldn't help as a last-ditch chance to ask, "Do you want to meet us instead later in town or something? I could keep him until you're ready."

"I can't hear you. I'm inside the educational offices already." And Katie's voice trailed off. She sounded distracted, like he didn't matter to her. Luke felt silly. Maybe it was baby fat on his arms, after all.

"Fine," he relented. "I'll drop him off. What's the address?"

"Thirty-seven Willow Lane."

Luke froze. "Can you repeat that?"

"Thirty-seven Willow Lane. It's in town, two blocks behind the CVS drugstore. A small cottage. The number isn't easy to find, but Huck will show you, just five minutes from you."

"I know it." Even when his mom was alive, both she and Frank had forbidden him to go near that house.

"Okay," Katie answered. "Thanks, bye, gotta go."

Click.

Luke's sun-kissed face turned ashen. Even little Huck noticed. He tugged on his shorts, asking, "What's the matter?"

Luke ignored the question and walked like a zombie to the end of the dock, carrying two huge bags of gear. Huck followed him, insisting on grabbing the five children's life jackets which engulfed him.

"We leave those on the boat."

"But I want to carry something, too."

"The bags are too heavy for you; it's fine. Quit it. Kids don't know how to . . ." He felt bad for snapping at this kid, the only one who'd offered to help out all summer. Most kids were so used to nannies and housekeepers, they left behind a trail of their own snacks, expensive new Patagonia wetsuits, and designer towels swiped from the family pool basket. Luke and the guys hadn't bought towels in years.

Huck looked up at Luke despondently. "I just really want to carry one thing."

The boy could only handle two wet, heavy beach towels before getting toppled, so Luke threw them on his shoulders.

As Luke and Huck walked up to the camp meeting area on the sandy shoreline, he knew that seeing Simone again would only bring those windy, gray clouds back. Still, he couldn't avoid her. She was now up there parading around in her turquoise thong bikini with her glorious ass, right in front of Kona and Kenny.

"Hey," he muttered, planting himself and Huck onto a towel in the sand.

"Hey." Simone smiled like she might just blow him one more time if he asked really nicely.

"What are you doing here?" he asked, coldly.

"Well, I was going to meet people in town, but I can stay . . ." She edged closer to him.

Simone had left him. He'd tried. Too late. Six weeks before, Simone had returned his texts three days late even though it said, "read," minutes after he'd sent them. She didn't text him back because she was too busy posting photos of herself with rich assholes nuzzling their noses between her big tits. Luke knew no one made her laugh the way he could. He made her belly laugh. And still she left him. She was thirty, and looking for a man to pay for anything she pointed at, he figured. Rather than spend time with a man of sterling character, she'd end up with a dickhead philanderer.

At that moment, Jake Chase drove up way too hot in his seventh car, a new Audi R8, with his youngest son, Richie. As the dust settled on the small group, Simone surmised this was an opportune time to lie in the late day sun rather than leave to meet her girlfriends in town as she had planned.

Jake and Richie walked up to the guys, as Jake shouted, "Yo! Dudes!"

Kona shot Luke a look, who, in turn, shot Kenny a roll of his eyes.

Behind the shield of his expensive dark Persol lenses, Jake focused his eyes on the spectacle of Simone on the towel. She was slathering herself with tanning oil and writhing her body on all fours, moving in weird contortions for no apparent reason other than to practice taking it from behind.

"We were just driving by," Jake said slowly as if in a trance. "Richie had nothing to do, and he was upset not to have a lesson earlier. Just thought we'd check in." Jake surveyed the beach, pretending not to notice Simone.

Luke breathed in through his flared nostrils and thought *I'm going to murder Jake if he touches her.* Luke had never once sat on the beach with Simone, looking at the waves and feeling like "he had her." Chasing her around the bedroom stuck out as the only realm where he could pin her down, physically make her writhe and succumb, like a victory he couldn't get enough of. Once they left the bedroom, it was a constant case of failure to conquer anything. He knew he wasn't the first man to get sucked into that fucked-up, soul-crushing pursuit of the entirely wrong girl.

"Richie, go check out the water, would ya? Is it cold?" Jake asked.

"I don't want to."

"Daddy needs to ask these men about something that's going on and you need to walk to the water's edge, put your toe in, and come back. Walk *very slowly*."

"I didn't do anything wrong, Dad!"

"You think that matters? Go!" Richie walked to the shore with his head drooped low.

Kona elbowed Luke in the gut. "Play nice. We need Jake. Don't forget, he said he'd call the town board."

"So, I'm out here a day and I'm fuckin' bored already," Jake said to the instructors. "I thought I'd take some days off, be with the family. The wife wanted it that way. Not like I need to be working and pumping out more cash, heh!" He slammed Luke's back really hard, conveying their buddy status. "Thought I'd see what you guys were up to." He then raised his eyebrows at Simone, who was now lying on her back, raising her hips in the air in rhythmic motion.

"So first I have breakfast, read a little news, then I'm restless as shit, then . . ." Jake detailed his lazy day off, oblivious to the fact that the guys would themselves like to have the opportunity to enjoy a little summer boredom. Instead, they had to drag entitled kids around a bay in a shitty boat they couldn't afford to fix.

Kona started in. "So, thanks for that lunch. Since you do have free time, maybe you could take a morning, and we can go into the Town Hall offices when they have public grievances meetings, then, we can together lobby for . . ."

Jake ignored Kona to study Simone, who was suddenly on all fours again, her back arched, making sure her thong was as far up her ass as possible.

"You know guys, I came down here to show some appreciation for all your hard work in the water. And sure, yeah, let's go to a meeting sometime. I'm busy, I mean I'm not, but I am. But I'll find a time to go with you. Sure. Just, you know, not today."

Chapter Twenty-Nine

Drop-off Drama

W hy are we just sitting in the car?" Huck was so in awe of Luke, he didn't want to say he thought it strange to be sitting there with no answer for several minutes. "I mean, it's okay. I was just wondering if you want to go inside with me and see if the neighbor is there because I don't see her now and I'm not allowed to stay in a house alone. She played with me yesterday for a little."

"Yeah, I think, we'll just, uh, sit here for a minute more to see if the babysitter comes out of your house." Luke tried to figure out his moves. Thirty-seven Willow Lane. It was too much, too strange. "Why did you guys move here? Why this house?"

"Um, my mom said it was time for us to move East. We lived with my grandma. She died. Did you know she died?"

"I'm sorry I didn't."

"We lived with her. It made my mom sad. She said she could only be happy if we moved for the summer. So we did. Mom has a new boyfriend. I think. I've only met him like four times, but I know that's why we're here. But sometimes she says he's not her boyfriend. Then I saw them kissing two times."

"Where did you see them kissing?"

"On the porch. And once in the kitchen. It was gross. He was kind of eating her face."

"Okay." Luke let that disgusting image sink in for a moment. "Whose house is this? Is it the boyfriend's, or did your mom rent it?"

"I think we rented it, but I think he had something to do with it. He picked it out before we came. It was hard to move and my mom was too busy to find us something, I think. But I'm not sure."

"What's his name?"

"What's whose name?"

"The guy, the guy who was kissing your mom."

"George. He's a little bit weird, but he's also nice sometimes, like when he buys me a donut or something."

"George who?" Luke asked.

"I don't know. He works a lot. He comes for dinner or breakfast, that's about it. He bought me a Demolition Lab Triple Blast Warehouse once. My mom got mad because I didn't say thank you."

"And why didn't you say thank you?"

"I told you, because he's weird," Huck answered.

Luke couldn't help but laugh. "Well, how is he weird?"

Huck flipped his palms in the air, as if to say *adults could be so stupid*. "I don't know, can't you just tell when someone's weird? He's just weird. He's not fun, but he acts like he is. Sometimes he makes me laugh a little."

Luke didn't want to get out of the car. He was stalling in case Katie pulled up behind him and he'd have a chance to say hello. Or, he might get a look at the boyfriend, though he wasn't sure that was a good thing.

Most of all, Luke sat in an idling car in a driveway with an eight-year-old for ten minutes because this house gave him a long, historical case of fear.

His father had told him that he must never step foot in the house at 37 Willow Lane. Luke's mom had worked here gardening before she died; something had happened with the owner, an older man, Luke never knew what. He was pretty sure it wasn't anything physical—rather a very bad misunderstanding.

He'd asked Frank if she'd gotten hurt, and he said no and left it at that; it was important to stay away. In his twenties, Luke had gone to the buildings department in Southampton town to see who owned it, but LLCs and estate trusts were listed and he couldn't tell the exact owners.

"Can we please go inside?" Huck couldn't wait any longer.

"Yeah, sorry, let's go."

They walked up to the front deck of the small house, Huck leading the reticent Luke. Music muffled in from the back area and Luke could see the neighbor's teenage daughter reading and sunbathing. All of the gray wood window frames were weathered, the steps slanted with age, and walkway stones badly cracked and in need of repair. A few quaint window boxes filled with geraniums lined the windows. On the small covered entrance, a white wicker rocking swing with a tattered cushion swayed slightly in the wind.

The hair on the back of Luke's neck stood up. He smoothed it down. It was just too damn crazy to admit that he felt his mother's presence. But he did.

Chapter Thirty

Violet Underground

Y ou want to stop by?" Julia Chase asked Katie over the phone a few afternoons later that week. "I was going to ask you on the docks earlier but I got distracted with all the kids and equipment. I just now thought, hell, I'm going to call her and make a plan."

"I'm in the car, just finished a meeting."

"Ever had a lavender-infused martini?" Julia asked.

"No, but it sounds good," Katie answered, pressing her cell phone headphones into her ear. She was driving back toward Southampton in a work-fueled daze. "I could use one right about now. You're so kind to reach out."

"Of course, you told me you don't know many people here," said Julia. "I'm terrible I didn't push earlier, it's on me. I'm a native."

"Regardless, you're good to do it. I just finished a session with a terribly dyslexic tenth-grader, who could not get through more than ten lines of *The Odyssey*. By the time we got to '*When they ate the oxen of Hyperion the Sun*' the kid was in tears. Anyway, poor kid, sorry to yammer on about work. Yes. Definitely need a break. From everything."

"Let me make you my favorite girls' drink called a purple pillow," Julia pressed. "It's got vodka infused with lavender from my garden, a little lime, and muddled blueberries . . . medicine at sunset after a harrowing day with husband and kids or work. You'll see. I don't make them too strong. Just right. You want to come over now?"

"You know, there's this other spot if you don't mind," Katie told her, not in the mood to be a guest in a strange home. "It's my little beach entrance where I walk for downtime, down at the end of Briarcroft Lane. I go at 5:00 p.m. when the sitter comes and I have a little break on Tuesdays and Thursdays. There's this big piece of tree trunk washed in from some storm where I sit. Maybe you could just meet me out there?"

"I actually know that tree trunk well," Julia said, laughing. "It's a place where I think about the messed-up elements of my life and how to plan my way out of them. See you in fifteen."

Katie smiled, wondering what exactly was "messed up" in the life of a woman with a glass mansion on the ocean, a super model figure, and limitless cash spitting out of her family ATM.

This late afternoon, as Katie slammed the car door shut and walked down toward the peeling waves, Southampton felt like it belonged to her. This beach entrance was narrow, with about ten parallel parking spots on each side. A lone couple—a nice-looking woman in her thirties with a long blond braid tucked behind a sun hat, and her handsome boyfriend in swim trunks—walked off the beach laden with towels and tote bags, their faces bronzed by a long afternoon in the sun.

Katie left her sandals by the side of the pavement. She walked along the dunes where the sand swallowed her feet to work her calves out more.

She walked down to the harder sand near the water to watch the light penetrate off the Atlantic. Huge sprays of mist spewed off the tops of large waves crashing on the wet shoreline. The ground beneath her shook with each pounding, curling roller. She held her forearms tight as if to give herself a hug, then placed her hands on her knees and exhaled a pound of stress.

It was quickly becoming cooler than normal this late afternoon, and fog drifted in, covering midsummer's heat and glare. Her four weeks in the Hamptons had passed with shifting weather patterns, summer squalls that turned into two days of downpours, the ocean flat one day and roiling mad the next. It was no longer the beginning of summer—she was *in it*.

"Hey!" yelled Julia from about fifty yards down the sand. She grabbed a martini shaker from her straw bag and shook it in the air, banging around the ice and vodka inside. "I've got some medicine for that glum face down there!"

Katie watched Julia plow down the beach, and thought about her own mother and how she veered toward honest, lively women as well. She'd always told Katie not to judge, not to assume that the housewives in Hood River who drove Katie insane with their P.T.A. bake sale demands weren't offering a solid chance at friendship. Her mom would have liked Julia's straightforward approach, just like the women Katie grew up with who held the world tightly in their clutches.

Julia sat on the log and spread her curvy, tanned legs out, the wind blowing her blond locks behind her. She was wearing jean shorts, a bohemian light blue blouse with blue flowers in varying colors, and an indigo short poncho. She pulled two cashmere orange blankets out (they matched her vintage Porsche and she kept them in the trunk for moments like this) and placed one on the sand for Katie and another to cover her own bare legs. "Sit on the blanket, it's more comfortable. Here, let me pour you a drink. Take a glass."

"This is civilized," Katie remarked, as Julia poured a chilled, violet-hued martini out of a large shaker into a hard plastic martini glass. "Oh, do I need this. It's been a strange week, a long week. Thank you." She laughed a little and sipped the drink. "I really appreciate your reaching out. I was thinking about my mother, and how gregarious she was."

"You mentioned her before. I'm sorry."

"Anyway," Katie went on, shaking her head a little to cast off sadness, "she always pushed me to be more open to different people."

"You saying I'm different?"

"No, you're not different, as in something bad," Katie backtracked. "Everything in Southampton is still an adjustment for me."

A filthy, wet Labrador down the beach chased a flock of seagulls and leapt over a wave, his four legs stretched out front and back. The sun, not yet ready to set, was covered in a line of clouds that turned the sky light pink.

After a few moments of small talk about kids and the weather turning unexpectedly colder, Julia asked, "And this George guy?"

"Well, I came to the East Coast to find a new place to work, and possibly at the same time, conveniently, to be with a lovely man. It's just George is a bit different from when I met him out West. He's a little hard to read," Katie explained. "Clearly, I'm so resolved!"

"It's so true that environments can change people."

"Well, take his club for starters." Katie nodded her head toward the fortress on a distant dune.

"Seabrook?" said Julia. "He's there?"

"Hmm-mmm."

Julia nodded, looking down at it. The beach was dotted with

other mansions atop rising sand dunes, haze smearing them into the landscape like a fuzzy camera lens. Some of the immense homes had shingled sides with white windowpanes, several chimneys shooting up, and circular porches rounding out the second floor bedroom suites.

Interspersed among the older-style houses, contemporary structures jutted out from the sea grass, constructed like intersecting cubes. Right angles were the rule, and all beachfront views were lined with huge glass panes. Either style reigned, no architectural creativity in between.

"No offense to your guy, but the Seabrook members are locked into their old world, Mayflower deal. It's a little hard to get past that. I get it. Don't forget, though, those clubs do so much for the town in terms of restoring historic homes and keeping land preserves safe from too much development. They are very active with people here in need, you can't deny them that. The hospital and the library wouldn't exist without the decades of support from that club."

"His mother is introducing me to women who chair this fundraiser for the library." Katie shook her head. "I've been put in charge of table dressing ideas, even though all I know about table settings is the fork goes on the left and knife on the right . . . and then I hear it's not settings, but decorations for cocktail tables. Maybe I'll suggest a friend like you help me?"

"They wouldn't like that." Julia laughed. "I promise you. There's no potluck type of inclusive anything going on over there."

Julia poked her finger hard into Katie's back. "Looks like someone is into you." Luke Forrester was walking toward them far down the sand. "One question, I've wondered about, especially as you talk a little wistfully about George. You and Luke?"

Katie was mid-sip, as she took the opportunity to pause. "We aren't, I'm here with George. Luke is just, we are friends."

As Luke walked into earshot distance, Julia said loudly with a little too much force, "Totally, agree, it's cooler now, needed these blankets!"

"Hey," Luke said, not sure this was a good idea barging into girl time. He sensed he'd interrupted something more than weather talk.

"You want to sit down?" Julia asked. Katie remained silent, her mind flashing on the day in the boat when he'd been so fun with the five boys. And then, reluctantly, on that turquoise bikini stripper act.

"I just have a question." Luke paused, his fingers playing with his cleft chin nervously, wanting very much to tell her that Simone was a former friend, no matter what porn scene she'd acted out on the docks. "I wanted to take Huck to make s'mores maybe one night soon, maybe on one of those Friday beach cleanups the biology department sponsors? I promised him. Julia, you and Richie could come, too."

"At night?" said Katie. She wondered if Simone would be there.

"It's just a whole group of us who care about the environment and try to get people psyched up for beach cleanups. We surf a little, grill dinner."

As Luke got more and more excited about the plan, Julia banged Katie's knee with hers and raised an eyebrow at her. *Oh, really? Not that into you?*

"I take my students when the weather is warm in spring and fall down near the jetty at the inlet. We have a bonfire. I have these little cast-iron skillets, and we heat up strawberries and pour it on the s'mores to melt the chocolate. We played a marshmallow game once at camp and Huck literally finished the whole bag; he'd love it. Maybe this Friday, there's a big cleanup and I could take you?"

"Well," Katie answered, knowing George was coming this Friday and she'd promised to make him her special grilled lamb roast. "This Friday I can't, but I guess Huck . . ."

"No, fine. I mean, yes, fine, I just wanted you to see the cleanup, too. But, sure, I could just go with Huck."

Julia banged her knee at Katie so she'd save him. Katie obliged. "It would be better if we went together. Soon, not this weekend, but sure, that's really nice, if Huck and I could go together."

With three different people trying to salvage the invitation, Luke bowed out. "Anyway, I gotta go back."

"Not into you? Really?" Julia raised an eyebrow. "After that performance, you're going to maintain that? His friend Simone knows it and doesn't like it. Just telling you my vantage point. I watched her disrobe on the docks the other day. I think that was for you, not Luke."

"You don't think they are still together at all?"

"I thought you weren't interested?"

"I'm—" Katie had to laugh a little. "I don't know what I am, to tell you the truth."

"That's allowed."

"Well, you're a gorgeous woman. I'm sure you have your fair share of men after you, even though you're married," Katie retorted, yanking her Portland Sea Dogs baseball cap down. "That Kona is after everyone. I'm sure he hits on you. I'm sure all the men out here do."

"Listen, I really love my husband. He's brash but he pours his love on me and the kids all day, and I like that. I need it, actually. We've got a good thing. He tries to act all macho and fight me on family decisions, but we both know he's going to let me win on anything that counts.

"But I play with Kona's mind because he deserves it." Julia leaned into Katie and touched her shoulder gently with hers. "Nothing better than controlling a man who is used to controlling way too many women. As for you and Luke, just saying, looks to me like there's more *there* there." Julia shifted her head toward Luke, now marching away from them. She neatened up the items in her Balenciaga tote bag, which cost more than all the jeans, sneakers, and sandals in Katie's entire closet. "Who is this George anyway? Do I know him? You know the Hamptons are all one small town and big town at once."

"His name is George Porter."

"I know him—or, I know *of* him." Julia nodded slowly, trying to place his face. "He's good-looking and holds a ton of sway over at that club. It's not a club we are part of, so can't say I know him well. But his name is bandied about, and his mother, Poppy, is very well known. What does he do?" Julia was worried for her new friend that George had the reputation as a man with many women chasing him. She couldn't remember if he'd ever been linked to someone.

"He's into investing. Not sure it's really working. He seems frustrated on that front, working too hard."

"Where does he live? And do you know anything about former girlfriends, was he ever married?"

"Never married, doesn't ever discuss former flames. He's very elegant that way, very gentlemanly. He lives in a small cottage, over behind town. And his family or mother owns a second one on Willow Lane where I am staying," Katie explained, forcefully, "I'm paying rent."

"Hey, I don't judge. Whatever system works, it's fine."

"Well, anyway, I just don't want to be totally beholden to him, you know."

"I do know. It causes you to owe him and that adds a layer of complication. I get it. You're smart to pay for it on your own," Julia replied. "Many of the people at the feared and famous Seabrook don't have any real net worth to speak of, except the cottages they inherited. I'm not saying having money should be important."

"It isn't. But I'm interested in you saying they aren't very wealthy in there. I can't tell."

"In that club, you've got guys who are fifth generation Harvard or Yale and everything's been handed to them in life. Some of them didn't do so well as adults, never got used to having to do work that required actual effort and accountability.

"Many of those men are frustrated the markets didn't treat them like their fathers and grandfathers—in the sense that making money is harder these days with the economy so unstable. So they are hanging fiercely onto their dwindling inheritances. They for sure have power at the club. But I'm not sure that power really translates anywhere as it used to."

Katie didn't care about George's financial stature, but she didn't like that he might be more desperate than he let on. Or that he was hiding something, which Julia seemed to be alluding to. Katie took the last sip out of her glass and brushed her lips. "You know, he's a wonderful man, and I'm grateful for his kindness. I'm just making sure I have my own source of stable work. Which, by the way, Jesus! People here spend a lot on tutors. I've never heard of charging so much an hour for dyslexia coaching. Back in Hood River, it's like a quarter or a fifth of the price here. Even the bigger Portland areas don't charge nearly as much."

"Well, you're an accomplished, published learning specialist. They should pay. But, coming here, it's fun, isn't it? Exploring something new?" Julia smiled warmly. "And don't think I didn't notice that you never really answered me on Luke, but that's what girlfriends are for. Ignoring the obvious while stating the obvious."

Chapter Thirty-One

Patio Party Gauntlet

The Patio Party Decorations Committee Chair flung open the frail front screen door of her cottage. While forcing out a huge breath, Topper Tobin announced to Katie with a transparent smile, "We are so glad you could join us, we're just desperate for the help."

Topper was a blond, Stepford wife with three low-functioning, teenaged boys. They were fourth generation students at the Hotchkiss boarding school, the eldest residing at the Tobin Hall, a dormitory donated by their grandfather. Two of them were on academic probation, and the youngest minutes from requiring rehab for his early-onset marijuana addiction. This summer, she'd sent them all on expensive Outward Bound trips to learn to step up to the plate a little in life. Topper asked Katie to come in and lured her into the gauntlet of the planning committee.

In the hallway, Katie noticed Topper's felt, baby-blue, three foot by five foot Hotchkiss Bearcats school banner. Topper thought it "cute" at age forty-three to display an emblem of her past. She had chosen not to exert herself much ever since her field hockey heyday when she had peaked in every psychological and physical way on that hallowed team. Katie followed Topper's portly frame out to the back deck.

Two spoiled King Charles spaniels pranced around, sniffing at Katie's ankles. The Tobin house was small by Hamptons standards, more the size of the Porter cottage. It had no pool, only a small lawn and a patio filled with gardenias in run-of-the-mill red clay planters. (Why waste money replacing something that lasts?)

"We are so happy that our handsome George Porter plucked you from God-knows-where's-ville out West," Topper yelled back at Katie without turning to look. "We hear you both just hit it off. We wanted to make you feel part of the efforts of our club to give back because that's soooooo a part of what we do."

Katie may have been a relative ingénue with the clubby crowd, but she knew helping the less fortunate souls of Long Island sooooooo wasn't part of what they do. Katie wondered right away whether this whole committee was a ploy to make these Ivy League graduates feel like they'd done something with their lives besides spawn blond children with good teeth. She was ready to play the part, and walked onto Topper's deck in her best Seabrook imposter outfit.

George had been very kind during Katie's third week, and had taken her to a store called Calypso St. Barth's in town that sold high-end Indian paisley-style blouses. He told her when socializing with the club women, she'd feel more comfortable wearing similar dressy-meets-dressed-down clothes.

"It will go smoother for you. Trust me," he'd said and kissed her forehead at the counter, feeling victorious. He'd purchased four silk caftans, two bright cashmere shawls for chilly Hamptons nights, and one pair of silver sandals. "I want you to feel comfortable. Just as you'd want me in a rugged type of Patagonia jacket out West and not some seersucker blazer from my club looking like the Eastern nerd I am."

He'd squeezed her arm softly to reassure her. And though he kept figuring out ways to keep that paper napkin COME EAST, NO STRINGS aura in conversations and actions, Katie couldn't shake the feeling that George wasn't as laid-back as he let on.

She knew laid-back people didn't notice clothes. And they didn't go into a specific store to buy exact clothes so that someone looks the part. A few other times, when he'd asked her to confirm three or four times that she wouldn't be coming to the club, she'd wondered if there was another woman there. Or, if he had been concerned that she wouldn't fit into some lunch group he had.

When she'd called Ashley in San Francisco for her opinion, she had countered, "Remember, George is a man who likes making sure the plan works. He's showing kindness, and taking care of you and your needs. Looking great is a need in the Hamptons. He's subtly helping you ease in, fit in. He's sexy in his knowing ways. Don't come up with little nitpicky arguments to fuck this up for no reason."

The two women already sitting in uncomfortable wrought-iron chairs smiled at Katie as if they'd just sucked on a huge slice of lemon. They radiated that orgasm-free lifestyle so unique and universal among Seabrook women. Both women matched in white shorts, Jack Rodgers sandals (circa 1971 Jackie Onassis in Capri) and a collared tight polo shirt. The super-fit Anne "Cricket" Fitzgerald had a short brunette bob, held back by a tortoiseshell hair band that she'd been using for fifteen years now. She was bone-thin and resembled a praying mantis. Very disciplined and military in her timing schedules, Cricket starting guzzling down cheap club Chardonnay starting at 2:00 p.m. each day during her child's tennis lessons, running off the alcohol with a seven-mile sprint every morning down Beachwood Lane.

On the right sat Bitsy Fainwright (named because she had "itsy-bitsy" toes as a baby and the moniker stuck forty-two years later). Bitsy didn't talk much, she more often reacted to conversations by smoothing down her 1950s bouffant-style ponytail that made her look twenty years older than she was.

"Let me serve you a refreshment," Topper said, as she poured Katie a too-sweet lemonade powdered drink. Both the glasses and pitcher had faded yellow daisies on them, and were a little cracked inside the plastic, looking very Sears 1963.

"The cottage is a little bit in need of an update. We keep meaning to redo it," Topper went on aimlessly to no one in particular. "But I've been so busy working on the books for the local children . . . well, we are grateful for the club Patio Party help because we desperately need volunteers like you, Katie. We have a committee, several chairs of that committee, different planning groups of that committee, the society photographers coming, the invites out."

"Those invites . . . the back and forth over which color, design, Jesus!" exclaimed Cricket, topping up her white wine to the rim for the third time in fifteen minutes. Topper patted her wrist to remind her of her plan to cool it with the Chardonnay during daylight hours.

"And do the children whose families can't afford to buy books come to the party with their parents?" Katie asked, just to poke these women a little where it counted.

Topper sniffed in for a very long while at Katie's pointed question. "Well," she answered, pursing her lips in a *fuck you lady* way. Katie noticed everything these women said to her ended in a question, connoting, *Don't you know that, you moron?* "You know, it's really just our crowd at the Patio Party?"

Bitsy nodded silently in agreement.

"But we do show some photos of the less fortunate families who come in the library, on Wednesdays when the mother-and-child center brings the little darlings to read," Topper explained. She huffed a little. "I guess we could invite a few Hispanic families to parade around a little. Or is it just all those Brazilians out here? They don't speak Spanish in Brazil, right? It's Portuguese?"

"Just curious," Katie persisted. "Who are we helping exactly? Which families, where do they live?" Katie had the sudden urge to run and tell Luke every phony detail about these people. He would then try to top her with a story of his own about some camp mom he'd encountered. She trusted Poppy's assertions: the old guard values of the club stood for preserving the town and helping those less fortunate. But some members were simply playing the part and planning parties for the society flashbulbs.

"Well, there's a mother-child center, way off," Bitsy Fainwright finally piped in. "I've been there, beyond the train tracks. It's a shelter of some kind. I hear some of the mothers, who are cleaning ladies, have kids in the public schools. They don't have husbands. A few of them have cancer and need some kind of medical help. I just *know* the extra help with their children and reading is life-altering for them."

"Enough with all this depressing talk!" Cricket Fitzgerald yelled way too loudly, waving her arm in the air, the sagging chicken skin underneath the bone wagging as she did.

Topper quickly moved the Chardonnay bottle on the floor, and added, "Let's talk about what we are *doing*. Katie, you've had your assignment to decorate the table . . . we could guide you, of course? The Patio Party, as we call it, is so alliterative, we just love the name! Just think: beach extravaganza!"

"So it's beach themed." Katie struggled to comprehend. "But on a patio or on the sand?"

"On the patio at the library!"

"But you said beach."

"Well, beachy feel is what I mean. We have a great guy with ducks and bunnies and a petting zoo for the kids, a few authors read their children's books to our young children, who just looooove it. The dads have a grand time, debating golf and grilling techniques."

"I'd love to help," Katie offered, trying to hide that she didn't mean that at all.

"The tables are sooo fun? Each table is themed!" said Cricket. "Of course no one is sitting at them. It's all about how they look, how they add to the atmosphere, how they help give the party a little boost of patio pomp."

Poppy was way cooler and more on the ball than any of these women, and Katie bet, so were her generation of bridge-playing girlfriends. She felt they could share a little giggle about the seriousness with which Topper took the table décor.

"You know, I know this woman who has great taste," added Katie, thinking of Julia, just to test her insistence that they'd never accept her kind. Clearing her throat, she said, "She isn't a member of the club, but Poppy had said a few others can buy tickets, and I know she's very generous. Her clothing is gorgeous, I bet she could help us."

The three women at the table rolled their lips inwards, in deep distrust, and looked at each other. Cricket listed sideways and closed her eyes for a minute, while Bitsy sensibly rammed a pillow between the iron grate chair and her elbow, propping her up a bit.

Katie went on, "She has a really spectacular home on the ocean."

"Oh, soooo great?" offered Topper. "Where on the ocean?"

"Middle of Beachwood Lane," answered Katie, knowing Topper was trying to make some kind of social totem pole calculation.

"Which house *exactly*?" Bitsy squinted her eyes at Katie, leaning in and grabbing the edges of her chair with her porky hands. Bitsy hoped to avoid an uncomfortable moment with George Porter's latest, sweet, but, out-of-it, Pacific-bred frontier girl. She hoped the woman's house was traditional and old, preferably with an owner-ship deed passed on by a great-great nana.

"I don't know the street number," Katie responded to the pit bull clothed in a pink polo to her left.

Cricket put her hands on her knobby knees and leaned in for the inquisition, taking her eightieth gulp of wine. "Okay, well let me ask this, is it old or new construction? Meaning is the house modern with glass like a, say, really goddamn tacky Saudi shopping mall?"

"Cricket, please!" said Bitsy. "Don't swear like that!"

Cricket grabbed the bottle of wine under the chair, almost tip-ping over her own, filled her glass beyond the brim so it overflowed a bit, took three huge gulps and continued, "Or is it kind of cute and shingled and gray with white trim on the windows? Maybe some sweet window planters like . . ."

Katie knew exactly what this gauntlet was getting at. Anyone with a hint of trendiness wouldn't be wanted in their ossified world of conventions.

"It's a new home," Katie admitted boldly.

The three women gasped as if they'd just sniffed a pile of fresh, steaming cow dung.

"Her name is Julia Chase. I think she'd love to help out."

"Nope?" answered and asked Topper matter-of-factly. "We know of her. She's just lovely as can be, but the committee is full?"

When Katie had walked into this stifling, decrepit back patio, hadn't this very same Topper Tobin said they were soooo desperate for volunteers?

Chapter Thirty-Two

Home Is What You Make It

"H oney, I'll pull the chair up to the sink. You can't reach like that from the floor," Katie told Huck that Friday night as he stood on his tiptoes trying to wash just-pulled-from-the-earth lettuce.

As he did with most nights, Huck wandered into the kitchen around 6:00 p.m. when he first heard his mother searching for oils, sauces, and spices, the cupboards opening and shutting. The two were used to this nightly ritual of Huck working alongside her on setting the table, putting water in glasses, and finding the salt and pepper shakers. His daily obsession with building Legos translated into a love not for clean order, but for the *order of things;* and he was drawn to the step-by-step process of preparing a meal.

Like her son, this night, Katie also yearned to understand the order of things and the reasons behind them. Namely, why George couldn't confirm if he'd be there for dinner when he'd said all week he was looking forward to time with them. Or, more disturbingly, why she'd landed on the farthest tip on the East Coast having lived and planned her entire life out West.

Katie checked her phone for the nineteenth time since 4:00 p.m. when it started to seem like George might not show. He'd texted:

> Trying to get there in time, something came up at work and also at the club, just need to check on a few things . . .

Did that mean, there was a chance he wouldn't come at all? Or, that he'd be late? Katie had asked that very question directly in a text two minutes later. It was now six forty-five, and there was no answer. Maybe he was still in Manhattan working, or was he already playing golf? If he were at the club talking to people (where rules prohibited cell phone use), that would mean he hadn't looked at his.

Flustered at no reply when she'd added four simple, slightly pushy question marks on the text reply again to George at 6:48 p.m.:

> Any time frame for your arrival????

Katie slammed the lamb roast onto the wooden cutting board and stormed out of the kitchen.

She started to open all the windows all over the cottage as if to blow some fresh insight into her life. The air conditioners banging in both rooms had kept her awake all night, wondering and wanting a plan that felt more solid. As she turned off the cold air and slammed open several rickety windows, Huck asked from the kitchen sink, "What's the matter, Mom, are you mad at me?"

"No, honey, it's just the dust; it's cooler out than I thought and the fresh air is so nice. I just want to let a lot in and if I open both sides of the house's windows, then it will blow through better."

"But why are you doing that all so fast like you're mad at someone?"

"Honey. I'm not." *Slam, slam, slam.*

"You are, but whatever," Huck answered.

As she shook the white curtains out a bit at each window, her anger at George's inconsiderate behavior swelled inside. *Where was he? How long does it take to text? Who doesn't check their phone in three hours? Well, that cute Luke Forrester wouldn't do this, for sure. Why hadn't . . .*

"Honey, can I just wash the vegetables tonight?" Katie asked, as she entered the kitchen again. The setting sun now illuminated the room with a sideways orange glow. "This lettuce is different from back home; it's from local farms and really dirty. Just, George is coming soon, I'm so late because of my tutoring . . . can I just wash it, please?"

Katie felt the heat of tears in her eyes, but willed them to cool and dry. She blinked a dozen times, cracked her neck left and right, and rolled her shoulders. In a trance, she stared at the yellow tiled linoleum floor with her hands on her hips, then shook her head a bit to disperse her foul mood. She would not cry, not now. Maybe in the bath later, but not in front of Huck, not with George (maybe) on the way. The cold water in the pot before her waited to be boiled for fresh summer peas. The ruby lamb begged for rosemary and garlic marinade she hadn't had time to prepare.

Katie knew dinner would have been better with marinade soaked on the meat hours ago, but the tutoring hours had stacked up last minute. Splashing it on now would coat it a little, but no flavor would sink in. This whole meal was feeling a little like her relationship with George: the flavor fresh and powerful, but the foundation rushed.

"Why?" Huck persisted. "I want to wash it, put it in that dryer thing, then I want to push the button to make the lettuce dryer go round."

"It's just—" Katie didn't want to squash her son's culinary talent, but she also didn't want to serve a sandy salad to George. "It's dirtier when we get it at a farm stand, filled with worms and bugs and dirt." Her eyes heated up again; she blinked hard.

"No, I can . . ."

There was no appeasing this child when he wanted to do something, and she didn't want to deny him his will to help. Katie's own mother, now three months, three weeks and four days gone, often told her, "Do these two things every day for Huck: number one: make him feel good about himself, and, number two: allow him to figure out how to do things on his own. Those two simple steps. Every day. It's all he needs to plow forward and grow into a strong, happy man. Single mothers, with far less than you, have had triumphant children. Children only need one good parent."

All they need is one. But, Katie plus her mother equaled two adults in his life, not one. And both of them understood that reality as her mom started to fade in her last month on earth.

"All they need is one," her mother had reassured her.

Katie had spent the final weeks asking her mother again and again to remind her of the steps for her son, knowing the steps would work on her, too.

Katie huffed loudly. She'd persist. She'd slam the dust out of the furniture fifty times a day if she had to. She'd get Luke's fingerprints on that beach-ball Simone butt out of her head. Tonight, she'd direct her innate sensuality on that handsome George Porter, assuming he showed up.

"Okay, fine, honey. If you really like washing the lettuce on your own and you feel you can get the mud out," Katie told Huck. "Then just do it. Wash it well. I don't want to eat a worm!"

Huck laughed at the sink, washing it again. "I'll do it, Mom. You think I'm such a baby." And he tried his very best to rinse the leaves, then sat on the floor in a little puddle of just-washed lettuce water, pushing the knob up and down as the still-insect-filled lettuce spun round.

"How come you are dressed up, Mom?" Huck asked, his legs spread out around the salad dryer. "Is Luke coming, too?"

Katie wondered how kids felt the earth rumble before the rest of the world even perceived a stir.

"No, why Luke? That's a strange thing to say. I mean, I get Luke, he's great, honey, but dinner isn't necessarily . . . well, he's more someone we would see on the boat or beach. Dinner here at the house, George's house, is not for Luke."

Katie knelt down to Huck's level on the floor to be absolutely positive he heard her. "Honey. George is coming. He's a wonderfully kind man. This is his house. He's not my boyfriend, as I said the other night when I put you to bed, but he might be at some point."

"You kissed him."

"I'm allowed to see if I like him, right? That's what that kiss was for, honey, kind of to see how he feels as a boyfriend. That's what grown-ups do, they . . ."

"Stop, Mom."

"Okay, no more kissing talk. You're the one who brought it up." She stood and rubbed his white-blond hair. "Let's just be really nice to George. And . . . let's not . . . let's not hurt his feelings by acting like we'd prefer Luke or anyone else."

"But I'd like Luke to come, too. Can he? Can he and George come together? He's been here, dropping me off."

"Not together, honey. Luke stays at the beach and his house, and George, well, he works so hard in the city. He's so nice to us. Remember that first day when we picked those cherries back home, remember how he helped you reach them and pick so many?" Katie pleaded. "Let's focus on him, tonight. Just like you tell me to focus

Chapter Thirty-Three

Blue Video

With Huck long asleep, the lamb still marinating in the fridge, the unused, washed but wormy lettuce packed tightly in a Ziploc in the bottom fridge drawer, Katie now lay propped up on her bed. The television's glare had turned the entire room a haunting blue tint. She felt lonely, and disturbed that George hadn't shown. A man had to work; she had no choice but to understand. She'd texted him back that it was fine.

In the closet, undressing, she'd found the carved pinewood box with her mother's remains. She hadn't wanted to hold it much this summer, preferring instead to forge on on her own. Tonight, she needed her mother. She felt raw, uncared for, completely alone.

The summery, spaghetti-strap dress with the tight bodice and cascading silk skirt she'd saved for tonight's dinner fell on her curves in a way that made her want to twirl. It was not meant to be worn in a dark cottage, alone with one's child. She now hung it, wrinkled for no good reason, back in the closet. Everything was unappreciated this night, even the fireflies. While they'd waited for a text, the dinner prepped, Katie had suggested they play out-on you only, not my phone or my tutoring papers. Same for George, he was so nice that other afternoon, with the Lego destroyer wing, when you couldn't find the piece, and I couldn't, and then he got on his hands and knees for like ten minutes and found it beside the plant? You wouldn't have ever finished that thing properly and *he found it!*" Katie added a little hysterically as if George had yanked Huck off a sinking boat. And then with more measure and calm, "Let's just give him a chance."

That advice was meant for everyone in the room.

Finally, as Huck finished setting the table, a text from George came through.

I'm so sorry, I'm delayed with a deal. Traffic to the Hamptons will be deadly. I'll call in the morning.

side. Huck had caught nine fireflies for George and kept them in a mayonnaise jar. He'd had to let them go before bedtime.

On her bedside stood a three-quarter filled, very special Wölffer Estate Vineyard rosé wine that Katie opened for dinner with George. She wasn't much of a drinker and had been in a rush to get home to Huck, but she'd tried a few varietals and bought this good bottle. Now she wished she'd saved it for Luke. She placed her fingers on her silk underwear, letting them softly caress the fabric until it moistened a little, wondering how Luke's own fingers would do the same.

Chapter Thirty-Four

Midweek Mojo

In the heat of the July sun, a Filipina housekeeper in a starched white uniform raced down Beachwood Lane on a child's bicycle, a tennis racket in the basket. The bike was so small she had to ride with her elbows bent upwards, her back hunched over. Her knees bounced up and down furiously as she pedaled.

"Look at that poor woman," Luke said to Katie. "Imagine her boss: some horrible woman blaming her because her child forgot his racket at the club. The kid has probably never once done anything on his own."

"I'm sure you're right. That bike is so small, she looks like a circus clown," agreed Katie. "I feel bad for her; she looks so sweaty and worried." She thought about her first day when she was hopeful Southampton wouldn't be that different from Hood River.

The shores of the bay were now peaceful, as if after a hurricane. After a beach walk to her favorite log, Katie had strolled up to camp to get her son. She and Luke were now sitting on a bench at the end of the dock, all of the exhausted campers having left, while

Huck rinsed off the life jackets. She wore her tank top wrapped around her neck, falling down the sides covering the front of her pink gingham bikini. Luke noticed Katie's creamy skin glowing in the afternoon light and wondered if he'd ever touch her for real.

A silenced ensued. Finally, Luke dove in with something he'd wanted to say for a while.

"So I was thinking about the last time we were on this dock and Simone . . ."

"Not important." Katie felt awkward, but intensely curious.

"It's important to me. I just want you to know she's an old girl-friend, or, really, a tormenter of men."

"It's fine, you can do whatever . . ."

"I know I can do whatever I want. So can you. I just want you to know it was a period in my life, that's all. She's not even a friend. I don't want people thinking she's my friend," Luke said.

"Why?"

"Well, can't you answer that, kind of?" Luke challenged.

Katie laughed, feeling the ice break loudly. "Yeah, I get it. She's a lot to handle. Takes up a lot of space."

"Like all these kids and parents at camp," Luke agreed. "They all take up a lot of space. That's the last thing I need in a partner. It's so nice with them gone at the end of the day."

"You know," Katie went on, "you hear about everyone over-scheduling their kids, people do that back home, but here it's just another level. That poor nanny on the kid's bike, in such a panic over his activity. I'll always think about that image when I try to describe the Hamp . . . I mean Southampton."

"There you go!" Luke answered. "Good job. Kona and I always say, 'If you're a rich kid in Southampton, the more lined up your schedule is, the less your parents love you.'"

"Why?" Katie smiled. She shielded the late day sun from her green eyes and turned to him.

"Rich people will do anything to get rid of their kids," he explained. "When we have sudden summer monsoons, lightning, and torrential downpours in the middle of the camp day, the richest of the rich kids never, ever get picked up early."

"Really?"

"Yeah, the moms would rather have them shivering in the back of my van with a rusty, metal floor bed and Chinese coal factory level emissions pumping out the back than miss their core crunch Pilates class. We're talking children whose parents have enough funds to finance a presidential campaign. Even the little ones huddled in the back, with rain pelleting the roof and lightning blazing all around us, ask, '*Why isn't my Mom here?*'"

"Well, why don't they come really?" Katie asked.

"The only answer we can come up with is that heavy hitters *really* need their downtime. Even if we all had T-shirts that said, 'we are all child molesters,' they would still say, 'hey, it's only three hours.'"

Katie laughed again, while Huck walked up to them.

"Thanks, Huck," Luke said, and handed him two one-dollar bills.

Huck's eyes bulged. "What's this for? For me?"

"Well, honest pay for a day of honest work."

"But I didn't work the whole day, I just helped clean up like you asked," Huck answered.

"Well, do you see any other kids here? Does anyone help as much as you?"

Huck kept his eyes open without blinking and shook his head left and right.

"In fact, I'll go help you spend it if you want. What about it, Katie, can I take him into town?"

"Mom, please?"

"Don't beg like that, honey, give me a second to figure out what we're doing after. It's so nice, you know, just us," Katie said to Luke.

Just us? Luke thought to himself, looking at the way her bare back curved beautifully as she placed her elbows on her knees.

"It feels like heaven today," Katie continued, not aware of the wishful *does she or doesn't she like me* loop going on in the man's head next to her. "During the weekend it feels like a bus terminal of people trying to flee some natural disaster."

"I get it. At pickup, we always wonder, *what is wrong with you people?*" Luke felt victorious making her smile so much, and even laugh at some of his observations on life here.

Katie took her hat off, and nervously put her hair in and out of a ponytail.

Luke felt an unusual confidence take over, possibly because Huck had climbed from the back of the bench onto his shoulders now, half distracting him, and he could talk as if the questions were no big deal. No more lame proposals as when she was on the beach with Julia.

"So, can we possibly hang out somewhere that isn't my job on a boat?" Luke asked. "Can I show you both around a little after camp or, make Huck those s'mores?"

Luke couldn't size up the roadblocks presented by this George guy Huck had mentioned. He knew that he came out only on some weekends, never showed his face at camp, and somehow helped Katie rent the house his father forbid him ever to step foot in.

"Huck, do me a favor. Go get me my phone in the boat, I left it there, and my glasses. You can get on the boat yourself now. You're learning well, just hold on, if you can wipe the cabin a bit too, please."

As Huck climbed back to the ground and bolted back to the boat, Luke figured the tasks would take the kid a good five more minutes, so he went even further, "So, can you do that, or is that George guy going to get mad?"

Shit. "I, uh, he's not out here now," Katie said, then blew out a little oxygen. "George is not really here much until August. I just met him this spring and we had this idea, I'd come out."

"An idea? Where he is? What do you mean?" Luke stared at the other end of the dock and jammed his tongue into the roof of his mouth, trying to displace the tension building inside him.

"I mean," Katie said, faltering, "I mean, he's just not really here much . . . and I didn't really expect it to be so different from . . . like all these crazy rich people like you say, with their poor nannies having to ride their children's miniature bikes in a panic, or be fired. All the huge homes, even Julia who is great and so welcoming to me, but she's still living in this enormous compound."

"Can I ask you about your cottage? George's family?"

"I'd rather not. I don't know them well," Katie answered.

"Do you know who lived in the cottage you're staying in before? Like, fifteen to thirty years ago?"

"God, I don't think it was anyone from the family. They only have guests in there, I think."

Luke wondered what his father had been alluding to, saying he could never step foot inside. It must be a guest with a sordid past. "Okay, I won't ask about the family."

Katie fidgeted with her ponytail again and went on. "And I didn't understand how far the city was—too far to drive out for dinner. Not that I miss George when he's working in the city."

"You don't?" Luke was loving all this making her nervous. If he could only be this confident more often.

"I just mean"—she swallowed hard, trying to explain—"for getting together plans, logistics, it's more spread out and complicated than I . . . But then, he works so much in New York and he's busy with golf and his projects and . . . so we don't really see him much."

"What projects?" Luke gained more nerve; seeing her so flustered had to be a good sign in his favor. He stood up in front of her to feel tall and just move a little. "So, he's out a lot or not that much or . . ."

"I don't know, there's stuff he's always running to. He has responsibilities that I don't really understand, and then he wants to be with all these people. And . . ." she said nervously as he edged closer to her. "Honestly I don't really like that many people out here."

"You don't like anyone?" Luke pressed. The more nervous and apologetic she got that she was even with someone beside him, the bolder he felt. He took another step so he was standing with his toes touching hers, and now bent a little so his knees grazed hers. "You came for a trial summer and gave up the gorgeous snow-covered Cascade mountains and not one person even makes you smile or . . ."

"You like Luke, Mom!" Huck knew he was flipping open the bottle cap of pressure between these two grown-ups. "You told me so!" He'd crept back to their end of the dock to listen and now grabbed her neck from behind the bench with both arms.

"Honey, I thought you were back at the boat."

"You told me Luke was nice. You ask me all the time how he was at camp; you almost never ask about Kenny, or Kona, or that kid who helps."

"Of course I do, I ask about camp all the time, not just . . ."

"Can I go into town with him, please? And can we have dinner with him too instead of George this time? It's Luke's turn, you said it, right?"

"No, honey. It's getting late. I'm sure he has things to do."

Luke brushed his knees onto Katie's again. "We're actually going to do a beach barbeque, down by the jetty at the inlet. If you want to come, you can bring Huck, too. Sometimes we even surf before the sun sets. I'll take Huck in for a few waves on a boogie board. You like marshmallows, right, Huck? I told the guys that I would bring some dessert food, so he and I could go get marshmallows in town now and you can meet us?"

Katie put her head in her hands.

She had to say no.

"Okay. We'll come," she answered. "And Huck can go to town with you. I'll see you at the jetty at six?"

Chapter Thirty-Five

First Date . . . or Is It?

Luke had instructed Katie to wait for him and Huck at five forty-five by the entrance at the end of Beachwood Lane. She'd arrived early, passing private driveways leading to houses titled Pelican Dune and Blueberry Gardens. A helicopter pad stood across the lot on the bay side, weeds jutting up from the cracks in the landing circle. She heard the thud-thud-thud of propellers in the distance from the inside of her car.

Katie had never been this far down Beachwood Lane where all the wealthy people landed. A dark black helicopter arrived, the words *Blade* marked on the side. She covered her eyes, sand whipping hard into her face. Not familiar with the art of helicopter arrival, she was now doused in dirt. As the propellers came to a stop, a beautiful woman descended, the type who would not do well with a flake of dirt on her all-white Hamptons outfit. She walked to a handsome man in a convertible Mercedes who had pulled up to the lot with perfect timing.

And then, just like that, the Blade helicopter was gone. Minutes later, the convertible was parked in a garage down the lane. And the woman, having her chilled Chardonnay poured, was miffed that her stylist hadn't picked out earrings for the new Gucci cocktail dress she'd just changed into.

After wiping the dust off her face, Katie figured she'd go down to the sand to get some air while she waited for Luke and her son. She walked out along the sea grass, trying to find a pathway to the ocean through the weeds and trails. She wondered what it would be like to take Huck into Manhattan on a helicopter, how many tutor sessions she'd have to teach to pay for two seats.

She stopped for a moment and leaned over, hands on her knees, thinking, *This is fine. It's cool. George is in the city, what does he expect me to do, not make some friends? This is just a little Wednesday night adventure. It has nothing to do with the fact I need a man who would never wear khakis.*

When she couldn't find a clear route, Katie decided against a walk into the trails between the lot and ocean, and sat on the log railing of the parking lot. Her nerves made her tap her feet and hit her knees with her hands as if there were a jazz orchestra behind her.

Her phone rang.

"Hey, baby," George said. "Manhattan is a concrete furnace this week. I just wanted to hear what you're doing."

Katie fumbled with her earphones nervously and jammed them into her ears.

"Oh, wow, glad you called, just at the beach with Huck."

"Can I talk to him?"

"I mean, I'm waiting at the beach for Huck."

"Well, who's driving him there?"

"Uh, just a, uh, mom, from the club, they . . ."

"That's great, nice, which one? I'll be sure to thank her for welcoming you."

"There were some moms there and a play date with a bunch of kids, and I'm not sure which one was driving. It's really hard for me to remember."

"Hey, that's fine, Katie," he said kindly. "This isn't an inquisition, I'm just wanting to know how you're doing. I want you to know I miss you, if I'm allowed to say that. I hate working this hard."

"I work hard, we all do. I get it." She played nervously with long leaves of sea grass, pulling threads off them and twisting them tightly on her fingertips. "Are you coming out, because we haven't seen each other and, well, I'm fine, but hopefully by August you'll be out more." She wasn't at all sure she meant that.

Katie heard the sound of tires against gravel, and turned to see Luke's van roll into the lot.

"George, they're arriving. Let me call you later. Bye." She hung up more abruptly than she would have liked.

As Luke stopped, slamming on the breaks, clouds of sand and dust spewed all over her again. A White Stripes song from eight summers ago blasted out of his van.

Luke rolled up to the edge of a trail and got out to reduce the tire pressure before driving on the sand. "Over here! We gotta go in by this lane. Hurry up, the sun won't be out much longer and I promised Huck I'd get him into the ocean a bit. We can body surf."

"Boogie board," yelled Huck assertively from the filthy side seat. "The *Star Wars* one."

Katie walked slowly up to the van while Luke knelt at each tire. "Huck, you're in the front seat? What is going on?"

"There's no backseat, and no air bags. This is a 1989 surf van. He's good. Get in," Luke said, smiling, the sun from behind lighting his hair as he looked at her.

Another helicopter landed, and both Luke and Katie shielded their faces from the dust.

"That's the second one tonight," she told him.

"Usually not many land on a weeknight," Luke answered. "You do know there's an Uber-type of helicopter company?"

"No way."

"Of course. It's the 'Hamptons,' as you call it."

"I don't!" She smacked his shoulder. "Not anymore."

"It's an app called Blade. You push a button, pay like seven hundred bucks, and book a seat on a flight. Or, for like five grand, you can get the whole helicopter. Kona checked it out and even got an account, because it seemed too crazy."

"You're serious? Uber-style app for helicopters?"

"Yep."

"I think I just saw a Blade helicopter before you arrived or I wouldn't believe you."

She hopped in the car on the passenger side, while Huck moved and crouched on the center console. It was nearing six o'clock, but the sun still beat down on her face. She held her hand out the window, allowing it to brush along the bushes that lined the trail. As they reached a clearing at the top of the dune, the salty breeze from the ocean caused the temperature to drop by ten degrees.

"I wish you could windsurf by the jetty. I'd love to see you do it."

"I told you, it's way out toward Montauk where I go. I like to do it alone. But, that's a shame because it's better than surfing, I promise, so fast and the ride is forever."

"Nothing's better than surfing, it's just you and the water, not all the sails and contraptions. Pure. Simple." He winked at her. He felt a little bolt of Kona in him for once.

"Are you sure these are houses down here and not hotels?" Katie asked, looking at the homes with landscaped decks and infinity pools. "They must have ten bedrooms. It's straight out of *The Great Gatsby* or something."

Luke stared at her until she had to turn his way, which she did for a moment before looking back at the houses to her right. He drove a little more down the sand, then said, "I always wonder how much money you have to have in the bank to own one of these houses, another huge apartment in the city, and a house in Aspen. And of course trips to France in the summer even though you use this house for only three months. What do you think, how much? A bunch of the families at Tide Runners seem to live like that."

"No clue," Katie answered, shaking her head. "Maybe fifty million? Maybe a few hundred? On the news they were saying the richest one percent in the United States now own more wealth than the bottom ninety percent," she answered, looking at Huck beside her, and signaling to Luke this wasn't the best conversation. She changed the subject, and asked, "What did you boys do in town?"

"We bought chocolate and marshmallows and orange soda for me," Huck answered, knowing she didn't allow sugary sodas, and irreverently toasted a glass bottle of frosty Orange Crush at her.

"That's healthy," Katie responded. "Lots of protein, low sugar. Great."

"Oh relax, Mom," answered Luke. "We'll get a hot dog that'll fill him up."

In the distance near the jetty, Katie saw pickup trucks and jeeps, some vehicles backed into each other to create more side by side space for coolers and grills.

"Who are those people?" she asked. "Do you know all of them?"

"Most, yeah, pretty much all. We all share the same secret: it's magical down here at sunset and the best place to eat a meal."

The acrid smells of crackling flames, burgers spitting fat, and burnt marshmallows overpowered the salty air. A few larger Weber grills planted in the sand were glowing red while two different bonfires roared, a hundred yards apart from each other, spewing off curls of black smoke. Out at sea, a dozen guys in neoprene wetsuits bobbed in the waves on their surfboards as the sky turned from pale blue to light violet. Lined up against the sea grass, way past the last three estates and the evening picnic group, dozens of

Winnebago-style travel trailers were parked up against the dune, Katie noticed.

"People sleep down here? I'm so confused."

"Yeah. It's an odd mixture, I know." Luke smiled. "It's a state park at the tip of Beachwood Lane, so you can camp out on the beach for seventeen dollars a night, about a hundred bucks a week. Families all over Long Island come down here, put a trailer on the back of their pickups, and roll it down to the sand. They cook, camp out, socialize, have family time, and stay the whole week with the Atlantic before them. Apparently the spaces fill up in a few days once they release them online in the spring."

"Near all the big houses? Do the owners complain about trucks down here?" she asked. "Just seems like it doesn't make sense, the juxtaposition of the trailers, your trucks, and those huge homes."

"Oh yeah. Big issue in Southampton right now. The people who own those houses have organized all kinds of meetings to try to kick the trucks off the beach, or at least reduce how many. This is only the most beautiful beachfront property in America. Why shouldn't everyone enjoy it? That's my view, at least."

"Who is down here now?"

"Everyone here tonight grew up here, makes their living here. We think we have the right to fish, surf, cook dinner, and enjoy the same view. Only the locals have to do it from a truck, not a four thousand square foot kitchen with Viking appliances."

"How can they kick you off? Isn't the beach public?" Katie asked.

"They want to reduce the trucks, but fuck, yeah, it's public."

"I heard that!" Huck said.

"Sorry," Luke laughed. "State park, public beach, belongs to all taxpayers. Just like our camp. There's the Seabrook Club next door on our public beach, and they want to shut our camp down so we don't ruin their view. But, we've had the camp for ten years now. And a hundred of their beach chairs is okay? The same attitude is at play in both situations: we got more cash and, therefore, we get our way. But they don't even live in Southampton year round, what right do they have to . . . well . . . the more time you spend here, the more nothing will make sense."

They drove by a home that had twenty-four rooms facing the sea. Katie then asked, "Didn't the owners see the trucks, the helipad, the trailers at the park down by the jetty when they purchased these homes?"

"That's what I say!" Luke was getting more animated. "They bought it sight unseen on realtor dot com or what? They knew what they were getting into. Many of us are volunteer EMTs and firemen, too. The city people want the fifty million dollar home, but they don't want firemen living in the same town to enjoy the same views. They only want them to put out fires, the cops to handle a burglary, and the plumbers to save them from leaks. But no eating a grilled hamburger in front of a pretty view, that's only for people with a fifty million dollar second or third home. Bullshit."

"I heard that, too!" Huck said and toasted his Orange Crush at the air. Life was just beautiful when cool people cursed.

"I think," Katie answered, "if the owners are complaining afterwards, they gotta be thinking they got the house and it gives them the right to get whatever they want next."

"Yeah, like ruin summer nights for hundreds of families who've been coming down here for generations. Fuck those fucker vagrant city people, they . . ."

"That was the third f-word!" Huck yelled.

Katie knew Luke brought out the sloppy male side of Huck. It was good for him. It was good for both of them.

Chapter Thirty-Six

Playing with Fire

Luke parked his van near the gang of local water sports instructors and surfers, along with their friends and girlfriends. Katie put her flip-flops on the dashboard and looked at the Atlantic stretching out before her. She felt a slight chill and remembered she'd left her sweater in her car back in the lot.

Luke grabbed Huck out of the center of the van, and after helping him into his sandy, cold wetsuit he'd worn earlier at camp, tore into the sea without a word to Katie. First he held Huck's hand and helped him leap over the small crashing waves on shore. Katie watched them bounce in the white water for a while as Luke pushed Huck into a few waves on his boogie board. She then grabbed Luke's gray sweatshirt with a faded NEW YORK SUNSHINE logo on the front and walked timidly over to the bonfire.

A few younger women in their early twenties, about five years her junior, talked in a small group and didn't say hello. She looked for the friends of Luke whom she'd met—Kenny, maybe, or an instructor she knew. In the distance, she spotted Kona out in the waves cruising down the line and besting every surfer out there. He wasn't her type, but she watched his muscles glistening on his bare, wet skin, and his long hair flying behind him. Faster on his short board, and with tighter turns than anyone, he raced ahead of the crashing white water as if it were a pack of dogs behind him. She got why young, old, married, single, and wavering women fell in unison like dominoes before Kona. With no one to talk to, Katie turned to walk back to the van until Luke and her son got out of the water.

She felt a tap on her shoulder. "Wow. He got you to come to beach night." Kenny grabbed a beer from a cooler on the sand and twisted the top off for her. "Take it. Relax. Come meet my wife."

"Seriously, I'm fine."

Kenny knew better. "You don't look fine."

"I'm good."

A girl still in her short wetsuit had walked by her on her way to a cooler in the back of a pickup next to Luke's van. As she grabbed two more beers, she said, "Hey, I'm Sarah. I don't think we've met."

"I'm Katie."

"Are you here with Luke?"

"Yeah." Katie took a big breath to act all relaxed. "I mean, he's just a friend. We're here for the summer, my son and I. He had asked me to come to this cookout you guys do here on Wednesdays I guess."

Sarah looked at Katie like she was lying. "Yeah, we just kind of come here and chill. Great you could come."

"Don't mind her," whispered Kenny. "She's best friends with Luke's old girlfriend Simone. She was just sizing you up. Let's get you situated." He smiled kindly, and put his strong arm around her shoulders.

"Thanks, Kenny. I'm good."

Luke startled them by grabbing Katie's waist from behind, soaking her with his wetsuit. She laughed and pushed him away. He felt good against her, despite the soggy cold. She then raised her eyebrows unnaturally high, said in a high-pitched, chipper voice, "Let me dry off Huck and put him in new clothes. Then I'll come back to the fire and we can grill a hot dog. Sound good?"

THE NIGHTTIME DESCENDING fast, Huck, having eaten half his weight in chips and hot dogs, now sat between Luke and Katie on a huge tree log that lay beside the bonfire. The threesome suspended their grilling sticks for the marshmallows above the roaring coals. The gooey white stuck to their hands, and the hot melted chocolate dripped all over their jeans. A small cast-iron pan at the edge of the fire held bubbling strawberries.

Luke mushed a marshmallow onto a graham cracker with a block of Hershey's chocolate on it, placed another graham cracker top of that, then dipped the sides into the strawberries. Luke then held Katie's chin with the palm of his hand so the mess wouldn't drip everywhere. She took a huge bite that caused the whole creation to crumble into the sand. Luke put his arm tightly around her shoulder. "That's how you're supposed to attack one of these. I like it. Let's make another." He looked at her for a long time straight in the eyes, like he was going to kiss her right then.

A few moments later, Katie's perfectly caramel-crusted marshmallow fell into the flames. Luke laughed and started to hand his to her, rubbing his shoulder hard against hers.

"You're too gallant," said Katie, marveling at his masterpiece in the glowing firelight. "I couldn't, yours is too perfectly cooked. I'll start another."

"Take it. Here." He tapped her knee with his.

"I'm not taking yours, Luke!" She grabbed the sandy bag of marshmallows and stuck one on the edge of her stick. "I'm gonna start again, that's the whole point, patience and then, reward!"

Suddenly, a massive ball of flesh brushed Katie's cheek, and then a hand grabbed the marshmallow out of Luke's fingers faster than a frog would catch a fly with his tongue.

"Well, then I'll take it," Simone said, sitting down on the other side of Luke. She placed his perfect marshmallow he'd made for Katie onto a graham cracker. Then she started licking the melted sweetness off the sides in round circles, as if she were in the prelude moment of what would become an epic blow job.

"What are you guys doing down here?" Simone asked.

Luke didn't look her way. "What do you mean, 'what are we doing down here?'" Then he shook his head in disbelief. "I've come here every week. All summer. Ever since I was like fifteen years old. Why wouldn't I be here?"

"Whoa," Simone answered sarcastically. "Sorr-eeee. I just meant like the whole family down here. I've been doing the bonfire my whole life too and I was just, like, how come the newcomers, you know? Not that it isn't nice to have anyone—I'm just starting a conversation is all. Relax, Luke. Hey, Katie." She stretched her head around Luke and Huck to face her competitor in the ring head-on. "You want to come meet my girlfriends? We brought some wine. You might like that better than beer; most girls do."

"Hey, all. What's up?" Kona barged in. "Simone, why are you sitting by the fire? You always say the smell ruins your clothes? How come you're not with your girls?"

"I'm waiting for Jake Chase. I told him you all would be down here. He was looking for you guys by the bay and the docks."

"C'mon, Simone! That's so foul. Why would you tell him that?" Kona demanded. "Shit. Now we have to talk to him."

"Why is that so hard?"

Kona cocked his head sideways at Simone—and then grabbed her elbow and lifted her off the log. "Hey, Simone, let's get a drink. I got something to show you."

"I'm not going anywhere, Kona," she challenged.

As if on cue, Jake's $120,000 silver Defender Land Rover, a vehicle most often seen barreling through the Tunisian Sahara in the Paris-Dakar rally, bounced up and down over the bumps in the luscious Southampton sand. Jake had bought it to replace the Scout that had been destroyed in the sand earlier in the summer. He tried to maneuver it in the tire tracks, just as his driver waiting in the parking lot had instructed him to do, but the car proved to be too powerful. So he swerved left and right until he skidded in the sand just inches from Kona's Jeep. Kona had stood up a few moments before, as he had a sense this guy wasn't going to slow down in time. Thankfully he did, and Jake jumped out of the front seat as if he'd just parachuted out of a plane onto Omaha Beach.

"Whew, that was intense," Jake shouted to the group, as he saddled up to his newfound posse. "Jesus, that thing is hard to steer. But it's great. *Just great.* Handles brilliantly in the sand. So useful on a night like tonight. Don't know how I lived without it."

As he waddled over to the group, he thought, *Why the fuck anyone would want an airplane engine full of exhaust and noise in their ears is news to me. No shock absorbers, a ride where you hit your head on the roll bar, I don't understand. Plus you can't control the fucking thing because it slides right and left if you're not driving in tracks like a jet locked onto a target, not to mention your fucking driver has to come to the parking lot to get the air in the tires down.*

At this point, a dozen of Luke and Kona's friends were sitting tightly together on towels and low chairs around the fire. Jake stood behind Luke's friend who painted houses for a living, grabbing his shoulders in a hard Spock treatment. "Hey, buddy, you wanna move over for me, can you do that?" Jake sat down on the other side of Simone and made sure his thigh touched hers. She, in turn, brushed her ample bosom (everything was ample on Simone— thighs, ass, tits, lips, hair,) onto Jake's thigh as she grabbed a few marshmallows from the bag.

"So, hey, can't believe I'm out during the week," Jake yelled to anyone around the circle who could hear, trying hard to think of a joke to make them laugh. "You know, I've always wanted to spend a July week here, working on my thigh tone, taking some spin classes with all those dykes that flock to them. Nothing against lesbians! I'm as politically correct as the next guy, just, you know, their short hair, kinda, maybe they should grow it a little?"

All the local guys and their girls around the fire looked at Luke and Kona, wondering why they had invited this kook. Several shook their heads visibly. Kenny stood instantly. "Hey, guys, I'm gonna roll out."

Luke rolled his eyes at Katie, whispering, "She's such a nightmare, why would she ask him here? It's not his place."

"So I actually took a class!" Jake yelled out to no one in particular. "It was awful. Who needs Soul Cycle classes with those teachers yelling at you, all the candles and shit, right?? I like nature! The fire! I mean, I like hanging out with people like you, who run on the beach and shit, right? You just fuckin' work out in the outdoors, you bike on the roads, you swim in the sea right here? I love the beach, I mean the sand is getting ground into my ass, but fuck it, I even like that!"

Reminding himself these guys probably didn't have a caterer down here, or even, fuck, a server of any kind replenishing the drinks, Jake looked behind him impatiently at the setup: empty chip bags and smoldering hibachis lined on two pickups, two coolers with three Coke cans and two beer bottles, a Tupperware pan of mostly devoured seven-layer dip, the refried beans getting crusty and the guacamole now brown, grocery store baggies of hot dog buns, and three flat hamburger patties on wax paper, now being eaten by flies.

"Anyone got a pitcher of tequila or something? I could use a drink. Some margaritas on the rocks, who's got . . . you guys hear about that Moët Ice Impérial champagne they launched recently? It's very bubbly, you're supposed to drink it with ice like hip-hop stars do on their yachts in France. Champagne is really fuckin' tasty with ice, forget the name of the drink they call it. Don't want you to think I'm not macho, but I like it. Ever tried it? I could bring a case next week?"

Chapter Thirty-Seven

Take Back the Night

Luke blared a happy Red Hot Chili Peppers song from several summers ago on the way home. He wanted to boost the mood back to where it had been when he was driving down to the beach at sunset, then cozying up to Katie in front of the crackling embers, when she'd actually pushed up against him for a fleeting moment.

The night had mostly unfurled as he had planned: playing in the water under the moonlight, introducing Katie to his way of life a bit outside camp, and constructing his expertly executed s'mores for her just as Frank had taught him. He'd expected for that charged moment to start about now, when he'd feel like a teenager, trying to figure out how to kiss her good-night. Her eyes, the way she walked, her soft voice, her kind way—all of it made him think of nothing but her. Yet the good planning had gone south—instead of Katie included in his clan on the beach, she felt repelled by Simone, and so much by Jake, that she'd stood abruptly and said it was time to go.

When they arrived at her cottage, the sitter came out to Luke's van and asked Katie if she needed help getting Huck to bed.

"Yeah, that would be great. My car is actually out by the beach still, and I should go get it with our friend here," Katie answered, careful not to disclose the name of the man driving for fear the sitter would tell George.

Luke noticed that Katie was cagey with the sitter, and he wasn't so stupid he didn't know the reason. He was only grateful to get her out of the driveway, because the 37 Willow Lane cottage gave him creepy shivers.

As Luke drove backwards out of the driveway, he placed his right arm on the back of Katie's front passenger seat, and his fingers touched her right upper arm. She moved her shoulder slightly away, but he pushed his fingers into her flesh a bit.

She turned to him. "I just need my car."

"I know." He felt it was now or never. The guy she was with was clearly in the city.

"I thought I might be going out tonight so I asked the sitter to just wait, and that I'd pay her," she said. "I wasn't sure Huck would be with me, or what we were doing." She hoped he'd just pull over and kiss her already.

While he drove, Luke looked down at her thighs, her right knee bouncing against the van door to the music. Her legs were spread out in an inviting way he was sure she didn't mean. But, damn, they looked firm and fleshy all at once. Her shorts were riding up the seat, so they pinched the flesh on her inner thighs in a way that made him very much want to touch her. Feeling a rise in his pants, he pulled his shirt out from his stomach so it covered his midsection. "Who were you going out with when you booked the sitter? I thought you said you had nothing planned tonight. Do you usually get a sitter when you are there?" Luke asked.

"Just some women I met who were having wine at the vineyard tasting, from the tutoring place, they do it every week." Katie answered slowly, as if there weren't any plans with him in her mind when she booked the sitter. "The neighbor needs the work and she's been great, so I wanted to give her some hours and I thought maybe . . . I don't know, Luke." She paused, deciding to get real. "Honestly, I don't know what I'm doing here. In Southampton. In your van. I mean, I'm getting my car. I do know that."

Luke turned up the volume on a corny Justin Bieber song he hated admitting he loved. He tapped his fingers on the steering wheel, trying to come up with a suave riposte to her dangling question. He wanted to change the station to find something cooler, but the beat of the song was good.

At least he'd made some progress: he'd succeeded in washing away that ugly Jake and Simone scene. Now, he had Katie captive, no kid in the car. They had time on their hands with the sitter chick planted in Katie's living room. Back on some sort of track here. Just how to get her alone somewhere and out of the van? His shack was fine, but not necessarily the kind of place you want to bring a woman first off; he'd rather lie on the beach. In college, he'd had an old Yukon, and during the summers he'd put a futon in the back and would open the back trunk and the sunroof when he'd drive a girl on the beach. This musty van functioned for his job with all the boards and coolers, but didn't do wonders for seducing women.

They were now mere minutes away from her car. Luke tried to make it seem normal that he was now driving about eight miles per hour, so that he could avoid being seconds away from having to drop her off. Suddenly, he pushed on the accelerator and boldly drove past her car, down three lanes, and up a short dune hill with a drive-able dusty path. In front, the peaks in the small waves sparkled in the moonlight. It was a hill where surfers checked the surf break sandbar before deciding whether to suit up and go in. Katie didn't say anything while he put the van into park. She let him hum away, while he tried to figure out how to get her on the beach.

"Do you want a drink?" he asked. "I have iced tea, or a beer, a half bottle of wine in the cooler . . . or, way in the back, a couple hundred warm mini boxes of apple juice?" That made her laugh, which settled him down a little.

"Sure. I wasn't drinking much on the beach earlier because I didn't know if I was driving somewhere or what, but sure . . . I'll have a little glass of wine."

Luke opened the back door and got a blanket, his bottle of wine, and two coffee mugs, which he cleaned out with some ice and a filthy, sandy towel. Then, he reached into the front window and turned the keys. "Hey, let's go look at the moon for a little, then I'll drive you right back to your car."

Katie bit her bottom lip hard. "Sounds good. I love wine and moons." *Wine and moons?* "I meant, like plural nights with a moon or like lots of wine kinds." *Lots of wine kinds?* Ashley back home would tease her over these fifteen-year-old nerves rising up.

They walked down the beach to the shore, where Katie kicked the calm water up a bit with her bare feet. She told herself she needed to behave like a grown woman, not like a bumbling tenth grader. The cold water on her toes and the salty, damp breeze woke her up a little, and reminded her that she was indeed able to make a decision and take action. Maybe even talk like a grown-up.

She wasn't sure if Luke knew she was starting a relationship with George, nor did she know if he cared. She was sure that mentioning George would be a huge mood killer. So she gave herself leeway to do as she pleased. How was she to figure out how she felt if she didn't venture out a little?

When they walked back to the dunes, Luke laid down the blanket where the sand rose and poured two glasses of wine into the coffee mugs. After splashing the ocean water and staring up at the stars, Katie seemed happier.

She took a sip out of a dirty mug full of the horrible, slightly above room temperature white wine. It did its duty, instantly calming her down, maturing her spirit.

Luke leaned in her direction so his chest brushed her left side. She could smell the wine on his sweet breath. He told her, laughing a little after a moment, "You know, I kind of stalked you through town that first night I saw you in the store."

She turned and acted surprised. "What?" Katie felt invigorated suddenly, like she could make some mistakes in life and then fix them, and that was okay.

"The week after Memorial Day. You had these really preppy yellow shorts on, and the guys and I were hanging on a bench in front of the shop in town. We couldn't peg you. You didn't look like a stuck-up city person, but then you weren't from here, so we couldn't tell."

Katie laughed a little, wanting to know more. "So the stalking was just that night?"

"No. It went on a little. Then you brought Huck to camp and I had to act cool and figure out something to say."

"I don't remember what it was."

"Glad it was memorable. I just thought you were really pretty. And hot."

She looked at him, her mouth a little crooked. "Both?"

"Yeah."

"I'll take both. That's nice." She pulled her hair behind her ears and rubbed her ear lobes to massage some more calm in. She took another sip of wine and cupped the mug with both hands.

Luke had enough waiting. He took the dirty mug of wine out of her hands and put it on the far edge of the towel. He placed his hand gently on her cheek, turned her face toward his, and kissed her softly. First he pressed his lips on hers, then played with her lips and teeth with his tongue. With his hands on her cheeks in what-the-hell mode, he finally kissed her deeply as he'd wanted for six weeks now.

He guided her back down on the blanket, laid partially on top of her, grabbing her butt tight. Katie arched her back and pushed into him. He then reached inside the back legs of her shorts while she dutifully pushed his hands to safer grounds.

After he drew back his hands for a short while, he then glided his fingers in again to feel the outer boundaries of her ass and inner thighs, and tried to creep his fingers farther inside, but she pushed him away again. They tussled on the sand, grinding sand grains into their hair and clothes. He started to kiss her stomach suggestively, to line her shorts with his tongue. As he did so, she looked down at his handsome face silhouetted by the flickering reflections of the moon on the water. His manner was at first soft, then more aggressive than she'd have expected, then softer again. She liked all of it. A lot.

"I don't want to do everything tonight, here," she said. She placed her hand on his wrist, and pulled it from the edge of her panties.

"Well, I'm so sorry, Miss, but I actually want to do everything here tonight," he countered, which made her laugh a little.

"Well, I'm not going to let you," she said gently.

"I can't stand it."

"I'll succeed in not letting you."

He smiled and kissed her forehead. "Tonight you will. But not for long you won't."

Chapter Thirty-Eight

Steps of Doom

At 12:30 on a bright August day, Luke walked up the steps of doom. Only a woman would get him to tread on the dreaded Seabrook turf. He'd pulled his baseball hat with the Mets logo on it down to his eyebrows, and jogged from his van to make sure he could get past the walkway and ropes without any of his "colleagues" from camp seeing him.

Katie had refused to sleep with him, but their time together was nothing short of exhilarating: stolen moments in the back of the car when little Huck had been dropped off, furious make-out sessions on the beach at night, on a sandy towel, Luke gently fondling every body part he could. Katie always watched his dark profile as he kissed her breasts, the moonlight reflecting off the rippling currents below. He carefully took steps to make her feel cared for, but not crowded or forced. Every day since that Memorial Day in the shop, something about Katie flashed through his mind: her delicate gait, the crystal green of her eyes, the curve of her inner thigh, the way she smiled back when he flirted. He'd prevail, he'd just have to. His heart ached with a need to will it so.

"Can I maul you for real, please?" he'd asked her that very morning. "I'm not going to survive if you say no anymore."

She'd been weighing going full steam sexually with Luke when George suddenly started calling more at night, checking on her, as if he could feel her pulling toward another man.

"Hey, baby," George had said just the night before. "I bought you something today. It's a red garter belt. I'm going to FedEx it to you. I want you to wear it, with the matching bra, under that silly sundress you wear. Put it on under that. Play with yourself a little; drink half a bottle of wine before I get there, so you're ready for what I'm going to do to you."

Today, with George still in the city, she sat beside the Seabrook pool, the sweet lifeguard giving Huck tips for another swim meet. Huck now decided he liked swimming competitions more than he thought—so much so that he'd begged to have Luke come watch his progress in the pool. Katie figured sharing a grilled cheese with a guy from town was fine. It wasn't as if she and Luke were going to hold hands under the table; he'd come only to see Huck swim. The ladies at the club, Topper, Bitsy, and Cricket, would all be gathered at a far table, not even noticing.

As Luke bounded up the steps after the morning camp session completed, the guard immediately stopped him.

"Which family?"

"I, uh, it's Katie Doyle. I'm not sure she's with a specific family."

He smiled forcefully. "She gets whatever she wants . . . or I'll lose my job."

This seemed strange to Luke. This club, with their staunch membership committee that checked the pedigree of people's great grandparents, didn't let anyone in for the summer just because they rented a house nearby. Luke had always heard they actually kept

the non-Christians out by insisting every member have a grand-
parent who was also a member . . . and in the 1920s when those
Southampton grandparents were eating deviled eggs and ham
hocks, diversity wasn't exactly a catch phrase.

The more steps Luke took into the club, the more his apprehen-
sion set in. At the next entry area from the lawn to the clubhouse,
he saw a kid he grew up with working on the hydrangea plants that
lined the front of the clubhouse.

"Yo," Brian yelled and put his shears down in the posies by his
knees. He stood up. "Didn't know you were working here now? Are
the boats broken for good?"

This was why Luke didn't want to come here. He knew he'd
bump into people working he knew from grade school, the waves,
or town. "No. I don't know, Brian. It was a bad idea. I'm just meeting a kid from our camp. I've never been inside here so when they
suggested it, sure this is my last and only time."

"Yeah. Well it's a trip inside for sure, stuff you can't see on the
outside." The kid wiped his brow with the back of his gloved hand
and went back to pruning the bushes.

Luke walked into the clubhouse. The rug beneath his feet was
a hideous, tattered carpet with designs of flowers popping out of
baskets in the center and a pink, yellow, and green border. A silver
tub stood on a round center table, filled with inexpensive carna-
tions, roses, and baby's breath. Wooden plaques lined the walls
announcing the winners of the club singles, ladies, men's, mixed,
and member-guest tennis matches over the decades. The gallery
before him looked like a 1920s beach house that never had been
updated: wicker chairs with faded striped fabric; polished wood
side tables with coffee-table books first published in the 1950s;
and small Chinese blue-and-white pots with spare, sad bouquets.
Walking like a masked burglar, he tiptoed through the galley and
headed to the paned doors, where he could see the lunch patio

and pool, and then beyond them, the ocean, sparkling in the noon sun.

A gray-haired woman looked over her reading glasses disparagingly. "Can I help you?" she asked.

Luke, though dressed in real shorts and a clean shirt, knew he looked like he did not belong here, even as a guest of a member. She maneuvered around her mahogany desk. It had a 1970s style Rolodex wheel with the name and club number of each member. "Did Laurence check you in at the gate, was he there when you stepped onto club property?"

"I'm here to see Katie Doyle. Her son, Huck, wanted me here for the swim meet only, love that kid."

"Oh." She actually smiled. "Of course. Miss Katherine Doyle. I wouldn't step in her way."

So strange Katie, the newcomer, held sway. Sure, she could make yellow preppy shorts sexier than anyone, but why all these fawning comments from the gatekeepers?

Luke plowed forward out the paned glass doors, paint chipping in parts. He walked down twenty steps to a pool area teaming with little kids, their blond hair now a greenish tint from eight weeks of summer chlorine. It being Thursday, the fathers were few and the tables by the sea were mostly populated with women and kids of all ages: au pairs in from Sweden, moms, aunts, and grandmothers, all here to consume cold hamburgers and boiled turkey with like-minded people.

Luke spotted Katie at a table in a corner bordering the gate before the sand. She didn't present airs like she belonged here in her casual pants and T-shirt, but she didn't entirely look like she felt out of place. Katie timidly stood up and waved, then nodded to Huck, who was running from the pool to latch onto Luke's thigh.

"My mom made you come because there's a swim competition. It's a swim meet, and I'm going soon." Huck's white-blond hair had grown unruly since he'd arrived, his tummy was fuller and his cheeks chubbier from all the summer corn and ice cream.

Luke knelt down. "You think there's any other reason I'd be here, but you? I can't wait."

"Really. I appreciate it." Katie smiled. "I know it's not your scene, but Huck drove me so crazy. I told him okay, that I'd ask you to try your hardest to show." She looked deeper into his eyes. "And, I did know you'd show. So thanks."

Luke rubbed Huck's head and neck affectionately and pulled him into his leg. "I'm starving. I've a waterskiing private just after—do you mind if I order some food? A grilled cheese or two?"

"Sure. Let's sit and order."

As his lunch arrived, the American cheese only half-melted on the inside, Luke explained how this very club tried to kick the guys off public sand, and how Kona always clarified that it was a public beach and tried to convince them they had no case. He was about to explain how this tool, Bucky Porter, policed the beach like a dickhead Marine sergeant when he saw him coming toward their table.

Luke pulled his cap down as far as it would go and started wolfing down his sandwich—anything to go unnoticed. Bucky might say something terrible about him to this beautiful woman that he'd grown more attached to by the hour.

Unfortunately, Bucky headed right for their table. Worse, he slowed and crept up behind Katie as if he knew her. Luke could not believe what happened next: Bucky put his hands around Katie's eyes.

"Guess who?" he said, in an exaggerated deep, male voice.

He figured Bucky thought the new girl in town was cute—how could he not? Luke, cap further down, bowed his head and slurped on his 7UP straw to remain incognito. Katie placed her fingers on Bucky's trying to guess who was behind her. Luke could see her playful upturned smile transform into a literal upside-down U, like a cartoon character.

"I thought you weren't coming until the weekend because of your work?"

"I thought I'd surprise you in time for Huck's swim meet. Is that a problem?" Bucky looked at the guy at the table with the baseball hat covering his face. "Who's this?"

Luke stood up so fast, his chair bounced back on the floor. "Oh, hey, Huck wanted a lot of attention today." He knelt over to pick up the chair while a few nearby members, several Southsides deep themselves, wondered if he had been over-served.

"And you are?" Bucky asked. And then, when he realized it was Luke from that godforsaken camp, he added, "Yep, I know him from the beach."

Katie spoke up. "He's the instructor who got Huck into the ocean. The one who got him over his fears. He's rooting him on today."

Bucky sat down and waved frantically at a waiter with his hand in the air like a kid in the back row of class. "I'm hungry." He turned to Katie and whispered playfully, "What am I supposed to ask him, *if he got tubed today?*"

She whispered back, "He's been very kind. Stop."

Bucky chuckled, rolled his eyes and leaned back in the chair facing the sea, considering his options.

He turned to Luke. "And you make a real living in the water?"

"Yes, I make a good living all summer," Luke answered. "And then, in the fall and winter, I work as a biology teacher, seventh grade. But my specialty is marine biology."

"So, not high school?"

"Well, actually, I like middle school kids. They are so interesting, development-wise. And when they get antsy and difficult, the laboratory is right here." He pointed out to the sea, while Bucky squirmed in his chair. "When the kids are feeling cooped up all day inside, I'm the lucky teacher who gets to let them out, on this beach, this *public beach*." Luke didn't need to be grilled by this asshole in front of Katie, and he still couldn't figure out why Bucky had sat with them.

"Is this part-time or . . ."

"No, it's full-time."

"And you're free now because . . ."

Luke leaned in. "Um, well, let's see, it's 12:30, camp is done." *As if you don't know our hours, asshole?* "And, well, because August tenth is not usually a school day, school kids around here are off for the summer?"

But then, Katie put her hand on his. "George. Freelance is the economy. Everyone works several jobs part-time. Luke's got a full teaching degree that's stable, but then in summer, he's earning more with his camp. It's just the way people manage. Look at me this summer, it's hardly a secure pension and benefits deal until . . ."

George? This was George???

Luke glared at Katie.

"Excuse me." Luke could not help himself. "We've met. He's known as Bucky around here. But you called him George?"

Katie could imagine Luke would be upset and unnerved that George had surprised them. But Luke was more uncomfortable than made sense. Something was really wrong here. Luke and Bucky, or George, knew each other. They had a past of some kind.

"My real name is George Porter," he explained. "George Herbert Bradford Porter Jr. Most people I meet now call me George. You may only know me as Bucky from the club. Most people here refer to me as Bucky."

"Very true." Luke swallowed hard.

"Katie and I met last spring at a conference out in Portland, so she never changed it to Bucky. It's fine. She likes George, right?

What did you say, Bucky was too cute or . . ." He rubbed her shoulder and kissed her forehead. Katie cringed like a child being embraced by an unwelcome relative.

"I said Bucky was old-fashioned, but anything you want to be called is fine, it's all the same," Katie said, staring at her plate.

"I'm going to excuse myself for a moment." Luke walked over to the pool without explaining, too incensed and confused to stay.

After the meet, he hugged Huck, praised him for his eighth place ribbon in a field of eight, and walked to the entryway.

He again bumped into the kid Brian near the front gate, who asked, "Did you have a good lunch?"

"Yeah. Just great. Phenomenal. Outstanding fare."

"You know that guy Bucky? I saw him sitting with you. Everyone's scared shitless of him."

"I know of him, from the town board election, plus he usually screams at Kona, not me. He knows the family I came to see. I guess pretty well, though, uh, I guess they call him George." He paused, dumbfounded. "I was just watching the son in the pool. Just did the kid a favor. He doesn't have a dad, so . . . I don't know, the kid kind of likes me around. I guess Bucky doesn't do it for him."

"Well, that's good because that Bucky is such a piece of shit," the kid added, looking up at Luke from his knees and shielding his eyes in the hot sun.

"I know. Kona and I know all about him," answered Luke as he walked away. And then, unable to help himself, he turned around and went back a few steps to ask, "But why do you say that? How does he show it? We just kind of take his bullshit behavior, and fight it. But you obviously can't. You work here. Is he super abusive or what?"

"Yeah, well, I work for his club, not him technically. He's a member. There are employees here, I have a boss who manages the place. But Bucky Porter, he's a full-on creep. Ask the bartender, Henry Walker, one of the only cool guys around here. Henry is out to murder Bucky for being such a dick to all of us.

"Bucky's super polite to the women and they buy his game. But then, on the sly, he takes photos of girls while they're sitting in the lounge chairs in their bikinis. He has a whole selection of 'beaver shots,' that's what he calls them. He put a little telephoto lens on his iPhone. He showed them to Henry only, and then Henry told us. Fucking sick-o, they're all pretty young."

"Yeah. I got it. I get it. Thanks."

With that vile bit of knowledge swirling around his brain, Luke tore down the steps to his van, like the degenerate everyone inside assumed he was.

Chapter Thirty-Nine

Push the Pause Button, Please

Luke sat on the bench outside the Sun Spot Surf Shop in town, studiously ignoring his phone. Katie had called about ten times since lunch, but he had no intention of picking up. He enjoyed seeing missed calls, missed calls—all from her. How could a woman so cool inside and outside be attracted to a man like Bucky Porter? What did Bucky do for her? How did he charm her, see her a few weekends, and cajole her to come east for a whole summer?

He looked back down at his phone. Each time she'd called, she'd left voice mails. So far, he'd only listened to two:

I bet you made him feel threatened, like we were on a lunch date or something. That's why he behaved like that. I told you, my life was a mess when we met, my mom had died only a month before, he came in and handled stuff. He's just, honestly, please can we just laugh about how bad it was? He would have been much nicer if he'd been warned, but I didn't expect him to be out. He must have just had a hard week in New York and then wanted to unload and see me after ten days. Like I said, I bet he got a hint of . . . a good-looking man with me at lunch and . . . well, he got jealous. Can you blame him for being not so friendly?

And then, in the second one, she'd added: *You have to give me a break, Luke. I know you hate people like that, people who come out for the summer only and act like jerks. We laugh about it. But I swear, he didn't behave the way he did at lunch when we met. I don't know how to explain it. Maybe it's Oregon and how it just chills you out; it's magical out there. He was different, we spent the day in Hood River and he was amazing, I swear.*

In Hood River, he was kind to Huck, he told me he had a house with extra room, and we should see the East Coast. He said he wouldn't even be here much and I'd have a chance to create a new life, teaching here after all the mess at home.

He stopped listening to the second message halfway through. Women made Luke insane. He couldn't decrypt any of their motivations or reasoning. Simone had also given him some long justification for the fact that, though they had epic sex and he made her laugh all night long, she decided to leave him for no one in particular and everyone in general.

"Hey, man, you look bummed out," said Kenny, who took the seat next to him on the bench. "What the hell is up with you?"

Luke exhaled. "I don't know. Women. All of them."

"Who now?"

"Not talking about it. I just can't deal with it. They're going to literally kill me."

Kona walked out of the surf shop and slapped Luke's shoulder, joking, "Hey, man, does it still burn when you pee?"

"Shut up, Kona. No diseases here. I don't even know if they have a name for the infections growing on you."

Kona sat next to Luke on the edge of the bench with his legs spread wide, elbows resting on his knees.

And, that was a good thing because the lovely Julia Chase came strolling down the street and stopped right in front of the bench and, not surprisingly, chose to stand right in front of Kona.

She said, "I was thinking I need a boat ride."

"You get anything you want. You tell me the time and place."

"Stop." Julia smiled and combed her fingers through her honey-blond hair. "I didn't mean it like that. You're so bad. I just meant I need a water-ski workout or to get some fresh air."

Kona put his hands on the back of her knees and was surprised she didn't flinch. She did say, "You hopeless flirt," but she didn't pull away or stop him. Kona appreciated a married woman who ignored all those silly restrictions in life, especially when he could feel his dick going from six to twelve.

"You want to go down to the boat right now? It's nearing sunset, the wind is calm if you want to water-ski a little. Keep these beautiful calves firmed up; the water is so smooth, it'll be like carving butter."

Julia put on her sunglasses to hide her disbelief at his cockiness. "I'd like that. I might do that. Today might work, or maybe tomorrow."

Kenny elbowed Luke, who took her indecision for another housewife crush and whispered, "I'll tell you one thing: behind every rich man, there's a woman who's tired of blowing him."

Out on the street, before this merry little group, teenaged traffic cops, (called Brownies), stopped cars for crosswalks. They watched for illegal U-turns and ensured the mid-Main Street traffic jams of harried moms, demanding fathers, and fed-up workmen didn't result in any homicides.

While Kona and Julia did their sexual maybe-we-will-screw-one-day-maybe-we-won't dance, Luke's father, Frank, eyed the group from across the street. He walked into Halsey Hardware to get a faucet washer, muttering to himself that his only child, that motherless boy of thirty, would continue to give him acid reflux, high blood pressure, and possibly heart disease down the line if he didn't start behaving more cautiously with the city people.

Luke didn't see Frank watching him, nor did anyone on the bench notice Jake Chase's new Range Rover SV edging through town down Main Street on the opposite side of the street.

Jake started to stop and wave at the group, but noticed his wife there, with *his* surfer dude friends, not hers.

Wait a minute. *Was Kona touching her?*

Like any husband still madly in love with his wife, he was proud of Julia's drive and good looks. He didn't mind her walking around town looking like a hot forty-something smoke show. She was still catching the attention of most men, which only reflected well on him. But Kona actually touching her legs across the way was a step too far. She was a piece of art meant for looking only. But don't ever, ever touch.

Jake pulled into a spot directly across the street. He parked straight in, perpendicular to the sidewalk, not at an angle, and so took up two spots. And though he looked like an idiot in his orange driving moccasins that matched his orange linen shirt, Jake Chase wasn't an idiot and he had a plan.

The Brownie walked up to his window, "Excuse me, sir, you're taking up too much space, town is crowded, and you need to park like the rest of the people. Why don't you back up on the street and I'll hold the traffic for you and you can go in at an angle like every other car on the road?"

"Shhh, cut it out, kid. I got this," Jake demanded.

"Uh, sir, really, I'm going to ask you to back up now. Careful when you back up not to cross the yellow line while doing so, in which case, I'll have to issue a ticket for . . ."

"Do me a favor, kid: meet your daily ticket quota, write me up a ton of tickets any way you want, just do it quietly. Let me take both these spots, straight in. I promise you, kid, there's a reason for this. And when you grow up, you'll have a time in life when you are pleading to another man to leave you in peace."

The kid looked confused. "You know, man to man, that's okay, I feel you, I do, but I'm going to get into trouble if I don't write up a . . ."

"That's my point, kid, we got a deal here, right? An understanding. You're going to write me up for a hundred fuckin' simultaneous violations, you're gonna meet your ticket writing quota for the whole week in the next six minutes . . . only you're going to walk away and quietly and not draw attention to us." Now, at the right angle, Jake's trunk faced his wife and Kona directly on the sidewalk behind him. He slumped down in the front seat to watch the rearview camera.

Self-made kagillionaires like Jake Chase got to where they were for one reason: because they hustled. He did not work harder than the union leader, the lobster boat captain, or even the hot dog vendor jockeying for his spot outside the park. But, Jake's forté had one special coating: he played people who thought they were slicker than he, without them even knowing.

And so, on this sunny Thursday afternoon, around four-thirty, Jake Chase kept his car idling directly across the street from the bench at the Sun Spot Surf Shop. He sat there with the engine of his spanking new Range Rover on, the gear shifted into "R" for reverse, his foot on the brake. His eyes were glued to his rearview backup camera screen so that he could watch Kona, the guy who thought he had smoother moves than all of them, caress those famous legs that belonged to his wife.

And then, he thought. *I like this backup camera. I got an idea . . .*

Chapter Forty

Talk Therapy

The next morning, Katie and Huck headed up to Tide Runners drop-off. He tugged her arm. *"Faster, Mom!"*

She found Julia kicking down the stand of her Townie pale blue bike and then helping her son Richie with his.

"How did the meeting with the club women go?" Julia asked. "You were heading to a party planning meeting last time I saw you. Did Sissy or Fee Fee draw you into some preppy fantasyland?"

"You have no idea. Let's go sit on the beach a bit. I want to finish my iced tea before my two tutoring sessions and before I go into the Seabrook with George's mother, Poppy. I'm a little agitated today, and that scene is really getting to me."

"Okay, let's walk, what's up?" Julia yanked a $3,800 straw bag with original Massai warrior beading out of her bike basket. Designed by a posh former colonialist from Kenya, the bags had sold out at Barneys in two days.

"Just a perfect storm is all I can say," answered Katie, looking everywhere for Luke, who had not acknowledged a dozen calls and texts. "I'll find you in ten minutes, I have to talk to someone first." Katie trailed off in search of the furious Luke. She walked down near the docks, around several dozen cars and pickup trucks to make sure he wasn't changing into a wetsuit behind one—no Luke anywhere.

Julia could tell her friend was upset over men, not plans. "You want to ask Kona or Kenny or one of the guys where Luke might . . ."

"Nope." Katie shook her head. "It's just a little thing."

"Honey, it's never looked to anyone, not me, not the guys, like just a 'little' anything . . . just F.Y.I. . . . he'll show at camp. He has to."

"I have to explain to him," Katie admitted quietly. "It's horrible."

"It's too early for a martini, but I bet I can help. Then again, we can meet here after your tutor and I can bring a shaker full. Don't worry; we'll sort it out."

Julia and Katie walked down the sand in the morning sun, which already felt like it was burning their faces. They pulled on the brims of their hats as they got closer to the ocean glare.

"You don't have to tell me everything, but the headlines are blinking in bright lights with the way you and Luke hold yourselves. I've never seen you with George, but I'd wager it's not the same. C'mon. Sit. We're going to sort the whole thing out here and now. I can see you're in some heartbreak."

Julia flapped out her huge baby-blue towel with a six-inch Hermès silk horse bit trim. "Sit down, there's plenty of room for two." Katie lay down on her side, supported on her elbow, touching the exquisite silk with her fingers.

Julia lay on her back, playing with the indigo beaded necklaces cascading down her cleavage.

"Where did you get the necklaces?" Katie asked. "You have so many things I would have no idea where to find."

"Oh, God, they're just something I found in town." (She'd bought four necklaces at $2,200 a pop out of the Ralph Lauren antique glass cabinet the week before—amulets found on Native American reservations, now sold for a hundred times their original price.)

Katie, taking in the last sips of her iced tea, studied how Julia's necklaces played off the cornflower blue towel. "Julia."

"Yeah?"

"The towel, which I'm going to bet you didn't buy at Pottery Barn, matches your beads. You know that, right? Tell me you did that on purpose and I'm going to freak out."

Julia answered deadpan, facing the sun, "I did it extremely much on purpose."

"I knew it," Katie huffed loudly at the sky. "You make me smile even on a day I'm dreading something." She jammed her straw into the ice of her plastic cup and violently tried to stab the lemon wedge inside. "I'm not sure I can go into the club with Poppy today I. Just. Can't."

A sweep of sandpipers danced around the white water lapping the shore. Julia kicked her legs in the air and sprayed oily suntan lotion on them. The muscles in Julia's tight torso bulged together as she scissored her legs to dry them. She asked, slightly out of breath, "What's so much about a simple lunch?"

"I woke up feeling like George was an experiment. His mother and his ladies-who-lunch friends are drawing me into a community I don't like at all."

"That club isn't easy." Julia smiled kindly, then added, "I know some great women in there, but most of it is tough for an outsider."

"The Patio Party has now mushroomed like lives are dependent on it going well. I told them you'd know better than I how to best entertain at a party. I don't care about a table setting, but I simply wanted my own girlfriend team, just to walk through their girlfriend gauntlet. When you listen to the women plot and plan, you have to wonder if Harvard offers free lobotomies along with the art history degrees."

"I would have loved to see their expressions when you suggested me." Julia started laughing.

Katie bit into a piece of ice, a bit distracted by activity at camp down the beach: a few younger instructors unloaded surfboards and brought them to the shore. Suddenly, a tall, thinner guy with chocolate, shaggy hair, shuffled onto the sand. As he dragged several foam boards down to the kids who were treading water, Luke surveyed the view left and right, and pretended not to notice that Katie was lying down the beach with Julia.

Katie watched him with a hard tug in her heart, as he dove over a crashing wave and powered out to the kids sitting on their boards. No matter how far away, any mother can make out the shape of the shoulders and head of her own child, and she pinpointed Huck grabbing the back of Luke's shoulders and hanging on.

Katie said aloud, "I fall for men who handle my son well."

"Luke will cast a spell on any mother," responded Julia, blowing out Lamaze-style breaths as she held her legs out three inches above the sand.

"I mean even George, too. That first time I brought him to my Hood River loft, introducing him to my son as the new friend he was, he went straight into Huck's room to help reconstruct a lop-sided Lego *Star Wars* ship—some toy Huck was obsessed with."

"In our home it was the Lego Death Star that almost did us in. It was designed for sixteen-year-olds, and Jake bought it for Evan when he was ten. It took so long to build, Jake had it encased in a Lucite case in our front hall on Fifth Avenue, a huge sphere. People come in and probably think it's a pricey piece of art we got at auction."

"Okay, so you get how Legos take over a household with a boy," said Katie. "A man comes into mine, and, before I even have time to pour him a glass of wine, says to my son, 'Hey, I'm a new friend of your mom's and I came to see her. But clearly, there's a Lego crisis going on and she's going to have to wait.' I remember Huck's eyes saying, to the world, 'Finally a man in my house!'"

"Doesn't mean *you* have to love the guy because he pays attention to Huck."

Katie watched a larger set of waves curl and crash. The white water silently crept up the ledge to within inches of her toes. Katie threw her Patagonia knapsack over her head.

"Yeah. But I specifically remember George saying to Huck, 'You're never going to sleep right if it's upsetting you.' I'm telling you, he was in my kid's head in the first thirty seconds."

"Okay, I take back what I said. Anyone would want to jump into a man's bed who did that."

"George then spent forty minutes fixing the Legos from the inside out, something I just couldn't do. He sat on the floor in that uncomfortable way non-limber men do, with one knee folded sideways, another bent upwards jammed into his armpit, stretching his arms painfully to reach a little, elusive piece. I remember his reading glasses were half falling off as he turned the building manual this way and that to decipher the mess poor Huck had gotten himself into."

"Women will beat themselves up over anything," Julia reminded her. "It's not a bad thing to be attaching yourself to men who are fixated on your son. You just have to think about what you need, which isn't simple. You may not want to admit it, but I know you're watching all the kids trailing behind Luke down there. What single mother *wouldn't* fall for a man who possessed that kind of grace and talent with children? He makes my own heart beat faster when my kids smile up at him like he's Ironman and Batman and Spider-Man all rolled into one. Sometimes I want to go up to Luke, when my Richie is hanging off him, you know, and just say, 'will you marry me, please?'"

Katie's mind turned to Luke's world-class kisses, the gropings on the beach at night, and she wondered if ending up with someone her own age, and who was from her same level background, was just easier. Plus he was hot. And fun. And a teacher.

"You listening to me, Katie?" Julia asked. "You're in la-la land."

"So sorry, I appreciate your advice, I really do. And you're right, I'm falling for Luke harder than I can handle. I feel a little to a lot guilty because with George, my stomach just doesn't get into knots the way it does with Luke, you know . . . but then, when George comes over, and literally the way he grabs the wine bottle from my hand and opens it or pours it or stands when I get up to find the salt, I kind of melt for him, too. And then I think, okay, maybe my stomach does get into knots with George, too. Whatever, I've got to focus on the fact that my child is settled and I have employment. That's what counts," said Katie, slapping her knee.

"Yes, but your heart counts, too."

"Well, I know, but I prefer to focus on other things in life, like my child, and windsurfing, or my job. But, honestly I've never been so fucked up over two different men, or what to say to them. And it isn't sitting right."

"You got time. Just keep everything discreet, which isn't that difficult if George is gone half the summer in the city. Somehow you've found yourself matched up with a true local gem as well as an upper-class Hamptons gentleman. So just go for the ride. Go eat bad tuna salad with Poppy Porter, eat sandy hot dogs on the beach with Luke, and make them experiences to have had. You're not necessarily in them forever. Time will give you answers, nothing else really will."

As Julia packed to go, and walked up to the camp drop-off area, Katie walked fifty yards down the beach along the shore.

Unlocking her bike, Julia said to her mini-me daughter, Alexa, "I promised Richie we'd go for a bike ride all the way to camp this morning, so I missed pushing you out the door, but you shouldn't be so late, you were fully finished with breakfast at eight-thirty when we left, sweetie."

"It's fine, Mom. I'm here, I don't even really go in the water that often."

"That's ridiculous, get in the water. Soon. I gotta go to class now," Julia answered. She started to drive her big front handlebars out toward the road, and looked back to confirm Alexa seemed ready to surf. Instead, she witnessed her daughter veering straight for Kona.

Kona had planted himself on top of a cooler, where he studied the ledger clipboard, having gotten most of the kids settled. A few sixteen-year-old girls who tended to hang out before surfing or wakeboarding tried to flirt with him. He'd taught them to dive under scary waves at seven years old, forever someone's cute younger sister to him.

Alexa Chase, another breed of young woman altogether, walked up to him now, her sexuality so ripe it exploded. In front of Kona and two leering young men down the beach a bit, she leaned over and struggled a little to pull her Indian-print pants down over her round bottom. She let the pants pool up around her ankles as she arched her back. She sucked her twenty-inch tummy in, all the while squeezing her boobs in tight with each inner arm so her cleavage flowed out of her skimpy bikini top.

Julia stood ten yards back, her legs straddling the bike, feet planted firmly on the asphalt. Grabbing those wide Townie handlebars tighter, she watched Alexa do her disrobing in the bright sun, maternal worry pulsating inside. She noticed the two men couldn't keep their disgusting eyes off her daughter.

Her young daughter's buttocks were barely covered by a thong that had almost no elastic on the bottom part. As wind picked up, it flapped up high and signaled that entry was not only possible, but quite possibly welcome. Julia lamented that, in a fit of weakness in a little beachside shop the previous Christmas break in Mustique, she'd been the one who'd bought Alexa that miniscule piece of fabric. She'd given her a long wetsuit to wear at camp today, and of course Alexa, though she had promised, had never put it on.

Kona got off the cooler, walked down the beach ten yards and told the sleaze-bags with gaping mouths, "This girl is sixteen, cool it."

Kona then threw a towel around Alexa. "Kid, don't wear a bathing suit like that on my beach. You're going to get yourself in trouble with the guys who can't be trusted to behave. I'm going to buy you a burka if you don't get what I'm saying." And then he threw a camp wetsuit with long arms and legs at her. "Put this on, wear it just like the other kids do, and get yourself a board before I smack you."

Julia steered her bike down the lot, relieved the guys were fighting the tough match with her. She'd have to spend this summer getting Alexa in line. The kid clearly didn't understand the dangerous power of her body.

KATIE WAITED ON the shore in front of the children out at sea, knowing Luke would have to come in from the ocean at some point. With two twelve-year-olds by his side, exhausted from their seven hundred yard swim around the ropes, he finally rode a wave into the beach, holding the skinny boys under each arm.

"Hey," he said to Katie. "I'm working."

"I know, I just want to talk."

"I'm really not talking." He looked at her, his lower lip curling, not able to hide his humiliation from the lunch table Bucky surprise.

"Well, later? When is good because . . ."

"Yeah. Later." And he walked away without saying good-bye or when.

At that, Katie's heart clenched up so much, she instinctually rubbed it with her hand to try to disperse the pain.

Chapter Forty-One

George Is Baaaack

George "Bucky" Herbert Bradford Porter Jr. didn't see a need to inform Katie Doyle every time he showed up in town. It took him a day or two to get acclimated to an honest day's "work" running the club and securing more voters for his election to the town board.

At this very moment, on the deck of the Seabrook Club, Bucky was engaged in his favorite pastime. He aimed his iPhone special telephoto attachment lens discreetly between a high school girl's legs across the busy pool. She was reading her book, her legs thankfully propped up and separated just right.

Nice, tight, little pussy. Here, little pussy . . .

He kept his "beaver shot" collection in a special photo folder on his phone and computer entitled, cleverly, *Nature Shots*. His second favorite pastime (or, third if you count pleasuring himself to said photos) was sharing the photos and showing them off to the bartender Henry Walker, the only employee of real class here.

Bucky knew this southern gentleman in the club's employ could be trusted.

He took Henry's silence as astonishment at the caliber of photos, instead of the speechless disgust Henry actually experienced. It was a good thing Bucky would regularly leave his phone for Henry to charge behind the bar. Even better that he'd hand it to Henry before the password lock came up. Henry knew what to do; he'd document the photo folder entitled "Nature Shots" and use them in good time, at the right time.

A little beaver amusement got Bucky through all the requests he had to handle like those, that very morning, of Mrs. Bitsy Fainwright. The portly fifty-five-year old Patio Party chair, a woman who had "summered" at this club since she was an infant in her mother's arms, had complained again about the surf school that, in her mind, invaded club water. "You must really get the town board seat and get rid of those surfers. They look like human seals out there. Why don't they find meaningful employment and stop ruining our view?"

Bucky nodded with determination.

"And once you get elected, I want you to publicize photos of their camp headquarters on our beach," Bitsy continued. "All the garbage, along with those unseemly coolers from Kmart. It's the Hamptons after all. Can't they get those charming striped ones we all have from Lands' End? Don't they understand life is just more pleasant for everyone's eyes when things match?"

Bitsy's hair was pulled back in a tidy, teeny, bouffant-on-top short ponytail that stuck out of the back of her head, fastened by a pink bow. She wore a pink golf skirt that fell above her thick knees. Her exposed calves looked like huge blown-up water balloons, and, on her feet, she wore sensible white, very bulbous Reebok sneakers, circa 1994. She added, "I also want those filthy wetsuits and towels

off the dune fence. Surely there must be some kind of legal viola-
tion you can slap them with, Bucky? Doesn't a fence that could fall
affect piping plover hatchlings? Can we use that against them?"

Her entreaty gave Bucky Porter another opportunity to go
down the beach and stake his claim on ancestral property. He
hoped darling Huck wouldn't be there, in case those instructors
were "working."

Bucky surveyed the Seabrook scenes before him: little children
in bright Ralph Lauren bathing suits running around with im-
possibly white-blond hair; young teenagers batting their eyes at
each other in the assurance that they would all grow up within
these inhibiting, incestuous walls and marry each other. And
the adults: fresh off the tennis courts, having "earned" getting
sloshed with a few rounds of Southsides from dear Henry; and,
of course, fresh young beaver everywhere to document for his
"Nature Shots" collection.

Bucky breathed in an air of invincibility at the extraordinary
assortment of good American breeding before him. He marched
down the beach toward the camp.

Halfway down the beach, something more potent than slipping
on the soft sand in his loafers stopped him: young Alexa Chase
walking in the most revealing red bikini he had ever seen. Her
sexual, willful gait terrified him—not because he felt manly stirrings in his boxer shorts, but because she looked agitated in a way
he might not be able to regulate.

Worse, she looked like she hadn't kept their little secret so tidy.

Chapter Forty-Two

Everything Isn't Quite as Shipshape as It Seems

That same day, after her seventh difficult tutor session with little Jeffrey in the huge house, Katie rushed up the stairs to the Seabrook Club. She was running only ten minutes late, a time frame infraction that might equal ten hours in Poppy's rigid mind.

As she searched for her lunch date, Katie wondered if she should start calling George his nickname, "Bucky," instead. It might be nice for Poppy to hear her call him that; it would be a show of acclimation to the Hamptons planet she'd landed on.

"Bucky" was just . . . not that sexy.

A shiver ran down Katie's body as she tried to cast off any feelings of guilt about him. She had to focus on Huck's happiness and her job. Within a week, she'd hear if she'd been accepted into the school district as a substitute or even replacement. Those words of her mother rang in her head, *"Your greatest love should be your work, not your man,"* as she ran down to the restaurant veranda toward Poppy, two steps at a time.

After wandering around the club for ten minutes, through the bar area and back up to the top, there was still no sight of Poppy. Katie stood on a brick pathway with purple posy plants on either side, surveying the gorgeous Atlantic before her. She saw a bunch of instructors, including Kona and Luke, with about twelve kids dragging surfboards down the beach. And then, to the left of dozens of tattered yellow-and-white umbrellas, she spied Bucky in the sand.

This on its own was strange. He hadn't called or texted to say he'd come out on a Thursday. Still stranger: he was vigorously arguing with Julia's daughter, Alexa. In fact, from the looks of it, Bucky was yelling at her. What on earth had she done to deserve that?

Katie watched as he turned his back on Alexa and began to walk away. She ran after him and pounded his back with her fist. Bucky now turned back to her and got in her face, with his nose right up against hers. Alexa started yelling back again with her arms flailing at her sides like she was frustrated or furious or both.

Why would Bucky yell at a sixteen-year-old girl? Why would she scream at him? Had she hit him with a board out in the water, while he took a swim? Alexa, come to think of it, didn't have a wetsuit on, and her long curly hair looked dry as it flew about in the wind around her.

A tap on her shoulder. "Dear, you're late."

"I've been here, I was . . ."

"I see," answered Poppy. "I was looking at the young children swimming. I thought I'd see you at the entrance. Perhaps my error. Let's sit, way back at my table. There's too much wind by the sea." Poppy was unaware of the disturbance on the sand between her son and the young woman. Katie started to point it out, but decided against it. She sat down, hiding her angst with a tight smile and sunglasses and readied herself for a dissertation on the nautical skill sets of 1700s settlers.

IN THE GLARE of the sun down by the water, Bucky squinted at his Rolex Daytona, wondering how much time he would have to devote to calming down this unhinged, hormonally unbalanced girl.

"Why are you trying to shut down the camp? It's so horrible. Everyone was just talking about it at drop-off. I thought you were just giving them summonses, but now everyone's really saying you're going to do it. We all love camp, it's so cool."

"You don't understand, there are safety issues, they mess up . . ."

"No, you don't understand, *your* club lifeguards have to ask the Tide Runners surf instructors to save your drunk members, who get, like, totally hammered at ten in the morning. The surfers know the ocean better than anyone. They read currents, see riptides when no one can, so don't say they aren't safe because they are safer than the guys you hire. Maybe we should shut down the club because of *your* safety issues?"

"It's hard for someone to understand, someone who . . ."

"You don't need to talk to me like a child who wouldn't understand. You were seducing me with iced tea on the beach way back in early May, Bucky. I was thirsty . . . you knew how athletic I can be and need hydration."

He ground his teeth. All females were hysterical lunatics, from puberty to pregnancy to menopause. One needed to keep them properly bridled. And then, he could only think: *shit, fuck, shit, fuck, shit, fucking fuck.*

"And another thing altogether: you wanted me here, on your turf, in that disgusting little beach cabana, far away from my house," Alexa yelled at him.

"Whoaaa, young lady, *you* suggested the cabana that first time. Let's keep the facts straight here. You, young lady, came at me that day; don't act like I used you for some selfish . . ."

"I understand you have a lawyer." She put her hands on her hips, biting her bottom lip to see how Bucky reacted to that that. She'd heard him talk to him several times about inheritances.

"How do you know that?"

"Not telling."

"Well, everyone has lawyers." *What was she referring to, this little bitch?*

"Well, why do *you* need one?"

"Are you going to sue me for having my way with you in the cabana?"

"We did it there only because I'm not a little snotty member of your club. So I couldn't go upstairs on real club grounds. I had to stay in the sand, near one of those gross huts. All because my family isn't the right kind of family—we've got too much money. You said it yourself."

"Please, calm down, Alexa," Bucky pleaded. "I didn't mean too much money, I meant you haven't summered out here long enough to get through the . . ."

"We aren't the right family, Bucky. You said it, so own it. That's why you gave me fresh iced tea on the beach and never had me inside the club. My camp coolers don't have iced kombucha or iced chai latte, or anything I like, *ever*. You knew that, you plied me with iced tea, you told me I looked fit. You joked about my tits fitting into my wetsuit, or acting as a nice pillow on my board, or, come to think of it, you'd suggested a nice cushion for your face. Only then did I have the idea we could . . ."

"Yes," Bucky pleaded, whispering loudly. "Exactly. You did suggest you show me your expert tongue techniques. That's how it started, with you insisting."

"I'm not an idiot," Alexa said. "I just hinted I'm kinda good at blow jobs, *which is the truth*. But then you flirted and I thought, well, we can just hang out a little. Like on the sly."

Oh Jesus H. Christ, thought Bucky, another woman with her

goddamn feelings hurt. Now she too would want something in return. The emotional connection that women are wired for was the real problem on this planet. That Katie Doyle was so much calmer and cooler than any woman he'd ever met. She didn't get all wigged out when he didn't call nor focus the universe on her.

As for the Alexa problem, none of this was his doing. This little tramp had flaunted her body on the beach, and had sat with him in a beach chair when she was too lazy to surf. This was way back, one of the first weeks in May, before the season was in swing. Christ, they'd even laughed how competitive women were about their bodies or some such. Now, he couldn't even remember.

People were always blaming the man. *"Oh, poor little Polly-anna, she's so innocent, she didn't know, he took advantage of her."* She sauntered up to him in her overpriced bikini and asked him for something to drink. *That's* what led to using the club bathrooms (the ones on the sand, of course, not in the clubhouse), which led to giving her fresh towels and a chair even though she wasn't a member, which was insanely nice of him to do.

Then, she, not he, *she* started coming onto him, mashing those huge tits into her wetsuit that never once got wet, talking about *her* blow-job technique, how *she* gets off in the bathtub with the warm water rushing onto her little pussy. *She* told *him* all this. How she straddles the fucking faucet, legs stretched out "like a big V," she'd said, he even knew the position! The V! Who could forget that? That was proof it was all on her! He loved folding women in V's, his favorite!

Bucky, however, did start to question the wisdom of it all as he saw Alexa's father, Jake Chase, pumping his arms back and forth as he power-walked toward the arguing pair. Bucky hadn't properly gauged the big scene he and Alexa were causing mid-beach, right between the club and the public entrance to camp.

Jake was slightly out of breath by the time he reached them. "Do you guys mind telling me what the problem is? Did she do something with her surfboard that isn't allowed?"

This hairy orangutan did not say hello properly, which, Bucky knew, was the reason people like Jake Chase were not allowed into the Seabrook. People at the Seabrook said hello to each other even when there was a disagreement. Granted, Bucky did acknowledge to himself, this morning's fracas had the potential of being a little more than a disagreement.

"Well, uh, Dad, kinda . . ." Alexa tried to intervene before this got ugly.

"I'm talking to Bucky," Jake went on. "That's your fuckin' name, right?"

Bucky could just not get over how people from the great city of Manhattan introduced each other. Who was this guy, some cop from Queens or a gentleman owning an estate in the Hamptons? What was the world coming to when the landowners of Southampton could not even address each other?

"I know you have a reputation for thinking you control this entire beach. I saw you are gunning for the town board."

"I am," said Bucky. "I just had a meeting with the mayor, actually, which is why I'm standing on the beach with a dress shirt and my blazer here on my arm, just trying to keep Southampton in tip-top shape. There was a surfboard problem and now there isn't a surfboard problem, Mr. Chase. I assume that's how I address you? Your daughter was a little excited over that surfboard problem, but she and I have gotten to know each other this summer a bit—she's a well-brought-up lady, by the way—kudos to you and your wife on that, and we have worked it out fine."

"Bull-fucking-shit you worked it out," Jake spurted. Bucky took his sunglasses off and wiped Jake's spit off, using the bottom of his shirt. *Cro-Magnon in the flesh. No other word for it.*

"I can see my daughter's upset," Jake continued. "This caused me to come down here and ask one thing of you: tell me the goddamn truth about why she's so upset. Do grant me that man-to-man honor, Bucky. Have the decency to treat others with honesty and uphold the values of your anti-anyone-who-isn't-a-white-Wonder-Bread-guy-in-khakis club you run?"

"I don't know if I've ever been accused of and insulted like this . . . that's just inaccurate hearsay about our membership policies, Mr. Chase." But then, Bucky thought about being aggressive back, seeing as this man might pummel him if he knew his daughter had her tongue halfway up his asshole just a mere seven days before. Or was it five? Or was it yesterday, or was it the girl in New York who . . . anyway, one of them had her tongue halfway up his asshole for sure.

WATCHING THIS OCCUR halfway down the beach, Kenny had had it. He'd fallen off the wagon the night before (second time this month) and was hung over from too many Hopnotic India Pale Ale beers, a brand that got him wasted much faster than regular beer. Not a good day for some dickhead from the Seabrook to harass his campers.

In front of the instructors out in the water sitting on boards (and rapt at the shoreline confrontation), a quarter of the membership of the Seabrook sitting on their tattered beach chairs, about thirty random local and city people who happened to be strolling on the beach that day, Kenny shoved Bucky so hard he fell on his ass.

As Bucky wiped the sand off, he looked at Kenny and said calmly, "You messed with the wrong man. Say goodbye to your camp." He brushed off his ass and put his blazer on, rounding his shoulders a few times to have it settle right on his large frame. He then stomped off into a sea of yellow-and-white umbrellas.

Bucky's loafers slipped in the sand as he returned to the warm Seabrook womb. And, to think he'd been put in such a terrific mood this very morning by that little nymph who lived next door to the 37 Willow Lane cottage. Imagine, he hadn't even taught a thing to that Cynthia sitter next door. She'd come revved with a motor on her like a goddamn Ferrari. He remembered her tight legs wrapped around him, her little tits bouncing away. What a waste of a monumental lay to be put in a mood like this.

Now, with Bucky all hot from their argument, which kind of weirdly turned her on, Alexa decided to twist her little body around and start marching up the dune. As she did, she loved that she could feel her large butt move with force in that same direction and then jiggle back to position.

"Why was Bucky yelling, honey, what's the real reason, really a surfboard problem?" asked Jake, ruminating over whether to tell someone to tell someone to off him.

"He's just a prick, Dad." Alexa was over Bucky's bullshit. "You gotta make sure he doesn't shut the camp down."

"Honey, I don't like girls using those words . . . and I think there's something you're not telling me."

Her father wouldn't understand that she just wanted to see if her technique worked on an older man, too. And, the club cabana shot was just too good for her @DIDITHERETOO Instagram account. Plus Bucky was beyond handsome. And a gentleman sometimes. Not like guys her age. So mature. Kinda cool. But her father probably would disagree on that.

"Well, I learned the 'prick' word because you use it all the time. I left my iced tea cup on his beach yesterday. You know, and he got all mad about manners. Then I was kind of rude because I was sticking up for the instructors that he gives a hard time to. You have to help them by the way, it's getting bad."

"I will help them, but you sure that's it? That's all you were talking about with him?"

"Yep. Just a jerk." She batted her big brown eyes back at her rich daddy. "We all hate him, all the instructors, me, too."

Jake walked back to the parking lot while his daughter spread her towel back on the sand, leaving her long wetsuit her mother had bought her in her bag, having no intention of doing anything in camp that day except talk to people and cool down from her conversation with Bucky. She took a good selfie of her body (anonymous, no face) in the awesome $378 dollar bikini her mother had bought her over Christmas break. She captioned the photo, #LAPERLAPRINCESS, and posted it on her anonymous @DIDITHERETOO account. It was important people knew what she was working with in those cabanas.

Next, she posted a photo of Cabana Number Thirty-Two (where she'd blown Bucky) and had captioned it, #PreppyPorn! People would figure out it was the Seabrook—or, maybe they wouldn't. Didn't matter. It made people curious and horny, both good things.

When Bucky got all mad, he got her insides all anxious in a juicy way. Maybe they'd have a psycho-sexual makeup session in his house. She knew that screaming at him would only entice him to beg for her super special circle-the-tip, then suck all the way down technique that made him explode, like a bucket full on her skin. It was kind of gross, but also, kind of okay. You could just rub it in because it's supposed to be good for your face. Anyway, the huge amount that came out, like a month's supply, proved one thing for sure: she was *really* good at it.

Chapter Forty-Three

They Don't Make 'Em like This Anymore

Katie bit into her crab salad, mushy with too much mayonnaise, the chunks bland from being canned and processed. The watery iceberg did not help much.

"Take a Triscuit," Poppy advised, smiling, her crow's-feet creasing, handing her a red plastic basket filled with saltine crackers and white bread rolls (seven grain rolls would have been way too daring in their post 1970 modernity). "The crab is so summery on crackers. I eat this every day, have for about fifty years now."

"You are a creature of habit," remarked Katie.

"Then, of course," added Poppy, as she blew kisses at Cricket Fitzgerald, who looked thinner than a famine victim, now with her sidekick, Bitsy Fainwright. Both women clacked along the cement deck area in heavy white golf shoes with a leather flap on the top, huge sensible visors on their heads, and tight pale peach-and-pale green golf shirts that didn't do wonders for showing off their midsections (one with several rolls showing in the front and back fat bursting around her bra straps, and one with an undernourished concave chest and torso). "Good game, ladies?" asked Poppy.

Bitsy placed her tray of chef's salad a few tables away and yelled back, "Lovely to see you, Poppy! And you, Katie from out West! We only played the back nine. Cricket here shanked one off a tree on the seventeen and then holed out from a bunker to win the match!"

"Excuse me, I didn't mean to be rude," Poppy told Katie. "I need to say hi to everyone here. It's very important for the community." She winked. "I know you don't drink during the day, but one night you could join us for a ladies dinner with my friends, who are, honestly"—she leaned in—"a hell of a lot more fun than the Topper Tobins and Bitsy Fainwrights of the world!"

Katie smiled. "Well, I was so happy to help them and I know it was important to Bucky, which I've decided now to call him as it seems everyone does. And yes, I did, several times meet them, but, yes, they are a little . . ."

"Tedious?"

"Well," Katie answered, "they are lovely in their own constancy and effort to help."

"No, they aren't. But there's some good women here, just a little hard to find with the boring ones everywhere." Poppy waved her hand at a local seventeen-year-old kid from Southampton high school working as a waiter for the summer. He liked Mrs. Porter, but found her son's beaver shots of young girls his age beyond the pale of horrible male behavior. (Henry had taken photos of Bucky's phone when he'd charged it for him behind the bar and couldn't help sharing his shock.)

"Yes, Mrs. Porter," he said, keeping a safe ten-foot distance. "Your second Arnold Palmer is on the way."

"Thank you," Poppy answered. "Let me be clear with you, darling. I'm on the committee, or even I guess cochair, of the Patio Party only because my great, great aunt first . . . oh well, never mind with her, she was so drunk at the first event, she passed out in the rose garden and no one could find her!

"What matters today, is with Bucky running for town board, the Patio Party has got to have a huge crowd. He'll give a speech and remind everyone to vote. Like a politician, he needs his female companion by his side at this important event, and certainly around for the election."

"Well," Katie said, "I'm here."

"I want you to do your committee work. It's very important to the community we've built. You, linked with Bucky, need to set an example as a hardworking woman who gives back to our community and doesn't just pose for society flashbulbs. I like that your son, Huck, is already working in the whaling exhibit in my attic . . . the labels that Bucky's father wrote don't stick anymore, but I'm intent on keeping them. Huck taping them nicely is a way to display my husband's handwriting, now that he's gone." As Poppy got all excited explaining the uses of whale oil in 1692, Katie searched the beach again for Bucky. She would ask what on earth was going on down on the sand with Alexa. On top of that problem, she didn't want him to bump into Luke.

Poppy hit her glass with her fork. "You with me, Katie? Do you see why they had these huge homes in Nantucket with all those barrels of . . ."

"Sorry, I was listening, I was just wondering where Bucky is."

"And I want you to know I appreciate your committee work on the party, but I don't expect you to be friends with those women." She winked. "Social swans in my day worked tirelessly to give back. Whether you toil away in the home, at a job, or for a cause, the work should be serious and intentional. And that, my dear"— Poppy smiled—"is why I respect you so much. Paying rent even though I didn't ask for it, getting your hours set with the tutoring first week out, applying to the local school system, taking charge of your life as any woman should."

"Well, I think Bucky respected that in me as well."

Poppy adjusted huge white sunglasses she'd recently found that belonged to her mother in 1964. "I'm rooting for him to catch you as his very own, but regardless, you can stay in the cottage and pursue your career for years if you like. My friends and I are women supporters before anything. It'd be good for my son to work hard at earning your love; you're a substantial woman." And then Poppy's face softened. "I love my son. But he does have some traits of his father, George Herbert Bradford Porter Sr." She leaned in. "Too many of those passes in life, you know, ones George Sr. and I fought like the dickens over."

Katie looked down. "Well, Bucky seems to work very hard."

Poppy pulled her glasses down for this. "Bucky got handed the same things the same way his father did. And I never agreed with it one bit. Bucky had straight C's in ninth grade, only for lack of effort, not brains. He should have gone to a local school that handled him right, not be pushed into Exeter and Princeton, the most prestigious schools in the country. It didn't serve him. He's a terrific man, he's kind, but, you have to stand on your feet like you do."

"Well, I do because I have to."

"I have to as well now. One thing George the elder did for me was leave me in charge of the financial reins. He did respect me, and said I'd figure out the best way to handle any family trusts. There's not much left in them, but still, there's something there. A nice nest egg. Two cottages. We'll see how Bucky handles himself in the coming years. Perhaps you can help him. Teach him a little something about accountability and drive."

Before Katie could verbally tap-dance around that request, Bucky approached the table, several beads of sweat pouring off his sideburns on what was an unseasonably coolish, August day.

Right away Katie noticed something strange about him, starting with the fact that he didn't sweat in street clothes ever. He looked unkempt, with trails of sand on the back of his khakis, his shirt not neatly tucked in (as it usually was), and his hair askew. He looked, frankly, like he'd had a little afternoon romp in the hay. Katie wondered about the times he didn't call or check in. Was he with someone else? For the first time, she felt for sure he had been.

"What's going on, Bucky, all okay?" asked Poppy. "What on earth . . . where have you been, young man?"

"Mother, I'm forty-three years old. I was at a town meeting for the election, kissing the mayor's ass, if you want to know exactly."

"Bucky, please."

"That's why I'm in slacks and a dress shirt in the middle of the day."

"How did the meeting go?"

"Fine," Bucky answered, curling his lips inward with such force that his mouth transformed into a tight, trembling line. The salt-and-pepper gray wisps of hair just above his ears were now stringy, dark with sweat. "Mother, we need to talk."

"I can go." Katie started to stand. Bucky pushed her back down into the chair, a tad too hard.

"Stay," he said, and patted her hand. He then sat down and waved impatiently for a drink. "Jesus, these waiter kids turn into slackers by August."

"Well, then, she'll stay," offered Poppy, trying to diffuse the tension. "Your *friend* Katie and I have been having a lovely time. We've discussed the remarkable tutor hours she's put in place. We've decided to continue to bring Huck to do his labeling work in the whale exhibit."

"Fine. Just. Fine." Bucky shook his head. His mother gave her only son a frigid glare. Katie's eyes darted from Bucky to Poppy. She thought this was exactly the kind of exchange mother and son must have had when he was five years old and didn't want to sit for those Christmas card portraits, wearing this very same outfit.

"Do you have a problem with Huck's project?" Poppy admonished. "A young man working hard and showing appreciation?"

"I do not," Bucky replied firmly, rolling his lips in together again.

"Well, then what is your problem right now?" asked the matriarch of the Seabrook.

"Mother. Cool it. The problem will be solved."

Katie knew in the depth of her soul, as did mother and son, this "problem" was a big one.

Bucky leaned back on the two back legs of his chair, and smacked his lips at the tartness of his fresh Arnold Palmer.

"It's a cool day, but I'm feeling warm." He stood up. "I'm going to shed some clothes." Bucky then took off his favorite blazer, the Lilly Pulitzer one with the pink-and-yellow gardenia lining, and folded it on the empty seat.

Chapter Forty-Four

Trouble Leads to More Trouble

Luke, Kona, Kenny, Alexa, and a few of the other kids straggling after camp hung out by the coolers.

"Anyone seen Bucky?" Kenny asked. "It's been days. He must be plotting."

"He deserved it. Let it go," Kona said. "He can't be yelling at one of our kids. You were right to push him, he can't . . ."

"It's going to cause us so much headache." Luke shook his head, as his mind ricocheted between Bucky's rantings and why Katie would even consider dating him. "I got a feeling Bucky's onto more than he says. He's got the bay constable watching us through the reeds. They delayed the legal meeting with the board, probably just to hand us more summonses."

"Well, I want to thank Kenny," said Alexa, standing up, twirling her body toward Kenny in that jiggly way and slapping him on his shoulder. "Bucky Porter was being a dick that day, as usual, so, you did the right thing to shove him, and I appreciate it."

Kenny nodded, noncommittal, feeling his actions might mess

with the camp's future again. It was one thing to beat up drunk assholes in bars; but he shouldn't hit men on the beach. It was foul. They'd all agreed at the AA meeting he'd gone too far. He had to work on self-control.

Alexa's phone rang. She hit Ignore. It rang again. She hit Ignore. Six times more, the same deal. "My brother is so annoying."

"Can't disagree with that," Kona said.

Alexa's phone rang three more times. This time it was her dad.

"Honey. Where are you?"

"I'm at the beach, why . . ."

"With whom?"

"Uh, Luke, Kona, two kids you don't know, Jack and Teddy. We're . . ."

"Put Kona on the phone."

Alexa exhaled. Life was so taxing. She handed her new Louis Vuitton iPhone case with a little purse on it to Kona. "My dad wants to speak to you. He's riled up."

Kona picked up, his heart beating fast, reminding himself that Julia Chase had never come close to agreeing to drop her panties for him.

"Yes? You want us to come? To you?" Kona raised his eyebrows at Luke. "Right now? She's here. Yes, we can. Luke can, too. We'll meet you there. We might get there way before you if you're an hour away, but, yes, we'll get some lunch, then be on our way to you. Just Luke and me."

Kona knew Kenny wasn't jonesing for an invite back to the Chase estate. Right about now, Kenny was only thinking about the Sam's deli "Chaz Special" he devoured every single day after paddling in waves for three hours: French fries in the base, topped with popcorn chicken, then chili and melted cheese.

"You guys want to go to the Corner Gourmet for sandwiches?" Alexa asked, excited to be hostess. "We can charge it all to my dad's account, no problem, and then just hang by the pool and wait for him. He's always late. And, like, no one looks at the bills. We can order whatever we want."

"Yeah," answered Kona, anxiously. "I'm hungry as shit. Afterwards, I guess we'll have to see what your dad wants." *What could it be? Flirting with his wife? Fuck!*

As they walked to their cars, Kona said to Luke, "This is good on some level, I hope. Watch: maybe Jake is going to get onboard with the fight against Bucky and save our camp."

"I swear to God, if you've touched Julia . . ."

"No way," Kona answered, knowing he'd tried valiantly. Maybe he was even making progress.

At the fancy Corner Gourmet in Southampton, about twenty pissed-off city housewives and their kids waited in line to order their sixteen-dollar miniscule paninis (all thinking: *Me? In a line? This sucks. I should be able to cut*). Kona grabbed a wooden basket lined with yellow gingham that looked like it belonged to Little Red Riding Hood. He started piling in chocolates from Holland, biscuits in fancy painted British tins for high tea, and Saran-wrapped chunks of thirty-six dollar-a-pound truffle-flecked Asiago cheese.

"Enough," Luke whispered, having just gone to the cheaper, local deli on his own. He looked into the basket of things Kona wanted to charge to the Chase account. "Not cool, c'mon. You're gross. Stop."

"Who notices the bills? She said no one even looks."

"What are you gonna do, Kona? Add some espresso machines, too? Or these, whatever the fuck they are?" An array of mini Raclette makers stood on shelves for customers wanting that melted cheese and *Boeuf de Grisons* they'd devoured on the top of ski mountains separating Austria from Italy.

When the crew finally reached the checkout line to pay, the baskets were filled with six mini filet mignon carpaccio and watercress tea sandwiches for Alexa and Kona (sixteen dollars each); four bags of house-made red potato chips dusted with Mediterranean thyme in thick clear plastic bags with bright green ribbons (fourteen dollars each—even Kona didn't have the heart to mention they all preferred Funyuns onion ring chips); six lemonade and hibiscus tea Arnold Palmers (nine dollars a pop) and Kona's biscuit bounty. When the cashier rang up $278, Alexa signed her house account she'd had since she was eleven.

Luke looked at the ceiling fan, trying to pretend he wasn't part of this crew. The sandwich he'd paid for himself from Sam's deli was inside a white bag in his hand: boneless spareribs on a roll with barbecue sauce, pickles, onions, and cheese. His was called the "No Bones."

Chapter Forty-Five

The Dog Days of Summer

Kona and Luke laid their lunch spread out before them on the sleek loungers while Alexa went to the poolside bar for plastic glasses. Luke whispered to Kona, "You swear to God you didn't fuck Julia Chase?"

"I'm sure."

"You don't sound sure," Luke probed.

"Okay, I tried to make a move. More than a few times."

"Tried? How hard?"

"I took her in the Jeep to see a good place she could paddleboard with her friends. My dick was so hard out of my mind I was having trouble thinking straight. I just asked her if I could take her pants off. Told her I was masterful with my tongue."

"Jesus, Kona! We need Jake badly on our side! What's wrong with you?"

"What the fuck are you blaming me for? It took a lot not to fuck her."

"Kona." Luke held his hands together tightly. "Remember that *Fool* painting in his house, with the stencils?"

"Yeah, so what?"

"So, you dip-shit, maybe that's Jake's little joke. It's meant for men who think they can fuck his wife." Luke was incredulous. "You think she told him?"

"No way."

"So, then why did he call us here?"

"No clue." Kona nervously chomped an entire tea sandwich in one bite. There was hardly any meat on it. The watercress was too bitter. The dill mayonnaise sucked.

Luke pressed, "You think Jake is onto Alexa, that she isn't his little girl anymore? That maybe she's doing his guests in their stupid colored blazers at his own parties?"

Kona shook his head. "He wouldn't want us to know about Alexa. But something's up."

The guys lay there ruminating, neither saying a word to each other. Kona, nervous Julia had said something, busied himself with his iPhone. He tried to figure out the probable cost, based on previous art auctions, of the inflatable Jeff Koons lobster raft hanging in the dining room.

Luke broiled in the midday sun, made worse by his long track pants. The clean, freshwater pool lured him in, but he didn't have a swimsuit.

"You know, you guys just come here every day if you want," Alexa said. She twisted her waist just a tad so that the fleshy part of her butt could rest on her ankle. She took another selfie of her bikini top and posted it on her Snapchat story. "It's no big deal. You can order, like, perfectly copied Nobu food, or whatever you want." She smiled. "Our chef is *really* good."

"No. Thanks. The Corner Gourmet only for today," Luke answered for both of them. "This is it. We're here because your dad called, but most days we have to get a quick sandwich at Sam's Deli and prep for the afternoon private lessons."

Kona said simultaneously, "Yeah. Sounds good. Thanks. We'll do that."

Luke sneered at Kona. Kona kind of almost screwing the wife, the grab bag of fourteen-dollar chips . . . all this made Luke feel dirtier than the dried-up zinc oxide on his face and neck. He wanted to dive into the water and lie down in the deep end to shut it out.

The late August humidity coming off the sea and bay suffocated him in his nylon sweatpants like Saran wrap. Luke pulled up the pants above his knees, fed up with Kona's grabbing "free" biscuits for later and Alexa's boundless narcissism.

"Sorry, guys, I'm baking. It's like I have heat stroke or something." He threw his sandwich back onto the wax paper and stood up abruptly. "I think I'm going to go back . . . Kona, you took the call from Jake; you can talk to him for both of us."

"I'll get you a suit." Alexa jumped up. "We have, like, a hundred. I'll be right back."

Alexa then flew, gazelle-like, across the patio to the enormous sliding glass doors. She pointed her toes with each quick stride, thinking how good a *Vogue* photo shoot of her legs outstretched would look.

She ran up the stairs, two steps at a time, and went straight to her daddy's mahogany closet, which took up about fifteen percent of the house's square footage. She began riffling through his clothes: blue jeans with an ironed seam like he liked; rows of black velvet slippers with embroidery on the top of his initials, and angels and demons on either shoe, and martinis. He never dared to wear the velvet slippers in public (but so wished he could because they reeked of an elite set that would never accept him). Next, more rows of JP Todd driving shoes in fifteen colors he wore to death, and his collection of ironed zippered sweatshirts from Saint Laurent, Gucci, and Lucien Pellat-Finet.

Alexa could see him in her mind's eye pointing his little stubby finger near Edviane's nose, telling her, "Everything. I mean every goddamn thing that is made of cloth gets hung in here, pressed 'til the creases could cut a steak, you got it?"

She rummaged through fifty brightly colored Vilebrequin bathing suits to find one that seemed more cool than flashy. It was important that the instructors not be intimidated by the bigness of the house. She was absolutely sure she could make the guys feel comfortable if she had the whole kitchen staff bring them pressed juice so they weren't thirsty or anything. It wasn't her fault that everything her father did at his job just made him, like, totally even more loaded.

She found a navy bathing suit with big sea turtles on it. Tame enough for Luke, she figured. Not pink; not preppy. She might even give it to him. A free bathing suit would make him feel, like, more equal in the house.

Unfortunately, while Alexa was upstairs, her brother Evan was arriving and looking for the staff to bring him a homemade pink grapefruit spritzer to cool off. Evan cursed himself for leaving his father's Loro Piana shirt back in the car. He wasn't supposed to take his father's clothes, and now it would be all wrinkled in the back, but he did not have the energy to go back to the driveway, open his car door, reach into the back (which would now be so hot), grab the shirt, and give it to the housekeeper to steam. He too had fourteen messages from his father that he chose to ignore. Parents were so outrageous that way; they could *fucking wait*.

He kicked his hot kelly-green, suede, Berluti driving moccasins off by the front door, and sashayed into his home. He could barely lift his feet out of exhaustion. He slid his feet along the shiny, waxed-up floors in the great expanse of the front hall to the living room, and then the deck. The floor cooled the bottom of his feet just like he liked.

It had been a taxing morning for Evan: he'd read the gossip pages of the *New York Post* in bed (looking for mentions on Page

Six of his friends with hot chicks at clubs), and then had eaten a healthy protein-rich breakfast of scrambled eggs on red quinoa that Claudio made for him and his father. He had to listen to his father badger him for leaving too late on weekday mornings for his job, because "it didn't show initiative."

After that unjustified rampage, he'd had to go into town to get new tennis shoes (it was such a pain, you couldn't ask someone just to get them, you had to go and get in your car and deal with parking it and then try them on . . . and wait because they don't have your size). With all the activity before noon, Evan just wanted some chill time on his back deck to sweat a little in the sun and get his tan on.

Only when he got there, he didn't expect to see the parade of world-class moochers lying around his deck.

"Oh," Evan said, sniffing in briskly through his nose, trying to contain his disgust. Surely Kona and Luke didn't make enough in a day to pay for the lunch they'd just charged to his family. "The Corner Gourmet." He picked up a piece of yellow-checked wax paper and let it flutter to the ground.

"Hey, man," Luke said, standing up, and wiping his hand on his filthy Nike sweatpants still rolled halfway up his thigh. "Sorry, your sister . . ." He didn't want to apologize to this douche, but he did anyway, out of deference to God knows what lip service he felt he owed clients' families.

"My sister what?" Evan figured the guys could muster a little sweat equity for the beef carpaccio charged to his family, the cost of which would, technically, be reduced from his future trust fund. So, in a sense, Evan had paid for the sandwiches.

"Your dad called us." Luke felt so humiliated, he wanted to puke in the pristine infinity pool before him. "We haven't seen him, but it was he who called us here."

"He invited you? But he's nowhere?" Evan asked, in his perfected schmuck tone. "I mean, it's fine, I just was wondering if that's true, why he isn't here?"

"Yeah, thanks for hosting while your father is now forty-five minutes later than he said he'd be," Kona had to say. "We, you know, keep your siblings alive in the ocean when they don't understand currents and go flying into waves they can't handle. We do that, oh, I don't know, what is it Luke, like six times a week? Four summers now?"

Evan took a few steps backwards.

"Because, you see, Evan, for some reason Richie and Alexa aren't the best listeners, no offense to the way they were raised or anything or the respect they were taught to give to adults in charge . . . but anyway, they jump in when we say they can't. So anyway, *yes*, we are here in part because we keep saving their lives all summer long. Your sister knows that. And yes, in return, she bought us a sandwich."

"I'm sorry I didn't mean to sound like . . ." Evan turned and walked with soldier-like purpose back to his own lounger, about fifty yards down the patio.

He took his new Beats by Dre headphones he'd just bought in town for $149.99 (miffed since he'd lost a half dozen pair already this summer), and mashed them in his ears with equal purpose and determination. He found his favorite Nick Jonas song to zone out. He entertained the possibility, off chance that it was, that he'd been a real jerk just then.

Alexa ran back onto the deck, wondering where were the *Vogue* flashbulbs when you needed them. "Luke, here's a swimsuit. You can, like, keep it," she whispered. "My father won't remember."

"I'm going to take a quick swim and then return it," Luke answered. Being around this craven excess made his body yearn for salvation in the cool pool.

Five minutes later, as his loose limbs sank down to the deep end, Luke found he barely needed to breathe. It felt safer and quieter splayed out at the bottom, watching his bubbles rise in the underwater oasis. After breaching the surface, Luke swam several underwater laps to drown out the fuzzy world above. And again, he floated on his back at the surface, then went under for meditation. Spreading his limbs, he let the air out of his lungs to slowly sink to the very bottom of the deep end.

When he was halfway down, *splash!*

Kona cannonballed right on his stomach. It knocked the air out of him. At the surface, Luke screamed, "You scared the shit out of me!"

"I only wanted to make sure you were okay," Kona teased, stepping out at the shallow end and grabbing a plush Hermès periwinkle-blue towel with Maharaja elephants trim.

Luke tried again to sink far into his underworld. After several minutes of breaching for air and returning to the safety below, he jolted out from the deep end and onto the side of the pool in one graceful motion. He then sat on the edge, allowing the breeze from the ocean to cool both his body and attitude.

Water healed everything. He always knew that.

Except when it killed someone you loved.

Luke then dried off with his own plush $630 Hermès towel (from a basket of a dozen) and wondered if Jake would show before they'd have to leave for private lessons. He left the deck to put on his filthy sweatpants and get out of this creepy billionaire fun house.

Closing the door to the bathroom, he placed his hands in a pocket of the borrowed swimsuit and pulled out a small folded wad of hundred dollar bills, soaked and stuck together. He peeled twenty-five apart, then laid them on the sink. This cash represented weeks of work in a wetsuit that, no matter how many times he hosed down with Johnson's baby shampoo, still reeked of his piss.

He thought about his father, Frank, and how horrified he would be if Luke kept the cash. But the thing was, Frank would never find out.

And didn't he kind of deserve a good midsummer tip for making sure the Chase children were safe? And what about last summer, when the Chase family had booked about a hundred private lessons all summer and then went to Majorca for the last week of August? They'd skipped town and forgot to tip before leaving. So this wet, soggy cash was God saying, "Hey, just evening it all up as best I can . . ."

Luke sat on the toilet seat and put his head in his hands. He opened the door, resolved to keep the cash. He needed it; Jake didn't. In fact, technically, Jake owed it to him. His heart raced faster than the Porsche in the multi-vehicle garage below.

He walked back to Alexa on the deck and sat on the lounge chair next to her. He handed her the twenty-five hundred-dollar bills and said, "I found this cash in the suit."

"Dad will never know," Alexa answered. "You should totally, like, just keep it. Think of it as a tip. I'm sure my dad hasn't worn that suit since, like, last summer."

Behind him, Kona, apoplectic, raised his hands in the air, *what the fuck you idiot?*

Alexa continued, "There's, like, no way he knows that money was there. It got ironed into the pocket; he probably meant it for something last summer and just forgot."

Luke thought to mention that, actually, last summer they got stiffed. And funny thing you say this Alexa, just *maybe* that much cash was in his pocket to tip them. Maybe he had been rushing to the beach in this very suit, but his wife called him back to the house about packing for Majorca.

"I can't," Luke answered. "Are you crazy? Not that we don't deserve good tips at the end of each summer. But, I can't steal it, Alexa. He has to *want* to give it to me."

"You're the crazy one, Luke. Think of how many lessons that is. It's so easy, so easy to just say okay." She leaned over and squeezed her boobs together with her upper arms like a 1950s calendar pinup. "He would want you to have it."

"You know, Luke, there have been a lot of times . . ." Kona added, "We could ask . . ."

Luke shot Kona a look. "Kona. Really?"

Kona shook his head, knowing that no matter how much he hoped to mentor and protect his younger friend who'd lost his mom in tenth grade, Luke would best him on morals at every turn.

Luke stood up. "Sorry, Alexa. I can't wait any longer for your dad. I got a lesson."

He walked the hundred yards or so back through the house, down the Egyptian tomb steps, to the carefully raked driveway, the nylon sweatpants sticking to his thighs.

It didn't escape Luke that being in that forty million dollar house, lying on that eight thousand dollar lounger, wearing those three hundred dollar, dorky French swim trunks made him feel a lot grimier than he did now.

Chapter Forty-Six

The Plutocrat Has a Plan

Yo!" Jake yelled out the window of his Range Rover. "Why are you leaving if we had a plan?"

Luke slowed his van down, while Jake reversed. The trucks stood parallel in the middle of the road, holding up traffic. "Let's move to the side of the road," Luke said.

"Here is fine," Jake answered. "They can kiss my ass and wait."

"We've been at your home almost an hour," answered Luke, looking back in his rearview mirror at now four cars behind him. "I thought it was like a panic . . ."

"It is a fuckin' panic thing. If you can, please, turn your van around and come back to my house. That would be helpful to me and my family."

A few minutes later, Luke walked up the modern-day glassed-in tomb five steps behind the owner, wondering what the hell was going on. He prayed on his mother's eternal happiness, wherever she was, that this had nothing to do with Kona and Julia.

When they got to the back deck, Jake told Alexa quietly to leave them alone. She whined, but Jake put his index finger right onto her lips and said, "Don't even talk," at which she raced to her room on the second floor and slammed the door hard, like a six-year-old.

Jake stood before Luke and Kona. He was about six inches shorter than both of them, with a much rounder physique resembling Humpty Dumpty. He stared straight into Kona's eyes, as if Luke was invisible. Then he reached up his hand on Kona's shoulder. "Listen, dude, first things first: I drove into town the other day and saw you on the bench. Outside the surf shop. Way too close to Julia." He stretched his neck so his face was right under Kona's. "Don't fuck with me, don't fuck with my wife."

"I, I didn't, we're just . . ." Kona took a step back.

"Yeah. So here's the thing: you touch her legs again and I'll choke you to death with some Hawaiian puka shells. You got me?"

Kona nodded, man enough to let Jake know his point was made.

"That's good. Because we got a bigger problem with Alexa." And then, gesturing them to come sit, he yelled, "Evan, get off your ass down there, we're going to have a talk, the four of us."

Kona tried to relax. No one had seen him and Julia together in public. Okay, he'd caressed her oiled-up legs a few times on the bench, tried to sniff her pussy a little when she did a yoga down dog move four inches from his face. Maybe once or twice or three times, he grabbed her hips from behind and ground his hard dick into her ass just to let her know he was human. Maybe he placed his hand on her tanned and toned thigh in the Jeep on the way to a paddleboard lesson, proposed that butterfly trick with his tongue, as a joke, *kind of.* But he hadn't gone to work on her in a way that the husband could bust him for. Yes, he'd tried, but who wouldn't? *Ola ole loa awiwi*, life is short.

Jake grabbed Kona's elbow and yanked him into a little cluster on the deck with Evan and Luke on either side. "We got a huge issue. I need your help . . . all of you."

"Dad, you're not going to involve these guys in our family business," Evan pleaded. "It's private. She's my sister; I have some say in how we are going to handle this."

"Oh, fuck, yes, I am going to get their help," Jake said, crossing his arms with his chest out, his fists clenched tight. "I'm going to run this piece of shit dirt bag out of town, off the town board, and far away for good, like a fuckin' cowboy in a Western. Not even involving the authorities, just Bucky and I are going to talk when I have the goods, and he'll vanish, you'll see. But I need these guys. It's my baby he's touching. All hands on deck."

Luke nodded to show they were onboard.

"And don't think I'm a dickhead and forgot about your camp closing. My wife reminds me every day," Jake explained. "When the shit's hitting the fan for real, then I concentrate and step in. Maybe I should'a gone into a town meeting sometime this summer, that's right. But if it was a day from closing I would have."

Luke stepped in. "Well, thing is, it could be a day from closing. We have no way of knowing. Your kids have loved camp and there's like sixty families, plus our income . . ."

"Luke," Jake interrupted, grabbing his thigh in a vise clench that made Luke jerk back. "When I move for real in my business, I fuckin' pulverize the competition. We got an enemy here, and I'm using the same skill set. There will be no more summons from Bucky Porter. Ever. Watch this."

Luke breathed out and looked at Kona. "Well, okay then. We are onboard, Jake. Anything you need."

"Tomorrow, at the public lot, in the spot right across from the front bench of the Seabrook Club, I'm gonna wait with my car, back side out, the gears into Reverse so the rearview camera is on my dashboard. Then I'll use my iPhone to film the screen."

"Okay . . ." Kona looked at Luke, relieved this had nothing to do with a little pussy whisperer harmlessness, and everything to do with something more serious. "I get it. The reverse camera in your car is like a spy camera. And you are spying on what?"

Jake answered, "Bucky Porter, that preppy pervert who's all over Alexa!"

Kona elbowed Luke.

"Fuckin' lecherous creep, saw them together at the party I threw on Memorial Day, but I didn't think they were actually . . . well . . . can't even say it out loud," Jake explained. "And then the fight on the beach between them, you all saw. I'm not a dumb shit . . . that fight wasn't over her fuckin' board in the water. Face it: she's a spoiled rich kid, she goes in the water like four times a summer. It wasn't a board issue.

"So I confronted Alexa the next day, and told her I was call-ing the cops if she didn't 'fess up, which she did, finally. She's got photos of where she and Bucky, well . . . you know, they got to business. First, some cabana at the club, and in the sea grass near my house. These kids and their phones, documenting everything, Jesus. I played it cool with her, like, *'Okay, just please let's find you a boyfriend your age.'* I was all understanding and calm, *'This is your life, honey, I'll trust you to make decisions.'* I left it at that so she didn't warn him."

Luke looked at Kona . . . *The guy from the party with the jacket flapped open to the sky was Bucky? Holy shit.*

Jake went on, "I figured out I needed an ally inside that club where Bucky hangs out. There's this Seabrook bartender Henry, cool old black guy, his son caddies at my friend's golf club. I always tip this kid big because he's a good caddie, tells me when to use the seven or nine iron because I suck at golf.

"I happened to remember his father, Henry, has worked at the Seabrook for forty years. I needed someone who hated Bucky Porter more than we all do. I thought, if Henry has been there for forty years, and Bucky has been in that club for his whole forty year life, Henry might just want to annihilate this asshole, too."

Luke and Kona nodded while Jake went on. "I know you guys think I'm a tool . . ."

They couldn't help nodding again.

"But I got more street smarts than I seem, good at figuring out relationships and motivations, so stick with me here," Jake continued. "I'm right: turns out Henry despises Bucky Porter. Big-time. Wants to nail him, too. For another matter with young girls. Henry trusts me because I'm good to his son. The kid and I joke around on the course, I talk to him. He knows I come from nothing. Like him.

"Henry is going to signal me when Bucky leaves to sit on his bench. All day, apparently, he steps out of the club to get on his phone, because they don't allow phone calls inside. I'll be there with the Range Rover, but this is where you all come in."

"We're with you so far," Luke said. "You got the rearview camera targeted on Bucky on the bench."

"So, after camp, during camp, whenever the fuck I tell you Bucky's out there on the bench, you all are gonna get Alexa off the beach, down to the lot. Don't say anything, just get her to stroll over there to the bench. Tell her to get something in your car, park your trucks near there early, or come up with something, anything. Then she'll bump into Bucky, they'll talk. I'll be recording on the reverse camera of the Range Rover. And we'll do this again and again until that fucker touches my baby when he thinks no one is looking. Then I show him the tape, the photos from his iPhone that Henry has, and I run him out of town for good. Vigilante style. Your camp is golden. Win-win."

Luke asked, "I don't mean to sound hesitant, I've got my own reasons I'm not a Bucky fan. Believe me. We all do. But Jake, you hire so many people, how come you don't get a firm, or some private eye?"

"I'm telling ya, dude, and you don't listen." Jake leaned in. "I drove a fuckin' laundry truck all night to get myself through college. You can't build the biggest Laundromat business in America if you didn't once drive the fuckin' truck for real. This is my kid. I'm doing this myself. And I'm trouncing this creep my own way."

Chapter Forty-Seven

Nail Him

Henry Walker texted Jake the next morning.

> This isn't going to be that hard. Your man's out on that
> bench half the day in late summer. He's out there now.
> We got him.

Jake Chase's Range Rover was already in the parking spot across from the side entrance of the Seabrook. He'd been there since eight-thirty that morning, making sure his rearview camera could film the bench where Bucky got on calls every day, several times a day. He slouched in his seat so no one would see him, while he sipped his Macchiato in a metal thermos, and ripped off the top of a boysenberry chia muffin his chef had made him.

He'd told Claudio to pack a cooler for the whole day, two meals for him and Evan, extra Parmesan crisps for snacks. When Julia had asked why on earth they needed a full day picnic, Jake told her, "I'm on a roll with an idea, Evan's helping, a new software plan. I want to lie on the beach all day and visualize it in my head. Then I'm gonna hit the city in September and get the funding. Love you baby, but we need space to create this winner."

"But Evan doesn't like the beach, his toes, his hair, why . . ." Her guys were acting shady.

"The kid's a pussy, he ain't got a choice."

"Yeah, Mom, I'm a pussy," Evan added. "You know that. Dad's right. I need to snap out of it."

"Honey, you're not . . ."

"Just let him be, babe. He's going to hit a home run here."

Evan nodded. "Sure as shit are."

THAT MORNING AT 9:42 a.m., Bucky Porter walked out the side entrance of the Seabrook and sat on the bench exactly two minutes after Henry had texted. As he got on a call, Evan, already at the top of the camp headquarters, waved his hands wildly at Luke and Kona out in the water. He and his father had texted the guys to hurry up and get Alexa up here. One issue for this motley foursome: the instructors couldn't answer cell phones when they were battling waves. So Evan was there to signal from shore.

When Luke saw Evan, he paddled into shore, leaving three kids on the sand. "Sit here, kids. No more surfing. Don't ask."

"But we were out there, it wasn't break time, no fair!" yelled a ten-year-old boy.

"Shut up," said Luke, uncharacteristically short with the children. And he ran to Alexa, midway up the beach, who was lying on a foam surfboard scissoring her legs to keep her core taut, just like her mother had taught her.

"Alexa," said Luke. "I need help in the lot, can you come?"

"Not now, I'm working on my abs. I'm not surfing today, so I have to do this now."

"You never surf. You don't need to do this now."

"I do."

"Alexa. Get up. Walk to the lot; get my surfer sunblock off the dashboard of my truck, it's right in front of the bench of the club. There's a kid with skin cancer who . . ."

"Cancer, is, like, a really sad thing to happen to, like, anyone," she answered out of breath, counting to twenty-eight, twenty-nine . . . "But isn't it his nanny's responsibility to put on his sunblock?"

Luke looked up and saw that Evan was now making a motion to forget it, and he dragged his index finger across his throat to signal, *No go, it had been a short call, Bucky was back in the club.*

Jake Chase had a way of getting a little too excited about his ability to crush the opponent. Not having been formally trained in F.B.I., M-15, or Mossad surveillance tactics, Luke, Kona, Jake, and Evan found the sting operation more challenging than planned. Getting Henry to tell them Bucky was there, having Bucky sit on the bench for a long set of calls, urging Alexa to stroll up there at the same time, and then having Bucky make a lewd gesture on a rearview camera required a tad more lining up of the stars than Agent Chase had outlined.

At 11:00 a.m. on day two of the sting operation, or "1100 hours," as Jake was now referring to it, Henry texted,

Your man is exiting.

Two minutes later, Bucky sat on the bench and got on a call, and Kona this time got Alexa to walk into the lot on cue. Evan cheered silently and even high-fived his new commando-in-arms surfer dude teammate. They watched Alexa as she strolled down to get Kona's surfboard wax from his Jeep, parked right next to the Seabrook bench.

Bucky was on a call; Jake could tell from the rearview camera that he looked like he was talking to a woman or a young child. His eyebrows were raised, he was making empathetic expressions, pursing his lips like something was adorable; hopefully he was listening to a long story on the line.

Jake crouched down in the front seat, put the Range Rover into Reverse, watched the camera, and filmed it with his iPhone. He bit into some Parmesan crisps nervously, spilling crumbs all over his lap, more like the Cookie Monster than a Navy SEAL hero. He watched Alexa approach Bucky.

"Fuck!" he said to himself as he watched her go out of frame. He tried to maneuver the car a bit to get a few more inches of view. He then dialed Evan. "You see her, is she near the fucker?"

"No, Dad, I can't see, I'm hiding up here behind the beach porta-potty, it stinks of spoiling hot shit back here. I see Bucky, but she walked around him I think, maybe she's avoiding . . ."

A loud knock on the driver's window. It startled Jake so much, he dropped his Tupperware filled with crisps on the car floor. *"Fuck!"* Then he knocked his orange-flavored Pellegrino can off the center console onto the precious Range Rover mahogany.

"Daddy?" Alexa knocked some more. He rolled down the window. "Camp pickup is at noon, it's, like, eleven, are you . . ."

"Hey, baby. I just thought I'd watch your amazing surfing progress. Damn, you scared me. I just dropped my snacks."

"Since when do you eat crackers in containers like that in the middle of the morning?"

"I was hungry."

This is a fuckin' shit-show, Jake thought to himself as he watched Bucky leave the bench in the rearview camera.

"Okay . . . but you know I don't surf. Once in a while when it's super flat, I'll paddle out and sit and talk to everyone, but why . . ."

"I'm not allowed to see my baby girl during the day?"

"No. Parents don't come to camp, Dad. It's embarrassing. Can we meet in town later? I just saw your BEACH2 license plate because I'm getting Kona something. And, I was wondering why you were here? I bet you're, like, watching me? Because of my fight with Bucky? But, you said I should handle my business on my own."

"I'm not, honey, I was just wanting to . . ."

"Yeah, yeah. I got this, Dad. Go home now."

Fuck. She had him.

On day three at 0800 hours, Jake rolled into the parking spot with a rental car so his daughter wouldn't scare the shit out of him again. Day four, five, and six that weekend weren't much different: Henry texted, Bucky would come out, Jake would put the car in Reverse. But the instructors were pretty much out of excuses to get Alexa to the sidewalk, so almost a week went by without any progress.

Though God rested on the seventh day, this commando team could not. Henry texted, Bucky came out to make a call, Jake filmed from his navy, unrecognizable Ford Taurus, and Alexa, late to camp, parked her bike up at the lot.

Kona, clipboard in hand, told her, "Alexa, next summer, you should work as a counselor, love the help you've given this week. Do me another favor today, get me some more attendance sheets, they're in my glove compartment, go now."

Evan mashed his hands together behind the stinky porta-potty secret viewing point in prayer. Jake put the Taurus into Reverse in front of Bucky's bench. This time, praise be to God, Alexa walked up to Bucky, all hot and bothered. She started yelling at him.

"And your point is? That you were born way last century?" Alexa asked, putting her hands on her hips right in front of Bucky at the bench, right in the center of Jake's rearview camera. Jake crunched down, sweating like a donkey, his shaking hands filming the rearview camera with his iPhone so he'd have video proof. "I don't know what problem you have with Instagram."

"I'm not advertising my life on social media," Bucky explained.

"That doesn't mean I'm out of it. It's very showy. And frankly, immature."

"Just FYI, you're not the boss of me."

"My friend showed me, Alexa. Give me a break, the photographs are linked together and called, 'I Did It Today Here' or something? His son showed it to him, apparently that Instagram posting card is very well known."

"It's not a posting card. It's called an account. And, by the way, it's an anonymous account, so you can chill."

"What concerned me was seeing Cabana Number Thirty-Two, the one at the edge, where we, I mean in the high grass by your parents' house, I saw that too, you can't tell where that was, so it's less of a transgression." He shook his head disapprovingly. "But a posting about the Cabana? C'mon Alexa . . ."

"I'm not admitting to anything. My name's nowhere near that account. It could be anyone."

"The Seabrook Club was listed at the location. Southampton."

"That's called a Geo-Tag." She looked at him like he was a grandpa.

"It's a discretion issue that I'm concerned about. We had a secrecy pact, remember? And then this kind of . . ."

"Um, I seem to remember you get hot when we do it somewhere we shouldn't." She smirked at him.

"You're right. I should take blame here, too. It *was* fun with all the people eating lunch and you, well, driving me . . . you're just so unbelievably sexual in the way you . . . I'm just concerned about the social media aspect, it's not wise."

"Are you doing other girls in Cabana Number Thirty-Two, too? Maybe she posted it? Maybe it's *not wise* to do several girls in the same cabana. Ever think of that?"

"Stop. You are the only one who I was with in number thirty-two. The Instagram photograph clearly showed the club, the number.

It was a reckless move on my part to take you in there, I am now seeing. Your level of discretion, frankly, is not exceptional and I'd like to have you . . ."

"Isn't that, like, what that book *Lolita* is all about? My friend read it. Some old man, like, kidnaps some young girl and fucks her all the time. Maybe that's like you. Some super demented part of you."

"I'm simply saying perhaps the Seabrook pool boys will be blamed, someone will lose a job, some married man here will be accused. People talk and you're simply giving them dynamite with this Instagram business."

"I don't appreciate being told what to do like I'm your daughter. It's, like a total turnoff, and makes you no fun and like, really old."

"Oh, no I'm not." Bucky looked left and right. No one on the sidewalk, no cars getting parked. The guards down the way were facing the other direction. He grabbed Alexa's big bulbous butt with both hands and pulled her into him. He scooped between her legs, almost lifting her body up.

"Got him," said Jake, clenching his fists, rage running through his body. It took everything in his power not to get out of his car, grab a nine iron from the trunk, march across the street, and tee off on Bucky's fuckin' face.

And up at camp headquarters, on top of the lot, in front of the porta-potty, Evan actually fist-bumped both Kona and Luke and had the class (a completely, newfound, virgin character trait), to say to both of them, "I was so wrong, totally wrong, you bros are awesome!"

Chapter Forty-Eight

The Socialite Scene

Katie arrived at the library parking lot the morning of the Patio Party: 10:00 a.m. sharp, as regimented by Topper Tobin. She paused and faced the late summer sun, burning bright above her. The air was warm but not baking hot, a slight breeze heralding the September winds. During the party, that sun would wane in that lovely late August way, as the earth's axis tilted toward a new season.

Her marching orders from the Seabrook planning committee were to be seven hours early *just in case.*

On this beautiful Saturday, when she would have rather been at the beach making up with Luke (who still hadn't texted after seven days), or out in Napeague Harbor windsurfing, Katie took a box out of the back of her car. Inside: mini hurricane lamps made of mason jars filled with sand and sea shells and dried driftwood and seaweed tied in a wreath with long strings of beach grass. She walked under a small rose-covered trellis to the entrance of the Southampton library garden. In the back area, enclosed with a quaint picket fence, a flurry of women rushed around like little mice stuck in a shoebox, bossing around Latino workmen from the party rental company. Katie placed her arts and crafts artfully on a small cocktail table and waited for the planning committee judgment.

"It's just so *clever*," Bitsy Fainwright said of the six mason jars, wrapped in a coil of rope at the bottom, half filled with sand, shells, and nautical trinkets like mini compasses strewn around. She pushed the sea grass wreath over an inch, and then back this way, that way, and then back to where it was, but, then, better, two inches to the left. "My God, you have a *real* talent, Katie. Is it your education training that helped you have that chic little . . ." Her voice turned all staccato . . . *"Je. Ne. Sais. Quoi!?"*

That last little line in French came off so shrill and inauthentic that Katie almost told Bitsy to cut the bullshit compliments. Known now on both the East and West Coast for her cool, calm, and measured demeanor, Katie was feeling mildly homicidal only ten minutes into the party prep. The rental company men, possessing stratospheric patience, had already shifted the tables forty-seven times.

Across the bar, Topper poured the pink lemonade into large glass punch bowls with spigots she'd found at Pottery Barn Kids. Cookies and cupcakes were set out on bright Lucite trays that one of the resourceful Wharton School M.B.A.s had found at Pier One Imports for eleven dollars. Each treat boasted a letter from the alphabet written in frosting and typewriter font. This clever touch came courtesy of Cricket Fitzgerald. She, by 11:00 a.m., was so sloshed she was now salsa dirty dancing with one of the Latino workers because she was feeling *"so crazy!"*

Chapter Forty-Nine

Demands on the Docks

That Saturday, out near the docks to Peconic Bay, Kona asked Kenny, "Bucky did *what*? You're kidding."

"He's screwing with us for sure," argued Kenny. "I mean, he just told me he wants to rent a Jet Ski. I won't take him out. No way in hell."

Kenny slammed the boat ropes down on the dock and placed his hands on his broad hips. Looking up toward Bucky and Huck strolling down the dock, Kenny's nostrils flared, and his right lip twitched upward in the same way it did when someone provoked him into a fist fight.

"Hey, guys," Bucky said when he'd reached them. "I have a day with my favorite little buddy here; his mom is busy with a party. I promised him as a treat that I'd take him on a Jet Ski."

Kona walked in front of Kenny to keep him from pushing Bucky to the ground again. He looked around everywhere suspiciously, but didn't see the bay constable.

"Bucky," Kona stated clearly. "So nice of you to come across a dusty parking lot, venture over a hundred yards away from the safety of your club." They'd already pinned him with the video, but Kona had to bite his lip not to say anything.

"We're ready." Bucky smiled, now picking up Huck like he was his own child.

"Well," Kona explained, "there's a rule that says you've got to be sixteen years old to ride a Jet Ski in Peconic Bay. There have been accidents and problems so the town board, as I'm sure you know, doesn't allow it."

Huck looked up at Luke and Kona with pleading eyes. "My mom is busy all day with that stupid party. He promised. He really did. I swear he did."

Luke knelt down. "You know, we could get in huge trouble." Luke tried to focus on Huck, avoiding his desire to hold Bucky underwater until the bubbles stopped coming up.

"So, let's get this straight, Bucky—you're going to pay for a private instructor to take you on two Jet Skis," Kona asked, grabbing the keys of two Jet Skis out of the metal box that was nailed to a deck pole. He swung two keys in front of him.

"Yes," Bucky answered. "Yes. That's right. Of course I'll pay. I want a tour of the bay."

And so it was that the guys relented; Jake had told them to act as normal as possible around Bucky until he made his moves with the damning reverse camera video.

For good measure, they took Huck, now with crocodile tears in his eyes, in a little ten-minute loop on the boat around the bay, even letting him sit on Luke's lap in front of the steering wheel. This was never allowed in camp. And, in turn, Kona gave Bucky a short lesson in Jet Ski safety near the docks, explaining where shallow sandbars rose, how to avoid the jetty boulders underneath the surface, and respect buoy codes. He even took him out in the open water for about ten minutes, until Bucky suddenly wanted to get back.

During this short lesson, Bucky carefully studied Kona's and Luke's every move. He watched Kona, while explaining the safety rules, kneel down on the dock and lift a small piece of plank out of a section of it. Inside, Bucky watched Kona grab a small key. With that key, Kona had walked to the metal box that was nailed to the dock pole, and then opened it to reveal two boat keys and six Jet Ski keys inside.

Now Bucky could drive the idiots' boats and Jet Skis any damn time he wanted. And they'd never know.

Or, they'd know all too well.

Chapter Fifty

Planning Perfection

By 5:00 p.m., an army of preppies, freshly showered from a day at the beach or golf course, paraded through the rose trellis of the Patio Party. They pushed up against each other, more roughly than their grandmothers taught them, overdue for their afternoon cocktail. The women looked like they were attending a Lilly Pulitzer sales convention. The men, presumably hardworking professionals who expected to be taken seriously, wore hot-pink pants with green boats or shellfish on them, and bright linen button-downs. To any passerby, these people looked like circus clowns.

Poppy Porter, wearing a pink hat, flowered green pants, and a white starched shirt in a show of Protestant restraint, walked up to Katie and said, irritated, "Bucky left little Huck with the lifeguard at the club. I hear he took Huck to the water sports dock, on a boat, then brought him back to the club."

"He is taking Huck all day; he just texted me to say they were having fun. They should be arriving now, right?" Katie said.

"Well," Poppy answered. "Strange thing. He told everyone at the club he was going back to the docks again, something about a Jet Ski. Mrs. Calhoun, a mother I barely know, just called, and said she was bringing Huck now. She didn't have your number. I assumed Bucky had left the club early to deal with the party or his town board speech, but why isn't he here? And why on earth was he on a Jet Ski?"

"He's an ocean man, he's always told me," Katie said, keeping her cool. "And the men who teach on the bay . . ."

"Oh, enough with the horse shit, Katie!" Poppy whispered with a clenched chin and neck. "Bucky can't stand those men. Why on earth is he out with them now?"

Katie stifled her worries. "I cannot answer that."

"I like to think you are loosening him up. But not this much, for Christ's sake; he's forty-five minutes late, usually he's in the receiving line!"

As Poppy stewed, Huck ran up to Katie. Lizzie Calhoun and her son Xander had brought him straight from the club's pee-filled pool to the party. Huck was dressed in a swimsuit and wet T-shirt, along with his slip-on rubber sandals—the favorites with a big Power Ranger strap on the top.

"I'm so sorry," Mrs. Calhoun said. "I told Bucky we'd be fine swimming for an hour, and he said he'd be back around four-thirty. But I waited until about thirty minutes later, and he still didn't show. I texted him a few times, called, no answer, and then figured we needed to be here for the beginning. I didn't have a second set of clothes at the club for Huck and we were rushed, so I figured I'd just bring him to you."

Even Katie, coming from the foothills of a mountain range, didn't want her son dressed like this in front of the club community. Katie put her tangerine-gin-punch (which tasted like cough medicine) down on a table of mismatched grapefruits and Birds of Paradise. She then pulled Huck over to two chairs near the bushes and quietly, but sternly asked, "Honey, where's Bucky?"

"He got Kona and Luke to take him on a Jet Ski."

"Are you sure?" She cracked her neck to release the tension just hearing this answer. *Did Bucky know about Luke and her?*

"Yeah, and they said they couldn't take me too, and he got them to let me ride on the boat. Luke told me not to tell the other kids. I only told Xander so far."

"Did Bucky ever get on a Jet Ski?"

"Yes. But it was kind of like he just wanted to understand how they worked or where they were, or something like that. They weren't out for long the first time. Then I guess he went back again."

"What do I do, Katie? He's over an hour late!" Poppy's first Pink Lady drink was not sitting well. She hated presenting awards, but she would have to make the formal declaration of service award to Mrs. Bishop, the librarian, on her own. And then punish Bucky later.

As Poppy plotted to infantilize her forty-three-year-old son, Katie grabbed Huck as he was biting into a turquoise cupcake with a large "H" on it and pulled him away.

"Honey," Katie said, trying to remain calm, "do you want to stay here and play with Xander and his mommy, Mrs. Calhoun, and eat more cupcakes, or do you want to leave with me?"

"If I stay can I have another?"

"One more. Cupcake or cookie, but not both. But I need to leave. Right this minute."

Chapter Fifty-One
Anxiety Alert

In the car on the way to her cottage, Katie texted and called Luke and Bucky. Neither answered. Luke often left his phone for hours in a bag on the dock, so this was not unusual. She never understood how he could turn off the world for so long and manage his business with private lessons and a camp packed to capacity.

Still, she was even more surprised when she arrived at the cottage and found Luke standing on the porch.

"What are you doing here?" she asked him. "Why haven't you picked up or texted?"

"I haven't been able to deal with all the reasons why you're with Bucky. And now I'm forced to, I don't have a choice."

"What do you mean, forced?"

Luke stood looking into her sparkling green eyes, deciding it was inconvenient that he'd fallen so hard for her. "I've been pissed you didn't explain who he was. Let's start with that, what the hell, why didn't you inform me that your George . . ."

"I did explain. I told you I was kind of seeing him." She looked around to make sure no one was coming into the driveway.

"Not that you were with him in general. The problem is I didn't know George was Bucky Porter! He's been awful to us. He's a horrible person."

"Well, back in Hood River and in Portland, and, frankly, when I arrived, he seemed different, I told you that, too. And I don't really owe you an explanation of where I was in my head back in April and how I decided to try with him. You can't be judging other people's choices."

"Whatever he seemed is not who he is," Luke said firmly. "I know so much more than you, you have no idea. Can I come in?"

"Yeah, sure," answered Katie, looking over Luke's shoulder again. "Sure, come in."

Luke stepped over the wooden door saddle of 37 Willow Lane. He then stood before the Americana red cupboard in the front hall and stared at dusty frames of Poppy Porter and her husband, George Herbert Bradford Porter Sr. "Both my parents said something went on here and I never knew," he said. "There's bad blood, way back."

"Your parents mentioned thirty-seven Willow Lane? And you never told me?"

"I was only here twice to drop you or Huck off, and I didn't want to . . . I don't know, jinx anything between us."

"What the hell are you talking about?" Katie crossed her arms.

Luke didn't answer. The first time he was here, he'd seen these picture frames, but he'd been so rushed he hadn't realized the young man, with darker, more youthful hair, was indeed Bucky Porter. He picked up a small frame encrusted with old shells. "These are Bucky's parents?"

"Yes, Poppy Porter and her husband, George Sr." Katie answered quietly, getting nervous about what he was alluding to. The couple was standing in tennis whites next to a net about twenty years before.

Luke grabbed another frame with Poppy alone, holding a young boy in her arms, about six or so, on a beach chair. "Mother and son?"

"Yeah. Why . . ."

He grabbed other photos of Bucky in his twenties with his father in a canoe on a lake, surrounded by pine trees in what looked like Maine. Katie pointed to it, saying, "That must have been around the time his Dad died—1996 or so, a few years after he got out of school."

Luke looked at Bucky's father with a mixture of intrigue and fear. Frank had always brushed off the owner of the 37 Willow Lane cottage as a selfish man, who was not worth speaking about. The details were unclear, but Luke's mother, Lynne, had been in the house several times as the gardener. Luke knew whatever happened back then, he was dishonoring his parents' wishes by being in here now.

"Katie, let's go out back on the deck. I don't even want to be inside this house."

"Wait, just stop for a second and tell me what you are talking about. What do you mean, you know stuff, about *bad blood*? Like another woman with Bucky or some weird family thing? Or, like something bad?"

"I came here to inform you that your George, our Bucky, is 180 degrees away from who you think he is."

Katie undid and redid her ponytail two times in a row. "I only need to know if you saw Bucky today on the docks. I'm getting worried about where he went afterwards."

"I did." Luke grabbed her hand and walked through to the back of the cottage to two wicker chairs, where he fell into one and motioned her to sit in front of him. "I won't ever let you near him again. That's just all I can say right now."

A heavy silence churned between them on the porch, the pause in conversation so laden, they might as well have been screaming at each other.

Luke stared at the cramped backyard, the unkempt hedges and bushes that outlined the lawn. How could Luke explain to her that they'd caught him grabbing the ass of a sixteen-year-old, sliding his fingers even under the back of her swimsuit—and his famous "beaver shots" at the club pool that even the guard out front knew about.

He wanted an apology. *Really? Bucky Porter?* How could she let him seduce her with his vile ways?

But, Luke had promised Jake he'd keep silent. Jake had placed his balding, sweaty face four inches in front of Luke's and stared him down after the recording was complete. He said, "*We got footage in hand of that pervert palming my daughter's ass. And there's more: Bucky takes a photo of women and girls sitting around the pool, and then a tight shot of their crotches. That genius Henry got Bucky's photos off his iPhone and I got those now, too. You can't say a word to anyone. It's my daughter. You did your part, now know your role and walk away.*"

"Yes, I did see Bucky today," Luke explained. "He comes up to me and Kona and Kenny and wants a lesson on a Jet Ski. With your kid."

"I didn't believe Huck," Katie said.

"Yeah, on the docks earlier, he came by, I saw it."

"Not okay," Katie answered. "I mean, okay with my kid, but not right before a huge event he has planned for since the party last summer."

"He's been trying to decimate our camp. And with the town board election so near, we didn't want to cause more problems. So Kona met his wishes, took him out in a Jet Ski on the bay for like fifteen minutes." Luke stood suddenly, out of nervousness, and then slid open the back porch screen door. It screeched on castings that hadn't been oiled since forever. He went into the kitchen, grabbed two bottles of beer and an opener from a creaky drawer. Katie waited on the deck—dumbfounded, anxious, and knowing it was an inopportune time to be turned on by Luke in his jeans and T-shirt.

As he returned to the deck, Luke said, "I really don't want to be inside this actual house; my parents both told me never to step foot in here. The deck is better."

"That's so superstitious."

"I don't know, through the years, I've checked on the house so many times. It's all in a trust with a strange title, no recognizable name, and has changed hands, so, I'm not sure what they were talking about."

Katie grabbed his hands. "This is freaking me out, your father Frank forbidding you to be here."

"Yeah, literally right this second I'm disobeying the family curse or whatever it is because I have to talk to you alone. And you know what? I don't drink much, but I need a drink right now." He opened the beers and handed her one, adding, "Today, Bucky was nuts on a mission, like he had snorted a cereal bowl full of coke. He wanted *the derelicts he's trying to destroy* to take him out in the bay. You can't be with this guy. I won't allow it. I'll literally stand between you two."

"What are you telling me, that there's other women? Or there's what . . ." Katie put her head in her hands for a moment.

"I think there's a lot of other women. And a fair amount of them are really young."

And then Katie's phone pinged with a new text, a message from Poppy:

IF YOU SEE MY SON, TELL HIM HE'S DISOWNED.

Chapter Fifty-Two

A Reckoning to Remember

And now, like two castaways on a stolen afternoon, Katie and Luke dozed in the early evening haze. Katie draped her naked thigh around Luke's thin torso, curling her foot under him. He grabbed her leg and tightened her against him. Locking her arm under both his elbows, he made sure she couldn't escape.

A light snore rumbled through his nose, his gorgeous profile in relief against the pale yellow walls. A good Romeo-and-Juliet fifteen minutes remained before they'd have to confront the divisive madness in their worlds and separate.

Katie's heart ached in a way she hadn't allowed this summer; both of them finally in bed, naked and raw. She watched Luke lying beside her: rough stubble carpeting the beautiful square lines of his jaw, his hair covering half his handsome face, his lips chapped from all the kissing. She pulled her arm free from under his and, with her index finger, made a line down his strong nose, circling his full lips, and then pushing in the little divot of his cleft chin.

Then, with the back of her hand, she rubbed his three-day old beard in an upward motion, and twisted a long strand of his hair around her finger. His somnolent breathing continued, but he summoned the energy to push his lips against the tip of her finger. She smiled.

Earlier, up against the wall in the hallway, Luke lightly kissed Katie's neck. He buried his face in her hair, then hugged her tight for comfort. It had been a strange, long day already. They were alone, and he wanted her close. He held the back of her head for leverage, and this time kissed her hard and furiously. Their groping caused a nautical map to fall to the floor and shatter, both of them too possessed with each other to bother with it.

Minutes later, she let her body slip down his and faced his middle, resting her bottom on her heels with her knees spread. The glass from the frame crunched under her shoes. He was hard under the laces on his surf trunks, and she had to pull them with force to unleash him. He tried to slide down the wall as well, but she pushed his hips firm back against it.

In the past, when it was the first time with a man, Katie might usually let him start everything. But today, she wanted to show Luke how pent-up she'd been. The hemming and hawing, the excuses, and the waiting were now over. With his shorts open, she held him in her hands. Her own insides pulsated with jumpy anticipation as she caressed and pushed her lips against him, *Oh my God,* he sighed from above.

He placed both of his palms on the back of her head and pushed her against him, trying, hoping desperately, to penetrate her mouth. She resisted, keeping her lips firmly closed, taking her sweet time, knowing it was driving him mad. She caressed him firmly as a concession for his waiting, wetting her hands with her saliva so they moved smoothly and rhythmically over him.

Finally, Katie opened her throat wide so he felt she was endless, and let him slide inside her mouth. Her fingers cupped around him at the base. Luke pushed up against her lips farther, and she relented more, moving her hands back and forth gracefully.

"You gotta stop or this is going to be over too soon." He now grabbed her under her arms and lifted her to him, wrapping her legs around him, kissing her as he walked to the bedroom. Her legs fell to the floor just before the bed. She stood up against the mattress, their bodies pressed against each other. Their hearts raced from nerves—this was finally happening. In unison, they tilted over together.

Luke grabbed the comforter at the end of the bed and pulled it to cover their bodies. He kissed Katie deeply in the dark fort he'd fashioned, while shimmying down his trunks. She tried to touch him again, but this time he pushed her hand away.

It was his turn. He caressed her belly softly, his finger lining underneath the top of her jeans for an eternity. When she could wait no more, her pulsating inside becoming explosive, she opened the buttons for him. He pulled her pants down slowly, lightly gliding the back of his fingers along the now bare inner lines of her thighs. He grabbed her hips in his hands and spread her legs, holding them down with his elbows. He lay there for a long while, licking, sucking lightly on her thighs, slowly moving higher between her legs until he tasted every bit of her. He glided his body up against hers to kiss her mouth too, his tongue now salty and metallic.

Finally, he held her bare hips firm beneath him, and pushed himself inside her. Katie moaned in relief, finally giving in to something she'd wanted all summer. As the comforter tangled in their legs, Katie moved furiously, then slowly, both beneath and above him. His body felt exquisitely thick and gentle all at once.

And now, Luke slept as only fully satiated men do. While she waited for him to wake, she curled her fingers, imitating how she'd grabbed his back, pushing him in deeper. She pulled the sheets over her head, the pungent aroma of sex settling around her. A pillow between her legs rubbed softly against her and it soothed her body now. She felt as tranquil as the sea on a flat day, not a breath of wind disrupting its surface.

AND, WAY OFF in the distance amidst rose-covered trellises, guests lingered around mason jars filled with sand and shells. In her mind's eye, Katie saw her son running through the party with his newfound friends, savoring an evening to be naughty without her watchful eye. Cookies with the initial "H" in a typewriter font were surely crumpled all over his shirt, and kiddie punch dripped down his elbows. She would bathe him that night, push his nose in with her index finger in that way that made him snort, then laugh, and tell him he'd never go to sleep because of all the sugar he'd had for dinner. He would deny it, look up at her, and smile that crooked grin he cracked when he told a fib.

Poppy was surely on her second Pink Lady cocktail by now. The elder priestess would be ricocheting like a pinball between groupings of people. She'd welcome them, proud of her club's charity, all the while banging her enormous hat into the guests as she spoke of the library's good works with every sector of the Southampton community.

Bucky would have likely arrived by now, smacking the back of an Exeter buddy he'd aced twice on the tennis court the day before. He'd be checking on the three children from the shelter, who'd be showcased around like cute little creatures from a petting zoo. He'd kneel before them, assuring they looked him in the eye and reciprocated his firm handshake. He'd talk to the club children, inspecting their manners just as meticulously, as they stood in bright pants held up by needlepoint belts.

Katie closed her own eyes now, and turned to Luke for a moment. She placed one leg around Luke's middle again, and her mind drifted back to the sea. The post-sex hormones sloshed all through her body. The trivialities of tablecloths now trailed away.

Luke's earlier rantings about Bucky, she reasoned, must be due to simple jealousy. Men were territorial like that, always protecting their female "property." His outrage had to be greatly exaggerated.

She would move on from Bucky, but mostly because she'd never fall in love with him.

She'd find a new apartment, gather more clients, and land that job in the school district that was practically hers already. Each day, she watched her son ready for more adventure, wanting to stake his own claim as well.

Desperate to leave the sadness of Hood River, she'd convinced herself that the handsome, responsible Bucky Porter could, in some sense, save her. She now knew, she was never the kind to be saved, nor was Bucky the man to try.

Chapter Fifty-Three

A Mad Mother

Katie assumed she'd be safe with Luke in the cottage. Bucky would have shown at the Patio Party by now. Earlier when he was not answering, his phone was surely out of battery. She allowed herself to flash on him in a crisp button-down, perhaps still wet on the back from his just showered hair. He'd have rushed after his Jet Ski trip in the bay, apologizing to Poppy for being so late. He'd save the Patio Party with an off-the-cuff toast, winning them over with his deft and certain charm.

A mere six minutes later, though, a hard knocking on the front cottage door disturbed Katie and Luke's hard-won peace. She broke free of his strong hold and practically shoved him off his side of the bed.

Frantically, Katie told Luke, "Bucky is here. He's knocking. It's got to be him—he's the only one who ever comes here. Jesus, the Patio Party isn't over, I didn't expect . . . go to the back. Hide in the little playroom off the kitchen. There's a closet in there, filled with toys and puzzles. Run! Hurry!"

Luke scrambled, naked, grabbing his shorts and T-shirt, then sprinted into a small closet. Once inside, getting dressed first, he quietly moved the little flaps of wood on the door's shutters open so he could see out to the front hall. Katie smoothed her knotted hair down and mashed an old straw hat down on her head. She threw on a fresh T-shirt and slipped into flip-flops. Clumsily, she hopped to the front door, stubbing her toe on the way.

Bucky might be upset she hadn't waited at the party; perhaps he was coming to get her. She had a fine alibi. She could say she came home to look for him. That made sense. His phone hadn't answered for hours. She'd simply driven around to search for him and stopped here to check as well. He couldn't be that mad. He didn't own her. She could blame his own mother for bossing her around and telling her to leave and find him.

"Yeah?" Katie said, out of breath, swinging the door open way too quickly, trying to project an aura of innocence. The outlines of her story were true. Never mind the hot man who'd just ravaged her, now hiding in her closet.

Only it wasn't Bucky at the door.

Poppy Porter stood on the cottage front porch. The radioactive flowers on her pants almost blinded Katie after the hour under dark covers. Poppy smiled tersely, her head bobbing a tad from the late afternoon libations. *Where. Is. Bucky. Dear?*

"Um, I'm not entirely sure, I thought he was welcoming his . . ." Katie wanted to say "his tribe," but she thought better of it. "This speech is his big shining speech moment, isn't it? I figured he was there by now . . . maybe you left before he arrived?" Katie looked back to make sure Luke was still hidden in the closet. None of the cottage doors closed firmly in their casings, and she worried that flimsy closet might pop open. She offered, "I came here to look for Bucky, that's why I'm here."

"Well, who saw him last?" asked Poppy. "He didn't come home

to change. I was just at *my* cottage. I didn't see wet towels on the floor." She added, "He's been leaving damp towels on the bathroom tiles since he was four years old."

Hiding in the back playroom closet, Luke peeked through the wooden slats on the door. He saw Poppy's arms flying about. For a moment, he wondered if Jake had gotten rid of Bucky Porter, mafia don style. When Jake had said, *"It's my daughter, now walk away,"* he couldn't have meant, *"Now is the part where I bury the pervert alive."* Could he have?

Luke thought about Bucky provoking Kona and Kenny on the docks, and how he'd tried to calm his buddies down. Maybe Bucky would be getting him into bigger trouble with the law, framing him somehow. Maybe he'd lose his teaching slot. Bucky on the docks, then Bucky late for the party: these parts of the story had to be connected. Though Luke had never been to the trellised South-ampton Seabrook Patio Party, he knew enough to understand it wasn't something that George Herbert Bradford Porter Jr. would ever miss.

Chapter Fifty-Four

Day of Discovery

While the women's voices, muffled through the closet doors, volleyed back and forth about Bucky's whereabouts, Luke studied the interior of the closet. Board games and puzzles from Bucky's childhood were stacked on the shelves, cardboard frayed and ripped on the corners, surely missing key pieces: The Game of Life, a puzzle of the Montauk Lighthouse, Rock 'Em Sock 'Em Robots, and Battleship.

Farther down, a metal box on a shelf rested just under Luke's nose. Opening it, he saw that there were photos inside. He shuffled through them. Bucky naked at age two in a plastic kiddie pool, stomach resting on his outstretched thighs. Bucky in high school looking like a kid who might blow up a school. George Sr. and Poppy pushing a carriage under trees on a quiet Southampton lane. Bucky's father winning a golf tournament at a club with a friend by his side, a silver chalice, weighing down both of their arms as they thrust it in the air between them, and printed on a green stripe in the bottom of the photo: George Herbert Bradford Porter Sr. and Christopher Milford Winthrop McPherson, Men's Seabrook Member Guest Tournament Champions 1990.

The hair on Luke's neck stood up like it had in the driveway when he'd dropped Huck off weeks before. *There's goddamned ghosts in this house.* His stepfather entered his mind. Frank would never understand his movements, nor the strange coincidence that a woman he'd fallen hard for resided at 37 Willow Lane.

While the women argued in the front hall, Luke found another box lower down—he could pull it without much noise. This one was some kind of navy gift box from Shep Miller, an old Southampton retailer that had probably been replaced by a modern, price-gouging organic juice chain.

Another shot of Bucky dressed in a cap and gown, Princeton Class of 1994 diploma in his hand, smiling next to Poppy. She looked much younger twenty years earlier with dark hair and Joan Crawford eyebrows. Another of father and son, this time the younger George approaching adolescence, a tighter shot of their faces, arms clumsily draped over each other's shoulders, both in tennis garb. George Sr. with a cleft chin he hadn't seen on the other shots.

Luke played with his own chin, mashing the skin down as if to rub away an uncanny facial similarity. He then pushed the skin on the sides of his lower jaw together with index finger and thumb to make the cleft more prominent. Again, he pushed the stubborn line down as if to erase it.

For minutes, he massaged his own chin, manipulating it, pushing it together as if to consider its very existence. He rubbed the line harder now, more roughly than was normal, as if to scrub away an almost certain resemblance.

Luke knelt down all the way to the floor where more photos were haphazardly piled into corners. He closed his eyes to will away phantoms that Frank swore still lived in this house. He felt them, and he felt Frank somehow knew what he was doing, and he was furious now. Still, was there a chance Frank was wrong? Superstitions weren't meant to come true. They were stories from the past to be discarded and ignored, like these photographs stuck together, mildewing in this dank closet.

Like with all of his father's morality lessons, Luke tried to gain his rightful independence from their grinding grip. But then again, Frank's lessons were the very basis for how a man behaves. They were to be heeded: stay away from certain people and respect his warnings about 37 Willow Lane. Frank's voice clouded around him, strangling him like the musty air suffocating him in the closet.

Next, he looked beneath all of the shelves, his butt so far in the air that he almost knocked the door open as he dug like an investigator about to break a case. Luke found more photos. He shuffled through them, curious about the faces of the demons that surely lay here.

Then, stuck in a crack in the back corner, on the floor of the closet, he found a dusty manila envelope, looking like it hadn't been touched in decades. A string wrapped around the pale yellow disk and dark, yellowing scotch tape held it closed. Quietly, he ripped off the tape, unstrung the disk, and reached inside to find six more photos.

His heart pounded so loudly he could hear it thumping from inside his ears. There was Luke's own mother, Lynne, in a photo in the garden of 37 Willow Lane. She knelt in the bed of mud and mulch out front that hadn't much changed today. It was sparsely filled with red geraniums. His mother had been working here, in this very house in which her son stood hiding right now; Frank had told him that much.

Luke looked at the next photo, his mother with work gloves on, shielding her eyes from the sun, a straw hat, and a basket of weeds with cutting shears by her side. But she was smiling at the camera, familiar, friendly, casual with the taker of the photograph, like a friend. The Porters were her clients . . . Luke knew that. They paid her to garden. But then something happened. Something Frank couldn't tell him. Luke swallowed so hard his throat ached.

Another photo . . . now his mother Lynne in a pink sundress standing in the yard, smiling again. Not like a worker, but like a guest. And then, another photo of his mother in the porch swing of this very house. Next to her on the swing, Bucky's father, George Sr., closer than a boss and an employee would sit, closer than friends.

Bucky's father with a cleft chin. Like Luke's. Bucky's father with brown, unruly hair like Luke's. In the next photo on the beach, George Sr.'s arm around his mother Lynne, both of them smiling, looking like, well, they'd just gotten out of bed. Her hand grabbing his hip flesh as lovers do.

Still another photo of his mother, looking beautiful at a bayside bar, boats, docks, seagulls in the distance, toasting the taker of the photograph.

His mother on a date with George Sr., in an illicit moment, a stolen cocktail by the bay.

Chapter Fifty-Five

Resolution Time

Katie's knuckles tapped onto the playroom closet door, then she opened the wooden flaps to peer inside. "You in there?"

"Yeah. Yep, I sure am."

"Poppy left. This is too weird. She's going back to the party, Huck wants a sleepover with that Calhoun kid, she's going to tell him okay. It's just too hard a day on both of us to find Bucky, and handle everything. I told her I'd look around town for Bucky, then drive over."

"You do that," answered Luke in a trance. He was sitting on the floor, elbows on his knees, his head in his hands.

"Come out, it's fine." She knelt down and caressed his shins. "What's with you? It wasn't that close. She wasn't coming back here into the playroom, you know. We stayed in the front hall."

He looked at her, his face white like cake flour. "Frank is always right."

"Why? What did he . . . does he know about Bucky? Did he tell you something?"

"Katie, Frank knows a lot about the Porter family. A lot more than you and I could have imagined. We have to go see him now. Together."

"Now? Frank? We're going to . . . how do you know?"

"Let me take it from here. It's all starting to make sense. Everything." Luke grabbed the old manila envelope with the photographs and tapped her on her forehead with it. "It's all in here," he said.

Then he grabbed Katie's hand hard, and they almost tumbled down the front stairs of the cottage, he was dragging her so fast.

Chapter Fifty-Six

Breakfast Table Breakthrough

Luke spilled the photos onto the red linoleum dining table in the kitchen he'd grown up in. Katie was on his right, the man who'd raised him across the table.

"Talk to me, Dad."

"With Katie here? I just met her, son."

"You met her before. On the docks. She and I care about each other. I want her here."

"Well, I've said hello to her once or twice, but this is the first time . . . and, son, I think this is very personal . . ."

"I want her here."

Frank nodded. Luke's mom was obstinate in the exact same way. Frank flashed on a scene about twenty years before at this very table when they'd been in a fight about how he'd brushed her aside at an engagement party because he'd been hanging with his buddies. Lynne refused to move until he agreed with her side of the story and promised to be more thoughtful in social situations. He knew the woman he loved was wrong—she had plenty of girlfriends there to talk to, she just didn't want to. But that balmy summer night, nineteen years before, he had to give in if he wanted to go to sleep.

Lynne's son, Luke, sitting before him now wasn't budging either.

"Okay, fine," answered Frank prudently. "Katie stays. Where did you get the photographs?"

"I found them in a crack in the back closet of a playroom, hidden behind a thirty-year-old game of Parcheesi."

"Where, Luke? Where?" Frank shook his head and curled his lips inward, preparing for this moment that was doomed to arise at some point.

"At thirty-seven Willow Lane."

"You were there?"

"Yep. Katie rented it for the summer."

Frank breathed in deep, clasped his fingers together behind his head, and cracked his neck back while spreading his elbows out. "Just amazing. Who would have . . . you both are newly . . . ?"

"She's part of the story, Dad. Like really in the middle of it. And I have to know and I want her to know and it's, just, I want her by my side right now."

Katie grabbed the top of Luke's thigh and rubbed it hard under the table. "Frank, I know we don't know each other, but since I met your son, or your stepson or . . ."

"He's my son," Frank said, sternly. "Always my son."

"Well, we just had a strong connection and I think he feels . . ."

Frank offered a subtle smile. "I know my son. I can tell how he feels."

"So?" Luke asked. "What happened?"

Frank flattened his hands on the red linoleum table he'd bought with his girlfriend Lynne at a garage sale down the street before they were ever married. A sale from a long time ago, way back when they were together, living together, and she wasn't yet pregnant with the child of her employer, Mr. George Herbert Bradford Porter Sr. residing at 37 Willow Lane.

Chapter Fifty-Seven

Forgive and Forget

Y ou obviously forgave Lynne," Katie remarked.

"She was too beautiful not to forgive," Frank answered, staring at his hands. "Her face was so sweet, the kindest face you ever saw. Her eyes tilted down on the sides like a puppy. You just couldn't deny her anything. No one could ever say 'no' to that face, because she was so good inside. She had this thin body, this graceful way of moving around that was like a ballet dancer. I would often stop what I was doing just to have another chance to watch her walk across a room.

"So I had to forgive her," Frank continued. "I couldn't stay mad. It was only an affair with that George Porter Sr. He was a snake who seduced his pretty young gardener because she worked near his bedroom. She was prey and she didn't even realize it. George Sr. took her out for drinks, bedded her . . ." Frank's voice became stilted and forced. "She said it was about four times, then he moved on to some married woman, I heard.

"When I confronted her about another guy—I . . . I just had a feeling one night when she was late and flustered, your mother told me straight away and apologized."

"What did you do?" asked Luke.

"Well, I left her immediately. I couldn't take it. We were separated for about a year and a half. But I thought about her every day. I'd drive my truck by houses where she was working just to see her. Sometimes she didn't know I was watching her at all. And, other times, I'd bring her a coffee while she was working so hard in people's gardens all day. She always took it light with cream. She liked blueberry muffins for energy, too.

"Then, about ten weeks after the affair ended, she felt the stirrings inside her. We both knew it wasn't mine. When she told George Sr., he said he'd give her three hundred dollars a month to keep quiet. She took the money because she needed it, for about nine months after you were born, Luke. "

Across the linoleum, Luke stared at Frank and fidgeted with the loose metal casing around the table. He'd thought his blood father had moved away. He never knew that he'd died and fathered a certain Bucky Porter as well. Bucky, his half brother.

Frank went on patiently and slowly. "After you were born, your mother and I were in touch a bit, we went for drinks. I could barely stand to stay away, but I did as much as I could. And then one day, the baby—that's you, Luke—you did this crazy thing. We were sitting kind of near each other in one of those Wednesday concerts in the grass in town, about two groups away from each other. We waved hello. In fact, I think I brought her over a beer or something. It was one nice June day, thirty-one years ago I guess, son, some blue grass band playing up on a stage.

"We hadn't come to the concert together or even planned on seeing each other there. She was with a girlfriend who'd been very supportive of a young, single mother, and I was with a buddy from work, Earl, who's still by my side at work every day. But anyway, I swear, you, who were like ten months old or so, crawled fifty feet across the grass right straight at me and sat in my lap. And then, you looked up at me, and I looked at you, at your mom. And I thought, I'm going to take this kid on because I love that beautiful woman sitting there across the grass.

"So, to hell with George Porter Sr.'s three hundred bucks. To hell with that guy's loose morals. We don't need him. We can make our own family. Which we did . . ." Frank's voice cracked as he rubbed his forehead. "Which we did." Frank tapped Luke's hand. "So. Yes. As hard as it is to believe, Bucky Porter is a son of the same man, George Porter Sr. You and Bucky are half brothers, his mom is that Poppy Porter woman in the big hats. I've seen her around town, kind-looking woman, I'm sure she doesn't know a thing."

"Do you think Bucky knows?" Luke asked. "Do you have any idea? Did my mom ever say anything about George Sr.'s family knowing about me?"

"Southampton is small and big all at once," Frank said. "Of course your mother bumped into George Sr. over the years, maybe once every year or so. I remember a few times she and I both would see him and move to the other side of the street. But I think she only spoke to him twice in fifteen years. And she did ask once. George Sr. said the rest of the family never knew. But she pressed him, and he twitched a little, and, she told me she got the impression maybe someone knew."

"Who did George Sr. tell?" Luke asked, barely able to breathe.

"She's wasn't sure. She thought maybe he did, only because he'd said something about a brother should know he'd had another, but she couldn't tell. That Bucky Porter, you ever get a weird feeling from him? Like he knew something about you?"

"I don't know. This is all so nuts, and so hard to get my head around. He yells at Kona, and well, yeah, he kind of puts his back to me. He'll kind of confront Kona and Kenny, but never me."

"Maybe he knew something of the connection," said Frank. "He's had to have had a feeling. Maybe that's why he was running you off his beach. It was just too much."

"He said we spoiled his view."

"Well, maybe he meant he didn't want to accept it, or wonder about it every day." Frank held his son's hand. "I'm telling you, I'm your family, I'm always your family. And your mother loved you more than any woman on this planet ever loved a son. And when she died, it all got passed to me to give to you. So I've got enough for both of us."

Tears streamed down Katie's cheeks as she thought of Huck, of Lynne's devotion to Luke, of how a harrowing and lethal day in a boat meant she missed out on giving him decades of love.

"Your beautiful mother is now one with nature. That's why I just tell you to leave her be, resting in the sea. And leave those wealthy city people be. We don't need them. Never have. I always tell you that, son."

Chapter Fifty-Eight

Lifting Fog

The air at this late sunset hour often became wet and heavy when fog rolled over the edge of Long Island, sucking moisture from the ocean, inlets, and bays. The salty mist wafted through the homes, the scent of the sea swirling around people and their furniture. In Luke's van, condensation collected in the corners of the windows, his seats damp as if they had been lightly rained on.

Neither Luke nor Katie looked at each other as they drove to the cottage. Katie decided she'd move out from Bucky's cottage in a matter of days. Luke, meanwhile, touched his cleft chin nervously, now seeing the strong paternal resemblance in that tennis photo.

The photo of his mother, hands on her hips, in front of the Willow Lane garden haunted him most. She appeared steady and assured in that image. Did she know right then she was pregnant, that he was already growing inside her? Luke turned down Willow Lane, both of them silent with reckoning.

As Luke thought about the woman who'd made him, who'd perished in the sea that was creating all the mist around them, Katie remembered the woman who'd died in the spring. Her own mother never knew of her trajectory out East. Yet, perhaps she was guiding this whole adventure to Long Island, and, ultimately, into this soggy van.

Her mother wouldn't want Katie landing here without confidence. She wouldn't want her living with a nagging feeling about a man. Katie would finally burn through the fog in her own head, stagnant and stubborn until now. Perhaps Bucky served only as a vehicle to get here, a delivery system, a human catapult.

This fall, Katie would work at a solid school system without so many budget cuts, and give her son a new life in a town that suited him more as he grew into a teen. She could now swat away those pernicious furies buzzing about her. The same ones that had tricked her into thinking she should accept a relationship with Bucky—a relationship that had always felt amiss.

She'd move out of the ghost-filled cottage. Soon. She'd thank Bucky for inviting her. She was grateful for his providing a framework: from a pail of black bing cherries to sharing an old family Volvo to putt around in. She would not stoop to ask about the younger girls he supposedly chased after. He was, it now seemed, genetically wired to stray. It didn't matter. She'd get that job; she'd keep her son challenged.

One more step to take.

The carved pinewood box waited in her closet, the small velvet pouch inside holding ashes. An eastern resting place for her mother now made sense. During the funeral, Katie had not spread all of her mother's ashes in the clear, fresh water of Flathead Lake. She discreetly saved an equal amount inside the velvet pouch. At the time, she had no idea why.

Now she knew the Atlantic would be a second home for both of them. It supported Katie when she slipped from her board, the salt water more buoyant than the fresh lake water. This ocean provided a playground for her son, a salty elixir to dive into at the end of a long day, a surface for her to glide on. As she stood on her windsurf, manipulating her sail before taking off, she'd see horseshoe crabs scampering along the sandy bottom. The jellyfish, with big maroon centers and long tentacles, swayed with the water's wake around her. After dusting the Atlantic with her mother's remaining ashes, she'd dunk herself in nearby. She'd float alongside her anytime she wished. The ocean was amniotic, so many creatures thriving within.

Luke on her left, the sweet teacher of the sea, the guy in the frumpy shirts, would also play into her future on the Atlantic. Earlier, Luke's body had fit so perfectly with hers, just like a missing puzzle piece she'd been seeking. She'd be more open to him in the coming weeks. But only time could tell the autumn story.

Chapter Fifty-Nine

Police Palooza

When Luke turned the van into the cottage driveway several hours later to drop Katie off, a police car waited in front of the garage. Poppy sat on the porch, clasping her hands in her lap, pursing her worried lips. The bird feeder George Sr. had bought George Jr. forty years before swayed in the front yard tree.

Luke's seventh grade friend, who had become the respected public servant, Officer James Monroe, took several large strides toward his van. At first Luke thought he'd high-five him out the window, but when he saw James's expression, he banged his forehead against his steering wheel.

"Luke Forrester, I'm so sorry, but I'm going to have to take you in. We've got some questions about the disappearance of George Porter Jr."

"Me? James? Me? You think I?"

Poppy walked over to the car. "Katie," she said, "please explain to your friend Luke Forrester that he should not talk at all."

Luke got out of the car while Officer Monroe softly said, "I got to bring you in . . ."

"Why?" Luke said, confused. But then again, maybe he wasn't—

maybe, in fact, he understood clearly. Bucky had framed him. All of them.

"We'd like to ask you some questions about his disappearance. One of your Jet Skis was found upside down near the jetty wake this evening. It wasn't banged up, it didn't hit anything hard, which we found strange as well. We didn't find the driver. We do know a Mr. 'Bucky,' or a Mr. George Herbert Bradford Porter Jr., as his license reveals, was seen on a Jet Ski in the early evening. Mrs. Poppy Porter called to say he was missing.

"Several witnesses saw you all take him out in the bay today. But a few people also saw him on the docks later; it's unclear with whom. The witnesses were confused about who he'd gone with the second time. We assume you went twice? Once at about 11:00 a.m. and once at 6:00 p.m.?"

"I didn't go twice, no one did. I know that . . . Kona and Kenny don't do anything in the bay without me, that's just how we work. They're strong in the sea, and well, I'm just more organized with the ropes and vests and . . . but no, I didn't take him twice. I can assure you, James."

Poppy yelled, "Luke, stop talking. Now. He's an officer of the law."

In eighth grade, Luke and James had stolen their first beers out of his parents' garage fridge. They'd chased girls all through high school without great success, both of them awkward and shy.

"Luke, they also saw you and your partners physically challenging Bucky around the dock late morning," Officer Monroe continued. "One member of Bucky's club told us it wasn't the first time there'd been a scuffle, a physical one. Kenny, who we all know to be a big, strong guy, after all, roughed him up on the beach apparently a while back? Shoved him to the ground, pushed him around a few times this summer? Apparently this happened in the sand, in front of many members of the Seabrook. We already have seven or more confirming . . . you know about that? I'm sorry, I have to take you in."

"Is Bucky okay? You found him, right?" asked Katie, from the passenger side. She still hadn't registered that Bucky was truly missing.

"We didn't. We, uh, we didn't. I'm sorry. We're on a full-scale search and rescue mission. We got the bay constable, the Coast Guard, some of his friends in boats, all looking. We may find him tonight." He looked sternly at Katie. "But it's dark now."

"Oh my God." Katie put her head on her knees, not believing this could be happening.

Poppy waved her arms frantically behind the officer's head at both Katie and Luke. She put her index finger up against her mouth. She opened her eyes wide, beseeching them to obey her. "Do what Officer Monroe says, please, kids."

"He was with me!" Katie said to the officer. "Luke Forrester was with me. At 6:00 p.m. In the cottage, then we saw his father who can also confirm . . . he wasn't on a dock this early evening at all."

Poppy raised an eyebrow.

"Do you have proof, ma'am? It looks a bit like the water sports camp was involved in his disappearance. They may have left the scene, as clients go out with an instructor only. We all know about the sandbars and jetties in Peconic Bay. How would Bucky even start the motor on a Jet Ski on his own without a key? I'm going to need proof from you if you're going to contend, Miss, that Luke Forrester was with you."

Katie looked at Luke, who nodded at her to save him with the good old, tried and true, romp in the hay alibi.

"I do. I actually have physical proof that Luke Forrester was with me this early evening. If you want to get very personal with DNA samples of his, you know, his, well, his . . ."

"I get your meaning, Miss . . ." Officer Monroe stated, acting official, but elbowing his hometown friend who'd nailed a hot chick for once in his life.

"It's Miss Katie Doyle."

"Well, if you'd like to attempt to exonerate your, uh, your friend here, you can come down to the station as well. Kona and Kenny are already there."

Poppy Porter raised the other eyebrow.

Chapter Sixty

Station Stop

Luke and Katie arrived at the station, Luke in the backseat of a police cruiser belonging to his local pal, and Katie driving the old Volvo right behind them. Both of them were dazed and baffled.

Luke prayed that hothead Jake Chase hadn't actually hurt Bucky Porter vigilante-style. He wouldn't do that. Or would he? And where the hell was Jake now?

Officer Monroe placed Luke and Katie in chairs beside his desk. He sat at his desk looking for his notes. "A man's missing and we don't have a ton of time here. It's now dark, he's out there somewhere. And if you think you can guide us, save his life, help him or us, we'd like any more information."

Katie spoke first. "Luke was, he was . . ."

Luke shook his head at her, "no," and cast a look at his two buddies behind glass doors of two different offices. He wasn't letting Kenny and Kona go down just because he had an alibi in Katie.

"Luke," Katie pleaded. "I just, if I have something to say, I gotta . . ."

"You have nothing to say," Luke answered. "Nothing. We've just got to wait. Do what Poppy told us. There's someone else who's part of this story."

"Luke," said Officer Monroe, rolling the chair wheels closer with his feet. He placed his elbows on his thighs. "I know Kenny and Kona are your friends. They're in the other room now, separated, guarded. We can't have you all talking together."

"A man is missing. If this woman knows you had nothing to do with it, that's important. Kenny and Kona will find their way, right or wrong. The truth will come out. The faster our force can get a hold of what's going on here, the faster we can find the missing person. I'd rather keep this a search and rescue mission of a live man, than a search and recovery mission of a dead man."

Luke shook his head confidently. "Katie Doyle has no information for you. Sorry, Officer. We have no idea where Bucky is. That's the truth."

An hour passed. The men stayed silent. Stale Sanka coffees in Styrofoam cups were passed around several times. Stale Girl Scout cookies were offered from one of the officer's daughter's sale. The couple didn't budge. Katie protested again, but obeyed Luke.

FINALLY, THE FRONT door of the small Southampton station banged open. A man growled at the rookie front desk clerk, "You know how much fuckin' taxes I pay for this building? That shiny uniform you're wearing was funded by the revenues from the powder room alone in my ocean home. It's called Pine Manor, six acres, fuckin' six-figure tax bill. You can't even let me in to talk to my friends without signing some goddamn . . ."

"Sir, there are rules, there is protocol, there . . ." the clerk protested.

"I don't have time for forms," Jake Chase yelled.

"Dad, please, it's a police station, not a restaurant." Evan grabbed the clipboard and brought his hotheaded father to a row of vinyl chairs. He filled the forms out himself, shaking his head at his father. "You should know better, Dad. They're policemen. Jesus."

On his other side stood Jake's latest bromance crush, a certain bartender of the Seabrook Club, Mr. Henry Walker. "Your son's right," he said. "Just do what they say."

After the forms were completed, Jake Chase, Evan Chase, and Henry Walker were led back to Officer Monroe's desk. It stood among six other old wooden desks in the center room of South-ampton police headquarters. At this hour, three detectives sat at their desks working the phones. Fluorescent lights buzzing above, they called neighbors, vendors, and club members to see if anyone at all had seen Mr. Bucky Porter after 6:00 p.m.

"Can I pull over a seat, sir? And this one, and this?" Jake placed three chairs alongside Katie and Luke, before he got an answer. "I understand, Officer Monroe, you are in charge of this investigation?"

"I am. You look like you got some things you'd like to tell me."

"That I do." Jake rubbed his hands together fast. He was really, *really* excited about all this mess.

"Well, what do you got?" Officer Monroe leaned back in his chair with his hands firmly holding the armrests. He noticed this guy's lavender shirt matched his girly lavender moccasins.

"Henry Walker and I've been stalking this guy Bucky Porter all day, that's what we got. Actually, what, Henry, we've been on his case two weeks now? You and I?" He punched Henry too hard and went for a fist bump and let his fingers explode out. "Henry and I got this, right?"

"Yes, sir, that we do," Henry answered elegantly. It was excruci-atingly difficult for him not to roll his eyes.

Jake went on. "Okay, everyone, listen to me very carefully." He clapped his hands together like he was coaching a sports team.

"We are, sir." Officer Monroe raised his eyes at his partner scarfing down Thin Mints. *This was going to be very interesting,* he thought to himself, as he grabbed a half dozen Lemon Chalet Crèmes.

"I'm tellin' ya," Jake said. "Bucky Porter is a piece of shit. And, by the way, he's not missing. He's on the fuckin' Appalachian Trail with some underage girlfriend by now."

"And he would leave town, as you say, Mr. Chase, because . . ." Office Monroe was very intrigued, as were the three other officers who had been working the phones. They now stood behind Officer Monroe, hands on their hips, curious about this mismatched trio who'd ambled in like cowboys.

"We got footage of Bucky Porter with his dirty paws all over my daughter," Jake yelled loudly, sweat bouncing off his balding head. His face was getting redder as his rage exploded. "We got photos from his iPhone of underage porn, which, by the way, just this afternoon, I made very clear to a certain Mr. Bucky Porter what I had in my fuckin' possession!"

"No!" Katie said out loud. Luke patted her leg and gave her an *I told you so* glance.

"You talked to him today?" Officer Monroe asked.

"Yeah, I wouldn't say talk," Jake said. "I'd say I ripped him a new asshole. I also told him if he didn't skip town he'd be shamed and jailed."

"So, you threatened him," Officer Monroe stated calmly.

"I told him I'd fuckin' impale him. Is that a clear enough answer to your question, Officer?"

"Uh, yes, loud and clear." Officer Monroe looked back at the other officers. Never a dull day in summer with the city people running amok in his town.

"And also, put simply, Mr. Henry Walker here," Jake explained, spitting now, "he got some video he shot on his iPhone of a certain Mr. Bucky Porter helping himself to a Jet Ski after he'd had a lesson with these guys. In a plank of a hidden wood piling on the docks, Bucky got a key that went into a little metal box on a pole, and then on video helped himself to a camp Jet Ski, took one out for a ride." And then Jake leaned over and whispered, very slowly, for effect, *"Alone."*

"Alone? You sure of that?" Officer Monroe asked. "We'd definitely like to take a look at it."

"Yeah," Jake said, rubbing his hands more, "I got motive to disappear. You know, statutory rape and child porn isn't the greatest image for a clubby guy who wants to go on the town board. And, I got him on tape getting the hell out of Dodge. Where is he now? I'm not sure, but he's not sleeping with the fishes, I assure you. I bet that Jet Ski isn't even dented."

"It wasn't."

"The guy's fuckin' fine." Jake smacked the front of Luke's chest enthusiastically. Luke coughed to catch his breath. "You know that. I know that. He's just long gone. And he's framing some local dudes, just because he's a rich fuck."

Strange choice of words, thought Officer Monroe, *coming from a guy in head-to-toe lavender.*

And with that, Jake fist-bumped Henry Walker again, who, in turn, smiled, but this time winked knowingly at the local officers gathered before them.

Epilogue

The wind-whipped sand crunched under Katie's boots on the same beach that, months before, had swallowed her bare summer toes. She wrapped her scarf tighter against the chill of the autumn air. The changing season made the ocean murky, turning it from azure to a silvery green. The sea grass reeds swayed wildly in the wind. On fall days with an open midday hour, the sea beckoned as if Neptune himself called to her through the waves.

Julia walked beside Katie. She'd come out for the day to help her settle into a second-floor loft above an old water mill in Bridgehampton. In her new apartment, the light spilled through the triangular windows of the two-story living area. Luke had painted the wood floors a glossy white that made the sunlight reflect off it, illuminating the room even more. Katie was grateful to have the girlfriend help as well. Ashley tried to coach her on fabrics on the phone from three thousand miles away, but it wasn't the same as touching them, putting them out together.

"You know what I'm going to say, what it needs," Julia said.

"I actually don't, which is why you're here. I've put all my stuff in, but it's missing something."

"Think about the local environment," Julia said. "Think of the sea you're drawn to. Copy that inside. You have sunlight that's blinding on your white couches. If you want to soften it up, we need to add the deep blue of the ocean with the white frothy wake. I brought a bunch of indigo throws from Bali. That's pretty much all you need and we're set. It'll be cool and relaxed, like my place."

"I know you think your house is really chill, just like Kona and Luke would love, but it isn't," Katie said, smiling. "It's a huge, fancy, out of control estate."

"No, it's like . . ."

"Please. You live on another planet," said Katie, now laughing at Julia's naiveté. "My apartment is nothing like your house, but I'm happy with it, it's my little Pluto."

"Okay, your new loft is smaller for sure—I'll give you that—but no less chic. Let's get it a little bohemian."

"I'll take the throws gladly. I can't thank you enough. I know I'm not going to find anything so special," Katie said. Julia would solve the warmth issue in the apartment in about three minutes, and she was grateful. "And Huck's space is done. You saw it, it's a weird corner room, but it's boy everything. We took his exact room back from Hood River and replicated it here, even with his bulletin board he constructed in his second-grade woodworking class."

"Did Luke help enough?"

"He put together Huck's bunk bed before anything, so his friends could stay. He's already had half a dozen sleepovers in the first weeks of third grade."

"I'm liking all of this: your kid happy, your feet firmly planted in this sand. Luke, cute, single . . ."

"Well, Luke's been amazing."

"You're seeing him how much exactly?"

"A lot and not. Both. Two days in a row, then not for a few. I won't let him sleep in my room yet, because I don't want to get Huck's hopes up. He still sneaks out by seven in the morning," Katie explained. "But then he comes back with coffee and muffins for us fifteen minutes later, as if he happened to drive by. You know, we're both in the same school system, teaching often on the same days, so it's hard not to bump into him. He's in deep, I think."

"And you?"

"I think I am, too. To be honest, I think I even knew it from the first night I saw him in a store in town. But, still I'm taking it cautiously."

"Just don't push him away."

"I was so duped by Bucky," Katie told Julia. "You can't call that run-of-the-mill philandering. I'm glad the police investigation is continuing into his activities with women of all ages, frankly. I can surely cooperate; that is, if they find him. I feel punched in the stomach. I'm still not totally accepting he was hiding this life from me, from all of us."

"Look, we all hope he's brought to justice someday. My husband wanted Bucky run out of town immediately because he didn't want to involve Alexa in any protracted prosecution, you know, just get him out of the picture for good type of thing. But I hear the police are onto his scent anyway, he'll be brought in soon enough. But remember, you were always a little tentative about him; you weren't as clueless as you let on. I remember our first car ride to that exercise class. You told me then you were taking it super slow," Julia reminded her. "You didn't wait idly for his calls. When he didn't get in touch, you were more pissed than whimpering in the cottage. Don't forget that sense of caution you felt."

"I wish I'd listened to that a little more," Katie said, looking down. "I'm not the kind of person that doubts myself and I was constantly questioning something—not about coming here, but about coming for him."

"Exactly my point. You never fully committed to coming here for him, you always knew something was up." Julia stopped in the sand and grabbed Katie's shoulders and stared her down. "So just leave it at that. You're a brave woman who battles the wind, salt, and waves on that windsurf. You shield your son on your own like a warrior. All on your own.

"I can't imagine raising a child without Jake's help. He knew something serious was up with Alexa the night of our Memorial Day party. Way before I figured it out. And he took action."

"That's for sure." Katie shook her head at the memory of Jake explaining to six officers how to take a man down.

"I don't know how you do it all without a father for him, but he's a great, happy kid," said Julia. "With this change to another coast, you took a chance. Now it's time to move on and sink deep in, but not so slowly you lose Luke in the process."

Katie shook her head confidently. "He's not going anywhere. He's loyal. He makes his wishes very clear."

"He's so open and direct with the kids, and I'm sure to his students," Julia answered. "So I can see that. But, most importantly, he's kind to you and Huck."

"And how's Alexa?" asked Katie.

"She's calmer, thank God," Julia answered, looking out at the sea as if to summon an otherworldly force to support her. "We're trying, Jake and I are on it like you can't imagine. He's so good with her, and she tells him everything. I know Jake seems crazy, but there's nothing like it when he shines his love on you. I can tell she's happy to remember that her parents have her back, now that we understand how far she could go if we weren't watching as carefully as we should have been. She's going to be fine, just, Jesus, it was all a little hard to accept."

"Of course she is. And with all that's going on, you're so good to come out just for me."

Julia kicked her couture winter boots in the sand, the salt-and-pepper laces picking up the colors in her gray hunting jacket. "I'd like to say it was just for you, but . . ."

"Oh, God. Julia. Tell me."

"I had to talk to Kona. In person. It was just too mean on some level."

"Mean? Kona's got like four hundred women he's shuffling, though, I don't think he. . . ."

"It was mean to Jake. Kona goes on and on texting me proposals, with this *Kipona Aloha* bullshit, which means 'deep love no one else can penetrate' or something. He probably cuts and pastes the same texts to several women at once."

"So what did you say to him this morning that changed any of that?"

"I told him to stop. This past summer, I just wanted to screw with his head a little because I thought he deserved it. Then, I started liking the game a little."

"Liking it how, exactly?"

"Nothing happened, but I started wondering, how much can I lead him on? Fuck with his head? And then just ignore him?" She shook her head. "But it was getting messy."

"How messy?" Katie asked. "And Kona would be dead if Jake ever . . ."

"Just a little too much caressing my legs, a few close calls in his Jeep when he got me alone for a paddleboard lesson. The sexual tension was at a level that wasn't right if I want to call myself loyal to Jake."

"Okay, I get that."

"And you know what? Kona is a really good guy, and he's much less mature than Luke, less formed. It wasn't nice to lead him on either, even if I simply meant to give him a taste of his own medicine. Anyway, I love Jake. He flirts but he doesn't touch. Jake's a baby deep down, and I just know he wouldn't stray. Women are more layered than men, right? More nuanced, like your monotone, bleached-out apartment is about to be when I get done with it."

As they climbed up the dune closer to the lot, the twosome found Poppy Porter and Luke Forrester standing side by side.

"What a pair they make," noticed Julia.

"They've been hanging out," explained Katie. "He goes and has a cocktail with her once or twice a week after school. He doesn't even drink much, but he pretends to sip one anyway."

"That's really nice to hear."

"It is. He's trying to understand all about the family history, about his father by blood."

"Well, she lost one son, and found another."

"Luke is her stepson; she was married to his father," Katie corrected. "But I'm sure that counts to go on for hours about his whaling ancestors!"

"With Luke's integrity and all that, it is the son she never had. You know that, Katie. Looks like they have to talk to you. I'll meet you later at your apartment." Julia waved.

"Poppy and I have been meeting for a long time today," Luke said, pulling Katie to his side. "We came to look out at our favorite view, and tell you about some things."

"You both are talking a lot these days."

"Well, dear," Poppy answered. "We're family now. I figure with all these modern arrangements I hear about, I might as well have one of my own."

Katie studied this November odd couple: Luke and his constant stubble, those deep brown eyes luminous with the sea before him, a loose sweatshirt and a New York Mets cap holding down his unkempt hair. And Poppy, a kaleidoscope of fall colors: a bright red scarf tying her orange hat under her chin, ochre yellow pants tucked into sensible boots, her full middle section covered in a green windbreaker jacket. She looked like a human pile of autumn leaves.

Poppy started right in. "We have such a nice morning together, and you know I always believe in gratitude in life for what we do have. It would have been nice of George Sr. to inform me that Bucky wasn't his only son. But I'll just have to make up for lost time with my Luke, who, by the way, makes an excellent Pink Lady drink now."

"Really?"

Poppy smiled proudly. "He won't join us for bridge, but he will meet me for my 3:00 p.m. drink. Luke's a good man, someone I respect in a way I didn't fully respect my own family, if you want me to be honest." Poppy paused, looking for the elegant way to say the obvious. She crossed her arms over that plentiful bosom. "Both George Sr. and George Jr.'s choices were, well, just, off the reservation, and a lot of people suffered for that."

Just then, Frank Forrester's pickup drove by. He honked from the lot, an Eagles song streaming loudly out his window. He slowed and tapped his baseball hat at the group, smiling brighter than he usually did.

"Hey, Poppy! Sunset's at 4:38 tonight, and I don't like to be late!"

"Handsome fellow," Poppy remarked, waving back. "That Frank. I like a man who respects schedules."

Katie shot Luke a look. *Frank and Poppy?*

He nodded and now crossed his own arms.

"You and Frank both have been . . ." Katie asked, "visiting with Poppy? You didn't tell me that!"

"He wanted to hear the stories," Luke explained. "I'll always call him my real dad, but he was curious about my blood relatives, too.

So I told him he could come listen. He believes my love of the sea came from the whaling history in my ancestors."

"And what was that sunset reference?" asked Katie.

"Yeah, what was that?" Luke agreed, staring Poppy down. "What did that mean?"

"He's a good man too, like the man he raised here. He's got a nice way about him." Poppy smiled and kicked a small pebble with her boot. "Frank took me out."

"No!" both Luke and Katie said together.

"Twice, to his favorite lobster shack in Montauk. He likes to get there way before sunset because they have tables by the window. We have an early dinner at five or so after a drink. Turns out we both like to listen to bluegrass, not that I knew what it was before he introduced me!"

"This is just too strange," Katie said. "Frank is so, well, set in his ways, and you are, I guess, you're alike that way. He's in thick work pants and a utility vest, while you're in your own colored uniform. But I guess it's not as far off as I might think?"

"Stranger things have happened," Poppy answered, smiling warmly. "Who knows, we're just starting a friendship here. But, we do share a stepson in Luke. I've been looking for a solid man for fifteen years now. Frank's been looking for a stable woman, he's . . . well, I like a man with a strong sense of honor, and devotion to his family. I fear he's not very clubby, though."

"Not a country club guy for sure, Poppy. I told you that before I introduced him," Luke said. "*Very* different from those types."

"You know what? He's not that different from the old guard of the club. They're all just people who want to help the town and are understated about everything they do. He's a discreet, kind man, just trying to do the right thing." Poppy laughed and tightened her scarf against the chill. "I will say that I'm not exactly used to riding around town in a pickup truck. But, I've learned to adapt to changing tides all my life, so I'm good. And he's adjusting just fine to the crab salad at the club."

"Really, Poppy? You brought him to the Seabrook, too? You only said you both went twice to Montauk." Luke looked at Katie suspiciously. "How many times exactly have you both been out together?"

"Well, maybe it's been five or six times we've seen each other," she answered, uncrossing her arms, and placing them on her hips defensively. "Okay, fine. Yes, I did take Frank to my club, too. Several times on his lunch break. He doesn't like the Seabrook food, but he's a gentleman and tries to please me and pretend. He says that's what Tabasco sauce is for!"

"I can see that perfectly." Luke laughed.

"Henry Walker saves a bottle for him behind the bar. And I can tell, that Henry approves, and that means a lot to me. Henry understands gentlemanly class better than anyone I've ever met."

"So you're going to keep having meals, as *friends*?" Katie asked.

"Who knows, child?" Poppy continued, "I'm grateful someone is interested in my stories! Frank's a builder by trade, fascinated with boats, how they were made, how they tracked the whales off Montauk. So you can imagine with the harpoons and all, once I get going about the voyage on the Essex that slammed into the rocks, you remember? Where they had to survive in the smaller rowboats for days and . . ."

"We remember." Luke patted her shoulder.

"Anyway, this morning, I told Luke of some plans I have."

"What kind of plans?" asked Katie, curious where the matriarch might be going with this.

"Don't look at me like that, Katie," Poppy admonished.

"Like what?" Visions of a wedding with Luke on a pink-and-green patio flew through her mind.

"Like I'm making *those* kinds of plans."

Katie laughed nervously. "I just meant cool down, please."

"Just passing things on properly, with both Georges gone," Poppy explained. "The second cottage is, as of yesterday, bequeathed to Luke in the trust which I control. It's up to Luke how he wants to handle that property . . . I just informed him this morning. Bucky won't be getting anywhere near it, though apparently he was trying in ways I didn't even know about, turns out he had a lawyer."

"Did Bucky know about Luke?" Katie asked Poppy.

"Well, he'd been talking to a lawyer a lot. And, I told that lawyer, an old friend of George Sr.'s, that he should never have taken Bucky's call. I held the titles to all, but, of course, men will be men. They like to be in charge, and they did talk a bit about who owned what house." Poppy shook her head.

"Poppy can't confirm if Bucky knew about me for sure," Luke cut in, "but, I'm thinking yes. That's my gut. I'm thinking he couldn't ever face me in person. He always turned his back and talked to Kona. George Sr. must have told him. And, maybe, he just wanted me out of the picture, wanted to erase me out like an old chalkboard."

Katie grabbed Luke's arm. "Well, that didn't work," she said.

"So I went into town," explained Poppy, "and transferred the title of the Willow Lane cottage entirely and solely to Luke."

"And I told Poppy this morning, that I can't keep 37 Willow Lane," Luke answered, his voice a little stilted. The recent whiplash of never knowing his birth father, nor that he even had a half brother plastered all over his face. "Who knows if even George Sr. would have wanted me to have it?"

"I told you, young man. Stop that now!" Poppy instructed her newfound son. Katie was surprised with the harsh discipline she laid out. "My husband left all the financial decisions of his family trust to me. A woman is fully capable of making these decisions."

"Whoa, Poppy," Luke backtracked. "I didn't mean the woman

thing, I just meant my blood father wasn't exactly involved in my life. He was trying to hide me. And besides, the cottage belongs to his family and I was just offering that possibility that . . ."

"*You. Are. My. Family,*" Poppy answered, hurt.

Katie rubbed Poppy's shoulder, feeling protective of this woman who'd been on her side since she'd left a bucket of bing cherries on the doorstep.

"I appreciate it," Luke said kindly. "The moment I heard, I told you I'm going to stick with my first gut instinct, Poppy. I want the cottage out of the picture fast. I'm going to sell it, and split the proceeds all up. Give some of it for education needs to the shelter, the kids who need it, because they are part of all our story here. A chunk to me for a bit of future cushion, for the family I will create. A little for Huck's education, just to say, I care about that child, and I want him to know I'm here for him. And, finally, a little to Henry Walker's grandchildren who also could use a little education safety net. He had a role in this story, too."

"You don't have to," Katie answered. "I'm in charge of my son, it's not your duty."

Luke grabbed both her ears and kissed her forehead. "I know. But it doesn't hurt to feel safe. And that's what I want for you. With both of our mothers now out there in those waves, who knows? Maybe they're plotting and planning for us to be together, to feel secure in this crazy, modern world."

Poppy patted Katie's hand.

"Take it, honey, it's not much. Huck is a smart child, but he'll still need the best teaching he can get in his life. Save it for his future. Accepting a little something from Luke is just a team thing. Better to live life as a team."

"We might be doing that," Luke said. "She's hard to nail down with her work and Huck. But, once in a while, she gives me time to convince her that's all I'm after."

"I'm still settling here, there's so much . . ."

"I know, I know about it. Take your time, I'm patient." Luke put his arm around her tightly.

Then Poppy placed both of their hands together and nodded, her huge, orange hat flopping like a giant stingray in the cold sea breeze. "Think about that team, honey," she said. "Don't resist too much. I know some things in my old age. I'm watching out for both of you. You have a real, live third mother you can share in me. I'm watching out for both of you. I know it's a strange way to get one, but consider me family."

"Yes, we do make a good team." Katie laughed assuredly, knowing this unusual trio might become a new Eastern family she could count on. And suddenly, with the churning waves, the cold, salty air turning her cheeks red, and the wind whipping her ponytail around like a propeller, Katie felt grounded, and very much at home.

Acknowledgments

I have been a journalist for twenty years and work tirelessly to make every fact in my writing truthful, even in fiction. The details of how the old money stalwarts, the new money arrivals, and the rooted local community swirl around the Hamptons are as accurate as I know how to present them. No matter how out-of-this-world the scenes may appear to you the reader, I've seen pretty much all of them with my own eyes. Many people living amidst these three worlds discreetly answered questions to help me fine-tune scenarios and I am grateful to all of them. My love of the sea prompted me to immerse myself in the community that navigates the currents better than anyone—those who battle it every day. A group of surfers and watersports aficionados to whom I dedicated this book has become a second family to my own.

Thank you to my William Morrow publishers Jennifer Hart and Liate Stehlik for believing in the book, and to my editor, Tessa Woodward: your discreet yet forceful way of communicating makes for an elegant, pitch-perfect editor. Julia Meltzer in production editorial kept the book moving, Elle Keck handled all logistics and is herself a strong editor; to Becky Sweren and David Kuhn for helping to launch this book, and to Kaitlyn Kennedy for doggedly spreading the word along with Molly Waxman. Thanks to Grant Ginder who laughed me through a big edit.

To those of you who had the patience and generosity to purview early versions or sections, I am always grateful for your wise feedback: Lynne Greenberg, Juju Chang, Andrea Wong, Leslie Bennetts, Heather Vincent, Liz Smith (at age ninety-four, more eagle-eyed than a copy editor), Kathy O'Hearn, Ebs Burnough, Holly Parmelee, Carol Margaritis, Amy Cappellazzo, Darren Walker, Ashley McDermott, Alexandra Wolfe, Neal Shapiro, Perri Peltz, David Saltzman, Karen Lawson, Peter Manning, Electra Toub, Ali Wentworth, Kyle Gibson, and Joel Schumacher. Jay and Alice Peterson always generously talk me through the process of writing. Thank you to Dr. Dominick Auciello for learning support data, to Will Zeckendorf for windsurfing know-how, and to Xander, Beau, and Drew Peterson for automobile fact-checking (though my cars here were pretty on target in the first place…just saying). Thank you to my brothers Jim and David and Michael Peterson for authentic lingo of your astoundingly unathletic sport of golf.

To my four parents, Sally and Michael and Pete and Joan, for their bottomless support and encouragement of my professional endeavors and my mothering.

And, most of all, to my three teenagers, Chloe, Jack, and Eliza (although the feeling I'm going to bet is not always mutual), let me tell you this: the greatest opportunity, joy, and thrill in my life is being your mom.

Reading Group Guide

1. At the Seabrook Club, many members are from families that have been "summering" in the Hamptons for generations. The tradition of civic duty to the club remains strong, yet it is very insular. Do you think the Seabrook Club is ultimately a force for good or does it simply churn out entitled people who are programmed to get around the rules?

2. On Katie's second night in the Hamptons, she begins a flirtation with Luke, even though she's there on the invitation of George. Do you think she's cheating? If so, why? If not, do you think she owes George anything?

3. Appearances say one thing, words serve to convince us further. How can people who are looking for love avoid deception? Isn't it especially hard to decipher if someone is indeed the right partner when all feels romantic, and the pieces fall nicely in to place? Do we need to take a bite of the apple to test if it's right as Katie does with George?

4. From the beginning, Poppy is on Katie's side as a fellow strong, independent-minded woman. Poppy's wistful remembrances

of her peers from the first wave of feminism seem to clash with the women Katie is meeting in the Hamptons. Do you think women from the 1960s and the 2000s are all that different? What about women who live in communities like the Hamptons? Are there things we all have in common, regardless of place or era?

If you consider all the anxieties that plague a modern, single, working mom . . . how much weight should be placed on these three pillars of her life: raising a competent, value-driven child, professional success and sound work decisions, and her love life?

5. Female characters in literature and film often have to be "likable" according to Hollywood standards. This often means doing the right thing in most situations, behaving sexually in a way that is somewhat "expected," and having priorities balanced. Look at literature and film and think about examples of married women who cheat and what happens to them. Do audiences give women a break or are they judgmental? Katie is working hard to make the right decisions, but is, as her friend Ashley says, "intrepid and insecure" at the same time. Do you believe that female characters have a certain bar to meet in terms of appropriate, "likable" behavior?

6. Social media and the Internet in general have sexualized the life of teenagers. Sixteen-year-old Alexa Chase has had everything served to her on a platter since she was born. Is she is some ways a "normal" kid who isn't able to judge when she is going too far? Would her behavior and decisions occur in a teen in a completely different community, or from a middle-of-the road background?

7. The sea and the salt water play an important role in this novel. The ocean heals, it protects, it gives joy and salvation, and it holds those dear to us. How does the ocean, and dipping into it, affect you?

8. Jake Chase is a "new money," self-made titan who put himself through school driving a laundry truck. He's gotten much of what he wants in life by engineering it himself. Does any of that forgive the way he treats people? Is he despicable or kind of lovable in his need for constant acceptance?

9. The local community of the Hamptons relies on the wealthy summer invaders for their income. The surf community lures the summer people into their idyllic, simple word of pleasure and cool. When people of completely different classes start to mingle, what are the obstacles? Is it fair to say that both sides are posing, posturing, and using each other in this novel?

10. There are several twists and turns in this novel. How much of the ending did you see coming? What was obvious all along, what were the factors that kept you guessing? Who in your reading group predicted what and how early?

About the Author

Holly Peterson is the author of *The Idea of Him* and the *New York Times* and international bestseller *The Manny*. She was a contributing editor for *Newsweek* and editor-at-large for *Talk* Magazine. Prior to those positions, she was an Emmy Award–winning producer for ABC News where, for more than a decade, she covered everything from foreign coups to domestic trials of the century. Her writing has been published in the *New York Times, Newsweek, Town and Country, Vogue, Departures,* and other publications.

ALSO BY HOLLY PETERSON

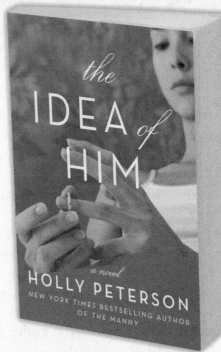

THE IDEA OF HIM A Novel
Available in Paperback and E-book

"A coming-of-age book for grown ups. It's fast-paced and intriguing, glamorous and real—not only a great, great read but a tutorial in how to be your own best friend."
—Elin Hilderbrand, *New York Times* bestselling author

Allie Crawford has the life she always dreamed of—she's number two at a high-profile P.R. firm; she has two kids she adores; and her husband is a blend of handsome and heroic. Wade is everything she thought a man was supposed to be—he's running a successful newsmagazine and, best of all, he provides the stable yet exciting New York City life Allie believes she needs in order to feel secure and happy.

But when Allie finds Wade locked in their laundry room with a stunning blonde in snakeskin sandals, a scandal ensues that flips her life on its head. And when the woman wants to befriend Allie, an old flame calls, and a new guy gets a little too close for comfort, she starts to think her marriage is more of a facade than something real. Maybe she's fallen in love not with Wade—but with the idea of him